DINAH JEFFERIES

Night Train
to Marrakech

HarperCollins*Publishers*

HarperCollins*Publishers* Ltd
1 London Bridge Street,
London SE1 9GF
www.harpercollins.co.uk

HarperCollins*Publishers*
Macken House,
39/40 Mayor Street Upper,
Dublin 1
D01 C9W8

First published by HarperCollins*Publishers* 2023
1

A catalogue record for this book is available from the British Library

ISBN: 978-0-00-8427085 (PB)
ISBN: 978-0-00-845872-0 (TPB, AU, NZ, CA)
ISBN: 978-0-00-864060-6 (HB, US, CA)
ISBN: 978-0-00-861934-3 (PB, US)

Set in Dante MT by Palimpsest Book Production Ltd, Falkirk, Stirlingshire

Printed and bound in the UK using
100% Renewable Electricity by CPI Group (UK) Ltd

MIX
Paper | Supporting
responsible forestry
FSC™ C007454
FSC
www.fsc.org

This book is produced from independently certified FSC™ paper to ensure
responsible forest management.

For more information visit: www.harpercollins.co.uk/green

For Caroline Hardman

PROLOGUE

The night train gathered speed, clanking and rattling, and the girl, poised on the cusp of a new life, held her breath. Eager. Hopeful. No turning back. The *clickety clack, clickety clack, clickety clack* of the wheels on the track beat a pulse in her head, the rhythm expanding around her until it was not only outside but inside her too.

Everything rested on this trip, this hope-filled dream, but now she was here, now she was finally off . . . everything felt so alien. The compartment, at first scented with cinnamon and mint, began to stink of sweat, oil, and something rancid. And as the train flew on through the night its whirring and beating only grew louder. Hurtling through blackness, hands over her ears, she longed to silence the racket, but still the noise soared as they went faster and faster, and each time the carriage jolted, her hammock tilted. Reeling, she clung on, but in the steaming heat the vulpine shriek of a whistle tipped her into fear.

1

The hot air grew saltier.

Her throat tightened.

Memories flooded her mind as the beat of the past mimicked the beat of the train – *thud, thud, thud* – hammering relentlessly in her head. She longed to sleep away the hours but her skin was on fire. She listened to the breath of people sleeping near her, trying to calm her mind, but when she slipped into moments of oblivion herself, she woke from dreams of hungry creatures rattling their cages. And oh, the thoughts she couldn't suppress, no matter how hard she tried.

Hours and hours passed, her mind growing dull and dark, until the squeal of the brakes signalled an end in sight. Thank God! And as the train pulled into Marrakech station, her relief swelled and she gripped hold of herself, tears heating her eyelids. For *this* was what she wanted, wasn't it?

CHAPTER 1

Clemence

Kasbah du Paradis, Morocco, July 1966

People still did occasionally flee and vanish into the mountains, just as once upon a time they had disappeared into the dungeons of the warlords, but if there were restless spirits wandering here, Clemence Petier had never seen them. In this place of infinite beauty, she had found peace of sorts.

She gazed out of her open bedroom window, hoping to catch the changing of the light; her daily rituals kept her steady, living in the present, and centred. And as she watched the sun rising, the mist burnt off, the mountains began to shine, and the glorious fragrance of wild herbs drifted in the air.

A perfect day.

Perched up high in the Atlas Mountains, the kasbah had once been a fortress built to withstand attack. Derelict and forgotten when she first found it, now it spelt safety for her. She loved the dazzling sunlight, the deep blue shadows, the glittering stars at night, and the blindingly white snow in winter.

Clemence wrapped the turquoise robe around her, fastened its ties, and as she did every morning, left the main house to walk across to the annexe.

As she crossed the terrace she paused only to run her fingertips over the velvety climbing roses. Blowsy, crimson and almost at an end, their petals dropped at her touch. *Like blood,* she thought, lingering for one more moment before walking on. She unlocked the door to the annexe, slid the bolts, and went inside.

At first glance, it appeared just as idyllic as the terrace outside, but something was wrong.

Birds were clamouring at an open window which overlooked a private courtyard with access to the mountains beyond. Two small copper-coloured butterflies were dancing in the sunlight, but the window should not have been open. And the room should not have been empty. Clemence glanced around, taking in the tray of uneaten breakfast – cooling French coffee, two pieces of freshly baked baguette, butter melting in the early sunlight – and the white robe lying crumpled on the rug. '*Touche du bois,*' she muttered and reached out to touch the gleaming wooden arm of a chair before she ran to the bathroom. *Touch wood.*

A tap had been left running but no one was there, so

she turned off the water and hurried to the living room where she found no sign of her.

'Madeleine,' she called, aware of the tremble in her voice. But all she could hear in response were the birds.

Then. Right then, she felt the panic. Madeleine had bolted.

As the distant past reared up her mouth felt dry, the old fear fluttering as if it were one of the butterflies. She dashed outside and called for Ahmed, her youthful assistant, whom she trusted more than anyone else in the world.

'Help me,' she pleaded as he approached. 'She's gone.'

She held out her hands and the young man enclosed them in his much larger ones for a few moments. 'She can't have gone far, Madame. I carried her breakfast in only half an hour ago and she was there. Has she eaten it?'

Clemence shook her head.

'She can only have been gone half an hour at most,' he said, his voice calm as they left the terrace.

'Did *you* unlock the window?'

'I'm sorry. She complained about the room being stuffy.'

Her heart sank. 'We have to keep her inside. She can't be allowed out alone. Not ever. I thought I explained.'

'The window was so stiff, I didn't think she'd have the strength to push it wide open.'

'I'll have to install bars. Or a filagree screen would at least look better. If we find her . . .'

'We will.'

But Clemence wasn't so sure. Madeleine could be devious.

'Ahmed, look for her as you head down the track. Take the motorbike to pick up my granddaughter,' she said. 'I might need the jeep to search for Madeleine.'

Her granddaughter might complain about having to take the long journey from Marrakech railway station to the kasbah on the back of a motorbike, but there was no time to worry about it now.

Clemence turned her back on Ahmed and set off to search the complex. With few remaining perimeter walls, her kasbah was at the same altitude as the last of the trees and nothing much grew above it, the mountain sides barren and rocky.

Looking down it was different. Looking down it was lush. The little village of Imlil huddled below, where the year-long supply of water from the river ensured the terraced hillsides would always be cultivated. From her vantage point she could see the walnut and pine forests where she collected cones for the fire. And lower down the agricultural land where villagers grew vegetables, potatoes, and onions, plus alfalfa for feeding a few cows, and below them the orchards of plums, figs, almonds and apricots. But there was no chance Madeleine could have gone that far on foot.

The air blowing down from the mountain top was thin and pure, and feeling the cool of it on her skin, Clemence glanced up at the rocky slopes. Where had she got to?

'And in a nightdress,' she muttered. '*Pour l'amour de Dieu!*'

She had felt so harried these last months looking after Madeleine. And of course this had to happen just moments before her granddaughter's arrival, which was already causing enough worry. Had it been foolish to allow her to come, this girl she didn't know? Not that she'd been given much choice.

Clemence passed through the bougainvillea-clad pergola, peered behind the rosemary hedge, checked in between the palms, and went back into the private courtyard where clouds of scented white jasmine spilt over the walls. Nothing. Not a sign of her at all. She ran to look down the steep downward track Ahmed had taken leading to where she kept her 1950s Hotchkiss jeep, close to Imlil. *Please, please, let us find her soon.* The heat could be cruel – so, so cruel – especially if you didn't know your way and the longer Madeleine was out there, the greater the risk.

Forty minutes later, there was still no sign of her. By now Ahmed would have alerted the villagers of Imlil on his way to Marrakech, and Clemence hoped they would help look. As she checked every nook and cranny of the building again, she heard Ahmed's sister Nadia calling for Madeleine too, her voice shrill and urgent. Clemence rubbed her forehead and took several deep breaths, trying to calm herself, but her fear was rocketing.

Suddenly she heard a pounding at the front entrance to the kasbah. She raced along the corridor to the door, flung it wide open, and saw Madeleine standing on the step. Still wearing a grubby nightdress, her white hair grey with grime, her face streaked with tears and her skin caked with dust, she looked absolutely exhausted. A man stood beside her, propping her up, though Clemence had barely glanced at him as she pulled her mother to her.

'Oh thank God,' she whispered, relief making her voice shake as she held her tight.

'Poor old soul,' the man said. 'I found her crawling on all fours not far from one of the tracks to the village.'

His voice was immediately familiar. Clemence would have recognised it anywhere, but surely it could not be . . . Hardly able to believe it and with dread already knotting in her stomach, she forced herself to look up. It was as if a bitter wind blew right through her, and even in the heat, she felt icily cold. He was dressed in smart grey slacks and a crisp blue linen shirt. Nothing remarkable – he could be any European, but Clemence knew he was not.

'Seems very frail and made no sense at all. I—'

He stopped speaking and stared at her. She felt a nerve twitching in her temple and fought the urge to run.

'Adèle? Adèle Garnier?' he asked, surprise clear in his voice. 'Can it really be you?'

She had not been called that name in fifty years. Could she deny it? His was a face she had not thought she would ever see again, had *hoped* she would never see again but there he was. She nodded silently and reached out to wipe the old lady's tear-stained face with her fingertips.

'Come on,' she said, her voice soft and low. 'Let's get you cleaned up.'

The man frowned, clearly expecting more from her.

'I'm afraid I have to go,' she said to him, maintaining a tight hold of Madeleine. 'These days, I go by my second name, Clemence, and I am Madame Petier. Thank you for bringing her back, Monsieur Callier.'

'Patrice.' He corrected her as if offended, wiping his brow with his fingers. 'If it's not too much trouble, may I beg a glass of something cool?'

'Of course. Nadia will bring it.'

Nadia, who was standing to the side watching, inclined her head. Clemence hurried her mother into the annexe, quickly ensuring none of the windows were unlocked and with shaking hands helped her to sip some water. How was it that Patrice Callier could still make her skin crawl?

She closed the shutters, unfolded a clean nightdress, and after rinsing her mother's hair and sitting her on the lavatory, she put her back to bed. Docile and exhausted after her adventure, the ninety-two-year-old woman complied without a murmur.

Clemence clasped her hands together tightly, digging her fingernails into her flesh. What was Patrice doing here? She had left him – along with the rest of her past – far behind her. She took several deep calming breaths, hoping he might have already gone, allowing the time to stretch out as far as she dared before returning outside. Her shame had been her undoing years ago and it must *not* resurface now. But whether he was gone or not, the only question that really mattered was . . . how much did Patrice Callier know?

CHAPTER 2

Vicky

Marrakech railway station

In the station yard, Vicky Baudin shaded her eyes from the dazzling white sunlight. She glanced left and right and then straight ahead through the chaos of donkeys laden with panniers, bicycles and motorbikes, and old men gathered in knots, smoking and gossiping. There was no sign of anyone who might be her grandmother. Her grandfather Jacques, a taciturn elderly man living quietly in their French village, had reluctantly given Vicky the woman's name and a PO number, but no description, insisting he had not seen Clemence for more than fifty years. And when Vicky had pressed him to tell her more, he had clammed up entirely.

She checked her watch. The train had arrived on time. 'Damn, damn, damn,' she muttered. 'What now?'

Although it was still early and not yet blazing hot, her skin was prickling. Everything around her was so very different to home, the air hotter, the sky brighter, the landscapes drier, but after the dazzling stone of Tangier, she had expected something more romantic. Instead Marrakech felt shabby and forlorn. The ground was littered, the painted windows of the station building peeling. But at least the train journey was over.

The jumble of voices eddied and peaked – alarming voices, as if all the short vowels had dropped out of the world. And yet amid the unfamiliar clusters of consonants she picked out a word or two of French. *Dommage. Jour. Demain.*

Although she assumed Moroccan Arabic must be the dominant language she felt lucky that some French was still spoken here. According to her grandfather, the country had once been a French protectorate and had only gained full independence from France a decade ago. But it meant Vicky should be able to understand and communicate a little. Or at least enough to buy a baguette or a croissant.

She looked around, taking it all in. She could not believe she was finally here. When her grandfather had let slip that she had a grandmother still living it had been a shock. There had never been a whisper of who her dead father's mother might have been. And when Jacques said this mysterious, long-lost grandmother was living in Morocco, it had felt like fate. Because Marrakech was also the favourite city of Yves Saint Laurent, a designer who meant more to Vicky than she could ever explain. And after the pain and hardship of the past year, she had suddenly felt certain that travelling to Marrakech to find them both might be the answer to all of her troubles. It might restore her belief in herself, leave behind her heartbreak over her boyfriend's callous rejection of her, and perhaps even finally find the answer to the mysteries her family had been hiding all her life.

In the station yard a few women dressed in black gawped at her, and heat rose in her cheeks. She held her head up and tried to remain aloof while furtively tugging at the hem of her bright yellow minidress. Splashed with large pink poppies, it did nothing to conceal her ample curves, and too late she realised that here in Marrakech, it ought to. On the train she had covered herself with a thin blanket but now she glanced around wondering if there was a public loo where she could at least slip into some trousers and put on a long-sleeved shirt. There didn't seem to be. One of the women came closer, made a strange cat-like hissing sound and moved off again. Vicky shrank back: so far, not the best of beginnings.

I am not afraid. I am NOT afraid, she told herself, forcing back the tears that seemed about to spring to her eyes. She prided herself on always appearing strong, whatever the provocation, whatever she was feeling inside. When the children at school had been spiteful about her parentage, she had not blubbed. When her mother had refused, yet again, to tell her anything about her father, she had not wept, and when her boyfriend Russell had cruelly insulted her dreams, she had not shed a tear. Well that wasn't entirely true, but she certainly wasn't going to start crying now.

Vicky marched forward, emboldened, and identified a taxi rank but with no waiting taxis. How far away did her grandmother live? Would a taxi all the way to the kasbah be expensive? From her pocket she pulled out the postcard Clemence had sent after she had contacted her via the PO box. Kasbah du Paradis – no address, just that and a few words.

Finally spotting a porter, she showed him the card. He indicated she should throw her case into a donkey cart, but she shook her head and feeling increasingly hot and sweaty, sat down on a low wall to wait in the hope her grandmother would turn up soon.

After what felt like hours a monstrous motorbike pulled up, hooting and honking, and the tanned young rider wearing a blue bandana and a stern expression held up a card with 'BAUDIN' scrawled on it. She let out a huge sigh of relief and dashed over.

'Ahmed Hassan,' he said and held out his hand. 'Sorry to be late.'

'It doesn't matter. I'm just pleased you're here.' She passed him her case and he tied it onto the back of the bike before removing a large black-and-white cotton scarf from his neck.

'Cover your mouth and nose. Wrap it around your head,' he said, and after he was firmly seated, he invited her to ride pillion. Vicky climbed on, grinning with pleasure, the scarf knotted firmly at the back of her neck. Her adventure was beginning at last.

Ahmed gunned the engine and shot away from the station, wheeling around a roundabout and speeding along an avenue of jacaranda trees. She felt light as a bird. She was in Marrakech. She really was in Marrakech, and on the back of a motorbike with a total stranger. Whatever would her mother say? She let out a great *whoop* of triumph and held on tight.

CHAPTER 3

Vicky

'Look,' Ahmed said, coming to a halt. 'Down there is the Ourika valley.'

Vicky contemplated the sun-drenched river valley below and saw a couple of dusky pink villages with citrus orchards threading around them.

'It's beautiful,' she whispered, and Ahmed nodded his agreement.

As the bike climbed steadily, a glittering landscape of terracotta slopes and craggy sun-streaked mountains opened up before her. In the distance, bleached by the blistering sun, they turned to the colour of ash. On one of the tight bends along the bumpy, unmade mountain tracks, Ahmed offered his apologies and told her to hold on tight. They were stuck in a pothole, the wheels spinning and causing clouds of sandy pink dust to spiral upwards, and Vicky wiped her stinging eyelids with her fingers. The scarf had not covered her eyes. Ahmed soon released the bike, and they carried on ascending until he came to a stop again. From there they continued on foot with him pushing the bike through a rabbit warren of steep and uneven alleys in a small Berber village.

'Short cut,' he explained, and soon after that he paused at the start of a rough track lined with wildflowers. 'Sorry,' he said again, indicating she path ahead. 'Up to the kasbah now.'

He stored the motorbike in a small shed, locked it, and deftly relieving her the case, began to move off. 'Very light,' he said as he swung it in the air.

'I'm banking on clothes being cheap here,' she said, handing him back the scarf he had lent her.

They climbed the track all the way to a low-built, rose-coloured building perched on a small plateau.

'*Voila! Kasbah du Paradis de la montagne.* Our gateway to the snow-capped Atlas Mountains,' he said with a flourish, pointing to the peaks.

And as she gazed around, she saw it was indeed a paradise.

'I'll take you to see gazelles if you like.'

'What? Now?' Vicky said excitedly.

He laughed. 'No. And the best time to see the Atlas is at sunset. Sorry it's not the season for snow.'

Up until now she'd only noted his stern expression but since arriving at the kasbah he seemed to have changed and as he walked her towards the building, his brown eyes had softened.

'Wow. This is so cool!' she said as she glanced up at the sky, feeling the warmth of the sun on her skin and her body unwinding as she watched a huge bird swoop for its prey.

'Golden eagle,' Ahmed said and smiled, and she saw he had the most beautiful white teeth.

'The kasbah has been restored in the traditional Berber way with rammed mud walls – pisé, we call it,' he said facing the building again.

She spun on the spot, holding her arms out wide and inhaling sparkling mountain air bursting with the energising scent of rosemary and mint. Made of several interconnecting parts and blending perfectly into its surroundings, the kasbah looked as if it had been lifted from the Middle Ages. It spread out almost like separate dwellings or a little village joined together by outdoor corridors or walkways. Indoor corridors too, she imagined. It was nothing like her stepfather's French chateau where, from the age of seven, she had grown up with her mother Élise. Nor did it resemble the big manor house near her aunt Florence and uncle Jack's cottage in Devon, where she'd spent school holidays playing with her cousin Beatrice. Vicky had grown up in the Dordogne in France but had just finished her course at an art college in London and this place was certainly not like anything there either.

Ahmed led her past a long terrace where beneath a cobalt blue awning a day bed covered in bright orange shimmered against the deep pink of the kasbah, the colours electrifying. Further along, a huge wooden dining table and matching chairs sat beneath a second identical canopy.

'Madame likes to sit out here,' he said. 'For the view.'

He opened a heavy wooden door at the side and took her through a long cool hall and into a large room with a fireplace and windows overlooking red hills. The stone floor was laid with rugs, paintings hung everywhere and the pale terracotta walls shone. Captivated, Vicky smiled with pleasure.

'*Tadelakt* plasterwork,' he said, breaking into her thoughts. 'The walls. Made from lime plaster with added colour pigment and finished with black olive soap. It came from these hills. Waterproof you see. Berbers used it to seal cisterns for storing drinking water, but now it is every-where. Beautiful, no?'

It was but Vicky, forgetting the walls, had turned to see that a tall woman had almost soundlessly entered the room and was standing just inside, seeming to catch her breath.

'Oh, you're here,' the woman said coolly while looking her up and down, her expression unreadable. 'I've had rather a busy morning and didn't realise, but I see Ahmed is showing you round.'

Her very nearly stern features did not match the smooth rich sound of her voice. She was smiling and yet there was something just a little off, a wariness maybe, as if she was trying very hard to control herself. At first Vicky was so awestruck she couldn't find any words: this woman didn't look like any grandmother she knew. Could they really be related? Vicky knew she wasn't bad-looking – her mouth was full, curling up at the corners, and she had large toffee-brown eyes shaded by very thick dark eyelashes – but she could see no trace of herself in this glamorous, elegant woman. *Her* hair was completely white, cut quite short in a crisp modern style and elegantly swept back from her face. Her eyes were hazel and a network of barely visible lines covered her lightly tanned skin. She wore the most beautiful silk kaftan in pink and gold, the colours shifting as she moved. Her feet were bare, but her toenails, painted rose-gold, gleamed and she wore an anklet studded with what looked like real pearls.

'Yes,' Vicky eventually said as she found her voice. 'Ahmed has shown me round a little.'

'I am glad,' she said, though Vicky could not hear any gladness in her tone. 'Welcome to my home. I am Clemence.'

Vicky couldn't help continuing to stare. It had only been a few weeks since her grandfather had revealed that Victor – his son, her father – had been born in Morocco and that Clemence was his mother. A woman Vicky had never heard mentioned, not by *Grand-père* Jacques, her mother, Élise, nor either of her aunts, Hélène and Florence. As a child it hadn't seemed odd not to know anything about the past. It was just the way things were. She hadn't had any idea what to expect coming here, yet still she found herself surprised and a bit taken aback.

'Come. Let's get you settled in your room. The cleaners came early today so it should be ready.' Clemence slipped on some sandals and held out an arm rather stiffly.

Vicky searched her grandmother's face in the hope of discovering something of her true feelings, either in her expression or her voice, but there was nothing. She followed her back into the hall and around a corner, passing an intimate terraced garden where the light fell on a huge clay urn from which startlingly pink geraniums cascaded. After entering another long, low part of the sprawling complex they reached a pale painted door and after Clemence unlocked it she ushered Vicky through ahead of her. The green window shutters were partially closed, to keep the place cool, Clemence explained, and they cast a welcome deep blue shade across the whole room.

'I have to see to—' Clemence said but broke off, casting Ahmed a strangely significant look. Ahmed nodded as if to confirm what had not been voiced and Clemence carried on more firmly.

'Well, I have things to attend to. Take your time unpacking and Ahmed will fetch you a cold drink. The bathroom is next door. We have our own hydro-electric power generator, although the water will probably run cold. Gravity brings our water from a spring many metres away.'

As she spoke, Clemence moved towards the door. 'Feel free to look around. I'll see you at about one for lunch.'

'Thank you,' Vicky said, feeling not the least bit welcome. Her grandmother sounded so aloof, so chilly. Why had she agreed to this visit if it was so tiresome?

'Oh, and there are spare kaftans in the wardrobe. Wear any you like.' She gestured to Vicky's skimpy yellow minidress. 'Best to cover your legs in Morocco, arms and shoulders too. We need to respect the Islamic culture here. And choose a hat. You'll need one, though we get most things done very early at this time of year before the heat traps us indoors.'

Despite those relatively kind words, Vicky felt as if the woman had been relieved – or even eager – to leave.

She felt the curiosity that had been ignited within her ever since she'd discovered her grandmother's existence flare even brighter. She needed to find out more about her. Much more. For why had Clemence never visited her own son in France, not even once? And why was her grandfather, even now, so reluctant to speak of her?

CHAPTER 4

After her bath Vicky perched on the edge of the bed, opened her bag and pulled out the only photograph she had of her father Victor. Perhaps nobody had thought of taking pictures during the war. She didn't know, but she treasured the one she had and it always brought a lump to her throat. Although it was grainy, she could still make out his powerful frame, dark eyes, and intense gaze. What had he been doing that day? What had he been thinking when the picture was taken? And had Élise taken that picture? She wished she could hear what they had said to one another. How they had been. Her mother had never really answered her questions about Victor and nor had Jacques, and she was desperate to know more. She knew they had both been proud of Victor, but maybe it had just been too painful to speak about.

There was a knock at the door and Ahmed came in with a drink. After he'd gone she glanced at the bed, which looked so inviting with its dark silky cover in this room imbued with a kind of woody incense, rather like liquorice. She craved sleep but checked her watch and saw it was nearly time for lunch, so she hurriedly picked out a purple kaftan and slipped it on.

As she returned along the corridor to the main house, she passed a room that looked like a library or an office – with leather chairs, bookcases and a coffee table inlaid with mother of pearl and ivory – before finding Clemence in the main room. Her grandmother was standing and gazing out of the window, two large black and tan dogs sitting obediently by her side.

'Lovely view,' Vicky said, eyeing the dogs nervously.

Clemence swivelled round and smiled. The smile seemed a bit more genuine than it had been before, as if some weight had been lifted from her in the intervening hours.

'So, you like it? My home.'

'It's wonderful. I've never been anywhere like this before.'

'It was a crumbling fortress when I bought it decades ago, possibly dating back to the fourteenth century. There was no sanitation. No electricity. It's taken years to rebuild.'

Vicky studied her, a thousand questions on the tip of her tongue, but where could she begin?

'The organic forms reflect Morocco's traditional architecture I feel and, wherever possible, I've used the geometric patterns and floral motifs typical of Islamic art. So, now you're settled, come and meet my boys, Coco and Voltaire.'

She laughed. 'Voltaire? The French revolutionary writer?'

Clemence shrugged. 'Why not? The dogs are Beaucerons, getting on a bit but still powerful. Fabulous guards but with a sensitive side too *and* minds of their own.' She smiled as she patted them.

Vicky edged gingerly towards the handsome black and tan 'boys', as her grandmother referred to them, but stopped a short distance away.

'What's that gorgeous smell?' she asked.

'Cedar, eucalyptus, and frankincense. Ambrosial, don't you think?'

'Ambrosial?'

'Especially delicious or fragrant. Worthy of the gods. I have it everywhere. Do you like it?'

'I love it.'

'The garden is full of bougainvillea, climbing roses, palms, plus jasmine of course. A garden is such an important place. I grow lemon thyme and rosemary, but there's wild sage, juniper and so much more around the place.'

Vicky felt in awe of this sophisticated woman, her gorgeous gardens, and the wild beauty of the harsh mountain landscape. As for the incredible aromatic air, she felt almost as lightheaded as if she were breathing a soothing, soporific tonic.

'Gardens teach us about the impermanence of life,' Clemence was saying. 'I'll show you later. Now . . . we will be having Maghrebi dishes with Moroccan drinks for lunch. I hope that suits you.'

Vicky smiled politely.

'For many centuries the Arab world referred to North Africa as Maghrib or the land of the setting sun,' her grandmother added.

The dogs followed as they wandered to the dining room where the tang of exotic spices made Vicky's mouth water, though she couldn't help feeling a little apprehensive. She'd never eaten African food before.

As they sat down Clemence said, almost too lightly, 'So, are you going to tell me why you've come here?'

Vicky thought for a moment. The day she had revealed she was thinking of going to Marrakech to meet Yves Saint Laurent, Jacques, white-haired and hunched into himself, had asked the same question. 'I want to be his apprentice,' she'd said. 'I'll even crawl around picking up pins from his floor if that's what it takes.'

He'd looked disturbed at her news and she hadn't known why, but he had stroked her cheek and called her *mon chou*, which always made her smile.

She took a long slow breath then glanced at her grandmother before saying, 'I've come to meet Yves St Laurent. And you, of course.'

Clemence's look was searching, as if trying to work something out. 'And that's all? Jacques did not send you?'

Puzzled, Vicky shook her head and no more was said. But she found it hard to picture her gruff grandfather being involved with a sophisticated woman like Clemence. But then, as Jacques used to say, *There's no accounting for folk*. She wondered how he was. How he felt about Clemence now. Surely he must be longing to see her, or maybe he still felt angry that she hadn't come to France with him all those years ago. She couldn't tell.

The meal was a Moroccan chicken stew cooked in a tagine, a round and shallow clay casserole with a tall pointy, conical lid. It was served with tender grains of couscous; Vicky found it absolutely delicious.

'So, you went to art college in London?' her grandmother was asking.

'Yes. I've got a diploma in fashion from St Martin's School of Art – a Dip AD they call it – and an offer of a postgraduate place at *L'Ecole de la Chambre Syndicale de la Couture Parisienne*.'

Her grandmother looked as if she was weighing up Vicky's claim. 'Then I find it hard to understand why you have come here instead?'

Vicky bristled. 'No. It's not instead. I'm not due in Paris until September. I wanted to spread my wings first and try to meet Yves Saint Laurent. I thought I'd have more chance here than in Paris.'

Clemence frowned.

'I wrote my dissertation on Saint Laurent,' Vicky continued, feeling she had to justify herself. 'He's such a brilliant designer and everyone in London says Marrakech is a hub of creativity and freedom.'

Clemence inclined her head but did not look as if she agreed and Vicky was still unable to work out what her grandmother was thinking.

The dessert arrived.

'Wow! That looks amazing,' Vicky said.

Her grandmother passed her a portion. 'It is an almond snake pastry, dusted with powdered sugar.'

There were a few moments of silence while they ate.

'They sometimes coat it with warm honey,' Clemence added. 'Do you like it?'

'Delicious,' Vicky said with her mouth still half full of the incredible almond sweetness. She had always been teased for her sweet tooth, and the way she could so easily put on weight because of it.

Clemence was looking at her unblinking.

Vicky shifted in her seat, feeling ill at ease under the scrutiny.

'What did Jacques say about me?' Clemence asked suddenly.

Vicky puffed out her cheeks at her grandmother's blunt question but answered calmly. 'Nothing really. Just that you were here.'

Clemence nodded slowly.

'I only found out you existed very recently, and I had plenty of time before September to come, so I did.'

Vicky was surprised Clemence didn't ask anything more about Jacques or say anything about her son, Victor. She tried to figure out the best way to bring up the subject herself and in the end she said, 'I never met my father. I wish I had.'

Clemence still said nothing.

This wasn't easy but Vicky tried again. 'Victor and my mother were involved in the French Resistance. Did you know?'

Without warning, her grandmother stiffened and changed tack, saying, 'Look, you need to be very careful in Morocco, child. Things are not what they seem here. And people are not who they seem either.'

'What?'

'I've lived in Morocco all my life. My family were senior civil servants as well as landowners and I know what I'm talking about. There is a great deal of unrest due to local politics. Hopefully things may change but for now no disagreement is tolerated. Anyone who openly opposes the regime puts themselves in danger.'

Vicky almost laughed. 'I'm not likely to be doing that am I?'

Clemence ignored her. 'Plus there is some understandable hostility towards all the European visitors who are flooding in. It would be far preferable if you returned to France.'

Taken aback, Vicky stared at her. 'No! I can't leave.'

'You are not listening to me.'

'But I've come all this way to meet Yves Saint Laurent. I want to work for him.' She thought, but didn't say, that she also couldn't leave before finding out everything about Clemence.

Her grandmother's voice was cold when she said, 'I'm not sure how I can be responsible for your safety.'

'I'm not political.'

'You don't know who you might encounter. You won't know who you're dealing with.'

'You want me to leave?' Vicky asked, dangerously close to tears.

'It would be preferable.'

'But I've only just arrived.'

Clemence seemed to soften. 'Look, my dear, I may at least be able to help you meet the designer. He's very relaxed. No fuss, no formality, and he has a little house in the medina. Dar el-Hanch, or the Snake House, it's called, although I hear he spends time at a studio in the Palmeraie, an area about half an hour's drive north of Jemaa el-Fnaa square. There are some luxurious but mainly run-down French villas there and thousands of palm trees.'

'You really might help me?'

'Maybe. It could take a little while as he's not here all the time.'

'As I said, I don't have to be in Paris until September.'

Clemence sighed. 'Well, if I do manage to introduce you, please promise to go home the moment you've done what you came here to do.'

Ahmed came in and handed Clemence a package. She glanced up at him enquiringly and he told her it had been delivered by a young Moroccan man. She looked towards Vicky and then put the package down. Clemence clearly did not want to open it in front of her. What was she hiding? There was something, Vicky could sense it. She had, after all, grown up with a mother who was constantly keeping secrets, who would refuse to confide in her daughter even when Vicky had begged to know about the past. It was perhaps ironic, then, that it was Vicky who was now keeping secrets from both Clemence and Élise . . . Because she had not told her grandmother the whole truth. For neither her mother, nor her step-father, had any inkling of her grandmother's existence, and Vicky was not going to tell them yet. Not until she had at least found out everything she wanted to know.

CHAPTER 5

Clemence

Kasbah du Paradis, the next morning

As crystal clear early morning light streamed through the window, Clemence reached into the back of the top drawer of her dressing table and fished out the packet again. Ever since she had first opened it – after her granddaughter had gone to bed the evening before – she had hardly been able to tear herself away from the contents. Inside the packet there was an envelope of old photographs and a brief note: *Thought you might want these.* She did not recognise the handwriting, no name was attached, and there was no clue as to who had sent it. Clemence wished she had someone to share these with and reproached herself for pushing away the love of her life, the only man she had ever truly wanted. Even now, all this time later, the thought of him brought her to a standstill, although as far as he was concerned, it was too late, far too late, and had been for a very long time.

The black-and-white images were all shots of her family and of their home. One stood out from the rest – her father's study the day after the fire. She screwed up her eyes, trying to remember who had taken the picture. Could it have been their family doctor, Patrice Callier's father, in the ruined doorway holding a camera? She studied the photo, forcing herself to remain calm. She could still smell the oiled leather and Havana cigars in her father's study, before the fire destroyed it. Whisky too, and his pungent cologne, and the sickly overripe apricots in a blue ceramic bowl. But the man in the doorway remained hazy. Shivering, she replaced the packet of photographs in the drawer.

Had Patrice Callier sent her these? It must have been him. Who else could it have been? But why? It had to be a message of some kind. Or was she being too suspicious? A creeping sensation of being watched made her pause and look around, although wasn't she the one who was watching? She'd spent her whole life keeping one eye open – always wary – the dread of discovery haunting her for so long she had become obsessed, but even if he really *had* sent the photographs, that still didn't mean he *knew*. Taking a decisive breath in, she stood up and headed towards the breakfast room.

She had not expected Vicky to be an early riser but once again she found her granddaughter there before her, already seated and gazing out at the view of the waterfall sparkling in the honeyed light, with both dogs by her side.

'Morning,' Vicky said, rising to her feet and smiling. She really was an attractive young woman. 'Hope you don't mind me starting without you.'

'Not at all. Do sit down. I'm glad you've made friends with Coco and Voltaire. I thought we might take a walk after breakfast, maybe pick some wild mint.'

'Lovely.'

Clemence gazed at her, unable to stop the questions in her head. Did Vicky resemble Victor? Were his eyes like hers? Did they share character traits? She had specifically asked Jacques not to send any photographs of her son and even though she resisted these thoughts now, they still bubbled up.

Ahmed's sister, Nadia, brought out fresh coffee and fruit for Clemence. The girl was slight with high cheek-bones, shining skin, and kind dark brown eyes, and she was marvellous with Madeleine. So far they had worked hard to keep Madeleine away from Vicky, for who knew what she might inadvertently say about Jacques or Victor?

'It's a beautiful day for a walk,' Vicky said. 'You're so lucky to live here.'

'You don't find it a little quiet?'

'I'd be happy sitting on the terrace and drawing.'

'You draw well. Light and precise. I looked at the sketchbook you left open on the table.'

Vicky pulled a face. 'I'm no artist but I have to sketch my designs. And I don't think the kasbah will be too quiet. The only thing is I'm not sure how I will get in and out of Marrakech living here.'

32

'We are very remote, so it is indeed a problem,' Clemence said, determined not to offer Ahmed's services too readily. And while she wanted Vicky to stay safe, she could not stay at the kasbah for long. Not now. If only she had ignored her granddaughter's letter when it arrived out of the blue, but she'd felt so curious she hadn't fully considered the complications. No, if she were honest, it was more than mere curiosity. Much more than that. But Clemence already had her mother to protect, and the photographs arriving like that had changed everything. If someone really was coming after her, the sooner she moved Vicky into Marrakech the better. It was truly unfortunate, but her granddaughter would have to go.

'By the way I heard some odd sounds in the night,' Vicky said. 'Like someone moaning or wailing.'

'A wild animal? Maybe a jackal. I heard it too. There are many animals here in the mountains,' Clemence said, doing her best to sound brighter than she felt.

Vicky took a deep breath. 'I wondered if you'd like to see this picture of my father?' She drew out a photograph from her pocket and held it out.

Just for a second Clemence saw the image of a dark-haired man but immediately looked away as a torrent of mixed emotions swept through her, the power of the image so potent she feared she might pass out. She felt an ache deep in her chest. Old wounds. Old hurts. A shard of ice piercing her to the core.

She backed off. Had to put a stop to this. 'Another time,' she said, trying to hide the tremble that would give her away, and it turned her voice unduly harsh instead. She was possessed of – or rather had developed – the ability to maintain her composure despite everything. This was no time to allow herself to crumple.

Vicky blinked rapidly as if to hold back tears at the rejection, and Clemence felt sorry to have to do what she had to do.

'As long as you're careful, you'll have much more fun in Marrakech,' she said. 'Meeting young people like yourself. You don't want to be stuck here with me when Marrakech is so vital. And when your cousin arrives, you'll want to be able to enjoy the city together. I've been wondering, did you leave a boyfriend behind in London?'

Vicky pulled a face. 'Russell. But it was more like he left me.'

'Ah. Well there is nothing like Marrakech to breathe new life into a person.'

'But—'

'I'll discuss it with Ahmed now,' she interjected as she rose to her feet. 'Much better for you to be where all the amusement is. Before long you really would be bored here. I have a good friend you can stay with. She'll keep an eye on you. And after all, Yves Saint Laurent is in Marrakech, or will be at some point.'

And despite her granddaughter's bewildered look she went directly to find Ahmed.

CHAPTER 6

Vicky

Marrakech

The following day, in the cool early morning, Ahmed drove Vicky and Clemence along the bumpy road from the high mountainside into the foothills, finally reaching the red walls of the Marrakech ramparts a couple of hours later. Weaving through the city's narrow streets, he parked as closely as he could to the centre of the medina.

'Blimey,' Vicky said as she got out of the car, gasping at the heat. It was a shock after the cooler temperature at the kasbah. Clemence smiled, handing her a large white hat.

When Ahmed opened the back to retrieve Vicky's case, she said, 'It's all right. I can carry it.'

He shook his head and stepped back. 'You'll get too hot. I'm used to it.'

She nodded her thanks and as she heard a mournful, hypnotic sound, she glanced up and across at a tall red tower.

'Five times a day you will hear the call to prayer from the Koutoubia Mosque,' Ahmed said. 'The tower has been standing guard over the old city since the twelfth century.'

As they crossed the huge square of Jemaa el-Fnaa Vicky paused to soak in the mixture of mint, orange blossom, and spice in the air, plus a more animal smell too. Camels? Pitched into a world teeming with so much life, her head was reeling.

'Amazing,' she kept saying. 'Totally amazing.'

She'd been expecting to stay longer at the kasbah and had felt a little hurt when her grandmother had high-handedly told her she would be moving to Marrakech without even asking if she wanted to go. It was hard not to feel nervous about moving to the city so soon. But now she was here, she gazed in wonder at this jewel of a place and understood why so many people were drawn to it. The Islamic buildings, the luminous light, the clusters of men in striped djellabas and women wearing purple, pink and green kaftans, the snake charmers hissing incantations, the water sellers in red robes with their bells and tasselled hats, the sound of water too, from fountains she couldn't even see – it was all incredible. Like nothing she'd ever seen before and yet . . . And yet, she was aware also of feeling an odd sort of recognition too. Lost in her thoughts, she realised Clemence was speaking to her.

'Sorry, what was that?'

'I was just explaining how camel caravans used to come here from across Africa to sell their slaves. It used to be the largest slave market in Morocco.'

'Gosh. How awful.' Vicky could picture the sun beating down on those poor men, women, and children tied up in heavy chains for hours on end.

'They still have camel trading days even now.'

They moved on and Vicky paused at the sight and smell of glowing red charcoal and glanced at her grandmother. She signalled that they could stop to eat hot doughnuts dipped in sugar – utterly delicious – and Vicky watched as more were cooked in front of them, licking her fingers, eager for another. But she didn't want to appear greedy in front of Clemence, who had not an inch of fat on her and seemed to think one was quite enough. Their doughnuts were followed by tumblers of freshly squeezed orange juice from a brightly painted stall on wheels.

Ahmed led them through the winding arched passages of the medina – *derbs* he called them – where Vicky heard rhythmic drumming and the delicate lilting notes of a reed flute rising over the top, and she felt as if she were listening to the heartbeat of Morocco. The dust in the air only flickered into life whenever a beam of light managed to slip through narrow gaps in the mysterious pinkish-red walls lining the alleys. Vicky couldn't work out what lay behind them: the only clues were the faded wooden doors, studded with metal. Would she ever find her way back?

'If you're wondering how to find your way,' Ahmed said. 'Just ask for the big square and people will point you in the right direction.'

She laughed. 'Do you always read people's minds?'

He smiled but did not answer.

'Exterior Islamic architecture in Morocco is simple to avoid envy from neighbours,' Clemence explained. 'Displaying wealth is considered disagreeable.'

Eventually, Ahmed knocked at one of the huge cedar doors. 'We are here,' he said.

An older tiny hawklike woman with olive skin, startling green eyes and dyed dark brown hair opened it. Boldly decked out in a long black dress, and with bright red lipstick, an orange necklace, and silver rings on all her fingers, she was eye-catching to say the least.

After a few words in Arabic to Ahmed, and kissing Clemence on both cheeks, she turned to Vicky.

'I'm Etta,' she said, and Vicky noted her expressive features and her pronounced New York accent. 'And you must be Vicky.'

'My granddaughter,' Clemence said, and Vicky was surprised to hear a note of pride in her voice. 'I'm hoping your little apartment is still unoccupied. Vicky is coming to stay in the town for a while.'

'Indeed. Follow me.'

It struck Vicky how different Etta and her grandmother were. Clemence tall and elegantly dressed in soft colours, Etta birdlike and dramatic.

'My home is actually one large house and an adjoining *dar* knocked together,' Etta said. 'One behind the other. *Riad* comes from the word garden in Arabic, and *dar* just means a house.'

Behind an arch they were enveloped by the magic of a secret courtyard garden where roses scented the air, frilly clumps of bougainvillea climbed the walls and bright red hibiscus flowers shot out from large clay pots. Vicky heard birds singing in the palm trees and water cascading from the mouth of a fountain in the shape of a fish. Refracted sunlight glittered on the blue tiled ground and in the little pool surrounding the fountain shifting reflections of waving palm leaves caught her eye. The entire garden enchanted her.

'It transcends time, don't you think?' Clemence said and Vicky noticed how much warmer and more relaxed her grandmother seemed now.

'That was my intention, but don't get your hopes up too much, honey,' Etta said. 'The garden is the best part.'

They climbed a small staircase leading up from the garden and arrived at a solitary door.

'These would be your own stairs, if you choose to stay,' the woman said as she unlocked the door. 'The apartment is self-contained.'

The peace of the interior surprised Vicky and after Etta had closed the door behind them, she stood with her arms flung wide as if revealing the sumptuous home of a film star, her gesture as dramatic as her looks. Although it certainly wasn't luxurious, it turned out to have two rooms with a faded painted wooden screen with three folding panels dividing the bedroom and a tiny bathroom.

'It's a *Zouak* screen,' Etta said. 'Needs restoring but I hope you like it.'

Vicky nodded enthusiastically.

The room at the back was painted blue and furnished simply with a wardrobe and two single beds. Ahmed placed her case on one of them. The living area at the front had orange walls and contained a tiny kitchen, a sofa, a chair, an old fraying rug, a brass coffee table, and a leather pouf. Also what Ahmed called a loggia, a gallery with one side open to, and overlooking, the courtyard garden, but with shutters that could be closed.

'I love it,' Vicky said, her doubts vanishing as she listened to the birds and gazed down at the lush hidden garden where dwarf palms and pots of giant leafed plants looked exotic and mysterious. She watched a little brown bird alight on a leaf and it seemed like a good omen. Once her cousin Bea arrived, she was sure she wouldn't feel so alone.

'Thank you, Etta,' Clemence was saying.

The woman inclined her head. 'So that's settled. Your granddaughter is most welcome at my riad.'

Vicky turned to her, suddenly worried. Bea could be terribly featherbrained and disorganised. 'My cousin will be arriving from England in a couple of days to stay here with me. Is that all right? She speaks French fairly fluently as her mother, my aunt Florence, is half French.'

'Ah, a mixture like myself.'

Vicky frowned, not understanding.

Etta laughed. 'Oh, I know I sound New York through and through but my mother was Moroccan. My Arabic name is Ettra.'

'That's lovely. You should use it.'

'It kind of got changed when I went to school in New York City, and it stuck.'

'Pity. Might you be able to teach me a little Moroccan Arabic?'

'Of course. And your cousin is welcome, as long as she behaves herself,' Etta said with a stern look and as Vicky's face fell, she let out a loud laugh.

'Just charge the rent to me,' Clemence said.

'Oh no,' Vicky said. 'It's all right, I can manage.'

'Nevertheless. And Ahmed will take you to the *souks*, where you may find inexpensive bits and pieces to make yourselves feel more at home.'

Vicky wanted to hug her grandmother but didn't dare. Clemence wasn't as severe as she had seemed at first, but she was still distant and at the moment seemed distracted. 'Could we talk?' Vicky said. 'Before you go?'

'I have business to attend to,' Clemence said, glancing around as if suddenly anxious to leave. 'But we can meet at the French Café for lunch. Ahmed will show you the way. We'll talk then.'

Despite her excitement at having this apartment right in the thick of things, Vicky couldn't hide her disappointment, but unable to voice the questions going round in her head, she nodded. There was so much she still wanted to know.

'Don't let yourself get cheated in the souks,' her grandmother added as she headed for the door. 'It is not respectable. Put up a good fight. And whatever else you do, be careful. The souks can be dangerous. They are not the place to forget where you are.'

CHAPTER 7

Vicky clutched Ahmed's arm as they edged through the throngs of people heading to the main arched entrance of the souk, a marketplace, Ahmed said, that had been trading for centuries. They entered and as they threaded through the dusty labyrinth of passageways shaded by palm fronds criss-crossed overhead, the swarming crowds felt overwhelming.

'I'm not sure about this,' she said.

'It's fine.'

His smile was meant to be reassuring, and he seemed very relaxed, but Vicky was in danger of panicking. In the intense heat her head felt heavy, and she rubbed away the sweat beading on her forehead as she attempted to get her bearings among the sights and sounds – and smells! Spices, tobacco, camels, mules, human bodies, drains.

'You must let yourself be lost. It's more fun,' Ahmed said and laughed at the puzzled look she gave him. 'Don't worry, I'm with you.'

Vicky did not like getting lost; she kept as tight a rein on her world as she could. Her grandmother had told her to be careful and this fierce place was challenging. She needed order and predictability. Not this.

Inside the souk there was everything from mountains of preserved lemons, tubs of turmeric and cumin, cones of spices she'd never even heard of, to meat and poultry, to clothes and furnishings. As she relaxed a bit she wanted to touch everything, although not the sheep heads laid out in a line; the noxious smell of the meat turned her stomach. She shied away from them, dodging a donkey cart and colliding with a man who fell backwards into a sack of grain. Everyone in the vicinity laughed.

'Oh *merde*,' she muttered under her breath, annoyed with herself, and glaring at the young man for being in her way and embarrassing her in front of Ahmed.

'Hello,' he said, blinking rapidly as another young man was helping him straighten up.

The one who had fallen was about her age: clearly English, with a shock of long reddish hair, freckles, and wire-framed spectacles hiding myopic forget-me-not blue eyes.

'I'm so sorry,' she said, switching to English and belatedly finding her manners.

'That's better,' he said with a grin as he brushed himself down. 'Are you always this short-tempered?'

'If you will stand around dithering as if you are lost.'

'I'm not lost. Are you?'

She tilted her head. 'I'm with Ahmed over there. I'll never be lost with Ahmed.'

'Well you should stick by his side forever.' He gave her a disarming smile. 'I'm Jimmy. Jimmy Petersen. And this is my friend, Tom Goodwin.'

Jimmy had kind eyes and an intelligent expression but also looked like a typical hash-smoking lad in a tie-dyed shirt – she'd hung out with plenty of them in London. Tom, however, was an intense-looking young Englishman of about twenty-three who was heart-stoppingly gorgeous with ash blonde hair, a light tan, and very dark eyes.

'Hello,' she said, instantly drawn to him.

'Tom here is a political journalist,' Jimmy said.

'Vicky,' she said still gazing at Tom. 'Vicky Baudin.'

'French?' Tom asked.

'The name does rather give it away, doesn't it?'

'Well, yes,' he said. 'That and the slight accent. On holiday?'

'Not exactly. On a mission.'

He raised his eyebrows and paused for a moment. 'Look, a few of us are getting together at a local bar later.'

'Oh?'

'You should come, meet a few people. Where are you staying? We'll pick you up.'

'I don't know you,' Vicky said, unsure. She had never found making friends terribly easy, but this was an oppor-tunity she ought not turn down.

Tom's mouth curled in amusement. 'We don't bite, you know.'

She smiled sheepishly.

Jimmy stepped in grinning. 'Ahmed knows us. Well, to be honest, Ahmed knows practically everybody. And you will too if you come.'

Ahmed smiled, rather enigmatically, and Vicky wasn't sure if it was true, but gave the thumbs up and told them Etta's address.

'Tom and I share rooms in the house of Jamal in a street a bit further back from her place,' Jimmy said. 'Only a few minutes away. See you later.'

As the two men wandered off, she and Ahmed moved on, past curtains of silky threads hanging in brightly coloured skeins, purple, orange, and citrus green. They bypassed the silk spinners, and finally discovered the silk dyers. Then they reached the large vaults of the rug and carpet merchants, their rugs – some flat and hand-woven, some with a soft shiny pile that made Vicky melt when she ran her fingers over them – stacked high or hung according to colour.

However, despite multiple sidetracks, she kept to her plan – following Ahmed's entreaties to haggle – took her time, bargained well, and paid roughly a third of the original asking prices. By the end she'd bought a blue throw with silver thread running through it, two patterned cushions in orange and pink, a brass lamp with a purple glass lampshade, and a mirror, because Beatrice would not survive for long without one. Her cousin was awfully sweet, but rather vain too.

An image of tall, blonde-haired Bea came into her mind, and she wondered what she would make of Marrakech. Had it been wise to invite her to come, or had it been selfish? Bea was a bit ethereal, rather clueless at times. She took after her mother, Vicky's aunt Florence – who wafted around with her head in the clouds rather like her daughter and seemed to think only of writing her novels and growing vegetables – and she was far less practical than Vicky. But she and Bea got on well and Vicky had invited her almost as soon as she'd had the idea of coming here. A mix up with their tickets meant they hadn't been able to travel on the same day.

Vicky glanced at Ahmed who was standing patiently waiting while she had been lost in thought. She already knew how calm he was and felt curious about him. 'I hope you don't mind me asking,' she asked, 'but why do you seem so unfazed by everything. Are you always this good-humoured?'

'I don't strive for success in the way you do,' he said with a smile

'Why not?' she asked, feeling perplexed. 'Shouldn't we all be striving for success?'

'It is God who will determine the future not you or I. While I have enough to live, to eat, why bother? We do not struggle as you do. Everything comes from God. Good and bad.'

'Good and bad,' she repeated and carried on thinking about it until she found the kaftans. 'Oh, I just have to look at these. Have we time?'

'If you're quick.'

She touched every single one, eventually settling on two, but only after Ahmed said she might need to leave now or she would be late for lunch with Clemence.

The Café de France turned out to be a colonial-style building overlooking the main square. Donkeys, ostriches, camels, and drifts of people were now wandering between lemonade sellers whose stalls stood beneath canvas awnings and women squatting on the ground with baskets of dried roses and irises in front of them. Ahmed left her outside the café and when she went inside, she was told she must go up through several floors and would find her grandmother on the roof terrace.

Up there the low walls were a deep terracotta, coffee tables were set out with blue cushions beside them, and draped muslin shielded customers from the sun. Clemence rose from her seat and came over to kiss Vicky on both cheeks.

'What do you think of the view?' she asked.

Vicky smiled and threw her arms out wide. 'Fabulous.'

The sky had an almost peachy look and Clemence pointed out Dar El Bacha, the Pasha's palace, and indicated where La Mamounia, the hotel for the rich and the chic, was situated, adding, 'Winston Churchill used to stay there, you know, in winter. They say he drifted from one balcony to another to catch the wonderful light in his watercolours.'

'I can believe it. But what's the Pasha's Palace?'

'T'hami El Glaoui was the last Pasha or governor of Marrakech, also known as Lord of the Atlas, and it was his palace. Not much more than a decade ago you might have seen rows of salted and severed heads set on spikes in front of his palaces. But the main square itself has quite a bloody and ancient history; Jemaa el-Fnaa used to be known as the Square of the Dead because of all the executions.'

'Good gracious.'

'The Pasha himself had been a mountain warlord controlling the huge trades of precious metals, spices, drugs and prostitution.'

'So he was on the side of the colonials?'

'Indeed. He had a kasbah in the High Atlas where he filled his dungeons with nationalists and other enemies who never saw the light of day again. Telouet Kasbah, it was called.'

Vicky gazed at her grandmother. There was so much of Moroccan history she did not know, but before she could ask any more questions Clemence was moving away.

'I think we need to go downstairs where it's cooler now that you've seen the view from up here. I've already ordered the food. Just a simple salad of vegetables with coriander and spicy olives chopped with cumin. Will that do?'

Vicky was sure it would, and they went down, a waiter leading them to a low table set for lunch where they sat on patterned yellow floor cushions.

'Did you enjoy the souks?' Clemence asked.

'Yes. Ahmed helped me a lot,' Vicky said. She looked at her grandmother then asked: 'Who is he? Ahmed, I mean.'

'He's a Berber boy I've known since he was five years old,' Clemence said calmly. 'He was always intensely curious as a child. I looked out for him after his father died and his family were experiencing hard times, and now it is he who looks after me.'

'Like a bodyguard?' Vicky asked.

Clemence laughed. 'He would love you to think so.'

It hadn't really been a reply but was probably all Vicky was going to get so she changed the subject. 'You said you might help me meet Yves Saint Laurent.'

Her grandmother nodded slowly. 'Yes.'

The waiter brought them an unusual kettle filled with water.

'It's for the ritual of *tass*,' Clemence said.

'What's that?'

'Traditional hand washing before we eat.'

The food arrived and apart from the clatter of spoons on metal plates there was a short period of silence. Vicky studied her grandmother as she served the salad, trying to pin down that hint of what was elusive about her, out of reach and unknowable. There had been a moment, at Etta's, when Clemence had seemed so much warmer, but perhaps Vicky had imagined it. Maybe Clemence didn't like her after all. Maybe it wasn't pride she'd heard in her voice.

'Will you tell me more about your mother? Élise, isn't it?' Clemence asked before Vicky could mention Yves Saint Laurent again.

'Of course,' Vicky said, surprised. But perhaps if she answered Clemence's questions, Clemence might answer hers. 'My mother is one of three sisters who all used to live together in the Dordogne. There's Hélène and Florence but neither of them lives there now. My mother does live in France, not in our old house, but in Henri's chateau – he's my stepfather.'

Vicky tried to keep her voice bright as she mentioned this last detail. She couldn't understand what her mother had seen in her rather strait-laced stepfather, Henri. To Vicky the marriage was a complete betrayal. Not that Henri was unkind, no, but he couldn't compare with her real father, Victor. Although Vicky had never known him, to her Victor was a hero of the Resistance and over the past few years the urge to know more about him and the connection she felt with him had grown stronger. She wished she could talk to Élise, but the plight of every waif and stray was more important to her mother than her own daughter.

'The chateau sounds very grand,' Clemence said.

'I suppose it is. My mother used to be in the French Resistance during the war but whenever I ask about it, she won't tell me anything. Although I do understand it must be hard.'

Vicky thought back to when she had pressed and pressed her mother to tell her something more – anything more – of her father.

'I begged her to tell me more last Christmas,' she said aloud, 'And when she refused, I said . . . awful things.'

'We all say things we don't mean.'

Vicky nodded miserably.

'Is she happy for you to be here with me?' Clemence asked.

Vicky didn't reply at first. She didn't want to reveal that Élise did not even know Clemence existed. She thought of her mother's glossy dark hair, her lack of interest in fashion, her rigid determination, and glanced down at the tabletop, her stomach tightening into a knot at the memory of their final dreadful row, her mother's unforgiving eyes – eyes that were beautiful when she smiled, though she rarely smiled at Vicky these days. She mostly complained about the amount of time Vicky was spending with Jacques, her grandfather. Once Vicky finished her final year at art college in London and revealed she was going travelling to Morocco rather than returning to stay at the chateau for the summer, her mother had exploded. She had accused Vicky of selfishness, of rejecting all the effort Élise had put into organising dinner parties with old school friends and with their neighbours in and around Sainte-Cécile. Vicky hadn't known – hadn't asked her to do it – but it had hurt her mother, nonetheless.

'I don't really get on with my mother,' she muttered.

Clemence looked at her with a puzzled expression and spoke in a gentle voice. 'She'll be worried about you, won't she?'

Vicky shook her head and felt tears prickling the back of her eyelids. But she ate her salad and instead of thinking about her mother she remembered playing cards with her grandfather. He usually won but her consolation prize was his wonderful homemade lemonade which they drank at a painted blue table in his garden in Sainte-Cécile.

'So, Jacques lived here in Morocco at some point,' she said, glancing at her grandmother. 'That's how you knew him.'

Clemence gave the slightest nod.

'How long has it been since you last saw him?' Vicky asked.

'Jacques? Let me see. Quite a while.'

'But you keep in touch?'

Clemence shrugged and changed the subject while

serving them both more salad and told her again about the unsettled political situation in Marrakech finishing with, 'The CIA and the French secret service are crawling around.'

'Spies? Why?'

'Who really knows? To help shore up the regime, I think. Sniff out dissidents. Just stay away from trouble, that's all I'm saying.'

There was a long pause.

After they had both finished eating, Vicky sighed deeply.

'That sounded earnest,' Clemence said.

Vicky glanced across and spoke tentatively. 'You never married again?'

Her grandmother just shook her head.

'Please will you tell me how it all happened? Why you didn't leave for France with your husband and baby. My father. Why you told Jacques to go without you.'

Clemence looked up at the sky before gazing at Vicky and saying, 'I was young and I made a deal.'

'With whom?'

'My mother.'

'So . . . ?'

Clemence was silent. She glanced at her watch and pushed back her chair, and Vicky knew the subject was closed.

'I'm sorry I have to leave,' Clemence said, her face revealing nothing. 'Do order dessert, or do you call it pudding, having lived in England? Anyway, have them put it on my tab. Will you be able to find your way back to the riad?'

Without waiting for an answer, she stood, leaving Vicky gaping up at her.

'Goodbye for now and stay safe,' Clemence said. 'Enjoy your time in Marrakech and of course visit me at the kasbah whenever you want to. Ahmed comes down regularly and always calls at Etta's, so she'll know what to do *and* more importantly she will look after you.'

Vicky watched her walk away, feeling stricken and with her stomach in knots. She pressed her fist into her belly hard and tried to twist the pain away. Since she had come to Morocco, she had not felt like this and had foolishly assumed she might at last have overcome it.

After she'd left home, she'd seen doctors for her low moods; depression was the label they had given her. She'd learnt to keep a tight grip on her emotions because how could she begin to describe the eviscerating hollow feeling hidden inside her? As a growing child she had yearned for the embraces her mother rarely offered. She knew Élise loved her, but she had no patience for what she saw as emotional indulgence, and as Vicky became a teenager the feeling grew. Though when she'd looked in the mirror during her mid-teens, her reflection never revealed the hopelessness inside her, and her mother hadn't seen it either – or hadn't wanted to. And Henri, courteous and affectionate but never overstepping the politeness of a stepfather, only ever said: 'Don't worry. It's a phase. She'll grow out of it.'

She had been hoping that tracking down her grand-mother would help fill that gap – somehow make up for never knowing her father *and* for her mother's distance.

But it was becoming clear to her that she wasn't going to bask in the sense of belonging she craved from knowing Clemence. And gazing around at the amazing square and thinking of her grandmother, she realised the past was holding its secrets tighter than ever.

CHAPTER 8

Clemence

Coward, Clemence muttered. *Coward.* She could still see Vicky's disappointed face. Why couldn't she have thought of something better to say, even if it was only to express how pleased she was to have this opportunity to get to know her granddaughter? The rising affection she'd felt was unexpected but, unsettled by the dense layers of the secret past lying between them, she had simply run away. The truth was she had only ever informed Jacques of her new name and the name of the kasbah. Nothing more. There had been no keeping in touch.

She closed her eyes for a moment, praying Vicky was sensible enough to stay safe. It wasn't necessary to scare the girl half to death, but she'd had to impress that caution was important. It wouldn't be easy for the girl. Vicky had a thirst for life and wanted answers to questions she had not yet even thought of. Caution would not be at the forefront of her mind.

Meanwhile Clemence had no idea how to accommodate herself to this immense change in her life. *A granddaughter. My own flesh and blood.* That Vicky was here, when Clemence had never even known her own son, Victor, seemed impossible. She had been a mother and she had not been a mother. How could you ever explain how that felt? And yet wasn't that the reason she had allowed her granddaughter to come?

She glanced around, searching for Ahmed and once she had found him quickly left the square, looking forward to the solace of her home. She didn't linger in town as they headed for her jeep, merely nodding at a few acquaintances here and there. These people considered her calm, unsentimental, well balanced, but even after all these years, they knew nothing about her. It was impossible to maintain anonymity but at least she could resist familiarity and she had done so. Word spread quickly here if you weren't careful.

As Ahmed drove the jeep up the potholed tracks around Imlil and she could see the outline of her home ahead, Clemence thought of their old family estate where, as a girl, she'd played with Jacques, Vicky's grandfather. It didn't take much to summon the sunnier memories of the past. The sound of whistling or the smell of apples would instantly nudge her back and there Jacques would be with his sticking out ears, mischievous brown eyes, skinny little-boy legs and the worst whistle you ever heard. She enjoyed revisiting those hot magical afternoons still sprinkled with stardust, even after all this time.

But her childhood friendship with half Moroccan, half French Jacques, the son of her father's driver, had been a closely guarded secret. Her landowning family and the other French settlers, along with their supporters in France, had tried to prevent any moves towards Moroccan independence and looked down on the locals as 'filthy ignorant natives' – her father's exact words. If her father had discovered their friendship, he would have ended it and Clemence's life would have become as lonely as it had been before she'd known Jacques. Although Vicky was now aware that she and Jacques had known each other in Morocco, she felt certain Jacques would not have told Vicky the rest of this story.

When Clemence was a child her governess, Mlle Lamorey, was the lazy kind who liked to doze in the heat of the afternoon. Clemence would creep out, hiding in the rose garden until it was safe, then picking her way through the apple orchards and running past the orange groves. And there Jacques would be in the little hollow they'd turned into a shady hideaway of mimosa branches and palm leaves. Both only eight or nine, with no siblings, they swore oaths of mutual loyalty and pretended to be brother and sister for it was what they wanted most in the world.

'Oh Jacques, Jacques,' she whispered under her breath. 'I am so sorry.'

She placed a hand over her heart and allowed the memories of him to subside although other aspects of the past continued to thunder alongside her and the photographs still disturbed her. *Thought you might want these.* Why? And what had Patrice really been doing halfway up the mountain when he found Madeleine? Had it been a coincidence? She doubted it. Still felt it must have been he who'd sent the package of old black-and-white photos. And unable to let go of the one of her father's burnt study which lingered in her mind, she closed her eyes to try to block it out. Her secrets must remain with her.

Back at the kasbah her dogs followed her to the kitchen where Nadia handed her a tray. She headed to the annexe, placing the tray on a tiled mosaic table kept outside. It was impossible to unlock the door while ensuring Madeleine did not slip out *and* carry a tray inside at the same time.

The dogs snuffled around her ankles. She gave them both a pat on the head and ordered them to stay. They sat and scanned her face with adoring eyes.

'*Maman,*' she called as she went in, wishing her mother was as easy to keep under control as her darling boys.

Her mother did not reply.

Clemence put the tray down and went into the bedroom where Madeleine was sitting in an armchair, her bony fingers pleating the cloth of her dress over and over. It pained Clemence to see her living like a ghost in a house where she had never belonged. Her mother would frown, straining to see, and then her eyes would dart around in search of something she recognised, something she could never find, while muttering over and over, *I want to go home. I want to go home. I want to go home.* But Clemence suspected the home she wanted wasn't a place at all. The home she wanted was her own self. The person she had once been. Or the person she might have been, or could have been but never had the chance to be. It was anybody's guess.

'Do I know you?' Madeleine demanded in a thin reedy voice.

Clemence sighed. 'I am your daughter. Do you remember?'

'Don't lie to me. You are not her. She ran away.'

Her mother began to sob, rocking back and forth, tapping her head and crying, 'Bats! Bats!'

All Clemence could do was stroke her back where, through the fine cotton nightdress, she could feel her bony spine and the awful scars. Once Madeleine stopped crying and looked up at her with a smile, Clemence dabbed at her face with a flannel and fetched a book of plants. Her mother loved flowers and liked to run her trembling fingertips over the pictures of roses and delphiniums.

She watched Madeleine touching the pages of the book tentatively, as if it were made of glass. Then she looked up and said, 'Adele, my darling girl. You should have told me you would be coming. I'd have prepared the guest bedroom.'

'Clemence, *Maman.* Remember?' She swallowed the lump in her throat but her eyes moistened anyway. These brief moments of recognition always broke her. She smiled at her mother and discreetly brushed her own tears away.

'Don't worry, *Maman,*' she said. 'I've already prepared the room.'

CHAPTER 9

Vicky

At eight Jimmy was waiting at Etta's front door and he and Vicky walked to the square. She was a little disappointed not to see his friend Tom with him but didn't say anything. In the square, enchanted by the feverish atmosphere on such a hot treacly night, Vicky listened to the staccato beat of drums, the clashing cymbals, the reedy pipes, and she gazed at the young boys with painted faces dancing suggestively while clicking castanets.

The aroma of meat, cinnamon and cloves filled the air and she noticed people sitting at long communal tables with shared bowls of lamb, couscous and vegetables. Her feet barely touched the ground as they passed knots of storytellers with huge spellbound crowds gathered around them, squatting women selling flat round loaves of bread, and acrobats in bright costumes building terrifying towers of human bodies.

Down the side of an atmospheric winding alley, lit by lanterns, they joined a dozen or so young people drinking beer. Vicky listened to their excited, earnest voices and felt awkward and left out. It wasn't really a bar, just the backroom of somebody's house; she wasn't sure whose.

'Look, there's Tom,' Jimmy said and they walked over to the intense young Englishman.

'Hello,' she said, so drawn to him she felt it must show.

Tom only gave her a vague nod before wandering off. Vicky watched him go, wondering why he was being so aloof when he had been so friendly before, but then she noticed Jimmy regarding her closely and felt her cheeks flaming.

'What?'

He winked and spoke in a whisper. 'I wouldn't get too keen. Tom can be like that sometimes. Too busy and preoccupied to have fun.'

'Oh,' she said.

'You're not disappointed?' Jimmy asked.

She shrugged. 'Why would I be? I don't know him.'

'So. What brings you to Morocco?'

'I know it sounds stupid, but I want to meet Yves Saint Laurent.'

Jimmy whistled and then whispered in her ear. 'It's not too much of a secret to say that all of us here . . . I suppose you'd call us rebels.'

'Like the Resistance during the war in France?'

'Sort of. And we all have to hide our views.'

'From whom?'

'Anyone we don't trust.'

'Why risk telling me then?' Vicky asked. She was not sure how serious Jimmy was being.

'I've done my research. Ahmed is a friend, and you are the granddaughter of Clemence Petier, and must be under her protection.'

'You know her?'

'I know of her. Plus you're staying in Etta's riad. She's a bit of an old-school bohemian, a creative like Virginia Woolf and the Bloomsbury set. She's half Moroccan, you know, and if you had right-wing connections, you certainly would *not* be hanging out there.

Vicky narrowed her eyes. 'Maybe I'm a spy . . .'

'Are you?'

'No, but I wouldn't tell you if I were, would I? Clearly you understand nothing about espionage.'

He chuckled. 'And you know so much?'

'Absolutely. Anyway, I'm flattered you've been checking up on me.'

'Don't be. I had to, before you came here with me. Frankly, we are all scared. The CIA and the French secret service have agents working undercover so you never can tell who is okay and who is keeping us under observation.'

'Why are they? Watching, I mean.'

'So they can identify communist sympathisers. You know how Americans hate communists. We have friends, dissidents, who've stood up against the government and they've disappeared without trace.'

'Not murdered surely?'

He shrugged. 'We believe so.'

'What do the dissidents want?'

'It's complicated but mainly education for all. Last year there were street riots originating in Casablanca but they spread to other cities. Of course, you have to choose who and what you believe.'

Vicky hadn't expected to hear anything like this. Her grandmother had told her to be careful. Is this what she had meant?

'Tom and I are digging for the truth about what happened to a man called Mehdi ben Barka.'

'Who?'

'He was the most radically outspoken opponent of the government, but ben Barka vanished from a street in Paris last year. He's not been seen since and nobody has any idea what happened to him.'

'So you are a journalist too, like Tom?'

'More of an activist.'

Vicky stared, shocked by everything he'd said, then let out her breath in relief as a buzz ran through the room. A glamorous girl with a cloud of bright auburn hair sauntered in, decked out in a scandalously sheer silk dress and gold high heels, and everyone turned to look.

'Slumming it tonight, Frieda?' one of the lads said.

She blew him a kiss and dug out an ebony cigarette holder from her bag. 'Got a smoke, darling?' she asked in a slow Texan drawl.

Jimmy lit one for her and she inserted it into the holder. 'Darling, come to my friend's party in the Palmeraie, Sunday evening. It'll be a gas. I promise. You've been there before, Jimmy.'

'Might well join you,' he said.

'Good. Bring your friend. Come and learn *dolce far niente*,' she said, laughing as she glanced at Vicky.

'The sweetness of doing nothing,' Jimmy muttered.

'So, who are you?' Frieda asked Vicky. 'And what are you doing with this English ragbag?'

'Vicky Baudin. I'm a fashion designer.' And even though it was almost true, it still rang rather hollow.

'Well, my darling, *you* are in the right place.' She eyed Vicky up and down. 'Pity you're not taller though.'

Vicky always tried to appear self-assured, at least on the face of it, but this woman's boundless confidence made her feel small and stupid.

'I'm so sorry about my lack of stature,' she said, her hackles rising.

'Don't mind me, sweetie. I didn't mean anything. I need models, that's all. Come to the party. Put on your glad rags and if you haven't got any, try my shop. *Frieda's Frocks* in Gueliz, the new town. I have some gorgeous silk embroidered folkloric dresses which would look fabulous on you. Fifteen per cent discount for newbies.'

She led Vicky to a cast-iron bench overflowing with plump patterned cushions. Frieda turned out to be nicer than she'd seemed at first, reminding Vicky not to be so hasty in her judgements. The woman had lived in Morocco for years, where she'd met Youssef who came from a wealthy Moroccan family connected to the sultan and didn't need to work. He'd financed her shop and they'd been together ever since.

'Of course, he's not allowed to marry me, a foreigner. And a white one at that. A mixed relationship isn't well tolerated.'

'Don't you mind?' Vicky thought of Etta, but of course she had grown up in New York.

'What would be the point?'

As she and Frieda talked, Vicky loosened up. 'I adore adventure,' she said. 'And I'm absolutely determined to go places.'

'You're like me. Driven. I didn't come from money, not like some.' She paused then added, 'Say, why not show me some examples of your work?'

'Really?' Vicky experienced a rush of excitement but hid it quickly and went for a nonchalant look instead.

'Sure. Come tomorrow. I have a seamstress who does amazing stuff for me. We might be able to make a few samples. See how they go. Well . . . I'd better split. Find Youssef. See you tomorrow. And come to the party – Sunday. Jimmy knows where my friend's place is.'

She disappeared into a room at the back and Vicky didn't see her again. When she asked Jimmy about her, he said, 'Don't be taken in by her performance. She likes showing off all right. But she's okay and she's well in with all the beautiful people.'

'Like whom?'

'Yves, my girl. Yves. Frieda could get you an in.'

'She invited me to her shop tomorrow.'

'Why don't I drive you then?'

'Really?'

'Meet you on the main road at ten?'

She smiled at him, delighted.

* * *

The next day the road was quiet as Vicky waited, nervously watching a couple of cyclists who both looked far too old to be wobbling past on their equally ancient bicycles. Next, a lorry came by loaded with planks of wood precariously tied on with rope and heading out of Marrakech old town. It was very hot although the sky was grey and heavy. Perhaps there was rain on the way. At half past ten, just as she was checking her watch for the hundredth time – she always liked to be on time – Jimmy screeched to a shuddering halt in a battered yellow Citroën.

'Ta-dah!' he said, as he waved at her through the open window, his long red hair blowing about and his blue eyes shining behind his spectacles. 'Welcome to my limousine.'

She laughed. 'Blimey! That thing actually goes?'

'Do not insult my pride and joy. She may have seen better days, but she does have feelings.'

'A sensitive car,' she scoffed, but she got in, and after stalling twice, Jimmy set off for Gueliz.

'Picked her up in Paris,' he said. 'Drove down through Spain and onward to Morocco by ferry. I share the car with Tom now.'

As they neared the new town Vicky scanned streets where wide boulevards lined with trees were connected by roundabouts, just like in Paris. The place was bursting with elegant apartment buildings, wide open parks, beautiful gardens, Art Deco villas, and modern shops. A world away from the winding narrow streets of the medina and the souks.

'Actually,' he said, 'this new town was built by the French in the early 1900s.'

'Not so new then.'

'No.'

Vicky drummed her fingers on the dashboard, impatient to show Frieda some of her designs. It wasn't much but it was a start, and failure was impossible to contemplate. Freida had been right, last night, to call her driven. She had been that way ever since she was very young. Ever since she spent every day at school with the other children taunting her, calling her a *bâtarde*. They used to laugh about her dead father, miming him being shot in the head.

'I'll show you,' she'd vowed then, teeth clenched together. 'I'll show all of you.'

Their cruel words echoed in her head, but it was a door to the past she rarely allowed to remain open for long, so she slammed it shut and stared out of the window instead.

Jimmy parked and pointed out Frieda's shop. 'I'll stop off for a coffee and we can meet back at the car in half an hour or so.'

Clutching her portfolio, she tried the shop door, but it didn't open, and she couldn't see if there were any lights on inside. She felt foolish standing outside on her own like this and glanced around to see if anyone was watching her. Maybe she'd mistaken the time or perhaps they were early. The street was quiet, so she narrowed her eyes and pressed her forehead up against the window. Definitely no lights. As she peered in and her eyes adjusted to the gloom, she saw nothing but empty dress rails, reams of untidy paperwork, and piles of abandoned boxes on the floor. Could this really be the right place? Jimmy had pointed it out, known it. She felt the disappointment keenly. But as she stared at the mess a little longer, an alarm rang in her head and her stomach knotted. She was looking at chaos. Total disarray. Oh God. A frenzied departure. Frieda had said nothing about leaving, hadn't even hinted at it.

She waited, wandering up and down outside the shop for half an hour, just in case, and spotted a man reflected in the window glass. A stranger with a shaved head and a thin, hollow-cheeked face, an unpleasant face, and he was laughing at her. It made her flesh creep, yet when she spun round to look, he'd gone. It was blazing hot, much worse here than in the medina, and with so little shade and so many reflections in the glass, she thought she must have imagined the man. Inside her loose cotton dress she was dripping with sweat. Time to move and find her way back to Jimmy's yellow Citroën.

When she told Jimmy about the shop and the man she thought she'd seen he was completely silent, his face grave as he glanced around.

'What are you looking for?'

He didn't reply.

'Frieda promised she'd be there,' she said. 'But honestly the shop looked as if it had been trashed, emptied. I don't understand. She asked me out here last night. Has there been some kind of burglary?'

'I'm not sure. Get in the car. I need to think, and we can't talk about this in the street.'

But even in the car Jimmy remained curt.

'It's odd, isn't it? Her vanishing so unexpectedly. You told me people were disappearing.'

68

'They are. I'm not aware of what Frieda may have been up to or who she was involved with, but I've got a good idea.'

For the rest of the way they remained in silence, but after a while she became aware that Jimmy was glancing repeatedly in his mirrors, his body stiff with tension. With a feeling of unease in her stomach, Vicky twisted round and saw a green jeep trailing about fifty yards behind them.

'I think they're following us,' Jimmy said.

'Really?' Vicky turned round to look again. The jeep had tinted windows, which did seem very odd in such a tough-looking vehicle.

'They've made every turn I've made. As I said, I share this car with Tom. If they have been watching him, maybe they think he's driving.'

'Might they have been watching you?' Vicky said.

Jimmy didn't reply.

After a moment, she heard him growl, 'Oh Christ, I bloody knew it! Hold on tight!'

The green jeep was suddenly bearing down on them at great speed. Vicky went rigid, her heart pounding. The jeep rammed into the Citroën from behind and Vicky lurched, her head snapping backwards and forwards from the shock of it. A deafening roar followed as the jeep smashed into them a second time. Gasping for breath, Vicky gripped the edges of her seat and was jolted back and forth again. The jeep pulled away. *Was it over? Was that it?* But far too quickly and before she had time to understand what was happening, the jeep tore into them again, slamming hard, this time right into the side of the Citroën. Her head emptied and her muscles turned to liquid. All she could feel was the tremendous force of the impact, the sound of crunching metal. Somewhere outside of herself she heard screaming. And then she realised it was her; she was the one screaming. Another vicious slam and they'd be crushed to death. Jammed against the door her chest tightened. She couldn't breathe. Could only smell the stink of scorching tyres and the hot chemical smell of mangled metal. The car rocked. Began to tip. And with a judder it finally gave way. She screamed again. And the Citroën pitched into the storm ditch while the other car drove off at speed.

CHAPTER 10

Vicky and Jimmy crawled out of the battered car. Trembling and breathless, they clutched hold of each other, doubled over at the side of the road. Vicky couldn't speak, but panted like a dog, shivering despite the heat.

'It's the shock,' Jimmy said once he'd caught his breath and straightened up.

She swallowed, holding her side.

'Does it hurt?' he asked.

She shook her head. 'Not much.'

'There's blood on your cheek.'

'It's nothing. My leg hurts a bit.'

'Show me.'

He examined her ankle and calf. 'Probably bruised. You'll be okay.'

'What the hell do we do?' she asked, too frightened to be embarrassed at the tears filling her eyes and spilling unchecked down her cheeks.

In reply he took her hand. 'Can you walk?'

She insisted she could, and he pulled her onto the road with him where he stuck out his thumb.

'We hitch? Is it safe?'

'You have a better idea?'

As they waited, she furiously brushed the tears away but they kept on coming.

'Beats me why you can't stop crying. It's freaking me out.'

'Getting rammed off the road is freaking *me* out.'

'Sorry.'

Ten minutes later, a lorry driver stopped for them.

Back at the riad in Marrakech, Etta, dressed in black as usual with all her silver rings in place, checked them both over while sighing dramatically.

'Well,' she said at last. 'At least it's only a few cuts and bruises. You're damn lucky you didn't break your necks. What in God's name was going on, honey? Was it a prank?'

Vicky could barely speak and only managed to shake her head, but at least she'd stopped crying.

'Look, I have to arrange for the car to be picked up,' Jimmy said, then turned to her. 'Will you be all right if I go?'

She squinted at him in bewilderment. 'I just don't understand why they did it.'

'To scare us.'

'Did you recognise the driver?' Etta asked.

He shook his head. 'Tinted windows.'

'But why me?' Vicky said. 'I could have been killed. We both could.'

'You were collateral damage,' Jimmy said. 'I—'

'Don't you worry,' Etta interrupted as if to shut Jimmy up. 'I'll make sure Vicky rests today. After all, she has to meet her cousin off the night train tomorrow morning.'

'We'll get to the bottom of it, Vicky, I promise,' Jimmy said. 'And I'll try to find out what's going on with Frieda's shop.'

With a self-conscious pat on her shoulder, he left.

His words did nothing to dispel how awful she was still feeling. For the rest of the day she lay on her bed going over and over what happened. She could have been killed. It was hard to believe, and how was she going to welcome Bea after such a day? How much should she tell her? She didn't want to frighten her with the truth of how she'd got the bruises on her legs and a cut on her face – but neither could she lie. Bea should know about the dangers that she too might be facing. Had Vicky been selfish to invite her? She had thought Bea might need the distraction just as much as Vicky needed the company. It had been only a few weeks ago that Bea had phoned her in London, weeping uncontrollably and blurting out that she had messed up her A levels.

'And my best friend will pass everything,' she kept repeating. 'With flying colours. I wish I was dead.'

It was then that she'd asked Bea to come to Morocco too.

Early the next morning there was a knock on the apartment door. Vicky opened it to find Ahmed. He explained that he had come to Marrakech to pick up something

Clemence needed, so while he was here he would drive her to meet her cousin Beatrice at the station. She hadn't been expecting this, had planned to take a taxi, and rather wished he hadn't turned up – especially when he spotted the plaster on her cheek and she had no option but to tell him what had happened.

'Your grandmother,' he said frowning. 'She is a good woman. You have to tell her.'

Vicky glared at her feet and scowled. 'I'd really rather not,' she muttered.

'If you don't,' he said, 'I will.'

She glanced up at him. 'Etta will probably tell her anyway.'

He sighed deeply and gave her a disapproving look. 'Honesty is always best.'

At the station Ahmed went ahead and Vicky followed as they made their way through the noisy jostling crowd. Vicky coughed in air thick with the acrid smell of cigarette smoke and laced with the smell of overripe pineapples. Right in the middle of the congestion, an old man sat on the ground, cutting the fruit into chunks and selling them in paper cones. There were quite a few Europeans milling around too, and she could hear American accents as well.

'Do you mind so many foreigners flocking to your country?' she asked.

Ahmed gave a non-committal shrug.

'Come on, you can tell me.'

'Well, it brings money I suppose. Work for people.'

'What about my grandmother?'

'She was born here and has lived here all her life. It is not just a passing fad for her. Come on. Follow me.'

When they finally reached the platform, the night train had already arrived. But where was Bea? Eager to see her and feeling anxious they might somehow miss each other among the swarming crowds of people, Vicky glanced around. Her cousin could quite easily make off with the first person who was kind to her. But then she spotted her dragging an overstuffed suitcase that looked about to burst. Vicky waved and ran towards her. Tall and thin, her cousin was the spitting image of Pattie Boyd, the model: pretty, with blue eyes, a delicate alabaster complexion, and long straight blonde hair flicked up at the ends. Vicky had always envied her hair – and Bea's cast-iron constitution and ability to eat absolutely anything without ever gaining a pound, while she herself continued to struggle.

Vicky gave her cousin an affectionate hug. Bea was wearing a sleeveless bohemian-style dress in clashing colours and looked amazing, her long hair smooth and styled. Even her false eyelashes were still in place. No mean feat after a journey on the night train. Eyes wide with excitement Bea spoke breathlessly and fanned herself with her hand. 'Oh . . . my . . . God, sweating already. So hot and it's still early. What happened to your face?'

'It's a long story. I'll tell you later.'

But Bea was barely listening. 'Is Morocco as romantic as we thought? Have you met Yves Saint Laurent? I didn't sleep a wink on the train. Oh my goodness, I can't believe I'm here. I was scared though, especially in Tangier, weren't you? Did it blow your mind?'

At nineteen, Bea was three years younger and seemed it as the gush of words spilt excitedly from her.

'Bea, slow down,' Vicky said, amused. 'I've only been here for five minutes so no I've not met Yves, but I have got us somewhere nice to stay and a party to go to on Sunday.'

Like a little girl bursting with excitement, Bea clapped her hands. 'Oh, I can't wait. Such a blast, isn't it? What will you wear? I brought a dress especially for parties. Orange, well sort of orange and yellow with a bit of blue. And silver sandals. They had gold ones which would have been better, but not in my size. Gold looks better with orange I think, don't you?'

'You're exhausting me, Bea. Take a breath.'

But Bea seemed not to have even heard her. 'Is it all frantically bohemian? You know . . . writers, artists and so on, like we thought? Does everyone smoke hashish? Mother must be pulling her hair out. Yours too. By the way, I really need to buy a hat. Big-brimmed to keep the sun off my face. A scarf too. Silk, I think or maybe cotton.'

Bea carried on talking the entire time they were in the car. Ahmed took them as close as possible to the riad, dropping them a few hundred yards from Etta's.

'I can carry your case,' he offered.

'Oh thanks,' Bea said, and batted her eyelashes at him.

'Don't be silly. I'm sure Ahmed has work to do and it's no distance. See you later,' Vicky said and picked up Bea's case.

After Ahmed had headed away to see to his errands and begin the journey back up to the kasbah, the girls were walking along a narrow alley, Bea still commenting on everything, when Vicky heard shouting and the sound of a skirmish.

She held up her hand. 'Shhh! Did you hear that?'

'What?'

'I'm not sure but it didn't sound good.'

As they rounded the corner to Etta's, they spotted something lying on the ground right outside her house. On closer inspection Vicky saw it was a hemp basket lying on its side, half of its contents strewn right across the cobbles. Some of the packages had been torn open, the contents now in the process of being wolfed by a skinny dog who snarled as they approached.

'Oh, the poor animal,' Bea said. 'He's starving. Can we—'

Vicky sighed. 'No. We can't rescue every homeless animal you come across.'

And Vicky noticed, among the mess of spilt food and partly eaten items, half a dozen perfect little oranges looking so bright and juicy but not loved enough to be retrieved. Or perhaps not having been able to have been retrieved. Vicky stared at them. What had happened here?

CHAPTER 11

Clemence

Kasbah du Paradis

Clemence picked up the thick white envelope Ahmed had just brought her and slid her fingernail under the flap. The wrapper from one of her father's Havana cigars fell out. With a growing sense of unease, she smelt once again the trace of smoke, the apricots, and the oiled leather in his study. She pulled out a sheet of white paper, unfolded it, and her breath caught as she read:

You think you have got away with it, don't you?

Still tormented by the photographs, this was too much. But who was behind it? Who wanted to frighten her like this? Because whoever it was, they were succeeding. With shaking hands she crumpled the note and flung it into the wastepaper basket. Then she glanced at the packet of photos again. She picked it up and laid the photos out on her dressing table, hoping to find a clue, anything to indicate or confirm who might have sent them. And, more crucially, help her understand why. There were eight in total. Two showed the beautiful ornate edifice of their old French villa, one was of her father's burnt study, and the others were of the orchards and gardens, including one of the well. Although she had sought to erase the past, her mind refused.

Even though Patrice Callier hadn't said anything to suggest he knew about what had happened, Clemence had not been herself since he first arrived at the kasbah. Even in his seventies there was still a shameless look in his eyes – a man who would step over the line as soon as look at you. Gazing at the photos again, chewing the inside of her cheek until she tasted blood, she thought about him as a child. Lonely. Unpleasant. Obsessive. She wasn't certain *he* had even sent the photos, but what if he had? What if he had come to confront her? It made her sick to even ask herself the question.

She was badly in need of a good friend, someone who loved her as she wanted to be loved. Someone who would hold her and tell her everything was all right when she revealed the terrible secrets she had kept for so long. But when she'd had that one chance in her life, fear had stopped her. Back then she had been strange and solitary, and so desperate to hide the truth she had pushed away the only man she'd ever allowed herself to fall in love with. Now she wished she could go back in time.

She arched her back and rotated her shoulders to relieve the tension and the stubborn fear coiling inside her. The harder she had suppressed the pain of the past, the more powerful it had become. It lay in wait, monstrous and terrifying. She'd fought so hard not only for her sanity but for her survival too and she feared having no control if the past ever pried its way out. Unhooking her mind from the memories, she slid the photographs into the envelope and put them back in the drawer. There had been nothing. No clues, except that she felt certain the image of her father's burnt study had been intended to send her a message.

When Ahmed arrived back in the afternoon, he drew her aside to sit in her private courtyard garden where the zesty fragrance of the citrus trees mingled with the sweetness of jasmine and rose. As they sipped the freshly squeezed orange juice Nadia brought them, he handed her a package from the Marrakech pharmacy containing Madeleine's medication and told her about Vicky's accident.

'So, you're saying it was definitely an accident?' she said frowning, catching hesitancy in his voice.

'Well, no, Madame,' he said and paused momentarily. 'It seems the car was rammed off the road.'

'Oh Lord! What should I do?'

'She's all right. A few scratches. Nothing more.'

Clemence immediately felt that she wanted to go to Vicky but was it right to leave Madeleine again? She liked to bathe her mother in the evening herself and then sit with her, singing softly while she fell asleep. And what if she did leave her? She couldn't rush into Marrakech every time something went wrong. Vicky would become too reliant on her, and she did have eagle-eyed Etta on her side. But still, Clemence felt tormented by indecision because being rammed off the road was hardly a minor occurrence. Who could have done such a thing and why?

She sighed. 'I think I should go.'

'Why not leave it for today and decide tomorrow?' Ahmed said. 'If she needs anything Etta will take care of her until then.'

The next day Clemence couldn't keep still. She did some desultory weeding and reluctantly attempted to cut back her trailing honeysuckle but soon gave up and over a strong coffee sat down to read a novel, *The Magus* by John Fowles. Although this literary thriller about a young Englishman who accepted a teaching position on a remote Greek island was fascinating, it didn't grip her because at the back of her mind she was worrying about whether Vicky was really all right.

She put the book down and rose to her feet, glancing at the burnished gold of her sun-drenched courtyard walls. The contrast with the cool depths of the shade where Madeleine lay asleep on a chaise longue was gorgeous, and the sound of water trickling from the little fountain had been gently soothing her mother, but Clemence still decided it was time to move her.

After Madeleine was settled with Nadia, Clemence circled the grounds. The sky was incredibly blue and the mountains bleached of colour. But when the shimmering heat became too much for her, she drifted indoors, a glass of water in hand, still unable to connect with her usually peaceful life. She had to go to Marrakech. It was the only thing to do.

At Etta's, Clemence met Beatrice for the first time and found it hard not to stare at how stunning the girl was as she stood smiling nervously.

'Hello,' Bea said breathlessly and held out her hand. 'I'm so happy to meet you. Wasn't it awful about the car? Honestly, I couldn't believe it. What do you think? I said to Vee, well more than once actually, that really, she should—'

'Let's forget about the car accident,' Vicky said, jumping in quickly.

Clemence sighed. 'Be that as it may, do you know if the damage is irreparable?'

'Not for sure, but I think Jimmy is getting it fixed.'

'Ah. Jimmy Petersen's yellow Citroën. I've seen it out and about.'

Vicky nodded. 'The very one. Do you know Jimmy?'

'Only by sight.'

'Anyway, now it's cooler, we're going shopping. Would you like to join us?' She paused and added rather shyly, 'Um, silly not to have asked before, but what should I call you? *Grand-mère* sounds so stuffy.'

'Clemence will do nicely.'

Fascinated by Vicky's quick recovery, she mentally compared the two cousins, wondering what innate traits Vicky had acquired from her mother's side that might be similar to Bea's, and what she might have inherited from Victor's side and therefore her own.

Vicky touched her arm and said, 'We're going to find a hat and scarf to go with Bea's orange dress. You could help us choose if you like.'

Despite her concerns for her granddaughter's safety, Clemence found it exhilarating being with young people. Not that she wanted to be young again herself, but it was tempting to bask in their glow for at least a little while as they flitted from stall to stall in the souks. Bea's childlike enthusiasm was infectious and eventually she found a hat and a flowery blue scarf she considered 'utterly groovy' and – with a defect that meant the pattern hadn't repeated properly – she was thrilled to get it half price.

It was as hot as ever and Clemence noticed Bea's constant chatter slowing as they moved on from stall to stall. Then, on their way back to the main square, they spotted Ahmed approaching. Vicky waved but Bea trailed behind, repeatedly complaining about a sudden headache.

'Really, Bea, could you just stop talking for one minute?' she heard Vicky mutter irritably.

'My head hurts. I'm not used to the heat. You could be more sympathetic.'

'Beatrice, this is me. If you wanted sympathy you should have stayed home in Devon with Aunt Florence and Uncle Jack.'

'Wish I had,' Bea said in a sulky tone.

Clemence smiled at their exchange and turned to them. 'Would you two like coffee?'

Vicky explained about Bea's headache.

'Oh, poor you,' Clemence said. 'In which case Ahmed will show Beatrice the way home and purchase some aspirin on the way. You should drink plenty of water, my dear. Vicky, you and I will go to the Café de France. How does that suit?'

In the square Clemence led Vicky to a table under an awning outside the café. She ordered for them both and when the waiter brought their iced coffee and almond croissants on a silver tray, she looked on as her granddaughter ate hers hungrily, watching the scenes going on around them all the time.

'Delicious,' she said and took a sip of the coffee. 'And this is too.'

'It's the local ice cream they use.'

They sat in silence, Vicky still gazing at the passers-by. Despite feeling curious about her granddaughter's life and wanting to ask all sorts of questions, her presence was also unsettling. Victor, whom Clemence had never talked about with anyone, was not far from her mind and she was wondering how much she could safely reveal to her granddaughter.

'I understand you're keen to know everything,' she said eventually, looking at Vicky, 'and there will be time.'

But before she had formulated what else to say she became aware of someone approaching their table. She glanced up and saw the man run a hand through his silver hair.

'I do apologise for the interruption,' he said, smiling broadly.

A tremor ran through her. She had hoped to have seen the last of him. 'Still here?' she said coolly.

'Indeed.'

She swallowed hard, hoping he could not see her discomfort. 'Vicky. This is Patrice Callier. Like you and I, he is French.'

'A former captain in the French Army,' he said, his eyes shining. 'I spent many years away but decided to return to Morocco recently. Loose ends to tie up, that sort of thing. Delighted to meet you, Vicky.'

Vicky inclined her head.

'And what brings you—' he began but Clemence interrupted him.

'You are a photography enthusiast nowadays?' she asked spotting the camera hanging from his neck. *Was there a link to the photographs? Was there?*

'Ah yes, my hobby, but I've been an art dealer for the last few years.'

Clemence glanced at her watch. 'Oh goodness! My apologies, Patrice,' she said without catching his eye. His smile remained fixed when she quickly rose to her feet and reached out a hand to Vicky, who pushed back her chair and stood up too.

'It had completely slipped my mind, but Vicky and I have rather an urgent errand to see to. I'm so sorry.'

'Another time,' he said with a slight bow. 'Once again forgive the intrusion. So nice to see you again, Clemence, and to meet you, Vicky.'

After he had gone Clemence needed to dispel the nerves Patrice's appearance at her table had sparked and wasn't aware of how quickly she was striding away from the café.

'Slow down,' Vicky called out to her. 'It's too hot to walk so fast.'

She came to a halt but couldn't help scanning the square to see if he was still there.

'Are you all right?' Vicky asked, looking worried. 'You seem to be in a tearing hurry.'

'I'm fine. I just wasn't in the mood for Patrice today.'

'Oh? I thought he was a friend.'

Clemence hesitated but then managed a smile and said, 'Not really.'

'Don't you like him?'

Clemence felt nauseous but recovered herself enough to say, 'Oh, it's nothing like that. Not at all. It's just me.'

Vicky gave her a narrow-eyed look. 'Were you and he once . . . you know?'

Clemence ignored the question, just turned, and marched on.

'I'll take you up on the roof,' she called out over her shoulder. 'It helps to have a wide expanse around one sometimes.'

At the riad, Clemence led Vicky up a different zigzagging staircase which eventually gave out onto the roof and Etta's secret garden. Beneath a shade made from woven bamboo, Etta had created a tiny pink paradise under which plants and people could rest in the cool of early morning, though now it was incredibly hot.

They took in hundreds of flat rooftops on differing levels looking as if they were linked together. You couldn't even see the streets below, but you could see the deep shadows and you could hear laughter and the sound of voices. The minarets rose above the riads and swallows flying low and fast could be seen snatching their prey in the air. On some of the roofs, women were hanging up washing and gossiping, but there were no men anywhere. In the distance palm trees swayed in the breeze and even further away the Atlas Mountains loomed over the landscape.

'You said you made a deal with your mother,' Vicky said suddenly.

Clemence took a long slow breath. Vicky was right. She had stupidly let that slip.

'Ah yes,' she eventually said. 'I was very ill after my son was born. My mother paid for Jacques to take my baby to France – he was half French, half Moroccan, you see, and that was the period when Morocco was a French Protectorate so he could move there with few problems. I was unmarried and couldn't keep a child.'

'Oh, I see. But what was the deal?'

'Oh, it was nothing really. It was wrong to say that. My mother simply suggested she would take care of everything just so long as I didn't make a fuss.'

Vicky looked at her, wide-eyed and incredulous. 'And you agreed?'

'As I said, I was ill. Delirious. I had no choice.' Then she added under her breath, 'He was better off without me.'

Vicky was narrowing her eyes, suspicion written all over her face. 'What did you say?'

'Nothing. It doesn't matter. Times were very different.' She paused. 'Or maybe not. It's still scandalous to have a child out of wedlock, however liberated we have become.'

They heard the door to the roof open and Etta joined them. Clemence reached out a hand to her and smiled. 'Etta is my oldest friend in Marrakech, Vicky. She helped me settle here many years ago in the same apartment you're staying in.'

Etta smiled. 'Your grandmother was a scared little thing in those days.'

And no wonder, Clemence thought. Clear as a bell, even after all these years, she could hear her father's words, *Next time we'll tip her right into the well,* but she managed to raise a smile. 'I was never little, Etta,' she said.

'Perhaps not, but you were terrified of your father.'

Clemence took her hand and squeezed it. 'I was a bit broken in those days,' she said. And while Etta was aware of some of her story and knew not to breathe a word about how she had changed her name from Adele Garnier to Clemence Petier, she certainly didn't know everything that had taken place back in Casablanca.

'Vicky,' she continued. 'You must understand it was hard in those days. Don't forget I was born in 1892. The male head of the household owned us women, completely controlled our lives. We had no say, no rights at all, although it was different for Etta.'

'How?' Vicky asked.

Etta shrugged. 'I was a young widow with a fortune. I could do what I wanted just so long as I never remarried.'

'So, you didn't,' Vicky said. 'Cool move.'

Tiny Etta roared with laughter. 'Wasn't it? Come, it's getting too hot up here,' she added. 'Mint tea downstairs beneath the trees.'

'I feel as if I've been in Morocco before,' Vicky said as they reached the bottom step and entered the cool court-yard garden.

'Maybe because of your relationship with Jacques?' Clemence suggested.

'But Jacques seemed to be so French back in the Dordogne. He never mentioned Morocco.'

'As I said Jacques was brought up here in a French-speaking world when the French ran Morocco. As he is half French, and pale-skinned, he would have easily obtained French papers and must have spent the rest of his life passing himself off as a full-blown Frenchman.'

Clemence could tell Vicky was itching to hear more but was tactful enough to let it rest.

Etta turned to Vicky. 'Has Clemence told you about Theo Whittaker? He asked your grandmother to marry him.'

Vicky shook her head.

Clemence smiled briefly and headed for the stairs.

CHAPTER 12

Vicky

In the early evening, light like liquid gold flooded their little apartment until it rapidly turned into shadowy darkness and they switched on the lamps. The melancholy sound of a flute drifted in as Vicky chose what to wear to the much-discussed party in the Palmeraie. On this occasion she wore silver hoop earrings and a kaftan in chartreuse green, the acid colour highlighting her rich brown eyes and chestnut hair. Bea dithered for an hour or more, finally settling on the orange dress she had originally intended to wear.

'*Merde*,' Vicky complained, swatting a mosquito. 'Let's go.'

Even before arriving at the square on this busy glittering night, they could hear the persistent drumbeat and smell the charcoal smoke and sizzling meat. They strolled arm in arm and before long Vicky spotted Jimmy sitting alone outside one of the shabbier cafés.

While Bea took off to watch the acrobats, Vicky approached Jimmy. 'Have you heard anything about what happened to Frieda?' she asked him in a low voice.

He shook his head. 'If anyone knows they aren't saying and whatever happened it must have been at night. But she's gone. Vanished. Youssef too. They must have upset somebody, for sure. Their place in the medina was ransacked as well as the shop.'

'How awful.'

'Yep.'

'And the car that rammed us?'

He shrugged. 'No idea. Shall we get a taxi now? I was waiting for Tom but there's no sign of him.'

'Perhaps he's gone on ahead.'

Vicky looked around and called out to Bea. As she did, she recognised the silver-haired man strolling across towards them and smiling.

'Hello,' he said.

'Hello. Monsieur Callier, isn't it?'

'Do call me Patrice,' he said. 'Off somewhere nice?'

'I hope so. A party in the Palmeraie. We were just on our way to find a taxi.'

'Well, I'm headed that way so why don't I give you all a lift? It's just a hire car, so not exactly luxurious, but still.'

'Oh, would you? That is kind.' She paused as Bea ambled over.

'I'm so sorry. I should have introduced my friend Jimmy and here's my cousin Beatrice.'

Patrice held out a hand to Jimmy then turned to Bea and kissed her on both cheeks. 'Pleasure to meet you both. I'm Patrice Callier.'

Bea smiled demurely.

They set off and by the time Patrice pulled up in the Palmeraie, the party was in full flow, the house lit up and noisy.

'Why not come in with us?' Vicky suggested.

With a laugh he demurred. 'I think my days of revelling are long gone. But have fun and be safe.'

'Well, thank you for the lift.'

'See you around,' he said and drove off.

'He seems nice for an old boy,' Bea said. 'How do you know him?'

'I don't really. He's just someone my grandmother knows. She seems funny about him and I'm guessing they might have had a thing, back in the day.'

They both laughed at the thought and with Jimmy entered the house. While he talked to owner, the girls went out through open French windows into a sparkling fairyland perfumed with jasmine. Dozens of moths were humming around the lanterns and in the hazy champagne-fuelled atmosphere the air was laced with smoke from hashish. For a moment it felt other-worldly, enchanted – and bewitching if you weren't careful. Vicky glanced around at the languid women wearing embroidered, irides-cent dresses. All of them smoking, laughing too loudly, dancing, or slumped on cushion-covered rattan chairs, quite clearly already out of it.

A man glanced across at them, smiled, and strode

over confidently. Tall and rangy, he had longish, dark-blonde hair, grey eyes and looked as if he was in his mid-thirties. Certainly older than she and Bea.

'Hello, I'm Oriel Astor,' he said. 'And you are?'

She was aware he was addressing his question to her cousin, but Bea was struck dumb, twisting the rings on her fingers and looking up through her eyelashes in a ridiculously coy manner.

Vicky took over. 'I'm Vicky Baudin, and this silent goddess is my cousin Beatrice.'

'French?'

'I am. Bea is almost entirely English.'

'But not quite,' he said and laughed. 'Well, we shall forgive her that. Morocco is still a meeting place for travellers from all over the world.'

'I *am* here,' Bea said and raised her head.

Although Bea's eyes were shining with delight, Vicky wasn't impressed by the man's easy glibness, and anyway, what kind of a name was Oriel?

'You look amazing, Bea,' Oriel was saying. 'Would you mind if I took pictures of you? I'm a photographer.'

Of course you are, Vicky thought, while Bea bit her lip. Although Vicky longed to be one of these shiny, glamorous people, the truth was her cousin already belonged among them far more than she ever would.

'Come on over and meet people,' Oriel was saying. 'Look, Bill Willis has joined us. He's a designer-decorator friend of Jean Paul Getty.'

As they made their way across, he asked, 'What is it you two do?'

'We're both in fashion,' Vicky said and gave Bea a look. 'I design and Bea models.' It was only a half-truth of course.

'Well, Bea, if all goes well I think you are about to become my next Marrakech victim.' He laughed at Bea's worried face. 'Or in other words, my muse!'

Oriel introduced the cousins to the rest of his friends, Bea suitably impressed and hardly daring to speak while Vicky moved off – no one seemed that interested in her, anyway – to look at the fabulous floating dresses and the fairy lights threading from tree to tree. The smell of marijuana grew stronger, much more so than any party in London she'd been to, and it made her feel slightly uneasy but apart from that the scene was magical. People swayed to the sound of The Moody Blues singing 'Go Now' and others lingered in the violet shadows having convoluted discussions Vicky was certain made little sense.

Then, as if she had sensed exactly where he would be, she saw him: tall, handsome, long-haired, wearing a white kaftan, and with the signs of an early beard. She couldn't breathe, just stood staring at the man who was so much more elegant than she had ever imagined. Yves. Nobody could understand how deeply she cared about meeting him, what he meant to her. Her dissertation had become a labour of love as she found out more and more about him. The fact that he had left Algeria for Paris where he met Christian Dior and ended up working for him, and the fact that he had only fairly recently launched his own fashion label. The fact that in 1962 his tuxedos for women had caused such a buzz – they wouldn't suit her of course, but Bea would have created a storm in one. More recently it had been rumoured he was designing a range inspired by Marrakech and that had been part of the reason she'd come here. She felt she now had the chance to act on her long-held fantasy of whisking out the designs and he'd be so impressed he would instantly invite her to his studio. And *putain de merde* her ex, Russell, could go hang!

'Is it him?' Bea asked in a whisper as she meandered back to Vicky. 'Is it Yves? Who's he talking to? Doesn't she look amazing?'

Bea was staring enviously at a woman with long thick hair, heavily made-up eyes, and wearing a smocked peasant-style blouse, flouncy vermillion skirt, hippie bangles, beads, and a band of silver bells around her forehead. Exquisite, though more artificial than Bea.

'Talitha Pol, I think her name is,' Vicky said under her breath. 'Girlfriend of Jean Paul Getty, but I'm not sure about the other man.'

'Do you think she's prettier than me?' Bea hissed.

'Oh, for God's sake. Nobody is prettier than you.'

'You're just saying that.' But still her cousin kissed her on the cheek.

Vicky, feeling blood pulsing in her neck and butterflies storming her stomach, was mustering the courage to speak to Saint Laurent, and was barely listening to Bea.

She took a few steps forward and arrived at his side. 'I so admire your work,' she said breathlessly, stunned by how beautiful he was. Like a shining god, all dressed in white. Her mind went blank then she managed to say, 'Do you find Morocco inspiring?'

'Who wouldn't?' he said with a bit of a shrug.

Tongue-tied, she scratched her neck, desperately trying to remember what she wanted to say now that the moment had finally arrived.

He stared at her for a moment as if he didn't understand why she was still standing there, but then he seemed to relent a little. 'It's the incredible colour that excites me, the blues, the oranges, and the brilliance of the light.'

She nodded but still felt afraid and out of her depth.

'Nice to meet you,' he said and turned away to his companions.

'Umm. I've just finished my fashion diploma in London,' she blurted out. 'I hope to work in Paris.'

He glanced back at her, a half-smile on his face. 'Ah. Then maybe we shall meet again one day.'

'Yes. I could show you my designs.' She began to dig inside her bag. 'In fact, I have—'

'I'm sorry we have to leave the party now,' he said interrupting her and checking his watch. 'But you must meet my assistant, sometime. She's a mine of information. Who to approach and so on.'

She felt the heat rising in her cheeks and backed off while he signalled to his friends. They all left together, and she stared after them in defeat, watching as they were swallowed up by the crowd.

Bea joined Oriel again and Vicky wandered off on her own, kicking herself for not telling Yves about her dissertation and not whisking out her designs quicky before he had time to leave. She yearned to achieve dazzling heights and if Yves Saint Laurent could just give her a foothold on the ladder, he would be key. She was sure of it. Because not only had Russell rejected her love, even after they had been sleeping together for eight months, but as an established designer he had also refused to give her an introduction into the industry.

'Darling,' the bastard had said. 'Your designs are pretty enough, but you'll never be a star. Too middle of the road.'

'I passed my diploma with flying colours.'

'Makes you competent at best. Mediocre at worst. Hardly the same as—' He shrugged. 'Well, André Courrèges, or Pierre Cardin.'

She had cried, hiding herself in the bathroom of his flat so he should not see how much he had hurt her. She had to make the grade in Paris, not just on her postgraduate course at the *Ecole de la Chambre Syndicale de la Couture Parisienne* – the place where Yves Saint Laurent had studied too, but also in the French fashion industry. She just had to.

Later, after she had danced for a while, she sat on a bench to recover her breath, still feeling a bit low, the sparkle and glitter seeming rather tawdry now. There were fewer lights at this end of the garden, but she still spotted Jimmy coming across and carrying a plate of food and a couple of beers, his distinctive red hair identifying him.

'I thought you might be hungry,' he said.

She smiled, took one of the beers and made space for him to sit with her. Food always helped relieve a touch of the miseries. There was a pause while they ate olives and savoury croissants stuffed with *merguez* sausage.

You wouldn't find the usual London party fare here. No pineapple and cheese chunks on skewers or the ubiquitous Mateus Rosé or Cinzano.

'Who is the sour looking guy over there?' she whispered tilting her head at a long-haired man who was swaying, clearly drunk, beside a tree a few yards from them.

'That's Georgio. The rumour is he just got the sack from Yves Saint Laurent.'

'Blimey. What did he do?'

'Not sure. Took the piss, I guess. He's been told to pick up his stuff from the studio though.'

There was a short pause while Vicky ate another croissant. 'I wish I knew what had happened to Frieda. You sure nobody knows?'

'Yep.'

'So, what are *you* really doing in Morocco?' she asked, wiping her mouth with the back of her hand. 'You said you were an activist.'

He sighed. 'Yes, but I also have a year to make up my mind whether to join the family firm or make my mark as a writer.'

'What's the family firm?'

He frowned and stubbed his heel into the ground. 'Everyone asks about that rather than the writing.'

'Sorry . . . Look, I don't suppose you saw where Bea went?' she asked.

'Yeah. She left with the American photographer guy. Pompous arse.'

'She left?' Vicky could not believe it. Bea could have at least warned her she was going.

Jimmy was grinning. 'Pretty girl, isn't she? Stunning really. A gazelle, all arms and legs, like Jean Shrimpton.'

Vicky rolled her eyes and despite her worry, couldn't help feeling a twinge of jealousy. 'Actually, she's like a child. Totally scatty.'

What on earth had Bea been thinking? She didn't know anything about Oriel, let alone whether he was trustworthy – Vicky didn't think he would harm her, but he was too glib and Bea too gullible. And her aunt Florence would be so mad with Vicky if she let Bea get herself into deep water . . . But what could she do about it now?

She sighed and rising to her feet said, 'If my cousin really has gone, and you can't find Tom, can you escort me home? If you're not too drunk.'

As Jimmy stood up, he discreetly removed a gun from his shoulder bag and slid it into his jacket pocket.

'Jeez Jimmy! Do you always bring a gun to a party?'

'Don't you?'

He smiled at her, and she couldn't help smiling back. But really – a gun! Did he always carry it? It left her with an uneasy feeling.

'Be prepared, my mother always used to say.' He gently nudged her with his elbow as he smiled again.

She shook her head. 'When my mother said that I think she was probably referring to clean underwear.'

After Jimmy left her at the riad with a peck on her cheek, Vicky wandered upstairs to their apartment, unlocked the door and went in. She turned on a lamp and threw her bag down on the floor. *Dammit. Dammit. Dammit.* Being with

Jimmy had helped, but alone again she felt hollow. *Perhaps I should have kissed him,* she thought.

The call of the muezzin at night only made her feel even sadder. She recalled her old fear of being alone, the empty flat when she was at college in London, the loneliness of Saturday afternoons when everyone else had gone to the pub, the feeling of being utterly friendless during the short holidays. And she knew it had all been of her own making. She had set herself apart from others, had turned people and their invitations down, had pretended to be happier on her own. Had thought she was better than other people. All of it to avoid ever feeling rejected. Instead, apart from the night when Russell had turned her down, it was she who she done the rejecting and she had lived for years with an undercurrent of pent-up misery.

She stared at her open sketchbook then began to draw, but paused to look down at the dark courtyard and listen to the night birds in the trees. She pictured the embroidered geometric and abstract patterns she'd seen women wearing at the party. Influenced by Islamic Arabic culture, no doubt. Once she began to sketch again, her thoughts still flew around like wild things. Even though she had done her best to act normally, nothing had really felt right since the moment she'd looked in at Frieda's trashed shop and imagined she'd seen the creepy bald man's reflection in the window.

CHAPTER 13

'You okay?' Bea asked, narrowing her eyes and studying her face. 'You look a bit—'

'I'm fine,' Vicky interrupted crossly. 'Don't fuss. What time is it?'

'About two in the morning.'

In fact, she had slept only briefly and had dreamt of salted and severed heads set on spikes in front of the Pasha's palace. When they opened their eyes and spoke she'd woken up, sweat soaking through her thin cotton pyjamas.

She swung her feet to the floor. 'God, I'm hungry though.'

'You should have come with us,' Bea said. 'We had great food. Oriel took me to a colonial house surrounded by palms where Saint Laurent has his studio, although he lives in the Marrakech medina. It had a portico with a balcony on top, you know, like you get in France. It was lit up with candles and the windows on the first floor were too. Magical. Guess who was there?'

'I don't know . . . Mick Jagger?'

Bea raised her brows and gave her a meaningful look. 'Better than that.'

'Who?'

'Yves himself. It's where he went when he left the party.'

Vicky groaned. 'Just my luck.'

'One woman had loads of coloured bangles around one ankle. I've simply *got* to get some exactly the same. Anyway, I come bearing gifts.'

Bea began digging in her enormous bag and muttering. In the end, chuckling, she pulled a bottle out. 'There's this . . .'

She passed it to Vicky who glanced at it and raised her brows. 'Vodka?'

'I nicked it.'

'We can afford to buy a bottle of vodka on the black market.'

'Don't flip out. It's more fun if it's free. Anyway, they had loads.'

Bea held out something else to her, wrapped in her new blue scarf. 'And there's this. Thought you'd like it.'

Vicky put the bottle down and stood up to take the scarf and its contents. She unwrapped it, frowned, and began leafing through the sketchbook her cousin had handed her, her mind racing. After a moment she flung it on the bed as if it were a red-hot coal. 'Fuck's sake, Bea. What have you done?'

Bea's pretty face fell. 'I . . . borrowed it. Someone had left a design studio unlocked. There were easels and drawing boards and a huge desk. It was just lying there so I had a look but heard someone coming along the corridor, and I panicked.'

'What do you mean?'

'I shoved it into my bag and hid behind the desk.'

'Why didn't you put it back after they'd gone?'

Bea shrugged. 'Should have, but I just ran.'

Vicky shook her head. This couldn't be happening. She was sick of having to be the sensible, problem-solving one when Bea always got to be the glamorous mess.

'I thought I could take it back later.' Bea gave her a beseeching look.

'Bea, the dates. They're recent.' Abruptly, she sank down on the edge of the bed, jiggling her foot while her cousin stared at the floor.

'Someone said he was overseeing the work of an apprentice. I thought, well I suppose I was drunk.'

Her anger, her loneliness, her envy of Bea boiled over. 'It's no apprentice. Look at the initials,' she exploded, jabbing a finger at the letters. 'Look! YSL.'

'Oh God. I'm sorry,' Bea whispered, fidgeting and scratching her skin.

Vicky balled her hands into fists and thumped the bed. How would anyone take her seriously now? 'Honestly, Bea, what an idiot!'

'What shall I do?'

'It's not brain surgery! If he finds out who stole it . . .' Bea's face fell.

'You really do not have a clue,' Vicky began, but everything was unravelling and she couldn't breathe for the upset blocking her throat. This was going to ruin everything – and possibly land them in serious trouble.

'I'm sorry,' Bea said again, sticking out her lower lip and beginning to cry.

'Oh, *merde*,' Vicky muttered. 'Shit! Shit! Shit!' She picked up a cushion and hurled it against the wall where Bea was leaning. It slid to the floor unsatisfactorily.

There was silence.

All Vicky could hear was the ticking of their little alarm clock but eventually she took a long slow breath and said, 'You must take it back. It's a crime. And these are his latest designs.'

'Will they arrest me?'

'Probably.'

'A Moroccan prison? Vicky, please,' she wailed.

Vicky felt her jaw tighten. Why had she encouraged Bea to come to Morocco too? She'd have been far better off on her own.

'Could we pretend to find it?'

'We . . . Beatrice? You mean *you*.'

Tears welling in her eyes, Bea slithered down the wall to the floor to sit with her knees drawn up to her chin, moaning, 'Oh God. Oh God.'

'Let me think,' Vicky said, relenting a little. Moving over to Bea, she squatted next to her on the floor and began to rack her brains. She had an inkling of an idea.

CHAPTER 14

That evening, after a rudimentary supper of bread and tomatoes, Vicky flipped the pages of an old Vogue magazine and looked up from time to time to listen to the noises in the street. Mainly cats yowling, people laughing, or someone shouting. She didn't want to deal with Bea's tears any more and yearned to get out of the apartment again and breathe freely, but it was too late to go out alone. She'd discounted the idea she'd had in the early hours when Bea had come home and hadn't had a better one, other than just binning the sketchbook somewhere far from Etta's house.

When she heard footsteps on their staircase, she rose to her feet and went to the door.

'Can't stop long, but are you hungry?' Jimmy asked as she opened up. 'Etta let me in.'

'Ravenous,' Vicky said, exhaling slowly, massively relieved it was only him and not someone asking questions about the missing sketchbook.

'Baked it myself.'

'What is it?' Vicky asked and reached for the plate he'd been holding. 'Looks like a giant doughnut.'

'*Meskouta*, otherwise known as Moroccan orange cake. It's too big just for me and Tom is nowhere to be found. We ought to have it with sweet wine, but I've only got beer.'

She cut the cake, handed out slices and in the following silence ate hers hungrily. 'It's very good,' she said between mouthfuls. 'I didn't realise you could cook.'

'Man of many talents.' He opened the bag he'd also been carrying and took out three bottles. 'I even brought a bottle opener.'

'We're not entirely useless you know.'

'I don't doubt it. Now . . . have either of you girls heard the latest news?'

Vicky, her mouth still full of cake, shook her head and went over to the sink to rinse her greasy fingers.

'What news?' Bea asked, perking up and sitting bolt upright.

'Well,' Jimmy said and pulled up a chair. 'I am the herald of something you will find hard to believe. Guess what's happened?'

'The Prime Minister of England died?'

'Harold Wilson died?' Vicky asked, having only heard part of the conversation.

Jimmy pulled a face. 'No. Someone stole Yves Saint Laurent's latest designs.'

Vicky, who was swallowing the last few crumbs of cake, began to cough. Jimmy thumped her on the back and Bea jumped up to hold a glass of water to her lips. She waved them away, doubling over.

'I'm all right,' she said when the coughing finally ceased and she straightened up. 'Sorry. It went down the wrong way.'

She and Bea exchanged glances and Vicky, desperate to somehow remind her cousin to keep her mouth shut, widened and then narrowed her eyes.

'What's wrong?' Jimmy asked, noticing her expression at the same time as Bea said: 'Well. As it happens—'

'Why would anyone do anything so stupid?' Vicky interjected. 'It's crazy. Not as if anyone else could use them, could they?'

'It was out of spite,' Jimmy declared.

Bea and Vicky spoke at the same time. 'Whaaat?'

'It was that guy Georgio. You remember he was sacked by Yves? It seems he took the sketchbook in revenge. And now he's skipped town without paying his rent. He'll never get a job in fashion again.'

Vicky nodded slowly while thinking rapidly.

Bea stared at her. 'But I should—'

'I suppose Saint Laurent will just have to start over,' Vicky chipped in to stop Bea from spilling the beans.

Jimmy announced he was heading off to see if Tom was back, then added, 'Okay if I take the rest of the cake?'

'Sure.'

He picked up the plate and made for the door.

As soon as they heard his footsteps fade, Vicky shook her head, feeling dumbfounded. 'Oh my God. Can you believe it?'

She began to laugh.

Bea stared at her, did a little jig on the spot, and then joined in with the laughter. Vicky, relief flooding her whole being, was unable to stop and laughed until her sides hurt.

'Owww,' she moaned, clutching hold of Bea and gasping for breath as she slowly recovered. 'I feel giddy.'

Bea went across to the cupboard and fetched two glasses and the bottle of vodka. 'This should do the trick.'

She poured them both a half glassful.

'Any orange juice?' Vicky asked.

'There's a little bit left.'

The vodka went down nicely, but with her emotions running so high, Vicky wanted another. Her fear over the stolen sketchbook and the delirious happiness at finding they were off the hook had triggered an unquenchable thirst. Thank God she was still going to be able to talk to Saint Laurent again.

'More,' Vicky said and waved her glass in the air. 'Now!'

'All right. All right.' Bea splashed the vodka into both their glasses and Vicky was the first to gulp it down. 'You should slow down,' Bea said as she sipped hers.

Vicky, feeling the alcohol fizzing and fiery in her blood, slapped her thigh as if in triumph and broke into a fit of giggles. 'Your face has gone red and shiny.'

Bea rushed over to look in the mirror while Vicky slumped back onto the sofa and closed her eyes.

'What are we going to do about Giorgio?' Bea asked.

Vicky pulled a face.

'He's been blamed, hasn't he, for what *we* did.'

'We? *We?*' Vicky said raising her glass. Some of the vodka sloshed over the sides. 'More vodka,' she demanded.

'Budge over,' Bea said and came to sit beside her on the sofa bringing the bottle with her.

'Lighten up, Bea,' Vicky said, adding, 'Got any dope?

Bea tilted her head. 'A little. Oriel gave me some. I'm saving it for a special occasion.'

'This *is* special.'

She hiccupped happily and began to sing 'You Don't Have to Say You Love Me'. Because bastard Russell hadn't, had he, even though she had?

'I adore Dusty Springfield,' Bea said and fetched the bits and pieces to roll a joint.

She sat down and Vicky rested her spinning head on Bea's shoulder. As they smoked, neither spoke until Bea said, 'We still have the sketchbook though.'

'Yeah.'

'And there's that poor guy Georgio,' Bea insisted.

Vicky twisted her body to look at her. 'Gotta get rid of the sketchbook then. What's the time?' she asked, her words slurring just a little.

''Bout midnight.'

Vicky rose to her feet and pointed at the door. 'Time to split.'

Bea blinked at her.

She grabbed Bea's hand and pulled her towards the door. The previous night she had thought of this, but it had taken a quarter of a bottle of vodka to give her the Dutch courage to pull it off. 'We are going to leave the sketchbook where you found it.'

Bea gasped. 'In the house?

'No. In the garden. Come on, *compañera*.'

'Didn't know you spoke Italian.'

'Spanish, you clot. Let's go!'

CHAPTER 15

Fired up on alcohol and hashish they reeled away from the riad and found their way to the road.

'Wow! It's vibrating. The sky is vibrating,' Vicky said, gazing up.

There were no streetlights, and the velvety night sky was alive with stars. Giggling and grabbing each other by the arm, they left behind the luscious smell of cumin drifting from the charcoal fires of the medina and walked a little further. Even well after midnight it was still hot and dusty.

Intent on hailing a taxi to the Palmeraie, Vicky peered into the emptiness and swore when she stumbled off the kerb.

'Anything? Bea asked.

'Dunno.' Vicky blinked into the darkness. 'Can't see a flippin' thing,' she said, reverting once again to the King's Road English she had picked up in London.

'Bummer! Use your torch.'

'No need. I can see a car's headlights.'

A taxi pulled up. Half an hour later the girls were in the Palmeraie, wandering along sandy trails in the dark surrounded by hundreds of palms inhabited by what sounded like millions upon millions of buzzing insects.

'*Nom de Dieu*! It's a wilderness,' Vicky said, flinching as a whining flying creature slammed into her cheek. 'Deserted, excepted for these fuckers!'

'And spoooooky.'

They both giggled but in the dead of night, the eerie palms felt impenetrable. The only light came from the moon and Vicky's weak torch. They passed a couple of ghostly abandoned French villas where the sickly sweetness of honeysuckle drifted in the air.

I am a teeny bit sozzled, Vicky thought.

'I'm itching all over,' Bea complained. 'The mosquitos are everywhere.'

There was a sudden crack from behind them. They both froze. *There could be anything out there*, Vicky realised, her muscles taut, her skin prickling. *Scorpions? Giant spiders? Adders? Not adders please*. Why had she never asked? She swivelled round, listening. All manner of living things were out there but the beam of light from her torch only lit up a lone dog and clouds of fluttering moths of every size and kind.

'Bloody hell,' she said.

They carried on looking, lurching over the stumps of fallen trees and blundering into bushes. 'Owww!' Bea shrieked. 'I hate these thorns. They just attacked me.'

'Tell me again about the house.'

'It's one of the French colonial villas, but all done-up. Surrounded by palm trees and bushes, and next door there's a mansion with huge grounds. Someone at the dinner told me the mansion once belonged to Olga Tolstoy, a relative of Leo Tolstoy's. I don't know if it's true.'

They stole on in the darkness not passing a single soul.

'There,' Bea said. She sounded excited suddenly. 'Shine your torch there.'

Vicky did so and Bea whooped in triumph. '*Et voila!*' she cried out.

The house had a beautiful portico with a balcony and six windows on the first floor, though they weren't lit up now.

'Wow!' Vicky let the light from the torch spread along a high wall. 'Don't much fancy climbing that. Talk about Fort Knox.'

'Looks like there's a larger house further along, also like I said.' Bea did a little dance on the spot.

'Come on, you clown. Let's see if we can get into the garden next door.'

'Get in? But why?'

'What do you think? To leave the sketchbook on the terrace of course. There was a terrace?'

'Yes but . . . you sure, Vicky? Is it possibly a teeny bit bonkers?'

Vicky laughed. 'Totally bonkers, but what a gas.'

What had seemed, only hours ago, deadly serious, now felt almost farcical. It was exactly the kind of riotous behaviour that would make for a great story one day.

Vicky imagined herself telling it to a group of glamorous, laughing friends sitting outside one of the great cafés in a pretty nook of Le Marais in Paris. Or maybe at an awards ceremony at La Coupole.

'Isn't that a car parked over there under the trees?' Bea said. 'Maybe someone is in.'

'Too far away. It looks as if someone's abandoned it.'

A little way along they discovered wooden fencing covered in a rampant climbing plant.

'This must be the start of the garden next door to the house you went to,' Vicky said and shone her torch around. 'It doesn't look well kept. Let's climb over, get into this garden, and then find a way into the back of the house we really want.'

'Sure! Just like that,' Bea said scornfully. 'And what if we can't get out again?'

'Bugger! I've just been bitten again. I'm bloody well covered in bites.'

Bea scratched herself. 'Me too.'

From the distant road came the sound of vehicles, but here the two of them stood completely still, breathing the heady claustrophobic perfumes of night-time, of wild animals, of the undergrowth, of smoke travelling on the air, of jasmine, and the night-blooming white flowers only visible when Vicky swept her torch light over the fencing. She felt the earth beating in rhythm with her own pulse. It felt strange but liberating too. They were explorers, adventurers, in an alien world about to unearth some wonderful new find for the world to admire. Bones, ancient coins, burial chambers.

Whatever. Vicky strained to hear signs of life, but there was nothing new except the gusts of wind picking up.

As she sneaked forward Bea pulled her back. 'Why not just throw it over the wall into the garden?'

'Hmmm. I don't know.'

'What's the difference where we leave it?'

'It'll get damp on the grass in the garden,' Vicky said although when she thought about it, Bea was probably right. It would get a bit damp wherever they left it. 'Anyway,' she added. 'More fun to leave it on the terrace. Can you imagine their faces when they see it in the morning?'

'I don't care,' Bea scowled. 'What if they've got guard dogs?'

'Shhh!'

'You shhh!'

Vicky ignored her. 'These creepers look strong enough to give me a foothold,' she said, but then shrieked as she stubbed her toe on a rock. 'Ow! Wish I hadn't worn these stupid flip-flops.'

'Watch out. There's a hollow there.'

But it was too late. With her eyes on the fence and not on the ground, her left foot slid right into the dip, she lost her balance and toppled over, landing on her bottom. 'Whoops!' she cried out, laughing as she leant back to lie spreadeagled on the ground.

'You okay?'

'Nothing hurts.'

'That's the vodka talking,' Bea said. 'I'll give you a hand.'

But from her vantage point on the ground Vicky had spotted something they might be able to use. 'Look, just along there. Seems like there's a hole in the fence! Maybe made by an animal.'

On her hands and knees, she crawled across to it. A dog began howling.

'There *are* dogs,' Bea whispered.

'No. Miles away. Follow me.'

Bea sighed loudly. 'Let's not. We don't have a clue what's on the other side of the hole.'

'I'll look.'

Vicky held the torch low as she wriggled through the hole. 'Only bamboo bushes here with enough space between them,' she called back to Bea. 'Come on. I'll shine the torch for you.'

'I suppose.'

'Come on, Bea,' Vicky called, feeling invincible and grinning at the realisation that Bea was being the more sensible one here, while Vicky herself was having fun for once.

After they were both through, scratched and dirty, they inched around the garden, skirting the edges until they were stopped by impenetrable brambles.

'Oh hell! Can't get through this lot.'

They retraced their steps to where they could see the bulky black silhouette of the house. 'We'll have to cross the garden over there,' Vicky said. 'It's the only way to get to the other house.'

Gradually they crept closer to where a line of shrubs divided the overgrown formal lawn from the area at the back of the garden where compost and stacks of mown grass lay in heaps. This wasn't the fragrant Moorish or French garden they might have expected but a pungent, unpleasant place smelling of dusty bone-dry grass and rotting vegetation.

'Yuck!' Bea muttered. 'The stink!'

Everything was suddenly louder than they expected. Birds shifted in the trees, animals scurried in the under-growth and a breeze rustled the leaves. Still too drunk to care about pain, Vicky squeezed Bea's arm, thrilled and scared at the same time. She listened carefully but there was no sign of anyone at all and the house remained in silent darkness. The garden was another matter: a cacophony of scratching, scrabbling, rustling creatures everywhere. *God but the undergrowth is seething,* Vicky thought.

'What are they?' Bea hissed.

Vicky didn't want to know. As they tiptoed on, the moon broke through the clouds again transforming the garden into a shiny silvery blue. They might be seen if anyone glanced out, but still none of the windows showed any signs of light.

Bea stumbled over a tussock and clutched Vicky's elbow to right herself.

Only another fifty yards and they'd reach the garden of the smaller house. They heard a sharp lonely shriek. 'Just some kind of dog again, or maybe a jackal?' Vicky whispered, her heart beating much faster.

Suddenly a light came on in a downstairs room of the bigger, run-down mansion.

'Quick, get down behind the shrubs,' Vicky hissed and switched off her torch.

'They're not high enough. They'll see us.'

'They won't be looking and it's cloudy again. Get down. They won't see.'

'I knew we shouldn't have come into the garden.'

The light from the room revealed a wide covered terrace, which gave on to the garden. They could see the French windows were already open but there were no flowers, no tubs full of plants, no miniature palms, and no garden furniture. Nothing to show the house was inhabited though through a gap in the shrubbery Vicky could see a tall man in the room talking to another man.

They appeared deep in conversation with one another, nodding and gesticulating. Vicky heard a few words through the window but when the tall man moved back behind a curtain his voice faded. Dammit. They'd have to sit it out until the house went dark again.

'What's happening?' Bea asked.

'Nothing. It's just people talking,' Vicky said, starting to sober up.

'I've got a cramp in my foot.'

'Rub it.'

Vicky yawned and she watched for a while longer.

'This is so boring,' Bea complained.

But suddenly the tall man moved forward again, and Vicky saw his face clearly in the light. She was surprised to see it was her grandmother's friend, Patrice. The man who had been kind enough to give them a lift to the party. Was this huge house his? She recognised his silver hair, remembered his bright blue eyes. On an impulse, and still tipsy, she raised a hand and began to stand up to wave. Bea pulled her back down.

'Don't,' she hissed.

Patrice was smiling and reaching out to somebody as if to assist them in some way. Vicky couldn't see the first man now, the one he had been talking to, but she heard him laugh. *Were they at a social event? A party or something? It didn't seem lively enough for that.* A third man came into view but with his back to her. His hair was red. Had he been the one Patrice had been reaching out to? As he turned slightly, Vicky could suddenly see the side of his face. It was Jimmy. Vicky was surprised. Apart from the time Patrice gave them all a lift, she hadn't realised they knew each other. Now Jimmy had what looked like a dark shadow across his cheek. No, not a shadow, a bruise. *Not another car accident*, she thought.

'What's happening?' Bea hissed.

'Nothing. Patrice Callier is looking after Jimmy. He must have been in a fight or an accident, or fallen maybe.'

But then all the breath left her body and the world went still – the tall grass, the leaves in the trees, the insects. Everything. Stunned, unable to even blink, wave after wave of ice coursed through her entire body and with one hand over her mouth, she managed to stop herself from screaming.

Patrice was holding up a gun. She blinked her eyes fast, certain that what she was seeing couldn't be true. Patrice had been so friendly. Was he really pointing the gun at Jimmy? He couldn't seriously be threatening her friend. She stretched her neck, desperate to catch a glimpse of Jimmy's face again to reassure herself, but now she couldn't see him.

Everything shifted, the garden moving once more, and Vicky strained to hear more of the conversation. A gust of wind whipped around her lifting and scattering the dead leaves across the grass.

'What is it?' Bea said and poked her head up to look.

'Get down,' Vicky hissed as Jimmy came into view again and she saw his face clearly; there was terror and blood all over it.

'Jesus!' she whispered. 'Jesus Christ! Patrice is holding Jimmy at gunpoint. He really is.'

Patrice looked as if he were focusing away from Jimmy, as if speaking to someone else, but his hands still pointed the gun unwaveringly at their friend. Vicky pressed a shaking hand to her mouth. What was Jimmy mixed up in? Patrice couldn't be seriously intending to shoot him; he just couldn't. Jimmy was political, she knew that, but Patrice wasn't. An art dealer, he had said.

Patrice was still turned a little away from Jimmy. And then, as if he were suddenly thinking better of it, he lowered the gun. Vicky almost passed out in relief, hardly able to breathe. It was all right. Jimmy was going to be all right.

But then Patrice twisted back and took aim again. A shot rang out shattering the air.

As if in slow-motion Jimmy crumpled to the floor. Uncomprehending, Vicky stared, pulse hammering in her ears so loudly she felt that Patrice must surely be able to hear it.

'I'm going to be sick,' she whispered as the garden tilted, tree trunks and branches creaking in the gusts of wind. *Had that really happened?* Jimmy. *Jimmy.*

'We've got to get out of here,' Bea hissed, her face shining white in the darkness.

She poked her head up to look around and right then, a dog howled. Patrice shifted slightly then looked out of the window. Vicky's entire life seemed to come to a halt as she tried to block him out. He was staring straight at them. Nauseating fear whipped through her again and again.

Rigidly silent, the girls remained rooted to the spot. How far into the garden could he see? Were they well enough out of his sight to be hidden? They couldn't tell. But Vicky felt as if she could almost hear Patrice breathing, almost feel his breath on her skin.

Minutes passed and then he turned from the garden. She choked back a sob as she watched him drag Jimmy across the floor and could just make out the soft *bump, bump, bump* of his lolling head. Sweet, decent Jimmy. Shot in cold blood. Vicky closed her eyes and she and Bea clung together trembling.

After a few moments of stillness, Vicky spoke.

'We should go now,' she whispered to Bea. 'Before he comes back.'

Bea nodded shakily, but before they could move, a cry rang out, once, twice. Sharp and terrifying. The light in the room flickered and went out, plunging the room into darkness. Vicky held her breath as she heard Patrice step through the open French windows onto the terrace.

'Who's there?' he called out.

CHAPTER 16

Clemence

Kasbah du Paradis

The mellow evening sun had long since set and though Clemence had gone to bed early and fallen asleep instantly, she had been plagued by dreams. So many dark dreams. She was back in her father's bedroom, the light too bright despite the semi-closed shutters, and her mother tiptoeing around, fixing this, fixing that, while the nurse took a break. Clemence had wanted to scream at her mother. *Just let him die. Why won't you just let him die?*

She woke up sweating, gasping, her strength pitching and plunging. The dream had felt all too real. Of course, it wasn't truly a dream, at least not a dream about unreal things that hadn't ever happened. They *had* happened, and she really had wanted her father to die. When the doctor – Patrice's father – had confirmed her father was on the road to recovery, she had been horrified.

'Strong as an ox,' he said, stroking his moustache and looking pleased. 'Sound constitution and fit as a fiddle. It will take more than this infection to finish him off.'

In despair Clemence had known it was true when her father began eating again. She remembered glaring at Madeleine from where she had been sitting on the window seat, watching her mother tempt him with this delicacy or that. It disgusted her. Her mother knew. She knew what her glare had meant.

She didn't want to be recalling all this – these were not golden childhood memories – but the dream had woken her and in the middle of the night she couldn't think of anything else. Flashes from the past continued to disrupt her every time she closed her eyes.

When her mother disobeyed him over some stupid minor rule soon after, he'd had her whipped in the court-yard under the blazing August sun and dragged Clemence out to watch. The man who'd had to do it was her father's henchman, a dour muscle-bound creature who never smiled except at the pain of others, animal or human. Clemence had recoiled in shock as the man tore the blouse from her mother's back and forced her to bend over the edge of the wall surrounding the well while the whip came down on her nakedness. Clemence had not yet turned fourteen, and terrified her mother might just jump into the well and drown, she felt incandescent rage exploding inside her. She dug her nails into her own flesh to stop herself screaming. But she could not prevent the terrible surging desire to strike her father for what he was doing. She didn't want him to have the satisfaction of seeing her weep, but her mother's pain and humiliation – and her father's enjoyment – was too much to bear. She could not help it.

She could even hear his voice in her head, the smug self-satisfaction in it. *See, girl, this is what we do with disobedient women.*

'Next time we'll tip her right into the well,' he had said afterwards, laughing at her. He had behaved like a barbaric despot, thinking himself above the law and human decency, worse even than the man who would become Pasha one day. As a young man in his early twenties he had visited their estate with some of his harem and she suspected her father had enjoyed those women too.

'They have spent too much time together,' her mother had said. 'They are not good influences on one another. Your father considers himself a warlord,' as if a ridiculous excuse like that could exonerate him.

The events of the past blurred together. She tried to remember if Patrice had still been around when the man had visited. His father, the doctor, had obviously been there but was it before or after Patrice had been packed off to school in France. Hadn't he been gone by then?

Either way, it had been Patrice who had put an end to the fun she and Jacques had shared when they were young, and she could never forgive him for it. He had been a strange, lonely kind of boy and they had refused to let him join in with their games when he found them in their hideaway. His mother was dead and perhaps the loss had changed him. She didn't know. But she remembered Jacques pushing him away and laughing at him. It seemed cruel now. But children were cruel.

'I'll get you back for this!' Patrice had shouted, red-faced. 'You'll see if I don't.'

The sky the next day was a beautiful cerulean blue and the sun was warm as Clemence weeded her rose beds, Voltaire and Coco nearby, growling as they tussled over a stick they'd found.

'Honestly, you two,' she scolded. 'Get another stick for heaven's sake. There's no shortage.'

She sighed and carried on for the sake of her sanity. In a life strewn with guilt, physical work always calmed her even when she was tired and her back twinged relentlessly. Except for when she had been with Theo, insomnia had plagued her, and even after all these years she still missed him.

But since Patrice Callier had appeared back in her life, she had hardly slept at all. She recalled the day when her father had called her to his study. Patrice was in there with his father and her mother too. All of them beaming as Patrice got down on one knee and asked for her hand in marriage. At first, she had been shocked that they all seemed to be acquiescing in this farce. But then she had burst out laughing at the joke they had decided to play on her. One look at Patrice's red-faced anguish stopped her short. His proposal had been in deadly earnest, and she had truly humiliated him. Why had he chosen such a public proposal? Had he hoped to intimidate her into accepting?

She found out later from Madeleine that Patrice had lied, told her Clemence had already said yes and was deeply in love with him. When Clemence turned Patrice down her father's anger had boiled over.

In her garden now she straightened up, stretched, lifted her face to the sun, then glanced down at the forest, recalling the first time she'd seen a yellowish-brown barbary macaque with a pink face staring at her from the low branches of a walnut tree. Taking a long slow breath and wishing she could bottle single moments of time forever, her spirits lightened. She loved the teeming earth, and the air also swarming with insects. It had taken years but gradually she had allowed herself to take pleasure in the beauty of her home.

She climbed the stairs up to the roof from where she could see the dramatic scenery of the valley, the rushing mountain stream, the yellow and green splashes of colour on the hillsides, and the traditional Berber village where a wonderful network of walking trails began. The natural beauty soothed her, gave her a sense of perspective. Below she could see Ahmed leaving the kitchen with a fruit juice on a silver tray.

'Put it on the terrace please,' she called out. 'I'm coming down.'

She thought of Vicky as she went back down the stairs and across to the annexe to help her mother dress. When her granddaughter had feigned not to care about the rift with Élise it had struck such a chord. After all, Clemence had done everything to try to forget her own mother for years after she had fled here from Casablanca.

She never could, of course. You couldn't, could you? A thing as dark as that scarred you.

But today was one of Madeleine's good days and Clemence decided to walk her around the garden for a little while. She tried talking to her mother while they were outside, but Madeleine only said, 'Oranges. I like oranges. Don't I?'

'To eat, *Maman*? You'd like an orange to eat?'

'Did I say that?'

'I thought you did.'

Her mother glared at her, unblinking. 'Who are you?' she said crossly. 'Where is my daughter?'

Clemence sighed. It was always the same. 'I am Clemence, your daughter,' she repeated for the hundredth time.

'Don't be ridiculous. My daughter is a little girl. Where is she? I demand to see her. I want to go home.'

Madeleine, agitated, was pulling at her own hair and Clemence had to bite back her temper.

'I have an idea,' she said far too brightly. 'We'll polish.'

Her mother had always loved polishing her favoured items of furniture with a natural polish fragranced with oranges and limes.

She encouraged Madeleine into the scullery and gave her a cloth. Her mother immediately calmed and began rubbing a marble worktop.

'Not here. We're going to the dining room,' Clemence said gently. 'Look, I have orange polish.' And she unscrewed the tin lid and held up the glass jar so that her mother might breathe it in.

Clemence encouraged her to dip her cloth into the polish.

The fact that she rubbed the same spot over and over didn't matter. It kept her focused.

Madeleine had loved her home on their family estate and hated having to sell up after her husband, Clemence's father, Claude Garnier, died the day of the fire. He had left half his estate to Clemence and half to her mother. And while Clemence had fled to Marrakech to get away from everything and everyone, her mother had stayed in Casablanca, moving into an airy apartment facing the ocean. She'd written saying how much she loved her lace curtains and the rugs in her new home, and especially how much she loved her little rascal of a dog, Simone. It had broken her when Simone died.

Madeleine stopped rubbing and turned to Clemence. 'Is it lunch time?' she asked.

'Not yet, *Maman*.'

'Why do you keep calling me that?'

'Because you are my mother.'

'Am I?'

Clemence felt her eyes filling with tears. She reached out a hand to Madeleine and this time her mother took it. 'You do know you must never say anything, don't you? About Casablanca.'

Her mother looked at her fiercely. Did she understand?

'Anyway,' she continued, 'we have your favourite today.'

Madeleine clapped her hands like a little child.

Her favourite food was a tart made with pears and confectioner's cream. She loved French wine with a meal and Spanish sherry before it. She loved strong coffee and almond croissants for breakfast, and she hated vegetables.

Nadia came in. 'Sorry to interrupt.'

'Not a problem. You have always been so good with my mother. Look, she's smiling at you.'

'My own grandmother was the same. I'm used to it.'

'Well, you'll never know how truly grateful I am.'

Nadia held out a thick white envelope and Clemence felt a tremor run through her. *Not another anonymous note. Please not another.*

'Can you take over with Madeleine?' she asked.

Nadia immediately stepped forward and Clemence left the room, tearing open the envelope as she walked to her office. When she pulled out the folded sheet of paper and read the note, she sank into the nearest chair, her whole being buckling.

You think your secret is safe? Think again.

CHAPTER 17

Vicky

Marrakech

Vicky only slept when exhaustion overcame her. She woke with a start a few hours later and in bright sunlight, sat up in bed, groaned and held her aching head in her hands. It had taken a long time to get back home. They had spent what felt like hours hiding in the trees, their hearts thumping wildly against their ribs, dreading that Patrice would drag them out at any moment.

He'd stood on the terrace, gazing around the garden with sharp piercing eyes. A cat with large ears and a pointed face came slinking past the spot where they'd crouched low on the ground. They hardly dared to breathe as it sniffed and sloped away from the shrubbery, sliding into the long grass of the neglected lawn.

It must have been the cat who had shrieked and brought Patrice out.

Vicky had been able to see him through a gap in the shrubbery, but he didn't move. He remained standing, still staring into the darkness at the back of the garden.

Surely if he really had seen them watching, hiding, he would have come down and searched the garden by now? The man inside called out to him, saying something Vicky didn't hear. Through the gap she saw Patrice hesitate then step forward, peering out with narrowed suspicious eyes, and shining a torch around the garden. The other man called again and Patrice quickly headed back into the house. The light came on.

A few minutes later, they'd watched him and the other man heave Jimmy's body from the room. When they heard the sound of a car being driven away at speed, Vicky had doubled over, groaning.

'Come on,' Bea said, pulling at Vicky's arm.

'Wait! It might be a trick.'

They'd hung on a bit longer before racing to the fence, tripping and stumbling over their own feet. Once they found the hole again, and ignoring how badly they were scratching their arms and legs, they scrambled back through, staggering on for an hour or more trembling, crying, holding each other up. But eventually a dawn fruit truck travelling to central Marrakech picked them up. The driver dropped them close to the square and they rushed into the riad, thanking God that their ordeal was over.

But it wasn't over, was it? Jimmy was dead. Murdered.

Edging to the side of the bed, Vicky twisted round and planted her feet on the floor, and the image of Jimmy's crumpled body reared up again. She screwed up her eyes. Jimmy. Dead. But why? If she hadn't seen Patrice shoot Jimmy with her own eyes, she would never have believed it.

She took a long shuddering breath. What on earth had they been thinking? Bea had been right because crawling into the garden had been a crazy thing to do, and she wished they'd simply chucked the sketchbook over the wall after all. She glanced at her broken fingernails, turned her wrists over and examined the scratches there and on her lower arms. If only there was a way to turn back the clock. But there wasn't. And the only thing to do was to get away from Marrakech as quickly as they could. They had to.

Nauseous and hungover, Vicky moved gingerly as she stepped over their filthy clothes on the floor. She reached Bea and shook her shoulder. As soon as she was awake, they stared at each other.

'What the fuck are we going to do?' Bea whispered. Her mascara was smudged; she looked as if she'd been at a sleazy all-night party.

Vicky sat on the edge of Bea's bed, rigid with fear. 'We've got to leave Morocco,' she said. 'If we stay, we'll always be looking over our shoulders, forever worrying whether we're safe or not.'

Images of the shooting kept coming back: the blood, Jimmy collapsing to the floor, his body lifeless, the soft *bump, bump, bump* of his head. The nightmare way Patrice had seemed to look her dead in the eye. Could they be certain he hadn't seen them?

'I'll ask Etta to help. They might only speak Arabic at the airport. I'll go down now.'

Bea clutched at her arm. 'What about the train? It would be cheaper.'

'I'll ask,' Vicky said, standing up and shaking Bea off her. 'Bolt the door.'

She ran downstairs and knocked at Etta's. The woman, wearing her usual black, ushered her into the kitchen and Vicky asked if she could help them book a flight. 'We have to go to England, today.'

Etta frowned, studying Vicky's face. 'How did you get those scratches on your cheeks?'

'I just took a tumble into some brambles,' Vicky lied. 'Too much to drink.'

Etta was still frowning. 'Honey, why do you want to leave today? What's the rush? I thought you liked it here.'

'I do.'

'So . . . what?'

'Please, Etta. I can't explain. Not now.'

'Right. Coffee on the go over there. Help yourself to a croissant.'

She picked up the phone and dialled. While Etta waited to speak to someone, Vicky barely took any notice of the cheerful jumble of paintings on the *tadelakt* walls, the overgrown potted palms, the brightly coloured crystal lamps. She saw them but felt too distraught to enjoy them.

Etta began speaking in Arabic. The conversation continued for a few minutes, and her brow furrowed at whatever the man was saying to her. 'Are you sure? France too?' she retorted, sounding impatient and reverting to French. 'None until the thirtieth – but that's in three days' time.'

She listened for a moment longer then slammed down the phone.

'What?' Vicky asked anxiously.

Etta sighed. 'Because England won the World Cup semi-final yesterday, everyone has booked a flight out of Casablanca or Rabat.'

'But it would take hours on the train to even get to Rabat. Isn't there a local airport?'

Etta shook her head. 'Only used by the armed forces I'm afraid. Seems like every man and his dog is either going to the final in Wembley or going to watch it on television in London or Germany, including, it seems, the entire male population of Morocco.'

'No!' Vicky groaned squeezing her eyes shut. *No. This can't be happening.*

'Nothing going for France either. Even at the best of times there are only a few flights,' Etta added. 'But with this . . .'

Vicky was standing and swaying, cradling her head in her palms.

Etta placed a hand on her shoulder. 'Come on, Vicky – whatever it is, it will be all right.'

'Tell me again what he said.'

'He said the flights are full of tourists *and* residents.' Etta shrugged. 'Who knew hippies and the beautiful people were so fond of football?'

Vicky swallowed hard, trying to control her fear. 'Please try the railway station.'

Etta dialled and spent half an hour hanging on while Vicky paced back and forth, taking in the embroidered wall hangings, the piles of magazines, and the intricate trellis work separating one part of the room from another.

Eventually Etta spoke and after a few moments shook her head and put the phone down. 'Sorry. All trains out of Marrakech are packed too.'

Vicky blinked rapidly, struggling to hold back her tears.

'What is it, Vicky? You look awful. What's happened?'

'I can't say. Honestly. But I need to see Clemence. She'll know what to do.'

She raced up the stairs to the apartment and passed on the bad news.

'Oh no! What are we going to do now?' Bea asked, her high-pitched voice tight with fear.

'Maybe Patrice didn't see us.'

'Maybe?' Bea wailed. 'We can't just sit here waiting for Patrice to knock on our door. Vicky, we can't!'

Vicky narrowed her eyes to think and knew her cousin was right.

'I'm going to find Tom,' she said. 'God, I wish more people had telephones here. Anyway, he needs to hear about Jimmy. Then we get out of Marrakech as fast as we can.'

'How?'

'I'll ask Tom to drive us to my grandmother's place. We can hole up there for a few days. He shares the car with Jimmy so I'm hoping it's fixed.'

'What if he says no?'

Vicky sighed. 'I don't have a clue, Bea. But if there's a knock at the door, don't let anyone in, even Etta. Keep the shutters closed too and don't make a sound.'

'How long will you be? I'm scared, Vicky.'

'Me too, but Tom lives just round the corner.' Vicky knew she had to be strong for Bea's sake and tried to soothe her.

'Don't worry,' she added, although she didn't feel strong or the least bit calm.

'What if he isn't there?' Bea asked. 'What if you don't find him? What if Patrice comes here while you're away? What if—'

'Bea,' Vicky interrupted, gripping her cousin's shoulder. 'Breathe. All right?'

Bea nodded.

'Stay quiet and remember don't open the door. Lock and bolt it once I've gone. Okay?'

'Okay.'

As Vicky left the riad she walked quickly, looking left and right, and twisted around to glance behind her. It was early and she didn't see anybody as she turned the corner into the next alley. It smelt musty with a metallic sickly odour she didn't instantly recognise. She quickened her steps. Blood. Was it blood? A dead cat maybe? Oh God. Keep breathing. A shadow moved. A shadow of a person?

She felt terribly exposed and too frightened to step forward, she watched as a man wearing a brown djellaba with the hood up came into view. He glanced at her and when he saw she was heading his way, he spun around and went back off in the direction he'd come from. What did it mean? Was she being paranoid? Had he forgotten something? Either way the banging in her chest was so violent she felt she might burst.

Only twenty yards and she would reach the bend and she'd be able to see Tom and Jimmy's place. Oh God! Jimmy. And she saw again the image of Patrice dragging his body across the floor. Poor sweet Jimmy.

She pushed herself to go on around the corner and saw someone standing in the shadow of a doorway next to the house where Tom lived. She slowed her pace and bent down as if to buckle her sandals as she waited for the man to move on. She spotted an animal lying against the wall. So the smell had been coming from a dead cat.

As soon as the man melted away, she checked the doorway before Tom's. No one there. She hadn't given a thought to what she might say to whoever answered when she knocked and was relieved when Tom himself opened the door looking bleary-eyed. Sleepy. His ash blonde hair sticking up in tufts. And despite the gravity of the situation, she could see he was just as beautiful as he had been before.

'We need your help. Me and Bea. Can I come in?'

His already dark eyes deepened further. 'I suppose.'

'This isn't a social call. It's an emergency.'

He raised his brows and the look said everything: *Stupid, hysterical girl.* He sighed dramatically and said, 'All right. But I warn you, I don't respond well to histrionics this early in the morning.'

'It isn't early.'

He shrugged.

Either way Vicky couldn't see him responding well to histrionics at any time of the day.

He led her through the inner courtyard of the house to a room at the back. 'Coffee?' he asked and raised the pot as she sat down on a hard wooden chair. 'I'll just heat this up.'

She shook her head. 'Leave it. I've come to—'

'No way,' he interrupted. 'I need coffee even if you don't.'

'For fuck's sake, Tom, stop. I've come to tell you Jimmy is dead.' She gulped back a sob, her heart breaking for their friend.

He frowned but there was almost a smile playing on his lips. 'What? Is this a joke?'

'Of course not. Please, please, sit down and I'll tell you.'

Vicky told him everything. She told him how Bea had picked up the sketchbook and why they were trying to put it back by going through the garden of the house next door. For a split second her galloping fear came back, real again. Mouth dry, she forced herself to swallow before continuing, controlled herself, and managed to tell him they'd watched Patrice Callier shoot Jimmy in cold blood while they'd been hiding in the garden.

Tom stared at her in shock. 'Jesus! Jesus!' he whispered.

'I know,' she said.

As he continued to stare at her, his eyes widened even further and beneath his tan, his face drained of colour.

'I'm sorry,' she added.

He didn't speak, just shook his head while she stared into the silence of the room, feeling awful.

'I can't believe it,' he eventually said. 'Are you sure it was Jimmy?'

'Positive. I'm so sorry.'

Tom stared at the ground, dreadfully distressed although swallowing hard, blinking back tears, trying to control himself. She couldn't think what to say. Didn't know how to make it any better and seeing him so terribly upset, her own eyes filled with tears.

When he eventually looked up, he gave her a small sad smile. 'Thank you for telling me. I'll have to let his family know.'

'Do you have any idea why he was killed?' she asked.

'He found out an awful lot of incriminating evidence against the government here and the security forces of France and America. If it got out, there would have been a whole heap of trouble for them.'

'What evidence?'

He look intently at her, and she felt as if he were working out if he could trust her.

In the end he said, 'The evidence that they abducted and murdered the activist ben Barka in Paris plus several other named men here in Morocco too. Jimmy was intending to publish his findings. It would have caused a massive storm.' His voice broke and he steadied it before continuing. 'And they have silenced him because of it.'

Vicky felt tears welling again and brushed them away. 'Who is Patrice Callier working for?'

'I don't know. Our rooms were broken into yesterday,' he said.

'Did you inform the police?'

He laughed bitterly. 'Hardly. We think they're in the pockets of the French secret service.'

'What did they take?'

'Jimmy's papers.'

'The thing is, Patrice might have seen us in the garden. We just can't be sure. He came out and it looked as if he had, but a cat yowled and then he and this other guy left with Jimmy's body.'

He stared at her horrified. 'You can't stay in Marrakech.'

'We tried to get a flight, but they're all booked because of the World Cup. I need to get to my grandmother's kasbah instead. She'll help us.'

He narrowed his eyes. 'How will you get there?'

Vicky swallowed hard. 'I wondered . . . well . . . could you drive us?'

He sighed and his shoulders drooped. There was a long silence. What were they going to do if he said no?

In the end she asked him if the car had been fixed.

'The engine works,' he said. 'So it more or less goes, but the bodywork still needs a bit more attention.'

'So?'

'Callier will have this place under surveillance too. May already have seen you coming here. We could meet near the garage. There's a back way, and I can make sure I'm not followed. I'll explain the route you'll need to take to get there without being seen.'

'Now? Can we go now?'

'Wish we could, but no. We need to leave early tomorrow morning while it's still dark. Don't go out, not for anything. I'll sort it with the garage owner. He's a mate and he'll fill the car and leave it where I can reach it. I have spare keys.'

'Thank you,' she whispered.

Tom looked dreadfully pale and agitated but was trying not to show it. She longed to throw her arms around him, pleased he wasn't the stand-offish man she'd thought he was the second time she met him. He was, in fact, someone whose real character was hidden beneath a kind of reticence. He had been a bit preoccupied, that was all, just as Jimmy had said. *Oh Jimmy. I'm so sorry that happened to you.* But his loyal friend Tom would help them if he could, though in her core she doubted he or anyone could be a match for a cold-blooded killer like Callier.

CHAPTER 18

Neither of the girls ate much that night, but they drank sweet mint tea and when it was time for bed Vicky reluctantly turned out the oil lamps but lay wide awake in the dark, her mind in turmoil. When she did eventually sleep, nightmare floods and fires of biblical dimensions tormented her, the red and orange flames rising to the sky with smoke sweeping through the streets. She woke with a shout when she really did smell smoke, but it was just drifting in from elsewhere in the city. Bea woke too and they lay silently until it was time, listening for footsteps on the stairs, neither of them daring to speak.

A little later, while it was still dark, they quietly dressed in grey djellabas – although Bea insisted on wearing her orange dress and flowery blue scarf under hers – and then they pulled the hoods over their heads. They had both packed their passports, a couple of bread rolls, a spare T-shirt, and a flask of water in each of their rucksacks, and Vicky had also slipped the sketchbook into hers. As foolish as it now seemed to her, the whole of Marrakech was still probably looking for it. She wished again that they'd just chucked it over the wall as Bea had suggested. No way would its loss or subsequent retrieval from the garden have come back on her. She could still have hoped to impress Saint Laurent.

They wrapped themselves in thin grey woollen blankets. crept out of the house and following Tom's directions, edged along the walls of the alleys as they made their way to the parked car. Hardly able to breathe, Vicky made out a dark silhouette and too nervous to take another step, she froze.

'It's all right, it's Tom,' Bea said, and when Vicky looked again, she saw that it was.

'Anyone see you?' he whispered, putting a hand on Vicky's arm.

'No. You?'

'There's always someone hanging around. Come on, let's get in.'

They piled in and Tom turned the key. Nothing. 'Shit,' he muttered. 'They promised the engine was fixed.'

Vicky held her breath as he tried again. If only Clemence had a phone, Ahmed could have come to collect them, but parts of Morocco were behind the times, especially in the remote mountains. The engine made an awful grinding noise, loud enough to wake the dead, but after several more attempts it finally spluttered into life.

'Well, how to wake up the whole of Marrakech,' Bea said. 'So much for being quiet.'

They set off into the chilly darkness, Tom driving them through the city, all of them aware of the noise the engine was still making.

'The steering is off too,' he said as the car swerved to the left and he fought to correct it. 'All we need.'

As the car stuttered through the dark streets and into the countryside, nobody spoke, though Vicky shivered as she gaped at the ghostly mists lying over the landscape. It was only as the first signs of dawn began to sweep across the mountains ahead of them that the car seemed to finally settle down.

'The car will take us only so far,' Tom warned.

They began to breathe a little more freely and as the sky turned pale blue with silvery streaks of cloud, Tom took the lesser-known tracks where he was able to. Eventually he was forced to join what people called the main road and they heard cockerels crowing and watched dawn painting the Atlas Mountain peaks rusty-red where they floated above the remaining mist.

'The local Berbers call the High Atlas *Idraren Draren*,' he said

'What does it mean?' Vicky asked.

'Mountains of Mountains.'

A little later, when the silvery clouds had melted away, Tom wound down the windows and – despite their unease – they savoured the crisp clean air, luminous with the distinct light Vicky had so often noticed. The risen sun had transformed the landscape; with no beginning and no end it glowed a deep rich yellow and the sky was a vivid cobalt blue. But their momentary feelings of relief could not last. And as Vicky watched the road climbing higher and the fields falling away, her mind could not help but turn back to Jimmy's death. She expected to recall it exactly as it had happened, in sequence as if it were a film, but it wasn't consistent or logical. Moments of the devastation came back to her, jumbled, fragmented. Her terror as she'd witnessed the unthinkable had somehow erased some parts, leaving the images threadbare. Was memory always so unreliable, freezing some things, exaggerating others?

She thought of Clemence and craved the safely of her kasbah. Strange that although her grandmother had been hard to pin down, she instinctively thought of her as a place of safety.

At a small Berber village Tom parked the yellow Citroën well out of sight of the road. Vicky walked about a bit to stretch her legs and stood in the shadow of a tree, glancing back at the spot where they had turned off. She frowned when she saw a large green jeep with tinted windows speeding by. Could it have been the one that had forced the Citroën off the road, or was it normal for some jeeps to have tinted windows in Morocco? Her grandmother's certainly didn't.

She followed the others along a narrow path of compacted earth to a spot where they bought bread and tomatoes and were offered mint tea by a local woman. In a simple village street and sitting on compacted earth in the shade of a tree, hoods pulled low over their foreheads, they kept a lookout. It would have been peaceful, had they not been in mortal danger.

For Patrice could be anywhere. Out there on the open road, hiding up in the mountains, or going about his business in Marrakech as if nothing had happened. As if he hadn't killed Jimmy. *What the hell is going to happen next?* she thought as a shiver ran through her. *And where on earth is this going to end?*

CHAPTER 19

Clemence

Kasbah du Paradis

Clemence, feeling exhausted from her broken night, lay back against huge striped blue and white cushions on the low day bed under the awning on the terrace. The note she had received inside the second thick white envelope had been similar in tone to the first and had been playing on her mind. *You think your secret is safe? Think again.*

She had torn it into shreds and cursed the sender.

Now she arranged magazines on the long copper-topped coffee table for Madeleine while they waited for breakfast. Her mother didn't spare them a glance, just dozed, or squinted at the mountain humming an old tune or complained how hungry she was and that nobody ever gave her anything to eat.

'Be patient. Breakfast is coming,' Clemence said more than once but the humming had drawn forth the ghost of a younger Madeleine and Clemence remembered more strongly in this moment how her mother's constant low murmur under her breath had used to annoy her when she was a child.

When Nadia brought out coffee and fruit, Clemence tried to keep her spirits up, but other images from the past kept arising. She sipped her coffee, picturing Jacques finding her weeping in the orchard on that terrible day when she'd been forced to watch her mother being whipped at the well.

The sound of voices broke into her memories.

At last! The builder, along with an assistant, walked towards them, smiling in greeting. For a moment she thought of hiding Madeleine away but really it would be too difficult with builders there. She would take the chance that if her mother said anything about the past nobody would understand her ramblings anyway. She had not seen the assistant before, but they had both arrived bright and early and were finally ready to start work. The beautiful filigree screens had been made to measure and the work had taken time, delaying their installation in Madeleine's rooms. The new man had unusually pale skin. And the same strong build as . . .

The memory hit her with such force. Theo Whittaker, the only man she had ever loved. She caught her breath as his precious image came back to her, almost as clear as if he were standing there before her.

Theo had been a little younger than her, fair-haired,

with sparkling blue eyes holding the whole world in them. He could be intense, serious too, but able to light up with irrepressible laughter as well. An American, he had that irresistible combination of being funny *and* clever, and Clemence remembered how intelligence combined with humour had actually been an aphrodisiac. God how she had wanted him! And she had fallen heart, body and soul in love, yet when she'd held back about her past, he'd insisted she was withholding an important part of herself.

'All or nothing at all, Clem,' he'd said, his eyes pleading as he spoke.

She hadn't dared tell him anything about her past, about Victor, and he had accused her of keeping secrets, said that she couldn't really love him if she wasn't willing to share who she was or where she came from. She'd been hurt, terribly hurt by it, but had held firm. And he could never have guessed why.

I wouldn't mind having all of myself too, she'd almost retorted in response, but what he asked was impossible, and she felt a part of her, the most vital part of her, fading when he left.

Much later he wrote to say he was divorced and had settled in Tangier where he was running a small private security firm. *Darling Clem, please say you want to meet up.* She'd memorised every word and she had wanted to see him again, very much, but what would have been the point? The outcome would have remained the same and she hadn't wanted to feel that misery a second time.

But the sensory experience of him stayed with her, ignited by memories of the music he played, the books on his shelves, the incense he burnt, the silk of his cushions, the touch of his skin, and his body slick with sweat. *Oh, that most of all.* And with each remembering, each story she told herself, she wondered how far from the truth she had strayed. *Perhaps if I'd told him? Should I have told him?* Had her fear made the past seem darker than it had really been? He'd always liked the less obvious elements of life, the hidden essence of people too, and she had agonised over her desire for him to really know her.

After only an hour or so, when they had finished breakfast, a crash followed by loud barking shook her from her thoughts. Moments later the builder hurried around the corner and explained how part of the wall had collapsed.

'We have to shore it up and rebuild,' he said, his face taking on an excessively sorrowful expression.

'Before you install the filigree screens?'

'Of course.'

'How long?'

He frowned. 'Two or three more days.'

Madeleine, humming again, was oblivious to all this but Clemence wondered how her mother was going to survive the week without her own familiar rooms to rest and relax in. The days would be long for Clemence too. Maybe today they could visit Ahmed's mother to at least break things up a little. The woman could barely speak French and Madeleine could not speak Arabic, so whatever Madeleine might say she was unlikely to be understood.

She called Ahmed and explained what she was planning.

'You wish me to escort you?'

'No, my mother should be able to sit on a mule for the short ride down.'

Ahmed looked doubtful.

Neither she nor Madeleine were in a hurry to move, though, and a little later the dogs began howling again. Hearing the crunch of approaching footsteps on the gravel track Clemence rose up to see who it was. *Dear God, what now?* Instinct told her to dash inside and claim a headache, but Madeleine couldn't move quickly enough, and anyway, she was already too late. As she screwed up her eyes against the sun and watched the man come into sight at the top of the final part of the track from Imlil, she stood her ground.

Patrice Callier. What the hell was he doing here?

'Ah, the old lady,' he said, his eyes narrowing as he glanced at Madeleine. 'No more wanderings, I trust?'

Clemence shook her head, remaining outwardly calm. Why had he come here uninvited? This was her home, her sanctuary. A bolt of fear ran through her. Did he know something? If he did and told anyone, the scandal would be on the lips of everyone in Marrakech within moments. People would pull horrified faces, profess to be shocked, but the thrill of it would be in their eyes and her life here would be over.

'I've come to talk to you,' he said. 'Old friend to old friend. I thought you might enjoy a catch up.'

'Are you living here? In Marrakech I mean?' she asked, not caring if she seemed ungracious, only wanting him to go.

He smiled that cool smile of his and remembering how easily he could get under her skin, her jaw clenched.

'I have a temporary rental in the Palmeraie,' he said looking around. 'Shall we sit?'

'It's too hot out here. I'll order tea.' She pointed the way indoors and taking her mother and the dogs with her, quickly found Ahmed and asked him to keep Madeleine out of sight until Patrice had left. In the kitchen she requested tea to be brought to the sitting room and then hurried back, trailed by Coco and Voltaire.

Patrice had made himself comfortable in what she considered her special reading nook. An alcove or small *bhou* at one end of the sitting room with a built-in sofa in navy and silvery blue tiles on the walls behind it, plus a kilim in a geometric Islamic pattern of blue and cream on the floor. Clemence ordered the dogs to sit – they helped her feel protected – and she pulled up an armchair opposite Patrice who was leaning back, legs spread wide.

'Well may I say you are looking especially lovely today,' he said, his eyes lingering on her body.

She glanced down at herself as if to check what he was seeing. She was wearing a subtle linen kaftan with a turban of coffee-coloured silk and, round her neck, a long chain of gold and silver spheres. Her nails were painted but the only make-up she wore was a pale pink almost translucent lipstick. She didn't reply to his comment. Could barely swallow let alone speak.

He smiled though it seemed more of a smirk. 'You were a fine-looking girl, Adele Garnier.'

'Clemence,' she muttered.

'I assumed you'd married.'

She shrugged.

'What with your change of surname to Petier. Yet you never married though, did you, Ade . . . I mean Clemence?'

'You're offering again?' she said, realising he must have done some digging.

'What would you say if I were?'

She shifted in her seat and stared at him. 'Why have you really come here after all these years?'

'Can't two old friends enjoy a glass of tea together?'

She felt a bead of sweat running down inside her kaftan.

'I'll come straight to the point, shall I?'

She wasn't clear what game he was playing, but convinced there was bound to be one, she had no option but to sit it out. In any case she needed to know.

'The thing is, I have to leave Morocco imminently.'

'Oh?'

'You may recall my father?'

'I do,' she said.

'Your own father's untimely death upset him. They had been friends. I hope you enjoyed reminiscing with the photos.'

So, it *had* been Patrice who sent them. The notes too? Withholding her true feelings of anxiety, she dodged the question and simply smiled. Inside she felt herself crumble. *Do not react. Do not react.* She glanced at the pale gold shine of the sitting room walls, wishing it were later when the sun would burnish them, and they'd turn a deep coppery terracotta. And he'd be gone.

'I believe you have some valuable property of mine,' he continued.

Time slowed right down. What did he mean? Still

thinking of the photographs and the anonymous notes, her throat felt constricted and unable to speak, she could only raise her brow.

Nadia entered with a pot of tea and a plate of Moroccan biscuits. She poured the tea and left.

'They were items your father promised my father,' he continued as he inspected the biscuits. 'I have a letter of intent, but when the will was read the document was ignored. I have no explanation why, but the items are extremely valuable. My father died recently and as it's now my inheritance, I've come to claim it.'

Clemence remained silent, looking down in astonishment, her mind racing. *What does he know? What does he know?* Could this be the truth? He was only here for gain? She felt his eyes upon her but fearing what else he might say didn't look up, only forced herself to breathe more slowly. In and out. In and out.

'A small rectangular casket made of gold inlaid with rubies and emeralds and inside it a very fine antique pair of heavy enamelled and silver gilt-hinged *khalkhals*. Priceless. You remember . . . the anklets?'

Her hunger to be free from the dread gnawing at her since the day of his arrival sharpened. She feared blurting everything out, opening her mouth, the words expelling themselves in a rush to fly about the room. Her guilt papering the walls.

He heaved a sigh of irritation at her silence but carried on. 'They are eighteenth-century Moroccan. Their surface is mounted with filigree silver wires and enamelled with turquoise, green and yellow enamel typical of Fez fine enamel.'

She had no idea what her father had promised, couldn't recall a single conversation.

'You have, what was it again?' she eventually said between gritted teeth. 'A letter?'

He withdrew a sheet of paper from his pocket and handed it to her. 'It's a copy. The original is in storage at the bank.'

She stared at him as images flooded her mind. Her father's burnt study. *His* father, their family doctor. Had it been a camera hanging round his neck as he stood staring at the ruined room? Now that she knew Patrice had definitely sent the photographs, it must have been.

'I have no way of ascertaining if this is genuine,' she eventually managed to say, gazing down at the thick parchment type paper with her father's stamp at the bottom. She tossed it towards him with as nonchalant a look as she could summon. 'And if it is genuine, why didn't your father contest the will?'

'I do not like to besmirch my father's memory but, in truth, he was far too weak.' He gave her a tight-lipped smile. 'I don't think he could foretell how much he was going to need that legacy.'

'I believed him to be a kind, compassionate man.'

'Well, it is rather a long story.'

She rose to her feet although her legs felt dreadfully unsteady – surely, he must see them shaking. Taking a sharp breath in she replied. 'And I feel yours may be a *tall* story. It makes no sense that your father did not claim it at the time.'

'As I said, he was weak.'

'I don't believe you.'

He stood up too and moved towards her. Was he going to hit her? She flinched, remembering the way he'd shoved her against the wall of an outhouse when she was seventeen, soon after she had rejected his marriage proposal, his hand fumbling inside her bodice. It had repulsed her. *He* had repulsed her. She had pushed him away as hard as she could and made a dash for it, calling loudly for Simone, her mother's little dog, so the servants would know she was there.

'Just answer me,' he was saying, jabbing a pointed finger at her. 'Do you have it?'

She took a moment and in a low voice said, 'I have no idea what you are talking about. I don't know anything. A casket, did you say?'

His eyes narrowed. 'You know what I said.'

He bunched his hands into fists and although he was still trying to hide it, his frustration was building. She wanted to run, call Ahmed, get as far away as she could from this man.

Even more tight-lipped than before he asked again. 'Do you have my inheritance?'

He took another step towards her and glowered, the muscles around his eyes tense, his fists dangerously close. She stood her ground, but almost passed out at the hatred she could see brewing within him.

'I do not have it,' she eventually said. 'Why would I?'

He was inches away from her, the broken veins in his cheeks purple, his mouth twisting, his eyes flaring. Who knew what he might be capable of?

She was still terrified he was about to lash out at her, but he only said, 'And your mother? The old lady you keep hidden here is your mother, isn't she?'

She bristled.

'You lied, Clemence.'

'I have my reasons,' she said.

'Just as I have my reasons for wanting what was promised to my family. I need the legacy. Immediately. My father died sick, penniless, and in debt and you just upped and vanished, taking his inheritance and mine with you. He needed that inheritance just as much as I do now.'

She held her breath.

'You made everyone think you had followed the driver's son to heaven only knows where in France. Jacques, wasn't it?'

'That was his name.'

'I never could understand how you preferred the son of a driver to me. Only, when I left for France too, I checked up on you but found no trace.' He tilted his head very slightly, as if considering whether to say any more. 'I'd rather not see anything go wrong for you.'

She let out her breath. His voice was chilling, and she felt herself shivering. Her hands, she realised, were shaking so much that all she could do was to squeeze them together as tightly as she could. He must not see her fear.

His eyes narrowed. 'Nor your delightful young grand-daughter either.'

She froze. Those eyes of his had witnessed cruelty, had probably been the cause of cruelty. There was an excruciating silence.

Appalled and barely able to contain her shock at his threat, she raised her chin and glared at him. 'Get out of my house.'

'You think what happened in Casablanca is a secret?' he said. 'I know what you are, Clemence.'

The shame and the guilt began to scream inside her and terrified by what he might say next, by what *she* might say too, she spat out the only words she could. 'I said . . . get . . . out of my house!'

She tasted blood on her tongue. Blood from fearfully chewing the inside of her cheek. She forced herself to stand firm, digging a nail into the fleshy part of her palm to hide the panic overwhelming her. She remained still for several minutes. Then she focused on the dogs. 'Voltaire, Coco, come!'

From a front window, she watched Patrice walking down the track until he was out of sight. And when he really had gone, she ran to her bedroom and collapsed onto her bed, where she sobbed and sobbed, gulping back the anguish and the fear. Weeping until her eyes were smarting and her throat so sore it felt raw. The dogs leapt up to console her, whimpering as they licked her face and hands. She could not lose all this. Not everything she had built. The life she had made. She'd lost so much once before and couldn't let this be the end. And at the thought of Patrice hurting Vicky she felt a rush of terror and got up to pace the floor. Not her granddaughter. No! No! Patrice Callier was capable of anything. His past dripped with blood. She could see it. Feel it. The violence in him. The rage.

A little later a noise outside drew her attention, maybe Madeleine coming across with Ahmed, and she paused, quickly wiping away her tears with her fingertips. An icy chill blew right through her but with it the fear gave way to anger. She would die rather than allow that man to harm Vicky. She would destroy him if she had to.

CHAPTER 20

Vicky

After leaving the Berber village, Vicky, Bea and Tom returned to the car and set off again.

'Why did you come here?' she asked him after a while. 'To Morocco I mean.'

'I'm just a political journalist looking for a scoop.'

'And Jimmy?'

'Jimmy?' His voice broke and he blinked rapidly before continuing. 'He used to tell people he was an activist and a writer, but he was more deeply involved in anti-government activities than I. There are young Moroccan agitators too trying to bring about change for the people.'

'I know about the riots.'

'Yes. And the CIA are here to identify troublemakers. We think the French secret service is involved too, though it hasn't been proven.'

'So you didn't come for the buzz and the fun?' she said, trying to lighten the mood.

She looked across at him as he shook his head and noticed a disdainful expression on his face.

'There is so much going on here to be worried about,' he said, 'but the rich Europeans, fuelled by champagne and hashish, see it as their own toxic playground.'

'I spotted that,' she said wryly, remembering how she had felt at the party in the Palmeraie.

'And despite those riots last year, not a word from the beautiful people.'

'You sound bitter.'

'Maybe I am.'

'How did the riots start?'

'With Moroccan students on a demonstration. They were demanding the right to public higher education for all. We take education for granted, don't we?'

She nodded.

'They were dealt with forcibly and the next day protesters vandalised stores, burnt buses and cars, threw stones, and chanted slogans against the King.'

'Wow! How frightening.'

'It all got out of hand and the army brought in tanks. Some say they had no choice.'

'What do you think?'

'I wasn't there. But European countries like France and Spain, Britain too, have tried for centuries to control Morocco and get a foothold in Africa and the independence here is fragile and fraught with complexity.'

'What about your family? Do they mind you being here?'

'Enough, Vicky. I need to concentrate on the road.'

She wanted to ask how he was feeling about Jimmy being killed in the way he had been. Being killed at all. She turned towards the window so Tom couldn't see her tears. He seemed to be holding on, but there had to be such a horrible mixture of emotions going on inside him. There certainly were in her. Misery consumed her, the worst she'd ever felt, but she also felt enraged by what Patrice had done. She tried not to think of Jimmy, focused on her breathing and managed to calm herself, but it wasn't easy as flashes from that night kept snagging, drawing her back.

She glanced over her shoulder at Bea on the back seat. Her cousin had fallen asleep with her mouth slightly open, looking so young and innocent. Vicky closed her eyes at the thought of what Bea's parents, Aunt Florence and Uncle Jack, might say about this. She had promised them it would be safe.

'Are you okay?' she eventually asked Tom.

'How do you mean?'

'I mean how are you feeling?'

'I'm trying not to feel. I'm trying to keep this old jalopy on the road until we get to the point where we'll have to walk.'

Vicky felt the sting of his tone. Were all men so uptight when it came to their emotions? She was still wondering about it when she spotted a young gazelle – maybe a gazelle – all on its own and rapidly springing towards them. She shouted, 'Watch out, Tom! Watch out!' But everything happened at once. The gazelle slammed into them, the car jolted, swerving wildly, spinning out of control and hitting a huge boulder. Tom plummeted forward, crashing into the windscreen. Vicky fell sideways into the door as she heard the screech and crash, the noise of metal re-arranging itself. Her door flew open, leaving her hanging half in, half out, and on the verge of losing consciousness. She struggled through it, pitching herself head first out of the car and straight into the dust and dirt gathered in a greasy heap at the side of the road. She opened her eyes and saw, just a foot away, the dead gazelle lying on the ground. Bea screamed, again and again. In the weird quiet when she stopped, Vicky was violently sick. She wiped her mouth and heard Bea sobbing now.

'I can't get out,' Bea wept. 'I can't breathe.'

Shaking from the shock, Vicky forced herself to her feet, opened Bea's door from the outside, then staggered round to see if Tom was all right. She stared, her body paralysed but her mind reeling at the sight of blood on Tom's cheeks, his jaw, his neck. She felt her chest tighten and tried to take some deep breaths. In through her nose and out . . . Oh God! The windscreen was badly cracked in a circle where his head had smashed into it. He hadn't gone right through but some of his hair was caught in the fissures radiating from the circle.

'Is he dead?' Bea's asked, her shrill voice rising even higher as she came round to look. 'Is he dead? Do something, Vicky. Do something!'

But Vicky was still unable to move. Tom was lying with his face in the shattered windscreen, bleeding, and she was just standing there gasping for air.

'I don't think he's breathing,' she managed to say.

Bea, shuddering, began to wail.

Vicky touched the side of his face. The air was thick with the sound of buzzing insects, some already attracted by the sweet metallic smell of blood. She felt his wrist for a pulse. 'Thank God! He's unconscious, but he is alive,' she said.

'Oh God! Oh God! Oh God! What are we going to do?'

'We have to get help.'

'Where the hell from?' Bea asked, looking around wildly.

Vicky shaded her eyes from the sun with her hand and surveyed the land. 'I think I can see buildings over there. It could be a village.'

'Or a fucking mirage.'

'This isn't the Sahara Desert. It's a mountain road.'

She opened her rucksack and tugged out a T-shirt to cover Tom's injured face from the flies and the heat of the sun. 'I'll cut across the ground to fetch help. You look after Tom.'

'No. We should stay together, keep out of sight.'

'I must go, Bea. There might not be a car along here for ages, and we have to get help for Tom.'

'Don't leave me. I can't bear the sight of blood. Let me go. I'm fitter. Let me go to the village instead.'

Vicky sighed. 'Okay. If it's what you really want but hurry up.'

Bea pulled out her blue flowered scarf from beneath her djellaba and tied it around her head, grabbed her rucksack and twisted round to Vicky. 'What's Moroccan Arabic for help?' she said, her voice quaking.

'Etta taught me a few words. It's something like *owni afak.*'

'Okay.'

'Don't go too far,' Vicky called out. 'Only ten minutes, fifteen tops. If you're nowhere near a village by then come back. We'll have to hitch back to Marrakech to get help.'

Vicky tried to stay calm, but she was breathing too fast and feeling the panic rising in her throat, she felt she was going to pass out. She checked herself over. Her leg hurt from when she'd fallen out of the car; her neck and shoulders were sore too, but she was fairly sure she hadn't banged her head.

The sun was high in the sky now, merciless, hot, and she was sticky with sweat and fear. Still shocked from the collision she couldn't help playing the moment of impact over and over. The horror of it welling up again and again. Terrified for Tom, a tremor ran though her, for if they didn't get help quickly enough, he might not survive. She glanced at him, silently begging him not to die while pleading with God for a car, for a village, for a woman passer-by. But there was nothing. She checked her watch. Bea had already been gone for fifteen minutes.

She surveyed the surrounding area and shouted for her, scanned the haze on the horizon too. Nothing.

'Oh hell,' she muttered, carefully picking up Tom's wrist and checking his pulse again. He was still unconscious, pale, and clammy.

About twenty minutes later she spotted what looked like a fruit lorry, with wooden sides at the back but no top, open to the air, and heading away from Marrakech towards the mountain. In response to her wild signalling, the driver pulled up.

Vicky said the few words she thought were right. *Owni afak.* She pointed at Tom, but the weather-beaten driver was already climbing down from his cab and running over to inspect the scene.

The man gradually shifted Tom's body away from the windscreen using a knife to release his trapped hairs. While he held Tom's shoulders, head, and upper body, he indicated she should take hold of his ankles. Together they lifted him from the car and shuffled across to the lorry. The man put Tom down on the ground while he released the catches on the back of the lorry. The tail gate fell open with an almighty creak. Between them they picked Tom up again and the man climbed into the lorry backwards, hauling up his deadweight while Vicky tried to help by raising his legs and feet.

Tom groaned and when the driver glanced back at him lying in the truck, he shook his head with an expression that suggested he thought her friend had little chance of survival. Without thinking, Vicky climbed in and crouched down to check on him. *Please be alive. Please.* His eyelashes fluttered briefly, and she spoke softly.

'It's all right, Tom,' she whispered. 'Hang on. You're going to be all right.'

She didn't like leaving him, but she had to get out and wait for Bea. As she straightened up, ready to jump down from the truck, there was a sudden jolt as the vehicle juddered into life. She lurched forward, landing on her hands and knees, and yelling at the driver to stop the truck.

As she attempted to stand up again he must have been going over a hole in the road for the jolt sent her flying once more. She yelled at him but he didn't stop. If she could just make him hear her . . . but there was no way she could jump out while the vehicle was bumping about with so much force. The driver was swinging around far too quickly and she could only cling on. As she gripped the side of the truck, she yelled again but he was picking up speed. Oh God. Bea!

CHAPTER 21

Clemence

Kasbah du Paradis

Ahmed and Madeleine had been gone for ages. With her frustration mounting, Clemence waited for them outside in case they'd gone down to the cool of the village. She could run down to the jeep but she ought to be here when her mother returned, although it was her granddaughter's safety dominating her thoughts now. She had to get to Marrakech quickly enough to warn her about Patrice.

'Hurry up, Ahmed,' she muttered over and over. 'Hurry up.'

The wait was interminable as she played Callier's threat over in her mind. She drank a glass of water and with her pulse beating wildly ran to her bedroom to unearth her pistol hidden in a lingerie drawer full of

168

rarely worn silks. The only good thing her father had ever done was teach her how to shoot. She had never held a loaded gun before her father had shown her, and after she had learnt how to shoot, she had fired his pistol only once more, and that had been long ago. Her own handgun, a *Pistole Modèle 1935A*, was a standard French sidearm used during World War II. She had obtained it on the black market and regularly cleaned and oiled it, so now all she needed to do was wipe its gleaming surface and slip it into her bag.

With shaking hands, she located an eight round, single stack magazine and slid that into her bag too along with a few overnight things.

Ahmed arrived back soon after, helping Madeleine down from the donkey and bringing her staggering across to Clemence.

'We did not go far. It was too bumpy, so we sat down under a tree and watched the birds.'

Clemence thanked him then said, 'Look Ahmed, I have to go to Marrakech.'

'I'll drive you, Madame. My sister will look after the old lady.'

'I know she would, but I need you to remain here and send your sister home.'

His eyes widened. 'Very well. I stay. There is a problem?'

'There may be. If the man who was here earlier comes back, do not let him in. His name is Patrice Callier, and he could be dangerous. Keep my mother in the tower room for her own safety and when you send your sister home tell her to ask your brother to come up here to help guard the house. Keep everything locked but let the builders continue.'

'Do not worry, Madame.'

Clemence went to her mother, kissed her cheek, and sprayed *L'Heure Bleue*, her mother's favourite fragrance, on her wrists. At first the scent had reminded Clemence of unhappy times but gradually she grew to accept its romantic, sweet spiciness and now it represented a much earlier time, a time *before*, when she had been thirteen and still innocent. A liminal time when she used to sit outside with her mother before her father arrived home, surrounded by the sounds of approaching night and before the first stars scattered the sky.

She felt melancholy when she thought of those days. The kind of melancholy that only came later in life when it was clear many things were done with. The hopes and certainties of early adulthood gone, replaced by the knowledge that whatever lay ahead would not be as pleasant. It wasn't a yearning for the past. No. It was a yearning for a time of life that could never be repeated. She would never again experience young love, never again taste champagne for the first time, and she would never know when she might be doing something for the very last time. Not really. For no matter how much it was expected, death always seemed to come suddenly just like sleep.

She squeezed Madeleine's hands, left the terrace, found the keys to the jeep and asked Ahmed again to please take care of her mother. He asked how long she'd be.

She shrugged. 'As long as it takes.'

The wind was getting up as she left, and the sky had

turned a strange pre-storm yellow. It didn't usually rain in the summer and although the garden was crying out for water, the tracks would turn slippery and muddy if the downpour went on for long. But whatever the weather, she had to get hold of Vicky and she had to do it with haste. Whether he intended to really hurt her granddaughter or not, Patrice's threat could not be ignored and the police, many of them corrupt or in the pockets of the CIA or French secret service, would be no use at all.

Once too often Patrice had trespassed on her life. *He must be stopped,* she thought. *And this time permanently.*

CHAPTER 22

Vicky

All the bumping, jolting way to Marrakech, Vicky held Tom's hand and used her own body to shield him from the worst of the sun's burning heat. Terrified he might die on the road, for once in her life she wished her mother were there. She would know what to do.

'Please stay alive, Tom. Please stay alive,' she whispered. 'I'm here. I'm staying with you.'

Thankfully he wasn't bleeding as much, though the sun had intensified the sweet smell of blood on his face. He had one huge cut right beside his left eye and the swelling was dreadful. Was he going to lose his sight in that eye? She wanted to wipe the blood away but didn't dare as there could be a shard of glass embedded in his flesh.

Still the images of the crash kept revolving in her head. The gazelle. The swerve. The collision. The noise of the windscreen cracking and the smell of the tyres burning on the hot stones. At one point she saw Tom's lashes flutter and he murmured a few words Vicky couldn't make out, for the noise of the lorry was too loud, and Tom was too weak.

She wasn't only worrying about Tom: she was scared for her cousin too. Why hadn't Bea come back as they'd arranged? Where had she gone? Imagining how frightened she must be, Vicky wished again she'd been able to get out of the truck to wait. She prayed her cousin would have the sense to hitch a ride back.

She heard Tom murmur again and glanced down to see his eyes were open. She gasped in relief and her own eyes watered.

'It's okay, Tom,' she said in a rush. 'We're taking you to hospital.'

'What happened?' His voice was very faint.

'An accident. But you're going to be all right.'

He closed his eyes again and went very still, the muscles in his face slackening, and her fear for him rocketed. She felt for a pulse at his wrist. Still alive.

As they entered the city and she saw life going on as normal – the clamour, the usual commotion – she could hardly believe it. How was it possible when this dreadful thing had happened? When they arrived at the hospital the lorry driver climbed down and went straight into the casualty department to alert the doctors. Vicky waited, watching people going in and out: a man on crutches, a nurse having a quiet smoke, two women gossiping, a young child in tears being comforted by an older woman, her grandmother maybe.

Moments later orderlies, doctors and nurses were rushing out towards them, looking at Tom, shouting to each other. The orderlies gently lifted him onto a stretcher and carried him through a pair of swing doors into the building. The racket inside was ear-splitting. Nurses were running to help and yelling for assistance. The whole place was completely packed with people waiting, crying, pleading to be seen. She tried to follow the stretcher, but a nurse put out her hand to stop her. A doctor with a wiry build and kind eyes led her to a different part of the hospital. He spoke French and had a gentle manner so in a halting, tearful voice she told him what had happened to Tom and explained how Bea was still out there on her own. He said he would ask a nurse to immediately call the police station.

It felt like hours had passed as Vicky paced back and forth in a ghastly olive-green corridor, listening to a child crying somewhere and the chatter of nurses in what had to be an off-duty restroom. She hated hospitals. The colour of the walls, the smell of disinfectant and bleach, the blood, the sweat, the stale second-hand smoke, and the stink of faeces and urine; all of it packed together like this made her feel ill. You could even smell the fear of the other people sitting and waiting, staring ahead blankly with drawn faces or otherwise with heads bowed and gazing at their feet. Eventually two policemen arrived, and a nurse pointed to Vicky. They came across and she stood up.

'Come with us, miss,' the older one said in French.

He took her to a stuffy but private waiting room. The heat was scorching, and she desperately needed a drink.

He sat down and indicated she should too, while the younger police man went to fetch her a glass of water. The older one looked as if he never smiled, and with a stern expression he questioned her about the accident and about who had been with her.

'My cousin,' she said anxiously. 'Beatrice Jackson, my cousin. Has someone gone to look for her? She's on her own.'

They kept on asking questions. Who had been driving the car? Had they been taking drugs? Where had they been going? Why were they in Marrakech? Who did they know? What was their relationship with Tom? With Clemence? With Etta? Frightened and terribly alone, she twisted her hands in her lap. Why were they asking all this? Had Tom died? Were they looking for someone to blame?

She answered everything but had to pause to remember she absolutely could not mention Jimmy's murder. *Must not* mention the murder under any circumstances, whatever else she said. At least not until she had spoken to Clemence. She remembered Tom saying the police were corrupt. Now she just wanted to find out if Bea had got back safely. She kept looking out for her, expecting the door to burst open and her cousin to rush in.

'All in good time,' they kept saying, and when she asked if they could hurry up, they just smiled at her. She wanted to scream with frustration.

'Please can I go to look for her?' she asked again. 'She might be waiting somewhere else in the hospital, or anywhere in fact, and I need to know if Tom's all right too.'

The policeman tipped back in his chair and she felt like pushing him right over. The overhead light was flickering relentlessly and the insects buzzing around it were giving her a headache. She rubbed her temples to try to relieve the pain.

When the doctor came in, he gave her a tired smile and exchanged a few words with the policemen in Arabic. She watched him impatiently, desperate to hear about Tom. He wouldn't be smiling at all, would he, if it were bad news?

He pulled up a chair and took hold of her hands.

'Is—'

'No. Mademoiselle, you'll be pleased to hear your friend is going to be all right,' he said.

Still overcome with self-recrimination, Vicky could hardly breathe for the relief flooding her body.

'A cut to his face,' the doctor added, letting go of her hands. 'Bruising and swelling, particularly along his forehead and around his eyes. He also has a broken jaw but it's a clean break so may well heal on its own. We've wrapped a bandage around his head and under the chin to keep him from opening his jaw too much. And he has concussion.'

'Is that bad?'

'He needs time to recover. My colleague is stitching him up and he'll have to remain here for a while, so we can keep an eye on him.'

'Can I see him?'

'Not today,' the doctor said. 'Maybe tomorrow.'

Vicky burst into tears. The policemen shuffled in their

seats, looking uncomfortable. She wiped her eyes with her hands, and the doctor patted her back.

The men were all smiles now it seemed that Tom was going to live. No charge of dangerous driving, or whatever else the police might have thrown at them.

Vicky rose to her feet. 'I have to find out where Bea is. If you won't help me, I'm going on my own.'

There followed an exchange in Arabic between the doctor and the police. One of the policemen turned to her. 'She is French, your friend, like you?'

'My cousin. I told you she is my cousin, and she is English.' She didn't explain the complex mix of English and French in their extended family.

'Why didn't you say?' the policeman said, getting up and slowly moving towards the door.

'What difference does it make?' she demanded, looking from the doctor to the policemen.

The doctor shrugged.

But then, like an avenging angel, Clemence burst into the room.

Vicky stared at her for a moment.

Then her grandmother held out her arms and Vicky flew straight into them. While Clemence was holding her, she was also speaking in a rapid, very fluent Arabic that brooked no argument. The policemen both nodded and after a few more exchanges they left the room along with the doctor.

'What's happening?' Vicky asked. 'What were they saying?'

'They've just explained that Bea isn't with you, and they are going to make sure she's all right,' Clemence said.

Vicky pulled away and made for the door.

Clemence held her back by the arm. 'No, you don't. You'll only get in the way. You need sweet mint tea for the shock. Then you need to get out of those bloodstained clothes and take a shower. We'll talk afterwards.'

'How did you know I was here?'

'I didn't know. I saw the wrecked car on my way into the city and recognised it. Don't forget when that yellow car was rammed off the road previously, you were in it too. I was worried you might have been involved again, so I came straight here. One of the nurses told me that you really *had* been in the car. Then she led me here.'

'Tom was driving and we, Bea and I, were trying to get away from the city.'

'Why?'

'There's a secret I need to tell you,' Vicky whispered. 'Something Bea and I saw. Something really terrible.'

An orderly came in to tidy the room.

'Don't tell me here. We're going back to Etta's.'

'How well do you know Patrice Callier?' Vicky asked.

'Don't say any more. Let's get out of here first. Then tell me.'

CHAPTER 23

Vicky saw her grandmother and Etta glancing at the filthy clothes still scattered on the floor of their apartment. The things they'd worn when— She closed her eyes, dizzy from the impact of the awful memory. In one way it seemed like an age ago even though it was not. She longed for it to be an age ago, craved for it to fade into the past rapidly, but would anything so awful ever diminish? Or would it eat away at her for ever, corroding her whole life?

'Vicky?' Clemence said, after whispering a few words with Etta who then left them alone.

Vicky blinked rapidly but couldn't speak.

Clemence rubbed away a fleck of blood from Vicky's arm and looked her straight in the eye. 'Right. What did you want to tell me?'

She took a breath. 'I'm not sure Tom will be safe if we leave him there on his own.'

'Because?'

Through the open window, Vicky heard the background noises of the city and stared at her grandmother. Patrice Callier was a friend of hers. Would her grandmother even believe her? She tried the words out in her head. They sounded crazy. She would sound crazy. With every ounce of her being she wished she had never come to this terrible place. Seeing Jimmy's murder had been the most horrifying, heartbreaking thing that had ever happened and now she was a fugitive too, so what on earth had been the point?

She glanced at Clemence who was now sitting quietly and gazing up at her.

'I'm tired, Vicky, so tell me. Or shall we find couscous to eat in the square and talk there?'

Vicky bit her lip and then the words just spilt out. 'I can't go out.'

'Because?' her grandmother asked again.

'Because Bea and I saw Patrice Callier shoot our friend Jimmy dead and we're frightened he may have spotted us. He may have seen us watching as he did it.'

'Good God!' Clemence exclaimed under her breath.

'We didn't feel safe here, so we were trying to reach the kasbah, you see. Tom was driving us to you. We told him all about it. We told—' The stream of words had poured out, but now her voice cracked and she burst into tears.

Clemence came to her and led her over to the sofa where she sat with an arm around her until her sobs finally subsided.

'Here,' she said handing Vicky a clean handkerchief from her bag. 'I see why you don't want Tom to be alone. You're frightened Patrice might do something to hurt someone else.'

'Yes,' Vicky whispered, and told her everything from the moment Bea had taken the sketchbook to why they were hiding in the garden, and how Tom had been helping them get out of town. Her grandmother sat quietly listening.

'Patrice will know we were trying to get away. If he really did see us watching, he'll also guess we told Tom about the murder.'

Clemence didn't reply for a moment, then she said, 'I think if he really had seen you, he would have charged into the garden with his gun.'

'Maybe, but we were so scared. We had no idea what to do.'

'You still have the sketchbook?'

'Yes. Saint Laurent thinks a man call Georgio stole it, but it was really Bea.'

'Don't worry. We can sort it out.'

'Now?'

'No, when all this is over. Now you need to have a wash.'

Later Vicky was slumped on the sofa with her feet up attempting to read, though her mind kept racing off in different directions. The gazelle. Tom. Bea. The police. Jimmy. Her mother. She wanted her mother. The noises from the street seemed different and unusually alarming: shouts that before had just been part of every day and every night felt threatening. A motorbike backfiring almost made her jump out of her skin. Clemence started too, spinning round towards the sound, listening intently. While her grandmother was doing her best to remain calm and in control, Vicky could see from the way she kept shifting in her seat and tapping her heel, she felt deeply uneasy.

'I thought Bea would have been back by now,' Vicky said. 'Surely, she would have hitched a lift. Or the police would have found her.'

'Etta has been with the police. She'll have found out what's happened.'

'But I need to look for Bea myself,' Vicky said.

'No. It's getting too dark now.'

'Oh God!' Vicky said as a memory came rushing back. 'I'd completely forgotten what with the crash and everything.'

'What?'

'We had stopped for a break, and I saw a jeep pass by.'

Clemence frowned. 'And?'

'It was green and had tinted windows just like the one that rammed Jimmy and me off the road.' Vicky covered her mouth in horror.

Clemence gave her a puzzled look. 'What? What is it?'

'Oh my God! Do you think Patrice could have got her? What if he was in that jeep waiting somewhere and spotted his chance?'

'You don't know if it *was* Patrice who rammed you off the road.'

'No. But it could have been. First Jimmy was rammed off the road and then he was killed.'

Clemence seemed to be trying to decide whether to say something soothing or something far worse than that. Vicky couldn't tell.

In the end what she did say was, 'Patrice is not a good man, so I hope nobody else has been hurt.'

'You knew he was a murderer?'

'No. Of course not.'

The anxiety Vicky felt was not anything like the fear of failure or perceived rejection she had lived with all her life. This was on another level. This was fear for her cousin's life, and fear for her own life too; a real threat to their safety, and not some unsettled anxiety based on nothing at all. Why had she spent so long worrying about things that did not matter? Why had she cared so much when people didn't seem to like her. Why had she feared being an outsider, when all along the real fear was this gnawing terror she felt in her stomach, this constriction in her throat and in her chest, this feeling of her heart no longer knowing how to beat properly?

She threw her book on the floor and glanced at her grandmother who was frowning, looking as if she was thinking a problem over or working out a solution. Whatever it was she seemed very edgy.

'What's wrong?' Vicky asked.

'Just trying to think,' Clemence replied and cleared her throat. Evidently having come to a decision she said, 'We must eat. I'm going downstairs to arrange some food and call someone from Etta's phone.'

'Who?'

'A friend. And if Etta is back now I'll ask her to sit with Tom until we can arrange better security. I assume not even Patrice would walk into the hospital and murder someone in cold blood right in front of everyone.'

'So you really do believe me.'

'Of course.' Clemence hesitated. 'The man I'm calling . . . he's an old . . . well I knew him some years ago. We may need his help with a situation this serious. And I imagine the police may have contacted Tom's parents by now. They'll want to be by his bedside.'

'Thank you.'

'You are not alone. Lock the door. I'll only be downstairs, and I'll ask Etta's cook if there's any food she can spare.'

'I'm not hungry.'

'You may think that, but if we are going to get through whatever still lies ahead, we both need to eat and sleep.'

The next morning, Vicky was still tormented by anxiety. She hadn't slept much, spending the night worrying about Tom and Bea.

A knock at the door interrupted her thoughts. Clemence told her to sit down and said she would open up.

'Is it your friend?' Vicky asked.

'Maybe. Take a breath and stay calm. I'll deal with this.'

Clemence opened the door, but it wasn't her friend standing there. It was the same two policemen who had been at the hospital. They spoke in Arabic, but Vicky could tell by the long faces and shaking heads it wasn't good news.

She couldn't wait a moment longer and rose to her feet. 'What is it? What are they saying?'

'They have found Bea's abandoned knapsack, but they haven't found Bea.'

Vicky felt her legs turn to jelly and sank back down but almost immediately got up again and ran to the bathroom, vomiting as violently as she had at the side of the road with the sound of sighing metal in her ears. She splashed her face and lay curled up on the tiled floor, weeping silently. A few minutes passed and eventually she picked herself up and looked at her reflection in the mirror, shocked by her red, raw-looking eyes and ashen skin.

After a while Clemence knocked on the bathroom door and told her the police had left.

When Vicky came back through Clemence handed her a glass of water.

'So what now?' she asked.

'We wait.'

Vicky walked over to the loggia, wanting to look down on the trees in the serene courtyard and listen to the birds singing. Wanting normality. Home. Anything but the reality of what was actually happening here and now.

In the evening Clemence called a French doctor she knew to look Vicky over. When he arrived, he checked the bruises on her leg and prescribed a sedative, saying how more than anything she needed rest. Vicky didn't want to take the tablets, but Clemence insisted it would be for the best and promised to take care of everything while Vicky slept. So Vicky ate some biscuits then swallowed the tablets and although she struggled against it, she fell into a dreamless sleep soon after.

CHAPTER 24

Clemence

Clemence had just looked in on her granddaughter, who was sleeping like a baby in the next room. *Dear sweet girl,* she thought. She was lying down on the sofa herself now. At aged seventy-four, although still fit and healthy, she sometimes felt dreadfully tired, almost as if the process of living had drained the energy from her. Sometimes she even envied her mother who surely could not go on for much longer.

She closed her eyes. Although she would give anything to forget her mind refused to, and the years slipped away as they so often did, and she was back in her rambling childhood home outside Casablanca. As a child she'd felt that both she and her mother only existed for her father's pleasure, or his displeasure, and they'd had to live with the threat of punishment at any infringement

186

of the rules. *Next time we'll tip her right down the well.* The trouble was he was unpredictable and changed those rules all the time. They'd had no life of their own. No autonomy. Her mother had been complicit until the dreadful day when she was not. If Clemence mentioned her father now, Madeleine either looked bemused, as if she couldn't quite recall him, or if she did, she would scowl, cackle and spit on the ground.

The change in her mother was incredible. She had always been so well turned out, wouldn't leave the house without one of her large Victorian hats and a matching pair of white kid gloves whatever the weather. She had a maid to fix her hair in the full pompadour style of the early 1900s, high, rounded and curved away from her head. Clemence had watched the maid, Circe, creating the shape, backcombing and rolling her mother's long dark hair into a wide pleat. Sometimes she used pads, or artificial hair, to reinforce the style. Every single day Madeleine had relied on a lady's maid and had kept to versions of that old-fashioned hairstyle her entire life.

Both Clemence and Madeleine had been careful about how they arranged their faces in front of her father. To be transparent in front of a dangerous man was to put yourself in the mouth of the tiger. Far better to remain opaque. Let him think you were exactly what he wanted you to be. Stay safe. If it meant living a lie, well, it was simply the price you had to pay for your survival. Not so bad really and Clemence had cultivated her inner world and the world she had shared with Jacques – until

Patrice had ruined it when he had told on them. She would never forgive him for that.

She felt for the pistol in her bag. Still there.

The next morning she'd just woken up, feeling stiff from falling asleep on the sofa, when she heard a gentle tap at the door. Not the police this time. It was Etta calling her name and opening the door.

'There's a man downstairs for you,' her friend said.

'Really? Who?'

Etta just smiled. 'You'll see. Come on.'

Clemence followed her down to the courtyard garden where Etta left her. The man had his back to her but when he spun round and spoke, she thought she might faint at the sound of him. Their first encounter after so many years.

'Clem. Clemmy.'

Over the years she'd tried to remember his voice and never quite could. But when he spoke those very first words, in that soft American accent of his, there he was, just the same as before, his voice hinting at a world of feeling within him.

Clemence pressed a hand over her heart, felt it pounding with disbelief and joy. Even though *she* had called him it was still a shock to see him standing before her. Strong. Solid. She couldn't speak – knew her own voice would let her down.

They stared at each other, Clemence so overcome she was blinking back tears that were threatening to fall. Neither of them spoke for several moments. She'd been anxious, aware how seeing him again might be a disappointment, that he'd have grown a paunch or have developed the purple nose and red cheeks of a drinker. But he hadn't.

His eyes were still a bright electric blue, although he wore different glasses; his face was even more freckled than before and his fair hair was liberally laced with silver. She longed to touch it. Touch him.

Perhaps his nose was ever so slightly bigger but basically, he really was the same in the way some people *are* always the same. He had wrinkled a bit perhaps, with a lived-in look, but he hadn't shrunk. Hadn't become less in any visible way. Had even become more. Perhaps because he had been so self-assured and solidly himself in the first place. Theo, the man she had loved above all others.

The man who had understood her in a way that required no words, in a way time could never erase. And yet here they were, standing self-consciously with each other, even though she had lived within his soul and he in hers.

She ran a hand over her hair and when he grinned, she burst out laughing. Couldn't help herself.

They began to speak at the same time.

Then, 'Sorry,' he said.

And, 'Come up,' she said. 'I'll introduce you to my granddaughter, Vicky.'

'Granddaughter?'

'It's a long story.' She had never told him about her child and of course it must be strange to hear the truth now, but she had no option but to continue. 'I had a son,

Vicky's father, Victor, long before I knew you. He died during the war.'

Theo looked visibly shocked but clearly realised this was not the time for that conversation. 'I'm so sorry,' he said.

'Thank you. But it's all in the past.'

He nodded.

Upstairs she withdrew just enough to allow him the space to enter and suddenly the years between them dissolved. Vicky's arrival had given Clemence a new lease of life, but this . . . this with Theo was different. She was *here*. Fully here again.

'You look just the same,' he said smiling.

She had kept up her outward appearance; it didn't take much – a good haircut, her lovely silk kimonos and linen kaftans, simple but elegant jewellery, varnished nails. Inside was another matter.

'Well, your hair's a different colour, of course, but you look just the same. Even more beautiful.'

Clemence felt her skin grow hot. When had she last blushed for heaven's sake?

'I—' But she found herself struggling for words.

He held out his arms to her and longing to be comforted she went to him.

Their hug was prolonged and Clemence realised how deeply she had missed being held by him. He smelt the same as before, spicy, with a hint of salt, and the tang of tobacco on his breath. She leant into him, soaking him up, and was instantly back in those heady days of laughter and long intoxicating nights of sex. Their bodies entwined, plotting their future, his warm hand always caressing a part of her – a memory so bold it took her breath away.

'So,' he said as they broke off and she felt embarrassed at what she had just been imagining.

He swept a hand across his forehead, lifting the hair away. A movement so incredibly evocative and intimately known that she felt like crying.

'My darling, darling, Clemmie,' he said and smiled his lopsided smile, a smile which always looked as if he were laughing at himself or was seeing the joke nobody else had spotted. 'Want to tell me what all this is about?'

She smiled back, unhinged by his proximity. She had always loved the way he called her darling. Nobody had before him, and nobody had since. She felt the tiredness drop away and remembered how it had been until he'd wanted to hear more. Not about her innermost self but about her past in Casablanca – the younger Adele she had all but snuffed out.

They settled on the sofa, and she quietly told him everything she knew about what had been happening in the here and now.

'And you believe your granddaughter?' he asked. 'She really did see this murder happen?'

'She certainly believes she saw it. And she believes the murderer may be aware that she saw it.'

'Is she a level-headed girl?' he asked.

'I think so.'

'And her cousin is missing?'

'Yes,' she said. 'Doesn't look good, does it?'

He sighed but didn't reply.

'Patrice Callier, the man she says pulled the trigger, has threatened me too – and my granddaughter – over another matter.'

He shook his head. 'Christ, Clem, what have you got yourself mixed up in?'

'Will you help us?'

'You know I will. Let me pull some strings and see what I can find out. I'm pretty much retired but I still have contacts here and a couple of guys who owe me the odd favour. I'll try to arrange for someone to guard the lad who is in hospital and someone to be here.'

'Actually, we may have to return to the kasbah soon. My mother is living there now, and she needs me.'

They talked a little about their lives. It had been thirty years since they'd been lovers when she had been in her early forties, and he'd been a few years younger, still married but separated. When he'd written telling her he was living in Tangier she had hidden the letter.

'You didn't write back,' he said, no reproach in his voice. 'I thought you might come.'

For a moment she wanted to cry. 'I thought I might too,' she managed to say.

'But you didn't.'

'No.'

'I never married again,' he said.

A short silence followed as that sank in.

CHAPTER 25

Vicky

Vicky had woken up but felt too heavy to get out of bed and continued to lie there listening to the hum of voices, although she couldn't make out what they were saying. The soft voices clearly weren't those of the police returning and all she really wanted was news of Bea.

She eased herself out of bed, but feeling woolly and hungover from the sedative flopped back down to examine her badly bitten fingernails. She hated this not knowing, this waiting. This awful fear. She picked at the skin, remembering the battles she'd had with her mother over the biting. It wasn't that Élise thought Vicky should be a perfectly presented little girl or young lady; her mother wasn't so fussy and most of the time knocked about in one of Henri's white shirts and a pair of old trousers. The things she harped on about were mostly to do with Vicky's attitude – and her nagging only had the effect of making everything worse. As a child, Vicky had adored her aunts, her mother's two sisters, especially haphazard, dreamy Florence, Bea's mother, with her blonde hair flying all over the place and her fingers always blue with ink. And her delicious food. She was an amazing cook. As a writer she was successful, even more so than her aunt Hélène who was doing well as an artist.

She heard her grandmother calling her and letting go of what she had been thinking, couldn't put off going through to the sitting room any longer.

A tall man with silvery blonde hair rose to his feet and held out a hand. He wasn't young, perhaps a bit younger than Clemence, but he was handsome in an older man way.

'Theo Whittaker,' he said. 'And you must be Vicky. I'm sorry you've been having such a wretched time.'

'You're American,' she said and shook his hand.

'Yes. An old friend of your grandmother's.'

Vicky sensed an atmosphere, not a bad one but a tangible *something*.

'You knew each other well?' she asked.

'We . . .' Clemence began to say but stalled.

The man glanced at her. 'Many years ago,' he said. 'Your grandmother refused to marry me.'

'I thought so. I was sure Etta mentioned that.'

Clemence laughed and Vicky noticed her grandmother's hazel eyes were sparkling and she was looking more animated than she had been before.

'If I remember, you were actually married at the time,' she said.

'But estranged. Separated.'

Vicky felt sure that whatever had happened between them it was most definitely not over.

But she decided to tread carefully, and aching to find out about Bea, asked if there was any news.

Clemence shook her head and squeezed Vicky's hand. 'Not yet, my dear. I wanted to tell you that while you were sleeping, Etta arrived back—'

'Tom's not—?' Vicky gasped.

'No. No! His father is now at the hospital and wants to talk to you, that's all.'

'Do I have to?'

'I think so. He wants to know everything. And Theo is about to make a call to Tangier from Etta's phone to arrange protection for you.'

'Really?'

'You too, Clemmy,' Theo said.

Vicky raised her brows. Clemmy? She had never thought of her dignified grandmother as a Clemmy.

There was a knock at the door and Clemence got up to open it and then stepped out onto the small landing

'The police are mounting a wider search,' her grandmother was saying as she came back in. 'They just told me Bea's passport was in the rucksack, and they've now contacted her parents. They will arrive tomorrow, or the next day, I hope.'

Vicky squeezed her eyes closed, her body filling with dread at the thought of what might have happened to

Bea. The only slight comfort was that the sketchbook was in her own knapsack.

'Her passport photo is rather out of date. They asked if you have a more recent one.'

Vicky opened her eyes, bit her lip. 'Oh gosh. No. I haven't. Neither of us has a camera so we hadn't got round to taking photos.'

'Pity, but they've also suggested her parents bring photos with them. It will slow things down while they wait. The police are trying to contact your mother too.'

Vicky felt hope and fear rising at the same time. Was that even possible? 'Why?' she asked.

Clemence shrugged. 'They didn't say. To tell her about the accident I suppose. I know they haven't reached her yet. But Bea's parents are flying over from London to Spain and taking the ferry to Morocco. Then a train.'

'You won't leave me on my own, will you?' Vicky said, feeling scared and terribly out of her depth.

'Of course, we won't,' Theo assured her.

'But first, breakfast,' Clemence said. 'Etta has offered to feed us all. Come down with us now and afterwards, Theo will drive you to the hospital.'

They made their way to Etta's apartment on the ground floor, following the alluring aroma of coffee which drew them to the open door where Etta stood waiting. Today she wore a long green dress with black jewellery and Vicky thought the tiny, usually hawklike woman really looked rather sweet and not quite so bold.

'Come,' Etta said. And they followed her through to the kitchen.

They ate seated at an ancient wooden table where the smell of spices from decades of cooking hung in the air. It had been laid with fresh French baguettes, *sfenj* dough-nuts sprinkled with sugar, *ghoriba* almond biscuits, a bowl of figs, several cheeses, and some pastries made with soft *Medjool* dates imbued with the fragrance of orange blossom and mixed with pistachio nuts.

For the first time in days, Vicky was starving and ate ravenously while Theo, Clemence and Etta talked quietly about the past. Vicky wasn't really listening. If Bea's parents were on their way, did that mean her mother might be travelling now too? In a way she hoped her mother *would* come to Marrakech, anticipated it with some pleasure even. But how was it going to feel, not only for herself, but for Élise, and for Clemence? Unless Jacques had said something, her mother didn't yet know that Clemence even existed.

Élise had stopped talking about Victor long ago – and if he were mentioned, simply changed the subject. Vicky's aunts had told her of Élise's utter devastation when he was executed and how afterwards she had sworn to do everything she could to make the world a better place. Vicky sighed. How come Élise had never realised that should have included looking after her daughter properly?

After breakfast Clemence, Theo and Vicky left the riad to visit the hospital. But only one step into the dusty alley, her stomach clenched, and she began to tremble. She placed a palm flat against the pink wall to keep herself steady, but the alley began to tilt.

'Help me,' she managed to get the words out in a choked voice.

'What is it?' Clemence asked.

Vicky's mouth and throat went dry, her breath caught, and her skin felt clammy. She could feel a hammering in her chest and her pulse was pounding in her ears. Light-headed and nauseous, it felt like everything was spinning.

'Help me,' she pleaded again and reached out a hand.

A passing woman turned to stare. Vicky doubled over, heard her grandmother speaking but, detached from everyone, she couldn't respond. There was a terrible weight on her chest, and now her breath wouldn't come at all. She attempted to scream but could only gulp at the air, her entire body trembling.

'You're safe, Vicky,' she heard Theo say. 'We're here. Squat down and put your head between your knees. It's fear making this happen.' When she was able to raise her head, he carried on talking to her in a calm, neutral, voice. 'Now, look around. Where are you?'

'I . . . ca . . . I . . . can't.'

'Yes, you can. Slowly. Hold my hand.'

She felt very small and very frightened but managed to say, 'In the alley.'

'Good. We're going to walk up and down,' he said and tentatively, still holding his hand, she straightened up.

'Well done,' he said as they took a few steps. 'Can you breathe now?'

And gradually Vicky regained her normal breath and she leant back against the wall exhausted.

'I thought I was going to die,' she said. 'I was so hot.'

'What frightened you, Vicky?' Clemence asked.

'Everything,' Vicky whispered. There was too much to even list. She kept on thinking of Patrice, of him pointing the gun at Jimmy. He could be anywhere, raising a gun towards them from the shadows. He could be planning how to harm Tom. He could have already killed Bea.

'Look, my car isn't far,' Theo said to Vicky gently. 'This alley is too narrow to drive down but all we need do is walk for two or three minutes. Everything else . . . we will solve in time. I'm working on our best course of action regarding Patrice. We will have to inform the police, maybe later today, but I just want to make a few enquiries first. Okay?'

'I suppose.'

'And we'll drive to the hospital in a minute where I will soon have a guard in place.'

Clemence put an arm around Vicky's shoulder, and they carried on to the car. Although her panic had subsided Vicky still didn't feel calm inside. She knew Patrice was out there. Somewhere.

CHAPTER 26

Clemence

As they sat together during the car ride, Clemence dwelt on Vicky's panic attack. She looked over to where her granddaughter was chewing her nails. A sign of anxiety? It wouldn't surprise her. She wished she could send Vicky to safety in France, but knew her granddaughter, potentially a key witness in a murder enquiry, wouldn't be able to leave Morocco.

Clemence looked over to Theo. He had always been thoughtful, full of ideas and inspiration, unlike anyone she'd ever met, and it seemed he hadn't changed: he had calmed Vicky so wonderfully, so gently.

He had done the same thing for Clemence, back in those halcyon days when they'd been together. After fleeing Casablanca, she had lived most of her years on guard, constantly anxious, constantly on the lookout for threats, but with Theo . . . It had been like being a girl again. They talked endlessly about where they might go, imagining the people they might become in another life. They talked about Rajasthan, Indochina, Burma. He was a count, she a countess, or an Indian princess riding a painted and bejewelled elephant. They talked about ordinary things and extraordinary things and as he spoke his voice seemed to sing inside her, as if it had become a part of her. He talked about his childhood, how his best friend had been killed in a riding accident. She had been knotted up inside herself, a tense woman, when they met, and he had gently unfolded her.

Vicky's panic reminded Clemence uncomfortably of her childhood, of her own hysteria the day she'd been told her father wanted to send her mother to a hospital for people who were 'sick in the head'. Clemence knew her mother was sick at heart, not sick in the head at all. There had been no help with breathing for Clemence when, hearing the awful news, she began to gasp and gulp for air. Instead, her father had made her hold out her hands, palms uppermost, and he had beaten them with a metal ruler until they were bleeding and she was weeping and begging him to stop. Thinking up ways she might engineer a cruel accidental death for her father became a fantasy. A game she played. Usually alone but sometimes with Jacques.

Theo was saying something, and it pulled her out of the past.

'Sorry,' she said. 'Miles away.'

'We're here,' he said, getting out of the car and coming

round to open her door where he glanced up at the sky. 'Looks like it might rain.'

Clemence welcomed the promise of rain. It would help relieve the intense heat and the pressure they were all under.

Through the glass door of Tom's hospital room Clemence saw a stocky middle-aged man with fair sandy hair standing with his back to them and looking out of the window. She opened the door and he turned instantly, frowning, hands on hips.

'Who the hell are you?' he growled.

'Clemence Petier,' she replied, with an outstretched hand. 'I'm with my granddaughter, Victoria Baudin. She was in the car with Tom.'

The man glared at Vicky, who was staring at Tom. Clemence followed her gaze. Tom's head was wrapped in bandages and his blonde hair stuck up above them, like a crown. The skin around his eyes was purple and one eye was so swollen you could barely tell there was an eye at all.

'You,' the man said, still glaring at Vicky and jabbing his finger. 'My son's accident. Whose fault was it?'

Clemence felt the need to protect her granddaughter. 'I'm so sorry for what happened to Tom, but it was an accident. A gazelle slammed into their car. But please tell us, how is Tom doing?

'As you see, he is sleeping.'

'So he is conscious, not in a coma.'

The man nodded.

Clemence held out her hand to him again, and he shook it. 'Lionel Goodwin,' he said in a gruff voice.

Vicky turned away from Tom to look at his father. 'For a moment I thought . . .'

'No,' the man said.

'It really was an accident, Mr Goodwin,' she continued, her voice shaky. 'I told the police everything I could remember, but it happened so quickly. One minute we were fine and the next . . . the next . . . the gazelle was coming too fast. We crashed, and Tom smashed headfirst into the windscreen.'

'And that is all?'

She gulped and closed her eyes for a second. 'We tried to get help. My cousin Beatrice went one way and I stayed with Tom . . .' Her voice trailed off at the thought of Bea still alone somewhere out there.

Clemence wrapped an arm around her. 'Vicky's cousin Beatrice is missing, Mr Goodwin. The police have made a search of the area but all they've found is her rucksack.'

'I'm very sorry to hear that.'

'Will Tom's mother be arriving today?'

He scowled. 'Tom's mother has not seen her son in ten years, so I doubt it very much. Tell me, Victoria, where were you heading?'

Vicky didn't reply. She was standing beside Tom's bed gazing at him. 'I think he's waking up,' she said.

Tom opened one eye. 'I . . . I . . .'

'Don't try to speak, son. They say you won't be able to open your jaw very wide for at least six weeks during treatment. I'm here to make sure they look after you properly.'

'Patrice?' Tom mumbled and closed his eyes.

Mr Goodwin turned to Clemence. 'What's this about Patrice? Who is he? Was he in the car too?'

'I think your son is muddled.' Clemence's voice was authoritative, cool. 'Vicky insists there was only the three of them, herself, Tom and Beatrice. I have no reason to doubt her.'

A moment later Theo walked in. 'All arranged,' he said. 'A guard for Tom will be here within a couple of hours. And I've identified the officer we need to speak to about the scene Vicky witnessed.'

Mr Goodwin stepped forward, aggressive again. 'What's all this?'

As Clemence edged away she watched Theo start in surprise then weigh up the situation. 'You must be Tom's father,' he said with a smile. 'I'm Theo Whittaker. I'm helping my old friend Madame Petier with a matter unconnected to the accident.'

'You're American,' Goodwin said, looking relieved to be among his own English-speaking kind again.

Typically bigoted, Clemence thought, but Theo just smiled and said, 'Indeed I am.'

'Thank goodness. I'm very pleased to meet you.' He held out his hand and Theo shook it, but the man did not let go. 'But if you are helping your old friend with an "unconnected" matter . . . isn't that how you just put it?'

Theo inclined his head.

'Then tell me why you are placing a guard in my son's hospital room?'

CHAPTER 27

'It's an astonishing view,' Theo said, glancing back at Clemence and then returning to scrutinise the rooftops and minarets as they stood on the roof terrace of the French Café. 'Especially now, while the air is so fresh and my goodness, the birds, so many birds. We came here before, didn't we?'

She stood a little way from him, occasionally casting sideways glances, aware he was doing the same in between looking down at the daily food market for mountain traders. Although Theo was usually a confident man, he looked the way she felt. Diffident. Wary. When their eyes met, she tried to unpick her feelings. He smiled and she felt suddenly a little more expansive, almost herself again, but after just a few moments the anxiety returned. *Come on, Clemence,* she told herself, *you're a mature woman.*

'Clem?' he said, gently reaching out for her hand.

'I remember when we came here before,' she finally replied, still not able to process how this shy spine-tingling exhilaration at seeing Theo could exist alongside her fear for Beatrice. There was still no further news of her and Clemence felt the constant dread deepening inside her.

'What is it?' he said. 'You seem, I don't know, distracted maybe. It isn't surprising.'

'No.'

'I feel it too. And me being here on top of everything else, well, it's a bit unsettling, isn't it?'

'I feel guilty. While Bea is missing, I shouldn't be feeling anything other than worry. Her parents must be going out of their minds. And I'm scared that Patrice Callier might try to hurt Vicky.'

He put an arm around her shoulder and she leant into him.

Theo and Clemence had wanted Vicky to stay with them, but she had insisted on remaining by Tom's side with a nurse keeping an eye until the guard arrived and a panic button if they were worried. Tom's father had gone to find breakfast, furious at the way Theo had simply fobbed him off and the fact that nobody else had answered his question. But he would be back soon and as he looked like a man who could handle himself and anyone else who got in his way, Clemence had given in.

'Do you remember our mountain walks?' Theo asked with the smile of recollection.

She nodded.

In the brief silence that followed she couldn't tell what

he was thinking, and wanting to steer the conversation away from the past she said, 'Why not tell me about your home?'

His face lit up. 'A beautiful cliff house halfway up Tangier's Old Mountain with an ocean view and a sloping garden. Took a while to restore but I'd love you to see it one day. Of course, Tangier can be rather cold and rainy so it's a warm house. Whitewashed on the outside and comfortable inside.'

She smiled at the thought of it. 'You still like reading?'

'Can you imagine me not reading?' He laughed that old distinctive laugh of his, a rich full laugh that had captivated her in the first place, that and the light in his blue eyes. From the start he had really seen her. Seen into her even, though not all the way to her secrets.

'You should never have left me, Clem,' he said, shading his eyes from the sun as he turned to look at her.

Surprised by how direct he was being and how swiftly he had approached the heart of things she gave him a quasi-smile. 'As I recall, you left me.'

He placed a hand on her arm. 'Worst mistake of my life.'

She sighed heavily.

'That sounded deep,' he said.

'I suppose it was.'

Unable to prevent her mind from straying back she thought of when she had fallen in love with him during the first precious days and nights he spent at the kasbah years ago. The start of all those months they'd been together. How the smell of him still excited her, just as it had done back then, how every time he touched her she felt exhilarated. And within moments she found herself back there . . .

Lying on an old sofa in the garden of the kasbah and waking suddenly after a dream of her own death. Not, she felt sure, because she was frightened of dying but because she wanted to be reborn with a different past. While she'd been sleeping, he had been reading but he noticed her discomfort when she awoke and rose slowly to his feet – it was too hot to do anything in a hurry – and he offered to fetch cold lemonade for them both.

'Thank you. I am rather baking.'

'Your cheeks are flushed.'

When he returned, he had joined her on the sofa where, still lethargic, she rested her feet in his lap.

'You have elegant feet,' he said, stroking each in turn as she stretched.

With a sharp intake of breath, she couldn't hide how deeply his touch affected her.

'I look after them,' she said as his large hand encircled an ankle. For a strong man he was gentle, and she felt lazily sensuous.

He laughed. 'My lady has highly erogenous zones in her feet.'

She had batted a hand at him, blushing.

'Do you like walking?' he asked. 'On these elegant, sensuous feet of yours?'

'In the mountains? Yes.'

'Shall we climb the high peaks together?'

And quite a few weeks later, when it wasn't hot, they were up in the mountains, dressed for the cold and staring at the shimmering high peaks covered in snow. He turned to her, took hold of her gloved hand, and deeply serious asked her to marry him.

She smiled at the earnest expression in his eyes and well aware she was sometimes hard to read said, 'Why don't we spend a little longer getting to know each other? I don't even know what you do in Tangier.'

He frowned for a moment but then his eyes sparkled with good humour. 'I thought you'd never ask. I'm attached to the American embassy.'

'And what do you do?'

'We analyse the political and economic situation here and report back to the Department of State in America. I used to train Morocco's police and military to implement better security.'

'And now?'

'France is somewhat more protective of their "protectorate" these days and is blocking anything they interpret as interference. I have a rather more clandestine role now. Rather dull really.'

'There's nothing dull about you, Theo.'

How desperate she had been when, eighteen months after they first met, she had watched him walk out of her life. She'd felt older than the mountains that day. Older and sadder . . .

'We never really leave the past behind, do we?' he said now.

She shook her head. They went downstairs and sat at a table on the pavement overlooking the square, ordering aromatic Moroccan coffee spiced with cinnamon, cardamom and ginger. Clemence always found this special mix a comfort. Across from them a group of men, sitting at a low table beneath a shady awning, were quietly playing a board game.

She viewed the bustling square. A skinny cat stretched and came across to weave around her legs, its fur warm from the sun, but seeing an old boy with a monkey on a chain was as upsetting as it always was. Clemence removed the beads from around her neck, threading them through and over her fingers again and again. She watched the *halqa*, a kind of street theatre, and found it calming. The circle of people standing around the acrobatic performer was small, and she could easily see him enacting his repertoire of stories and myths.

'What do you regret?' Theo asked quietly, seeming to pick up on her introspective mood.

Clemence didn't reply immediately, and when she did it was to shrug slightly and move on. 'When will Vicky be able to talk to the officer you mentioned?' she asked. 'The one you say is safe. It is urgent.'

He narrowed his eyes at the abrupt change of topic but said, 'Soon. Officer Alami is of town, so we just need to be patient until he's back. She mustn't say anything about what she saw to the local police. I mentioned the corruption?'

'Yes.'

'It's endemic. If someone knows where she is, they may pay the police to keep quiet or even to slow down the search. But at least they are conducting a wider search for Beatrice with uniformed officers out looking for her every daylight hour since she vanished. They don't need to be told the reason they were all on the road to the kasbah.'

'But as they don't yet know about Patrice, they won't be looking out for him, will they? He'll still be walking around.'

'Yes, he may well be. But if the murder was political in some way, it would be dangerous to say anything until Alami returns.'

'I'm thinking of Beatrice too. The High Atlas above the kasbah can be so treacherous.'

'Let's hope she didn't get that far, and they'll find her soon.'

'Alive?'

'We have to think so. Come, let's finish our coffee and see if we can find out when the parents are arriving.'

'I think they're flying over to Spain, and at Algeciras they'll take the ferry across to Tangier and then the train I suppose.'

'Quite a way.'

Clemence nodded. 'And I really need to get back home. My mother's memory is vague at best and sometimes she doesn't even recognise me.'

'That's hard for you both.'

'Yes. It is. I've given Ahmed, the young man who manages the kasbah, a list of who is allowed in when I'm not there. I'll add you to the list in case you come up to the mountains. You would need to show him some kind of papers to prove who you are.'

He raised his brows. 'Goodness. Glad to see you're well organised. Does he have a gun?'

She shook her head.

'I'll bring my own.' Theo pushed his chair back and stood up. 'Do you think this Patrice might really have the girl?'

'It's possible.'

At the station, Clemence and Theo took a few steps back to allow Vicky to greet the Jacksons. Bea's mother, Florence, looked exhausted. With a heart-shaped face, gunmetal grey-blue eyes, and pale skin, she was a pretty woman, but her anguish was visible. The dark purple circles under red swollen eyes told Clemence she must have been crying for hours. Her curly fair hair, lightly threaded with early silver, had been tied back at the nape of her neck and she gripped her husband's hand, looking as if she were scared to let him go.

Vicky ran to hug her aunt, holding back tears.

Clemence watched Florence, feeling immense sympathy for her. Poor woman. This must be hell for her.

The father, Jack, moved forward to hug Vicky.

'You all right?' he asked the girl when he let her go.

'Not really,' Vicky said, her voice shaky.

Jack gave her a compassionate look, squeezing her arm, but his words were businesslike. 'Look,' he began, 'please will you tell me what on earth has been going on here?'

'It's a long story,' Vicky said. 'But it started with a sketchbook.'

'How does a sketchbook end up with my girl's disappearance?'

Clemence saw her granddaughter really struggling to hold back tears now and stepped forward, putting a hand on Vicky's back.

'I'm Clemence Petier,' she said, holding herself very upright. 'Vicky's grandmother, and this is my friend Theo Whittaker.'

'Oh my God,' Florence said, noticing her for the first time and staring. '*You* are Victor's mother?'

'Yes, I am.'

Jack said hello and shook hands with Theo.

Florence was still gazing at Clemence. She opened her mouth to speak again but her voice broke and when she began to cry, Jack put an arm around her shoulders.

'My dear,' Clemence said. 'All our emotions are running high.'

There was a short silence.

'Is Vicky's mother – is Élise coming?' Clemence asked eventually.

Jack was the one to reply. 'Not sure. We called, but she wasn't there so we left a message with her husband, Henri.'

Clemence didn't say anything. On the one hand she yearned to meet Élise, the woman who had loved her son, Victor; on the other hand she felt such shame and guilt she was afraid to meet her. *What kind of person will she think I am*, she thought, *to abandon a baby like that and never even attempt to see him again?*

CHAPTER 28

Vicky

Her grandmother kissed her on both cheeks and then again for a third time. 'I must go, Vicky,' she said. 'I don't like leaving you, but I've left my mother at home. She's—'

Clemence coloured up, looking uncomfortable, as if she had said something she shouldn't have.

'Oh!' Vicky said, astonished by the revelation. 'I didn't realise she lived up in the mountains with you.'

Clemence gave her an uncertain smile. 'I'm sorry. I have tried to protect my mother from . . . well . . . from too much . . .' Her voice drifted off.

Vicky frowned. What was her grandmother getting at?

'Anyway, she's ninety-two and I need to make sure she's all right.'

'Of course.'

'I'll introduce you to Madeleine next time.' Her next words came out in a rush as if she were glad to leave the subject of her mother behind. 'Don't worry, I'll be back soon. In the meantime, the Jacksons are here, Theo too, and I'm sure Etta will step up if you need any help. You should soon have a guard and that will be a relief. But don't do anything on your own.'

Vicky swallowed hard and watched Clemence heading back to her jeep, the feelings of comfort and safety she had felt oozing away with her. It seemed as if her grandmother had even more secrets than Vicky had first thought. She couldn't help speculating that if her own mother did come to Morocco, *she* might be able to find out more about the past than she herself had managed to do.

But how would Élise react to what had happened? How could she possibly understand? Part of Vicky wanted her, needed her, but she also felt sure her arrival would only lead to more quarrels between them.

While Florence and Jack booked into their hotel, one of the oldest in Marrakech, Vicky and Theo were going to meet his contact, Officer Alami, at the police station in the new town. They would all meet up after the interview. Police were still scouring the immense high mountains asking questions, but early the next morning, the Jacksons would be joining the search party and the mountain villagers would be shown the photographs they'd brought with them. Vicky had already explained what her cousin had been wearing. Terrified for Bea and for herself she tried to still her shaking hands. When would this end? Everything had become so desperate here and she longed for London and for France.

On the way to the police compound, the streets were as noisy as usual, with a jumble of revving motorbikes, bicycle bells, and people buying and selling, or simply doing nothing. Élise would call it loitering. Vicky called it hanging out, although in truth she resembled her mother more than she cared to admit. Élise was someone who kept herself busy all the time, just as Vicky did. Seeing her aunt Florence had brought a pang of hunger for her own mother, so capable and strong in a crisis.

Once inside the utilitarian building, Vicky and Theo were shown to a stuffy high-ceilinged room with a fan slowly revolving yet despite that, the air still felt hot and tired. The stench from a drain just outside the open window combined with cigarette smoke didn't help. Vicky wiped the sweat from her brow with the back of her hand and stiffened when a tall thin officer entered the room. He gave Theo a nod of acknowledgement, pushed back his chair, and invited them to sit, then sat down himself, stretching out his long legs before him. He was middle-aged, stern looking, with bushy black eyebrows and a pronounced nose. When he took off his hat, she saw he was almost bald. Speaking softly in Moroccan-accented French, he told Vicky he was Officer Alami, and he asked her to describe what she'd seen the night Jimmy was killed.

She felt distressed and embarrassed, having to tell him about Bea stealing the sketchbook and having to explain why they'd been creeping through a garden in the dead of night. It sounded so stupid, and she could feel her cheeks flaming with shame. The officer listened carefully without interrupting but when she had to tell him about what had happened in the garden, what they had seen, a lump formed in her throat and her eyes watered.

'In the garden I . . . well, my cousin and I . . .' Her voice shook, and holding back tears she stopped, unable to continue.

'Take your time, my dear,' Alami said gently. 'There's no rush.'

She wiped the sweat from her hands on her skirt, took a long breath and began again. 'We, well it was actually me who saw all of it.'

Theo put a hand on her shoulder sympathetically.

'I saw . . . I saw Patrice hold up a gun and then I saw him . . .' She swallowed hard but her voice was cracking. 'I saw him shoot my friend Jimmy.'

She screwed up face to try to block out the awful image, but the tears dripped unchecked down her cheeks and onto her hands in her lap.

The two men sat quietly giving her time.

'I . . . we . . .' She swallowed again then furiously wiped her eyes with her fingers. 'We saw Patrice drag Jimmy's blood-soaked body across the floor.'

Again she heard the soft *bump, bump, bump* of Jimmy's head, and she began to sob, shoulders heaving with grief and the horror of seeing someone she knew die like that right in front of her. Theo pulled his chair closer to her and stroked her back. From his pocket he took out a white handkerchief and told her it was clean as he passed it over. She gulped at the air and eventually stopped crying, giving him a wan smile before dabbing at her wet cheeks.

After a good long pause, Officer Alami asked if she was able to continue, no pressure or judgement in his voice. She said she was.

'Good girl. Are you certain you recognised the man as Patrice Callier, the person you met when you were with your grandmother?'

'Absolutely. He gave us a lift to a party too.'

'And you think he may have spotted you in the garden?'

She told him why she thought so. 'I think he saw me and Bea,' she added. 'Or he *may* have seen us.'

'And you believe your cousin's disappearance is connected with this man?'

She nodded silently, unable to speak further. Awash with a torrent of emotions she thought of sweet, sentimental Bea. Her love of clothes. Her longing to love and be loved. She remembered the day Bea had bounced into the flamboyant Biba boutique on Abingdon Road in London, smelling of British Rail egg and cress sandwiches and with a copy of *Honey* rolled up under her arm. She'd gasped at walls decorated in black and gold Art Nouveau wallpaper, huge potted palms dotted everywhere and bright eye-catching feather boas.

'Wow! This is so groovy,' she'd said in her usual light, breathless voice. 'Totally fab.'

The dark, sombre dresses were displayed hanging on hatstands, in grape, mulberry, purple of course, and even a blackish colour rather like dried prunes. Vicky encouraged

Bea to try a few on and it turned out that the ultra-skinny designs could have been made for her.

She missed her cousin so much and wished again that she had never come to Morocco. Wished she had never had the stupid idea of trying to impress Yves Saint Laurent.

'I shall be assisting with the search,' Alami was saying. 'But my focus will be on tracing Patrice Callier's movements. Do you have any idea if he lives where the killing took place?'

'My grandmother may have an idea. I didn't get the impression he'd been here long. I don't really know if he lives in Marrakech.'

'He's a friend of your grandmother's?'

'She knows him, yes.'

'That's all?'

'She believes Patrice might have abducted my cousin. I saw a green jeep with tinted windows on the road that day, the same kind that rammed Jimmy off the road, then his rooms were raided, and then I saw Patrice kill him. Don't you think that might all be connected?'

'We will speak to her.'

'I can drive up to her kasbah tonight,' Theo offered, 'while you're tied up this end?'

Alami nodded. 'And Miss Baudin, Vicky, you will not be able to leave the country for the present. And we would be most grateful if you could identify the house where the murder took place. Can you do that?'

She agreed, hoping Theo would be with her when she met up with Bea's parents again. When she thought of them, she wasn't thinking so much about her aunt Florence and her obvious anguish, but rather her uncle Jack, whose bravery during the war was well known. He would know what to do. And he might have a gun too and that could be useful, although she didn't know if he'd have been able to travel with one.

Theo checked his watch. 'I'll stay with you, Vicky. Maybe we can all grab something to eat with the Jacksons.'

Much later, Vicky was driven out of the city in a police car with her uncle Jack and Theo accompanying her for moral support. They were heading for the Palmeraie, in search of the house where Patrice had killed Jimmy, while Florence remained in the cool of the hotel, nursing a headache.

They sat in the back squashed together and as they crawled along, Vicky remained frozen and rigid, dreading the thought of seeing the place again, this time in broad daylight. At first, still almost too scared to look, she wasn't at all sure where it was, but after a few more minutes of wavering she spotted it.

'There,' she said in a whisper, pointing. 'That one.'

Jack reached for her hand. Vicky glanced sideways at him, feeling mortified and guilty. He must think she was brainless for having got Bea and herself into this. She didn't want to be here, but she had to help so that was that.

Alami drew to a halt and twisted round to her. 'You all right to get out? Make absolutely certain?'

'I don't think she is,' Theo replied. 'You know where the house is now. She's done her bit.'

'I am already certain,' she said.

As they left the area Vicky looked out of the window

as images of that night flashed through her head again. The pair of them laughing as they stumbled around the Palmeraie in the dark. Their fear of the scurrying and scratching animals. The awful flying biting insects. The heat, even though it was so late. Their crazy drunken attempt to return the sketchbook via the garden. The shock of seeing Patrice holding a gun.

And Jimmy dying.

CHAPTER 29

Clemence

Kasbah du Paradis

As Clemence walked up the track to the kasbah, she heard screaming and quickened her pace. Arriving out of breath, she found Madeleine, hysterical, hitting out at Ahmed and scratching her own cheeks.

Clemence tried to soothe the old woman, but nothing worked until she gripped Madeleine's hands and gently said, 'Come. Do you remember how we used pick cherries together in our old Casablanca orchards? Figs and dates too?'

Madeleine calmed, beaming at her. 'And *Maman* came too, didn't she?'

Clemence realised Madeleine had disappeared even further back in time to her own childhood.

Years before Clemence had been born and long before Madeleine met Claude Garnier, the estate had belonged to *her* family. After they married, he took control in a manner nobody had anticipated. It began slowly with months of manipulation, and then before Madeleine or her parents knew what was happening, the old loyal staff were gone, her parents were living in a rundown villa on the edge of the estate, and a controlling regime had begun. It had grieved Madeleine profoundly when her parents died young from pneumonia. Claude frequently promised to rectify the damp and mould in their house, but he never had, and Madeleine held him entirely responsible for their deaths.

That night, her mother finally fell asleep but only thanks to a strong sleeping pill. Clemence loathed giving her such pills. It was one of the many reasons why she had rescued Madeleine from the old people's home in Casablanca. She had been sedated day and night and Clemence had sworn she would never resort to such inhuman behaviour. Now it was a crutch she only turned to occasionally. Although it was something they had both seemed to collude in, she still felt terribly guilty for their long estrangement, and when she had finally visited her mother's apartment again it was a neighbour who had explained that her mother was now in a home.

At least the wrought-iron grilles now fully installed at the annexe would keep Madeleine safe, and while she had been in Marrakech, Ahmed and his brother had fitted stronger locks and bolts on all the doors of the kasbah. She had given Ahmed an updated list of whom to allow inside, including Vicky, of course, Bea's parents, and her old friend Theo. Anyone Ahmed didn't already know had to show their passports or papers of identity before he would let them in.

A little later and back in her own room, Clemence couldn't sleep, her mind either obsessively trawling through everything that had happened or imagining everything that might still happen. She could see now that Patrice was a far more dangerous man than she could ever have imagined. Not just a blackmailer, but a murderer too. That night, Clemence slept with a knife under her pillow as well as her pistol because just knowing they were there seemed to help.

She could still recall the first day she had practised using her father's pistol when she was sixteen, her pulse racing, her palms sweating, but she had carried on and made a rational decision to learn to shoot well and had never regretted it. She had not been psychotic or crazed with the urge to kill but you never knew when being a damn good shot might come in handy. A memory floated in and out of her mind, inching towards resolution, and she felt certain the day of reckoning would be coming. And coming soon.

When she did finally sleep, she awoke from nightmare images of destruction – her house and her life exploding around her – but extracted herself from them as quickly as she could, forcing herself to become calmer and to think about happier times instead, using the technique she had perfected over the years.

She thought of the escape plans she and Jacques had created when they were young. After weeks of carefully skirting the boundaries of the enormous estate, Jacques had drawn up a map of the surrounding area, while she made lists of what to take with them, where to go when they left, and how they would get there when the time came. She'd been pilfering coins from her mother's purse and little by little the money was building up. She'd been filching supplies too: biscuits, cake-like macaroons, and dates, and if Cook noticed some items were missing, she didn't say. It made Clemence wonder if Cook had been stealing food too, and if she had Clemence wouldn't have blamed her. Her father did not treat the servants well, not with respect, nor with their pay.

Once Clemence had stolen half a bottle of sherry and she and Jacques had made a bonfire and drunk most of the sweet liquid before being terribly sick. She had gone home smelling of smoke, alcohol and rosemary. Luckily her mother hadn't noticed the lingering odour of vomit. But by then her mother wasn't noticing very much.

Eventually Clemence did fall asleep again, this time into a deep dreamless sleep. It was still completely dark in her room when a sound jolted her awake. She came to consciousness quickly and with her pulse speeding up she lay completely still, eyes wide open, nerves on fire. What had it been? She heard the noise again and while her eyes adjusted to the gloom, she silently slid her knife out from under her pillow. There was a pause, a few moments of silence. Had she imagined it? Dreamt it? A cat shrieked in the woods outside, and one of her dogs began to bark. Maybe it had been nothing, just the animals. When her dog stopped barking, she listened to the silence buzzing in her ears, laying her head back down on her pillow and closing her eyes.

Just as she was about to drift off again, thinking that from now on she would bring at least one of the dogs in with her at night, she heard light footsteps approaching her bedroom. She held her breath. With the knife in her hand again, she heard a key turn in the lock on the other side of the door. Cold terror consumed her. Only Ahmed had the other key – hers was on her dressing table for safety as it often fell out of the lock – but Ahmed would have knocked. Whoever this was, it was not Ahmed.

The door swung open, the thick warm air moving as it did. Silently, she slipped out of bed. Her eyes adjusted to the darkness and her heart lurched when she made out the shape of a man. Everything in the complex was as familiar to her as the back of her hand. Unlike the stranger, she did not need light to know her way, and while he still stood in the doorway, she was able to slip behind him and hold her knife at his throat.

'Move one single muscle,' she hissed in his ear, 'and you are dead.'

'Jesus, Clemmy,' the man growled. 'It's me.'

'Theo?' she gasped.

'Of course, Theo. For God's sake, take the damn knife away from my throat!'

She instantly did so. 'What the hell were you doing creeping into my room. I might have killed you!'

'Indeed.'

Her breath caught in her throat. 'Sorry. I'm a bit on edge.'

226

'You don't say!'

'Sorry.'

'I never had you down as a killer, Clem. Would you really have cut my throat?'

She didn't reply for a moment, and turned her back on him to light a lamp.

'Clem?'

She couldn't think of the right answer, any answer at all. It was not in her nature to lie and yet life had made a liar of her.

'We never know of what we're capable,' she eventually said, finding the words. 'So, yes, if it had been Patrice, I may well have cut his throat.'

He stared at her looking baffled, a mixture of horror, shock and . . . was that amusement in his eyes? Or even admiration? She wasn't sure.

'You still haven't told me why you were in my bedroom,' she added.

He shook his head. 'No.'

'So?'

'I was only coming to wake you. I drove out in the early hours. I gave the young man – Ahmed, I think he said his name was – I gave him my passport and he gave me the key when I explained why I'd come. He's right here in the corridor.'

She called out to Ahmed that he could go, and that all was well, then turned to Theo. 'Please never do that again. Or if you do, bring a lamp in with you.'

'Do you always sleep with a knife at hand?'

'Lately, yes,' she said.

'They're restarting the search for Beatrice very early. It'll be dawn soon and I thought you'd want to greet the Jacksons when they arrive. Also, the police want to ask if you know where Patrice lives. Vicky thought you might.'

Clemence led Theo out to the terrace and in silence, wrapped in blankets, they watched the sun rising over the mountains together. As the pinks and purples spread across the sky and gave way to yellow and orange, they both relaxed, the enduring power of nature reviving their spirits.

A little later Clemence was carrying a tray to Madeleine when she heard booted feet tramping up the top of the track.

Three policemen neared the house with Jack and Florence following behind. 'Good morning,' she said and looked for her granddaughter. 'Isn't Vicky with you?'

'Her mother Élise is due to arrive today,' Jack said. 'So, she's in Marrakech. Don't worry – she has an armed guard now.'

'Ah I see. Well in that case would anyone like coffee?'

They all agreed that they would, although Florence barely nodded, just sighed deeply, looking pale and utterly exhausted. Clemence headed straight for the kitchen, gave Madeleine's tray to Nadia, and returned a few minutes later carrying a huge jug of coffee and several cups rattling on a silver tray.

Theo came out from the house wearing a clean white shirt and charcoal-coloured trousers. His hair was still damp from the shower.

He greeted them all and then poured the coffee Nadia had placed on the table.

Theo's police contact, wearing a hat, drew Clemence aside. 'I'm Gabriel Alami,' he said. 'I need to ask if you are aware of where Patrice Callier might be living.'

She frowned. 'He told me he'd taken a temporary rental somewhere in the Palmeraie,' she said looking up at him. 'I'm afraid it's all I know.'

'What does he do?'

'How do mean?'

'His work. What does he do for a living?'

'He says he's an art dealer.'

Alami's eyes bored into her. 'You don't believe him?'

'I'm suspicious.'

'Of?'

'Well . . . I have the feeling he's really working for the French secret service. Or as some kind of mercenary. He was in the French military for years.'

'Indeed. Left under a cloud if my research serves me well.'

'I didn't know.'

'You'd be surprised how many disaffected men end up in clandestine activities. Sometimes as paid assassins.'

'Is that why he killed Jimmy?'

'Could be.'

Theo came over to join them and after Alami had acknowledged him he said, 'Well, if Jimmy Petersen's murder turns out to be political, it does make things more dangerous for the girls.'

Clemence took a long slow breath.

'We understand Jimmy Petersen was on the trail of

evidence connected to Mehdi ben Barka's abduction in Paris last year.'

'Weren't some Moroccan police involved in the abduction too?' she asked. 'Isn't that why Theo told us not to talk to anyone about the murder until you arrived?'

'Maybe. I couldn't say.'

Clemence stared at her feet, desperately wishing Vicky and Bea had not got themselves entangled in all this. 'I know how dangerous opposition politics can be,' she said.

'Indeed. It has taken centuries to shake off the control of foreign powers and now we have a Moroccan regime ruling with an iron fist. That may be what we need for now, but I believe our king may yet play a peacemaker's role in the Middle East where he has many allies. Hassan I died back in 1894, but he introduced a policy of internal reforms that brought the country a degree of stability. We hope our current king will follow suit.'

Clemence closed her eyes, just wanting it to all go away.

'The Marrakech police searched the house where young Jimmy was killed. Nothing. And no sign of Patrice Callier living there. We traced the owner though. She lives in France and hasn't been over here for months.'

She opened her eyes and studied him. 'So, you're saying the house has been cleaned up?'

He inclined his head. 'Spotless.'

She glanced across at the others, who had finished their coffee and were preparing to leave to begin the search. 'Are you going with them?' she asked Theo.

'Not now. Jack and Florence are ready to go. I thought I could lend a hand here.'

She turned away, unable to conceal the surge of relief she felt. Then she walked over to Florence who was sitting with her head in her hands.

'My dear, you're most welcome to stay here while the others search. You look all in.'

Florence glanced up at her with red-rimmed eyes. 'You're very kind but I think I'll go mad if I don't do something active, at least for a while. It's the sitting around waiting I can't bear.'

'Well, if you change your mind.'

She and Theo watched them leave and the way he gently put a hand on her arm and squeezed so reassuringly took her back to the first time she'd ever seen him, all those years before.

It had happened one afternoon: he had been standing in the square as if transfixed, his eyes wide with the thrill of Marrakech, but his relaxed stance suggesting he was no tourist. He'd spotted her and smiled.

'Don't tell me you live in this mayhem,' he'd said, running his fingers through his short fair hair. She liked his American accent.

'No, I have a kasbah in the mountains. Are you on holiday or working in Morocco?'

'I work in Tangier and have a few days off. It's quite a few years since I was over this way.' He rolled up the sleeves of his rumpled linen shirt and touched her arm gently, his eyes unswerving as he asked her to join him for a coffee. She had felt an instant connection and didn't turn away.

She had agreed, and they'd come up to the roof of the French Café and talked for hours. She couldn't remember about what, but they'd eventually parted when it grew dark, and she invited him to visit her at the kasbah the following day.

'Come to lunch,' she'd said. And he had.

CHAPTER 30

Vicky

Outside the famous La Mamounia hotel, in air humming with sleepy butterflies and bustling insects, Vicky paused. She'd been conflicted to hear her mother would definitely be coming: on the one hand desperate to see her and for once be comforted by her, but on the other feeling anxious at the thought of the grilling she was bound to get. She shook her head as she went inside, though whether in exasperation at herself or at Élise, she couldn't tell.

The receptionist explained that her mother had arrived and was waiting in the jasmine garden, so with an unhurried pace, Vicky wandered out among clusters of citrus trees and towering rose bushes, finally finding her way through a tunnel of jasmine where the air was cool and smelt delicious. Slipping off her sandals and wriggling her toes in the dry grass she watched a colony of ants crossing her path.

When she turned a corner, she saw with a jolt that her mother was sitting on a wrought-iron bench in a shady nook, leafing through a newspaper. Vicky couldn't read her expression. Was she angry? Tired? Playing for time, she edged back a couple of steps as quietly as she could.

But obviously having heard her, Élise glanced up and rose to her feet.

'I've come to take you home,' she said, her voice cool.

'I'm sorry. I didn't see you,' Vicky hedged.

'What's been going on here?'

Vicky swallowed the lump in her throat. *Please don't let me cry. Please, please, don't let me cry.* She opened her mouth to speak but the words died on her lips. Élise remained completely still. They stared at each other, the air crackling with unexpressed emotion and the strain between them so marked it was almost visible. Vicky's entire body felt tight, all her muscles tense, her throat dry, her mind about to explode.

'I can't go home,' she whispered.

Élise frowned. 'Of course you can. I've already bought the ferry tickets.'

'I can't go home,' Vicky repeated and gulped as she fought the tears. 'Not without Bea. And anyway, they won't let me.'

'Who won't?'

'The police,' Vicky whispered. 'The police won't.'

Suddenly Élise stood and strode across the gap between them, her arms outstretched. Vicky fell straight into them as if she were five years old again. She immediately began to sob, her reason disintegrating, and all the pent-up fear and anxiety streaming out as her mother held her tight.

When she finally stopped, they sat on the bench together and Élise handed her a tissue from her bag.

'I was only told you and Beatrice are in trouble. I had a garbled message from Jack and haven't been able to speak to Florence. I've been so worried, *chérie*.'

'We're in danger, *Maman*. Real danger,' Vicky said, and her voice shook.

'Come now, it can't be so bad, can it? Just some nonsense surely?'

'No. It's bad. It really is,' she said. 'And I really can't leave. The police won't let me and anyway my friend Tom is in hospital and Bea is missing. I have to wait until she's found.'

Élise rose to her feet and held out her hand. 'Come on. I think it's best if we go to my room.'

As she pulled Vicky up, she looked over her shoulder, a cross expression spreading across her face.

'What?'

'That man keeps looking at us. Do you know him?'

Vicky gave her mother a sheepish smile. 'Meet my bodyguard.'

'*Mon Dieu!*' Élise said and shook her head.

'He'll follow us and stand outside your door.'

As they were talking, the light changed, and the sky seemed suddenly to turn red. The guard ran to their side and hurried them inside.

'Sandstorm,' he said.

Inside the hotel they walked along twisting corridors reminding Vicky of the streets in the medina and eventually they reached her mother's room on the first floor. The glass double doors to the balcony were being swiftly closed by the maid who curtseyed and left the room. Vicky went across to look but everything outside was lost in the swirling red cloud. After a few moments she turned back to view her mother who was sitting on the edge of the bed, looking absolutely worn out.

'It's a lovely room,' Élise said glancing up. 'Henri organised it. He's so kind.'

Vicky didn't reply. When she was about thirteen, she had overheard Henri doing something in the kitchen and telling her mother, 'You do realise what's wrong, Élise? You and your daughter are far too much alike. Both truculent as hell.'

Élise had laughed. 'But you love me all the same.'

'For my sins.'

They'd didn't know Vicky had heard the exchange but might have guessed when she stormed off in anger, slamming the doors, and escaping to be with Jacques, not returning for supper.

In her mother's room now, Vicky took in the beautiful curling Islamic patterns on the terracotta, ochre, and green tiling rising halfway up the walls, the delicate lattice-wood screens, and the gorgeous amber *tadelakt* walls so like her grandmother's. The furniture was Art Deco French, the curtains a deep chocolatey velvet and her mother had a huge king-sized bed with crisp white sheets and a burgundy silk bedspread. Despite the insanity of everything going on, over which they had absolutely no control, she couldn't help appreciating the beauty of it.

'If you need to sleep, we can talk later,' Vicky said.

'No. Tell me what's been happening. The police didn't say much. I won't be able to rest without hearing the whole story. Come and sit down.'

She sat beside Élise who had moved to a sofa covered in an ochre linen fabric with big squishy burgundy cushions the same colour as the bedspread. Vicky told her everything, starting with Russell's brutal rejection, her plan to meet and impress Yves Saint Laurent, covering the story of the sketchbook, the terrible murder of their friend Jimmy, and ending with Tom's accident and Bea's disappearance.

Élise looked deeply shocked as she struggled to absorb everything, asking questions and wanting Vicky to clarify when she couldn't grasp the full impact of it.

'So,' her mother said, blinking back tears. 'The police organised the bodyguard?'

'No, Theo did. He's a friend of . . . well, a friend of my grandmother's'

'What is she like?' Élise asked quite calmly, not seeming at all taken aback to hear her daughter had a grandmother in Morocco.

For a moment Vicky was speechless. 'You know about Clemence?' she eventually said.

'Well, not really. Her existence was a complete secret. I was shocked when Jacques told me.'

'He told you! I begged him not to.'

'I pressed him hard, I'm afraid, after you set off. We were

very concerned and after Bea wrote, Florence was too. Although it was before all this happened.'

'We?'

'Henri and I.'

'Why? Why were you so worried?'

'Henri has contacts over here, so he's aware of what's been going on politically. He said it wasn't the safest place. He cares about you, *chérie*.'

Vicky bit her lip. 'I know.'

'So?'

'Clemence kept telling me it could be dangerous here, but of course she hadn't any idea Bea was going to steal the sketchbook. If it hadn't been for that bloody thing, we wouldn't have seen Jimmy being killed, and we wouldn't have had to get out of Marrakech in a hurry.'

Although of course Jimmy would still be dead. That was not her fault.

'Why didn't you come straight home?'

'We wanted to but there were no flights because of the World Cup final, no train tickets, nothing. I'm so glad you could come, *Maman*.'

'Are you?'

Vicky gave her mother a hug. 'You'll never know how much.'

Élise swallowed visibly. There was a pause as they held hands for a few minutes, the peace between them unspoken but there all the same. It had been such a long time coming and clearly they both felt it deeply. Vicky glanced across at her mother and saw her eyes were warm and thoughtful.

The sandstorm had died down, so Vicky opened the doors and went out onto a huge balcony, surrounded by a low terracotta wall with painted green railings and enough space for two wine-red rattan armchairs and a copper table. She ran her fingers over the dust on the table and surveyed the view, gazing across the lush gardens now covered in a reddish hue, the palm trees, the ramparts of Marrakech which seemed to enclose the gardens of the hotel, and finally the magnificent Atlas Mountains in the distance. Even after a sandstorm it really was heavenly. Although until Bea was found and they were all safely back home, if they ever *were* all safely back home, she didn't think she'd be able to breathe easily again.

CHAPTER 31

Clemence

Kasbah du Paradis

The search party returned, tired, dusty, and looking dreadfully despondent. Clemence tried not to fear the worst for Bea, but she was distracted, as it was exactly this moment that Madeleine, in a cranky mood, started grouching about her family's neglect of her.

'I want to go home,' she muttered, her hair wildly dishevelled, her clothes awry. 'They keep me prisoner here.'

The police had gone, but Jack and Florence were standing half turned away, clearly trying not to stare.

'I'm so sorry,' Clemence said. 'My mother, well . . . you can see for yourselves.'

Jack and Florence both glanced back at her and signalled in an embarrassed English way that they understood, while she attempted to discreetly lead her mother in the direction of the annexe. There was no point trying to keep Madeleine hidden any more and anyway she rarely made any sense now so was unlikely to divulge anything intelligible. Clemence had been worrying unnecessarily.

However, Madeleine did not just demur. She had other ideas altogether and was spinning about and flailing her arms like a whirling dervish. Ahmed came out to assist but Madeleine batted him off too. For an old lady, she could be unbelievably strong when riled and they were scared of hurting her if they used their own strength. Short of picking her up and carrying her away they were at a loss.

'Ahmed,' Clemence said, 'Please would you show our guests to their room – the one Vicky used before.'

He inclined his head.

'I'll take care of Madeleine,' she added. But when she asked Madeleine if anything was hurting, her mother whipped out a rolled-up magazine and slapped her across the cheek with it.

'Everything is hurting,' Madeleine whispered and began to cry. 'I want my mother!'

Clemence rubbed the sharply stinging spot. She had never aspired to being an especially 'nice' person. In fact, to Clemence 'nice' seemed a vapid kind of description meaning almost nothing, used when you didn't really know a person and wanted to appear 'nice' yourself. But her mother's senescence was testing her to the very limits of her empathy. She forced herself not to react.

'Come on, *Maman*,' Clemence said in a soft reassuring voice. 'Let's find cake.'

Her mother gave her a sly smile.

Clemence kissed her on the cheek and took hold of her hand. She knew the offer of cake wouldn't work for ever.

As she came out of the annexe a little later, she spotted Theo through the trellis. He was sitting on a bench in her small private courtyard behind a lovely *mousharabiya*, a delicately carved outdoor screen. Her bedroom opened out at the back of the complex to this little paradise where roses and fragrant jasmine spilt from the walls and mixed with the zingy essence of citrus in the air. Hibiscus grew wild here, attracting hummingbirds and butterflies. She felt at her safest in this spot, wrapped in deliciousness, and where nobody could see her. Ahmed had lit a candle smelling of honey, beeswax, and orange blossom, underpinned by the grounding woody aroma of cedar. Ahmed's mother made all the candles for the kasbah using plants she and Clemence herself grew and some of the oils they bought in Marrakech.

'Everything seems to be upsetting my mother,' she said. 'It's a struggle.'

Theo looked up at her and cleared his throat. 'Maybe I should be making tracks,' he said a little awkwardly.

'Do you have to?'

He studied her face. 'Would you rather I stayed? I was hoping to organise someone to look out for you up here, but I could stay on instead. Moral support?'

She looked down, overwhelmed by the emotional turbulence she felt. Worry for Beatrice. Anxiety for Vicky.

Longing for Theo. Compassion for Florence and Jack, and how could she even name the guilt and remorse about the neglect of her mother? Though it hung in the very air she breathed.

'Clem?'

She looked up at his once smooth face, now a network of fine lines, deeper laughter lines etched around his eyes, and of course the frown lines on his brow. His lived-in face, still utterly beautiful to her even after all these years. Perhaps even more so.

'Yes, please stay. I would like that.'

He smiled. 'Glad it's settled.'

Once the visitors had showered off the dust of the mountains and changed, they all sat down to dinner under the soft light of fretwork lanterns. The night was noisy with the sound of insects hitting the inner glass and creatures shuffling about in the garden, plus the two Beauceron dogs snuffling around their ankles eager for titbits as usual. The strain was evident on Bea's parents' faces and Jack did most of the talking, telling Clemence and Theo how they'd walked ancient trails between remote stone villages nestled into the sides of the mountain.

Florence stared at her plate, toying with her foot, clearly finding it impossible to eat at such an unspeakably hard time. Jack stroked her back, tried gently to encourage her to eat but she shook her head and didn't say a word.

He continued to tell them how in every one of villages the Moroccan policemen had asked people if they'd seen a girl who looked like Beatrice in the photos they'd brought with them.

'Some villagers barely glanced up and simply carried on with whatever they had been doing,' he said. 'But others offered us a glass of mint tea, asking questions about what had happened, and promising to keep their eyes open.'

Clemence kept an eye on Florence, whose head remained bowed.

'These people seemed to have figured out millions of years ago how to survive up here and life has not changed much since,' Jack added, taking up the conversation again.

'They are pretty self-sufficient,' Clemence replied, understanding how talking about the day was Jack's way of coping with his fear for his daughter.

'The size of the villages seems to be limited by the size of the nearby water source. Of course, limited water means limited farmland and limited farmland means limited mouths that can—'

'Oh, for God's sake,' Florence interrupted. 'Our daughter is missing. Can we please stop talking about the damn villages?!'

She still had barely touched her food and had stopped pushing it around her plate. Even though she held her hands tightly clasped together Clemence could see they were trembling.

'Sorry,' Jack said quietly, looking abashed.

'I don't know how to be,' Florence said with a note of abject despair in her already broken voice. 'I can't sleep. I can't eat. I keep imagining terrible, terrible things. She must be so frightened. What if she's lying hurt and all alone somewhere?'

'You need rest, my dear,' Clemence said, her voice soft. 'If it would help, I have sleeping pills for my mother. You'd be most welcome to try one.' And she remembered how for the first few nights after Jacques wrote telling her of Victor's death, she too had needed sleeping pills.

'Won't they make me groggy in the morning?'

'Not if you skip dessert and go to bed early. We have excellent coffee to wake you up tomorrow. And, of course, you're welcome to stay here during the day tomorrow, if everything gets too much.'

Tears slid down Florence's cheeks and as Jack wrapped an arm around her, he lifted the hair from her eyes with such a tender touch that Clemence felt a lump developing in her throat.

'I think a sleeping pill is exactly what you need, my love,' he said.

'You do?'

Clemence fetched the pill then Jack and Florence went straight to their room, utterly drained and propping each other up for support.

Theo held out his hand and asked Clemence if she'd like to stay outside with him.

They stood contemplating the millions of stars peppering the silky blue-black night. Gazing up at the sky like this often transported her to other such nights.

'Remember camping in the desert?' he said as if reading her mind, and wrapping an arm around her shoulders.

She leant into him. 'How could I forget? How old were we?'

'Young.'

'Not that young. I was forty-four.'

'No, but relatively speaking, we were young, even if we didn't think it at the time.'

She looked up at the sky again and was instantly back in 1936. Neither of them had any idea of what awaited them. And despite what had been going on in Germany, they had no sense of impending doom. They trekked across the desert on camels with a jeep following behind. Theo had told her to pack a thick sweater for chilly desert evenings and to wear long-sleeved cotton shirts and trousers during the day. She brought along a scarf to protect her eyes and head from the sun and sand and wore thick socks inside her hiking boots. But she hadn't broken the boots in well enough and towards the end of the first day was in agony from a huge blister, although her stubborn determination kept her going despite the pain.

The first night Theo had spread a blanket on the ground where they could sit and relax in the cooling desert air. She struggled out of her boots then took off her sock to show him the blister and he fetched a pouch from his rucksack.

'You can't walk on that. I'll have to drain the blister,' he said. 'If not, it'll only burst as you walk and risk infection. If I do it now, it should relieve the pain.'

She watched as he struck a match to sterilise a needle. He punctured the blister just at the point where it began to rise above her skin, gently pressing so the fluid would drain away.

'Thank you,' she said.

'Best to leave it uncovered so the air can dry and harden it. When you're ready to sleep, wear some soft, clean cotton socks and I'll dress it properly in the morning.'

'You're well prepared,' she said.

'I've been in the desert before.'

He had taken hold of her hand and didn't let it go as they watched the sun setting. The sky darkened slowly before it sprang alive with millions upon millions of stars.

'Incredible to think this is what our distant ancestors would have looked up at every night,' she said.

'It's a great place to wonder where we came from.'

The air filled with the smell of woodsmoke and dry dustiness underlaid by the aromatic traces of cinnamon and ginger. Was she imagining the spices, or the odour of tanning vats, or the animal smells from the city? She suddenly realised they were sitting downwind of one of the camels and jumped to her feet in a hurry.

'God, that's foul.'

He laughed. 'Come on, let's sit further away.'

Later, even after the others had retired for the night, the two of them were still outside lying side by side on the blanket and whispering.

'Tell me about your childhood,' he had said, and as her chest tightened, she struggled for words.

Her childhood had turned her into someone she had never wanted to be. How could she tell this beautiful man about it, this man she was falling in love with? She told him about the orchards instead, and the camp she had made with her friend Jacques.

'He sounds like a good friend. Are you still in touch?'

And there it was. Whatever she said it always came back to the same thing.

'Not really,' she said, shaking her head.

She leant into him, stroking his cheek, loving the stubble already growing there. He took her hand in his and they kissed. With others in tents not far from their own, love-making would not be on the cards, not in the desert. Nor would sharing a tent be allowed.

And yet . . .

'We'll pitch our tents further from the others tomorrow night,' he said, and she smiled in the darkness when he picked up the oil lamp.

Nothing could beat their first night sleeping at a desert camp surrounded by high sand dunes and with only the huge timeless sky above the tents, especially when he silently joined her.

'Is this all right?' he said.

'More than all right.'

'I'll go back to my own tent in a little while.'

She had woken to find him gazing at her, his eyes full of love and with such a look of wanting her. She kissed him and inhaled the fragrance of his skin, still with a slightly peppery note. Coriander seeds, cardamom, or caraway, she wasn't sure which, but his skin was musky, sensuous, seductive. His hair smelt of woodsmoke and she wanted to breathe it in forever, to wake up and see him every single day before she saw anything else or anybody else in the world. She kissed him again, long and slow, and despite everything they did make very nearly silent, breathless, utterly ecstatic love again before he slipped back to his own tent.

We're all a collection of stories, she had thought after-wards. *Some good, some not so good.* The question was, how did you allow a new story in, when just one of your stories already took up too much space?

Back then, she hadn't known the answer. But that had been many years ago, before World War II even began.

Now, all these years later, Theo turned to her, a question in his eyes, and she knew.

'Come to my room,' she whispered, trying not to worry about how he might see her now she was so much older.

'You're sure?'

'I don't want to be alone at the moment.'

'That's the only reason?'

She held his gaze. 'You know it isn't.'

As they walked back into the house, despite the hunger she was feeling for him, she could not forget the gravity of what was going on around them – Bea was still missing, Patrice was threatening her and maybe her grand-daughter too.

And yet later as they made love, she felt every nerve waking, her blood buzzing in her veins, her skin on fire. She needed this. In the face of the danger Patrice had generated, she needed to feel the power of life rising within her. Needed the joy of it. Needed the feeling of soaring and leaving the dread behind. Needed the sensa-tion of freedom, of lightness. And most of all she needed the feeling of being connected. To Theo, to nature, her own nature and his, and everything else that lay around them. No longer alone, she felt the decades slipping away and completely forgot she was not young. Her age didn't matter and neither did his. Love was ageless, timeless.

'How are you even more beautiful, Clemence?' he said, his head on the pillow beside hers.

She smiled. 'You always did find the right thing to say.'

'No, I didn't. Not back then. But now . . .' He paused. 'Clemence, I just want to be with you. The past doesn't matter.'

They slept but she was woken in the night by the sound of weeping. Florence. What a terrible ordeal for a mother not to have any idea what had happened to her child. And, of course, it made her think of Victor. All she had been told was that he had died during the war. For a long time that had been enough. Or so she had told herself.

And Clemence decided that while Élise was here in Morocco, she would find the courage to ask what kind of man Victor had turned out to be. She would finally hear the details of exactly what had happened to him and how he had died. Her son.

CHAPTER 32

Vicky

'Ah, glad to see you, Victoria,' Tom's father said, half frowning, half smiling as she and Élise entered Tom's hospital room. 'I was hoping to get back to my hotel for a short while,' he continued. 'I assume you can take over?'

'Of course. My mother will stay too,' Vicky replied, indicating Élise.

He nodded at her vaguely. 'The doctors told me Tom's injuries were just the result of an accident. But nobody has explained why there's a need for a guard on the door.'

Élise stepped in. 'Why not sit with Tom while I talk to his father?' she said.

'I can speak, just about,' Tom muttered, his voice thick through his bandaged jaw, though at least he had been propped up with pillows now.

251

Vicky drew up a chair, sat down, and touched Tom's hand. 'Does it hurt very much?'

He nodded.

Meanwhile she heard her mother properly introducing herself to Mr Goodwin. 'Élise Boudin Dumas. Pleased to meet you,' she said in her almost flawless English, holding out her hand.

Vicky only had eyes for Tom and, wanting to concentrate on him, she tuned out the conversation in the background, her mother telling the story from the start. She wished she had the courage to hold his hand but felt nervous of being too pushy, then he reached out and nudged *her* hand.

'Never been looked after by an angel.'

'Now you're laughing at me.'

'You're . . .' he groaned.

'Don't speak. I know you're feeling a lot better, but—'

'Not only gorgeous but also kind,' he managed to get out, interrupting her.

'I'm not you know. In fact, I'm rather a cow.'

There was a brief pause as a kind of chuckle rose from his throat.

'Jimmy said you didn't . . . well didn't have time for . . .' He said you were too busy and—'

His attempt at a laugh interrupted her but he looked tired from the effort and she felt guilty.

'Don't try to say any more,' she said.

Tom's father strode back across to the bed. 'Despite the guard at the door, I really don't want to leave Tom,' he said. 'But he's obviously out of danger, and as I said, I really could do with a bath and some clean clothes.'

'*Maman* and I will stay until you get back,' Vicky said, looking up at him. 'I've brought a book to read to Tom.'

But when she turned back, she saw he had fallen asleep.

'Very well. While he's asleep it's a good time for me to go,' Tom's father said.

While Tom slept, Vicky talked to Élise. In a low voice she made an effort to ask about Henri, which pleased her mother, but the only thing she could really think about was finding Bea.

Her mother's brow was furrowed with concern. 'I do understand. I'm desperate to see Florence. My poor sister must be beside herself with worry.'

'Of course,' Vicky said. 'Uncle Jack too.'

'I called Hélène in Malta the day before I left France,' her mother added.

'*Tante* Hélène?'

'Yes. She has always been brilliant in a crisis. Along with Étienne, she's going to join the search for Bea.'

Vicky hesitated before speaking but this was as good an opportunity as she was likely to get. 'What really happened between Aunt Hélène and Aunt Florence?' she asked.

Her mother regarded her with an uneasy look. The last time Vicky had asked this question, Élise had fudged her answer. But now . . . Vicky was hopeful things might be different and said, 'It was always there in the background, but you never really explained. All I remember is hearing a few whispered conversations and then whenever I came into the room the conversation stopped dead. And if I asked, you changed the subject.'

Élise sighed deeply. 'I think at the time we all were of

the same mind and agreed not to talk about it. But I suppose it does no harm to say now. They were both in love with the same man.'

Vicky frowned. 'Not Uncle Jack?'

'Afraid so.'

'Oh my goodness.' She whistled, shocked at the thought that her steady Uncle Jack could have been the cause of some kind of love triangle and a family rift.

'Trouble was Hélène had fallen for him first and couldn't forgive Florence.'

'Did Jack love Hélène?'

With a look of regret, Élise pinched the bridge of her nose. 'The thing is it was awful at the time because Hélène could not believe that he didn't. It was clear to me though, and Florence always said he was fond of Hélène, but that he'd never been in love with her.'

'Sounds messy.'

'It was very upsetting. But it was twenty years ago, you know, when our lives were fractured, and times were very difficult. Hélène was terribly hurt and didn't even come to Florence and Jack's wedding.'

'They resolved things in the end?'

'I think once Hélène met Étienne, she realised she'd been holding on to an illusion. No matter how much she had wanted it, her relationship with Jack had never been anything but friendship, at least on his side.'

Vicky lifted her chin and drawing closer she decided to bite the bullet. 'We never talk about what happened during the war, do we?'

Élise didn't meet her eyes.

'You don't tell me anything about how you felt,' Vicky added.

'Don't I?'

'*Maman*,' she said, giving her a look. 'You know you don't.'

'Aren't there more important things?'

Vicky shook her head. 'I don't think there are.'

Élise glanced at her and then away again. 'You really want to hear?'

'Well, yes, I—'

'Those memories aren't easy,' her mother interjected. 'My mother, Claudette, was hard to love and as a child I learnt to be guarded. I suppose it became a habit and continued when I grew up.'

'But my father. Victor. What about him?'

Élise frowned. 'How do you mean?'

'You loved him?'

'Very much,' she said, her voice low.

'Please tell me about him. All I've ever heard is that he was a Resistance hero, and . . .' She paused. 'And . . . I know how he died too, of course. My *grand-père* Jacques told me when I was growing up, but I know he couldn't bear to say very much. Is it like that for you too?'

Vicky watched as her mother swallowed, looking upset and sad.

'I'm sorry. It doesn't matter, *Maman*. We can talk about it another time.'

Élise seemed conflicted for a few moments but eventually she recovered and said, 'No. I'll tell you. Victor was brave, very brave, and so good-looking. Brown hair cut short, olive skin, the fire of idealism blazing in his eyes. Powerful but graceful too, you know. I think it was love at first sight although he always denied it.'

Vicky remained silent. Her mother seemed to be losing herself in the past and Vicky didn't want to interrupt her.

'Anyway, I ran a small café where people would leave messages for the Resistance – a letterbox we called it – and I met him through that. Later when we worked together our relationship became . . . intense. *He* was intense.' She swallowed visibly then with a pensive look she smiled. 'He used to say I smelt of carbolic soap.'

'Oh, *Maman*.'

Élise shook her head. 'You are your father's daughter, you know.'

Vicky frowned. 'Am I?'

'Not only do you resemble him as well as me, but my bet is you would also have been among the first to join the Resistance. I took a little while.'

'I'm not political.'

'Oh, Vicky. I realise you pretend not to be, but I've seen your eyes burn when you get the bit between your teeth. Anyway, it wasn't about politics, it was about survival. Your father understood that and he was one of the key figures from our area. It was either us or them.'

'How terrible.'

'Yes.' She stood up and added, 'I'll tell you more another time. I promise. You're right – you deserve to hear his story. But now I need to find *les toilettes* and then get us both a sandwich or something. Will you be okay for a little while? The guard is just outside the door.'

Élise left the room quietly and Vicky sat next to Tom's bed again, watching his eyelashes flutter as he slept and the movement in his eyelids when he was dreaming. She wasn't sure if her mother had meant it when she said she would tell her more, or whether her excuse to stop and leave the room had been genuine, but finally she felt the wall of silence was crumbling a little. She sighed, aching to really be able to picture her father, bring him to life in her mind's eye. It was dark outside now and she had no idea of the time. She heard the usual hospital sounds coming from beyond the door and managed to relax a little. She was safe here, wasn't she?

CHAPTER 33

Clemence

Kasbah du Paradis

She found it hard to picture Jacques as an old man, a grand-father to Vicky. The last time she'd seen him he'd only been twenty. Most of all she liked to recall their childhood games and every time they invented silly rhymes to go with those games, she had laughed until her right side cramped from a stitch. She began to sing under her breath:

> *Burn the witch*
> *Burn the wizard*
> *Burn the wicked ghoul*
> *Burn the wizard*
> *Burn the witch*
> *Burn the silly fool*

As she lay awake relishing the early morning light and the sound of Theo breathing, she could hardly believe he was there. Once this terrible period was past, this time, maybe this time, there might really be a chance for them. She heard sounds of movement in the house but couldn't bring herself to get up yet. She had too much she needed to think about before the day truly began.

Until recently she had trained herself not to dwell on Jacques and what they'd asked of him but whenever she thought about meeting and talking with Élise, he sauntered into her mind, whistling out of tune, ears sticking out. Élise must have not only known him as he was these days, but also had shared his suffering when Victor was executed.

When they were children there had been days when she and Jacques had pretended to be heading off on an adventure to India, or America, or France, unaware that one day Jacques would do just that along with her baby boy. Over the years Clemence had forced herself not to think of her child. Not his life, nor his death. It had been impossible at first when his sweet little face would appear in her mind, his dark eyes seeming to smile, and yet she had been clear there was no other choice but to let them both go.

Theo stirred beside her. He yawned, turned over and looked right at her. 'Hello,' he said and smiled.

'Hello.'

'Been awake long?'

'Long enough to find things to worry about.'

'You haven't changed.'

She laughed but began to slide to the edge of the bed. He caught her wrist. 'Stay.'

'I can't. I really have to see to the guests and especially Florence.'

'Of course. I'm being selfish.'

'No I understand. We have a lot of catching up to do.'

As she slipped on her silk robe, the bedroom door flew open suddenly. Theo's presence in the bedroom meant Clemence had not thought to lock it and now Madeleine burst into the room still in her nightdress, her white hair corkscrewing around her head, Ahmed following at her heels.

'Sorry, Madame,' he said to Clemence. 'I opened up her door to take in her coffee and she got away from me.'

Madeleine staggered over to the bed and stared at Theo, reaching out to touch his face, then narrowing her eyes in confusion. 'You are hiding my daughter?'

'No. She's just here.'

'I don't know *her*. I want to go home. Will you take me home?'

Theo glanced up at Clemence.

'Come on, *Maman*, let's get you dressed,' Clemence said as she reached out a hand to encourage her mother towards her.

Madeleine slapped her hand away. 'Get off,' she hissed.

Theo tilted his head towards Clemence as if to say he would handle this. Then he raised himself on one elbow and turned to Madeleine. 'Why don't we slip you into your dressing gown and then find some breakfast?'

Madeleine looked mollified.

Clemence raised her brows and looked at him pointedly. He was stark naked in her bed. 'Why don't we find *you* a bathrobe first, Theo?'

'Ah,' he said and looked sheepish.

With some difficulty he managed to extricate himself from Madeleine's clutches and once decent he took her off to the annexe. Worrying about what her mother might blurt out seemed the least of her concerns right now.

Breakfast was a sombre affair. The eggs were left, cold and unappetising, the toast merely nibbled, the apples peeled but abandoned and brown. Florence said she still felt groggy from the sleeping pill but had slept quite well and felt a bit better for it, although her drawn features and drooping shoulders told another story. She drank some orange juice and accepted a croissant but only took one bite.

'I did wake up once,' she said, 'and couldn't stop crying but I must have fallen asleep again. I hope I didn't disturb anyone.'

'Not at all,' Clemence said as she poured coffee for those who wanted it. Jack and Florence only sought tea and lots of it.

In the uneasy silence Clemence searched for how to offer meaningful comfort without being trite or clichéd. She caught Theo's eye, but he only gave her a sympathetic look and didn't speak. In the end she only said, 'Will you be joining the search again today, Florence?'

Florence sighed deeply as if from an exhaustion too deeply rooted for words. 'I have to. I can't just sit by.'

'Are you sure?' Jack said and put a solicitous arm around her shoulders.

Florence dipped her head and Clemence could see her tears were not far away. She felt a lump in her own throat because loss was loss. Bad enough to lose a baby, though really that was more about losing what might have been. A missing nineteen-year-old daughter was on another level altogether. A girl whom she'd nurtured and loved, kept safe and fussed over from her first stumbling steps through all the years of her life. Every birthday marked, every cake baked, every scolding regretted, every tear spilt, every moment of laughter gone, every sorrow felt. All of it gone. And not even to know what had become of her. Not to know if she were alive or dead. The anguish. Was it any wonder Florence could barely function? Clemence took a long breath and exhaled very slowly.

Nobody mentioned Bea's name, as if by remaining silent and not voicing their worst fears they might somehow keep her alive, although Clemence knew these mountains well. And the longer the girl was missing the worse the outlook was likely to be. In a weird way she almost hoped Patrice *had* taken her and was planning to use her to negotiate should he be caught.

Jack rose to his feet. 'We're meeting the police down in the village.' He held out his hand. 'Florence?'

His wife took a sharp breath, pushed back her chair, straightened her back and stood. Theo offered to help with the search, but Jack said they would manage, and reiterated that someone needed to be here at the kasbah given all that had been going on.

For the rest of the morning Madeleine followed Theo everywhere. She sat beside him whenever he was sitting, and she tried to follow him when he walked around the estate, although she had to give up when it became too much for her. Just before lunch Theo asked Clemence if they could talk.

'*Maman* usually goes to sleep after lunch,' she said. 'We'll have some privacy then.'

So far Madeleine had not let loose anything about the past in front of Theo. But Clemence, picturing the bats hanging in the attic of their old Casablanca home where her mother used to hide from her father, and the bats in her mother's head now, knew she still might. And then as the pudding was served, Madeleine spoke up right out of the blue.

'Apricots,' she said. 'Rotten apricots . . . He hurt you, didn't he? Your father.' And she spat on the ground and began rocking. 'Hurt you. Hurt you. Hurt you.'

Clemence swallowed but couldn't speak and simply stared down at her empty plate remembering the hated bowl of apricots he always kept on his desk because it was what she could always see and smell. Their rancid odour, *his* too, and the vile stink of his burnt cigars in the onyx ashtray. A door closing, a key turning. When she glanced up, she saw Theo gazing at her with a puzzled expression. She shook her head and he seemed to understand not to question her in front of Madeleine.

But when Nadia tried to serve Clemence her fruit salad, she pushed her plate away and hurried from the table.

CHAPTER 34

Clemence fled to her room, pain surging through her. She opened the right-hand door of her wardrobe and from the top shelf, took out a gold casket inlaid with rubies and emeralds. The box Patrice insisted was his. She placed it on her bed and opened the lid. The enamelled silver and gilt-hinged *khalkhals*, or anklets, Patrice had claimed were owing to him were long gone – sold by her mother soon after her father had died, Clemence thought. In their place were dozens of folded letters she had written, pouring her feelings out to Theo. Not one had ever been sent. She lifted them out and read one of the earliest ones, then ripped it up, shredding it into tiny pieces that floated in the air like little white moths.

She sat silent and motionless, the letters still in her hands. From the start she had liked Theo because he was different; he challenged her prejudices and really wanted to know what she thought about things. He'd always considered her answers to his questions carefully as if her point of view mattered. The sex had been special too, because they didn't just do it, they talked while they were doing it. No man before or after had asked her how she was feeling during sex. It was all about whether they could 'perform' or not, hardly ever bothering how she felt. But where did it leave them now? She and Theo had made love for the first time in all these years, reopening an intimacy she had run away from. And he'd want to know what Madeleine had meant about her father hurting her. He would ask her.

She read another of the letters, her hands trembling as she remembered. A moment. That's all it took to decide. Just as she had decided all those years ago when she hadn't sent them. No matter how much she wanted to confide, to open up to him, he could never see these. Not even one.

There was no time to tear them all up. Instead, she ran to the sitting room, quickly putting a match to the fire Ahmed always had ready in the grate for a chilly evening. The sticks didn't take long to catch and as soon as the flames began to crackle, she started feeding the letters into them one by one.

She heard the door open and raised her head for a moment to watch as Theo walked in and came near, though not too close.

'Clem?' he said. 'I've been looking for you.'

Panicked, she thrust an entire bundle of letters into the fire, but as she did it they slipped, one or two catching on the breeze from the open window. With a sinking feeling she watched them flutter and fall not far from Theo's feet. He reached over and picked one up.

'Can you give that to me?' she said.

He looked at it and was about to hand it over when something must have caught his attention, possibly his name. 'It was written to me, wasn't it? Can't I just read it?'

She couldn't speak.

His look bored into her for just a moment then he glanced down. As he read, he remained impassive, but when he had finished, he looked stricken, his eyes blurring with unshed tears that he hurriedly dashed away. There was a pause before he spoke.

'I'm so sorry. I'm so, so sorry.' He almost choked on the words

'There are some things,' she said and paused for a moment to take a breath. 'Some things I—'

'I understand. I should never have pushed you before.'

She shook her head. There was nowhere for them to go with this save for more pain. 'It doesn't matter.'

He remained where he was, and she realised she had never seen him looking so lost.

She rose to her feet and spoke calmly. 'Theo, last night should never have happened. It was a mistake.'

He took a pace towards her, but she held up her hand to stop him. 'I've made my decision, Theo. Please don't come any closer. I'd like you to leave the kasbah.'

'I thought—'

'Me too. I'm sorry.'

His face crumpled as they gazed at each other. 'Oh Clemmy. Won't you let me help you?'

It was like being offered water when you were dying of thirst. Water when you had no hope of ever drinking again. The day before, on their last whole day together, he had reached for her hand, traced every line on her palm.

'This one for everything that has gone before,' he'd said. 'This one only for me.' Then he'd smiled at her, his blue eyes bright as if he had somehow known what might be coming even though she had yet to think it.

'Clem, let me help you,' he insisted again now, his voice low and urgent.

What she'd had with Theo had been a connection they consummated in words and actions but did not rely on either of those alone. There had been more – another dimension to the two of them.

But she shook her head and said, 'No. There's nothing you can do. The damage was done on my fourteenth birthday all those years ago. Soon you won't be able to look at me. There are days when I feel so crushed by it, I can barely look at myself.'

'What he did was not your fault.'

She shrugged, couldn't bear to let him go. It felt unnatural and wrong . . . but let him go she must.

'Let me stay. What happened back then makes no difference to how I feel about you.'

'I'm sorry.' She shook her head.

'What about Patrice Callier? Will you be safe?'

'I have a gun and I know how to use it. And Ahmed will be here. Patrice just wants to dig up the past. I can handle him. Please, Theo, I mean it.'

Even though she had seen the desolation in his eyes,

she turned back to the fire, squatting there until she could hear his footsteps fading so he should not witness the tears running down her cheeks and falling to her lap. Because that was the last time she would ever see his face, and because there was so many more things she could *never* say . . .

And if Theo knew the whole of it, it would poison any chance of future happiness they might have. Better that he left now before it began. In truth she was broken, irreparably broken, and Theo need never know the rest.

CHAPTER 35

Immersed in her sorrow, Clemence walked automatically, without seeing anything, arms wrapped around her middle as if to contain the abyss grief had quarried within her. But whatever her own misery, the exhausted visitors staying at the kasbah had to be her priority and with Florence's sister, Hélène, and her partner due to arrive soon she couldn't dwell on her own problems.

The slopes of the mountain had turned golden in the late afternoon light, fading into purple with hints of deepest blue in the secret places within its crannies and chasms. Despite the sadness threatening to overwhelm her, Clemence gained solace from this time of day at the kasbah. It was the hour of relaxation, a peaceful hiatus while the rest of the world rumbled on, crumpled and tired, before the dark finally arrived. A moment full of nothing but itself.

She joined Florence who was sitting under the awning

at the front of the house, restlessly leafing through the pages of a magazine and jiggling her foot.

'How are you?' she asked and handed over a glass of sweet iced coffee laced with vanilla.

Florence took it and sipped before replying. 'Oh . . . you know.'

'I'm so sorry.'

Florence didn't speak.

'Would you mind telling me about your life with your sisters when you were young?'

'In the Dordogne, you mean, in France?'

'Yes.' Clemence didn't ask anything more specific, but she wanted so much to hear about the area where her son had grown up.

Florence spoke softly. 'Well, after *Maman* left to go back to England it was just the three of us. Hélène – she worked as a nurse. Élise ran her café and I looked after the house, the animals, the garden. I adored cooking. Still do.'

'Sadly, not my greatest skill,' Clemence admitted, and it raised the ghost of a smile from Florence.

'I'm sure you have many other talents. Anyway it was a truly magical time, and we were happy until the war came.'

'And then?'

Florence sighed and shook her head. 'Not so magical.'

'I imagine not. What was your home like back then?'

A dreamy look came into Florence's eyes and Clemence felt she had asked the right thing.

'Our house was a lovely old place on the outskirts of the village.'

'Sounds idyllic.'

'It was. As I said, the kitchen was my domain. It had a flagstone floor hollowed in patches and I used to hang herbs to dry from the beams.'

'I love the smell of drying herbs, especially lavender.'

Florence smiled. 'We used to swim in the river naked and dry ourselves in the sun. There was a track to get to the village, but you could also cross a small field to get there.'

'Was it a large village?'

'Not really. There were a few shops, and the square was . . . was . . .' Her words dried up and she faltered.

'Please go on.'

'Are you sure?'

Clemence nodded.

'I'm so sorry . . . but you see the square . . .'

There were a few moments of silence as Clemence blinked away the heat rising behind her eyelids

'The square was where Victor was executed.'

Clemence wanted to cover her ears with her hands, run from the conversation, but her limbs felt too heavy and anyway she had to stay for Florence. Once she had controlled herself, she said, 'Do you think Élise might be willing to talk to me about what happened to Victor?'

'I don't know. She never speaks of it. Never. It was the most profound loss for her, literally soul destroying, and eventually she slammed the door on that time of her life.'

'I see.'

'A few years later she married Henri. None of us expected it, but his first wife, Suzanne, was killed during the Liberation so they had both lost someone in terrible circumstances. It must have been a comfort.'

'Yes.'

'Suzanne didn't support the Nazis. Quite the reverse. It should not have happened. Anyway, Élise lives in Henri's chateau, not our old house.'

'Sounds very grand.'

'I suppose it is. But . . . I don't know, but I think Vicky resents him and her mother for marrying him.'

'Such a shame.'

'It would have helped Vicky if Élise had been able to talk about Victor, but she just couldn't.'

'I understand that.' Clemence paused for a moment, wondering how to keep Florence talking. Anything to help relieve the misery and fear the poor woman was experiencing if only for a few moments. So she said, 'And what about you and Jack? Where do you live?'

Florence gave her a sad little smile. 'In a beautiful thatched cottage called Meadowbrook in Devon. I'm very lucky.'

'And Hélène?'

'She lives in Malta, in an old palace we all inherited from our mother's sister, Rosalie . . . if you can believe it. Quite a leap for a nurse from our little French village.'

They heard footsteps and both turned to look towards the rugged track that wound up from the village. 'Is it her? Your sister?' Clemence asked as a tall woman came into view, followed by a dark-haired man.

Florence didn't reply, but tripping and stumbling in her haste she ran down the track and flew into her sister's arms. They hugged each other so tightly Clemence wondered how they could even still be breathing. When they stepped back a little, they smiled into each other's eyes.

'So?' Hélène said.

Florence nodded, as if knowing what her sister meant. Clemence had always wished for a sister herself and felt a pang watching them. There was tenderness, love and concern emanating from this strong athletic-looking woman. The sisters had already been through so much and it showed in the depth of their bond.

'Come and meet Madame Petier, Vicky's grandmother,' Florence said, clutching her sister's hand as if she might never let it go. 'Obviously none of us knew anything about her before, but this is her place. And Étienne too, come. I'm so sorry for ignoring you. Thank you for being here.'

The wiry looking man who had arrived with Hélène nodded. He kissed Florence on both cheeks and spoke with a strong French accent. 'We are here to do whatever we can.'

Florence gave him a nod of gratitude. The three came over to Clemence who had risen to greet them.

She held out her hand to Hélène who took it and looked her straight in the eye. She was taller than Florence, handsome rather than pretty, with a muscular build. Her firm handshake and the way she held herself, told Clemence that Hélène would be a steadying voice and a much-needed rock at this dreadful time.

'Welcome to the kasbah. You must be thirsty,' Clemence said. 'What can I offer you both?' she asked

'Cold water for me,' Étienne said, turning to Hélène. 'You?'

'Same, please.'

Clemence hurried to the kitchen where she asked Nadia if all the rooms were ready and to please prepare a tray for her new guests. While she waited, she reflected. It was fascinating to see the similarities and differences between Florence and Hélène, but she still couldn't suppress her innermost desire to meet the other sister, Vicky's mother, Élise, the woman her son had loved. The woman who had really known him.

Back in the shade of the awning the three, heads together, were talking quietly but they all glanced up as she approached. With all the turmoil going on inside her she felt naked before them, so simply smiled, placed the tray on the copper table, and left them to it. She needed time to deal with her own churning emotions.

At every turn, after every step, around every corner she saw Theo's shadow and it was tearing her apart. He seemed to hover close at hand and more than once she twisted round to speak, signal to him, or to reach for his hand. But he was gone of course. *She* had made him go. Sent him away, just like before. Though perhaps not really like before. *I'd rather gouge out my own heart than go through that degree of loss again,* she thought. Fighting the stubborn pulse beating in her throat, she craved the solace of her own bedroom where a trace of orange blossom fragrance would still linger in the air. It usually calmed her. She quickened her pace, almost ran the last few yards, opened the door, and glanced in anguish at the bed where she had so recently slept with Theo. She felt his touch, his love, even now, the pain of loss so intolerable she could do nothing but give in. She ran to the bed, followed by the two dogs who had slipped through the door behind her, tails between their legs, and whimpering to see her so upset. She allowed them to jump up and lie on top of her quilt with her. She plumped up her pillow, held it over her head and with one arm around Coco's neck and shoulders she wept, only stopping when she felt completely hollow.

Later, in her bathroom, she ran a hand over the gleaming *zellige* tiles in shades of greenish blue – sea glass, cyan, jade, teal. Their luminous shine usually lifted her spirits but not today. She splashed her face with cold water, dried it, unscrewed the top of one of her oils and dabbed its musky tang onto her wrists. What would the visitors think to see her looking so wretched? She stared at her reflection. *Stupid. Stupid old woman.* Why was she behaving as if she were Vicky's age and not seventy-four? It was beyond ridiculous. She was ridiculous.

Later, after dinner, breathing in the sweet vanilla perfume of stocks, mingling with the woody earthy smells of the land, she spotted Florence wandering alone in the dark wearing a nightdress with just a thin cotton robe thrown over her shoulders. She watched her for a moment, before moving forward.

'Can I help?' she asked gently.

Florence glanced over her shoulder, her face drawn. 'Jack's dozing and Hélène and Étienne were exhausted after their journey so they're having an early night. I came out to look at the stars.'

'I do the same sometimes. Come out here to contemplate the stars, life, everything.' She didn't mention how as little more than a child, she had often escaped outside where, bathed in starlight, she felt free from the fears of the night.

'I'm praying that Bea is looking up at them too,' Florence said then bowed her head.

There was a short silence, for what could Clemence say? In the end she simply said, 'Stargazing reminds me of how little we really know.'

'Yes. It's such a mystery. Life. Why does everything matter so terribly much to us when we are such infinitesimal dots?'

'I like to think that each one of us is part of the magic, part of the majesty.'

Florence raised her head just a little and Clemence thought she seemed to understand.

'But it doesn't mean we shouldn't feel desperate at times,' she continued. 'Grief-stricken, or afraid. We're human, after all.'

'And I am so frightened,' Florence said in a small voice. 'I don't often tell people, but now it seems pointless to hide anything. I was raped by thugs . . . violently, when I was nineteen during the war in France. I thought it was the worst thing that could ever happen to me. I was wrong . . . This is.'

Aghast, Clemence felt her own heart pounding. This was so hard for her to hear – to remember the feeling of being continually on her guard. She put an arm around Florence and held her tight. She knew exactly what the woman must be fearing and maintained the silence but then Florence herself changed the subject.

'We fell out, you know. Me and Hélène. Over Jack. Silly now. It was awful though, at the time.'

'But you're okay these days?'

'Oh yes. I used to feel guilty, but she forgave me eventually. Hélène and Étienne are so good together. He's the dark silent type, you know, but he watches everyone else interact and doesn't miss a trick. Hélène and he are both artists now and they climb together. They're going to hike up the mountain to look for Bea tomorrow.'

'Well let's hope a new day will bring us some good news.'

'You think it's still possible?'

'Anything is possible,' Clemence said, but as the night swallowed everything except for the twinkling lights in the sky, did she even believe her own words?

CHAPTER 36

Vicky

Marrakech hospital

In air thick with the smell of antiseptic and soiled bandages, Vicky closed her eyes. Outside an ambulance bell began to ring, setting up an unpleasant discordant clanging in her head. She heard raised voices, bringing back the moment she'd arrived in the lorry with Tom, when he had been injured so badly, she didn't even know if he would live. Yet he had, thank God, and seemed to be recovering quite well.

In the late afternoon Etta, wearing a dark green kaftan with scarlet beads, arrived at Tom's hospital room carrying a paper bag. Although only half Moroccan she spoke the language perfectly and had no trouble getting in. Etta seemed to know everyone. 'I brought you food,' she said. 'Nobody can survive on the stuff they dole out here.'

Vicky sighed. 'Tom is on liquids only.'

Etta wrinkled her nose. 'Pity. But *you* still need to eat. I'm betting you haven't thought of food all day. Here, have one.'

Vicky helped herself and took a bite. 'Mmm. Lemony and soft. *Ghoriba* cookies are my favourite.'

'Not too sweet?'

'Just right. Can I have another?'

Etta laughed, handed her the whole bagful and went to scrutinise Tom. 'Doesn't look great, does he?' she said frowning.

'Much better than he was. But he'll be fine eventually they say. Don't wake him. He needs to sleep.' Vicky, unexpectedly protective of her friend, could feel herself reddening as Etta raised her eyebrows.

'We're just friends,' she protested.

Etta smiled but with a shrewd look said, 'If you say so.'

She headed for the door and gave Vicky a wave. 'See you later.'

'Thank you,' Vicky said, holding up the bag of cookies before stuffing another into her mouth.

After Etta had gone, she settled herself on the chair next to Tom's bed and reached for his hand. She watched his chest rising and falling with each breath and realised how much she wanted to know him better. He was so different from Russell, quieter, more thoughtful. Kinder too, she hoped.

She sighed deeply, feeling so mixed up. Guilt and shame, worry too, were all muddled in with this concern for him. Was he really going to be all right? She savoured this time alone with him. They didn't have long together as Élise and Tom's father had gone out to eat and would be back soon. Vicky couldn't help thinking that two people less likely to get on could not be found.

Tom woke and attempted to mumble through barely open lips. 'You all right?' he croaked.

She stroked his hand, not quite hearing him. 'Shhh! Don't talk.'

'Tell . . . 'bout you.'

'What?'

'Truth. Why come here?'

What do I have to lose? she thought. 'Well, I suppose I came here to get over a disastrous love affair.'

She told him about Russell. He had been cruel; she recognised that. It hadn't just been at the end. He'd always found ways to belittle her, make her feel less of a person. Walking in the night too fast and far ahead of her back to his flat. Undoing her bra without asking. Teasing her with those long, experienced fingers between her legs. Then laughing and refusing to make love when she really wanted to. Sneering at her work with a smile on his face. *Darling, surely you can do better.* It had seemed acceptable at the time but now she conceded he'd enjoyed tormenting her, making her feel worthless. She felt glad she hadn't made a scene, crumpled, or pleaded, when he'd dumped her, but what a fool to think she had loved him. With an ache she remembered the pain, the sorrow, the anguish, but realised Russell was nothing to her now. Less than nothing. She didn't care about exacting her revenge any more. She still wanted success, but it would be for her and not just to prove Russell wrong.

Tom was drifting off and she closed her eyes too, fell asleep, and was woken a little later by Theo's contact, Officer Alami, leaning over her.

'Sorry to wake you,' he was saying as he took off his hat and edged respectfully back.

'I . . . I wasn't asleep,' she replied, feeling dull and groggy. She wanted to hide, didn't want to talk to him. 'Or . . . maybe I *was* asleep.'

He smiled. 'It's so hot in here, anyone would nod off.'

She swallowed, hurriedly draining a glass of water. Feeling less daunted, she said, 'I hate falling asleep in the day. So?'

'Can we talk? I don't want to wake the young man.'

She got up reluctantly and they went out into the corridor where he glanced around and spoke in a low voice so as not to be overheard. 'I thought you might want to hear the latest.'

Did she want to know? She sighed deeply, impatient for him to leave her alone in the little cocoon she had created with Tom where nobody else could intrude.

A nurse wearing a green uniform took a few paces towards them, opened a door, and disappeared behind it.

'Well?' Vicky said.

'Well,' he echoed. 'It seems that Patrice Callier has vanished into thin air. There appears to be no trace.'

'But there has to be. Do you know if he has got Bea?'

He shook his head. 'At the moment it's anyone's guess.'

Vicky forced herself not to cry in front of this man. 'So, we have no idea where Bea is, *and* the police haven't arrested Patrice for Jimmy's murder?'

'With no body . . .' He raised his hand and shrugged. 'It's deplorable, I know.'

'But they will go on looking, won't they?'

'Yes,' he said. 'They have your statement, but there's no physical evidence, nor anybody else who can give us information about the murder. Finding Jimmy's body is crucial.'

'But I saw it happen. Isn't that enough?' Vicky felt as if the room was suddenly spinning. She took several long slow breaths but still felt awful.

He averted his eyes as she gulped down a sob and took a moment before she could speak again. Then she pulled herself together to ask, 'What about Bea? She saw most of it too.'

He shrugged. 'Well until we find her there's only you. They are still maintaining a search party for your cousin but I'm afraid I don't know for how much longer.'

There was a long silence.

'They think she's dead,' she said eventually, her voice flat and her blood running cold with fear. 'Don't they?'

CHAPTER 37

Clemence

Kasbah du Paradis

At the sight of Hélène's troubled face when she and Étienne arrived back at the kasbah, exhausted after climbing all day, Clemence knew there had been a problem. She led them to her private courtyard and went to fetch cold drinks and some fruit.

While Hélène and Étienne had searched higher up the mountain, Jack had spent the day with the police probing the lower area where Tom had crashed the car and Bea had disappeared. The police had examined this area before, but Jack had insisted they try again. He was now bathing, and Florence had been persuaded to rest.

When Clemence returned to the courtyard with refreshments, Hélène and Étienne were talking in hushed tones.

'We need to speak with my sister and her husband,' Hélène said, looking up. Despite her tiredness and obvious worry, she still seemed calm and in control.

'You've found something?'

'Étienne did,' Hélène said.

'Not Beatrice?'

Hélène shook her head.

'I'll fetch Florence and Jack,' Clemence said, feeling sad and a little scared as she hurried off to wake them. As she neared their room she paused, wondering what Étienne had found because, whatever it was, she genuinely feared for Florence's state of mind. The woman was already at breaking point.

She knocked at their door and Florence stood beside Jack as he opened up, raking his fingers through his tousled hair, his green eyes widening the moment he saw her. 'Tell me. Have they found my daughter?'

Clemence shook her head, tried to keep her own anxiety from showing but the desperate look in Jack's eyes showed she had failed.

As soon as they arrived in the courtyard, Florence ran directly to her sister. 'What is it? For God's sake, what have you found?'

Hélène stood up, dug into her pocket, and drew out a blue and white flowery scarf. Clemence drew in her breath at the sight, recalling the day Bea had bought it.

'You've seen it before?' Hélène asked turning to her.

She faltered. 'I'm not sure. I may have overreacted. There might be dozens of similar scarves, but it does look like Beatrice's. I don't know. Where did you find it?'

'In . . . well I suppose a bit like a shallow cave,' Étienne said.

'Let me take a closer look. There was a defect, so she got it for a snip.'

Hélène handed her the scarf. Clemence examined it closely and found the place where the pattern had not repeated correctly. 'Unless the whole batch was faulty, I'm afraid this could well be Bea's scarf.'

Florence crumpled into a chair and hung her head. Hélène came to kneel in front of her.

'I can't bear this,' Florence whispered shaking her head. 'Tell me how to bear it.'

'Listen to me, Florence,' Jack said. 'This may not be a bad thing.'

'How?' Florence stood up again suddenly, taking a step back and knocking over the chair. 'How? For Christ's sake, will people stop telling me things will be all right.'

'I wasn't say—'

'No!' she interrupted, her voice rising sharply. 'No! Stop trying to pacify me. Stop grasping at straws.'

'I . . .'

'Just stop, Jack!' she shrieked. 'I can't stand it. Our daughter is lying dead somewhere in this godforsaken country and all you can say is that finding a scarf is a good thing. For once in your life face facts. Beatrice is dead, Jack. She's fucking dead.'

He held out a hand to touch her arm. 'Come on, Florence.'

'Get off me!' she screamed as she withdrew, her voice ragged with pain. 'Get away from me, all of you with your bloody platitudes. Can't you see I'm going out of my mind?'

'Jack might be right,' Hélène tried to say.

But Florence shied away, her red face rigid and her eyes wild with rage. 'You have no idea how this feels. To think . . . to think she might have been hurt by someone . . . our beautiful daughter, Jack . . . maybe violated by some filthy scum!' She gulped back a sob, bowed her head, and began to keen, rocking back and forth on the spot and moaning like an animal in agony.

For a few moments, nobody spoke.

'She . . . may not . . . have been hurt by someone,' Jack eventually tried to say.

'Stop it!' she yelled at him, tears pouring down her face. 'Just stop it!'

'But maybe it's not a sign that she's dead?' He tried to hold her, but she fought him off.

Then she turned and ran.

'Let her go, Jack,' Hélène said in a flat voice. 'Let her calm down in her own way.'

Jack blinked, eyelashes wet with tears, and he simply shook his head.

Clemence went straight inside and soon after came back with glasses and a bottle of brandy.

'I think maybe we need this tonight.'

She poured them all a glassful and turned to leave, wanting to give them some privacy.

Jack reached out a hand. 'No. Please stay.'

'It could be a sign telling us we're on the right track,' Étienne was saying. 'She has been there, maybe is still up there somewhere nearby. And we're going to look tomorrow. We may be close to finding her. Don't lose hope, Jack.'

'Thank you, Étienne.' Jack's voice was gruff.

Hélène touched his arm. 'Believe me. If it's the last thing I ever do, I'm going to find my niece.'

As it grew dark, Ahmed told them dinner was ready, but Florence did not appear. Jack went to fetch her and returned, worried. 'She's not in our room.'

Clemence stepped forward. 'I have an idea where she may be.'

'I should go,' he said.

'No. Might be better if it's a stranger.'

Jack turned and headed straight to the room he shared with Florence, taking the brandy bottle with him.

Clemence found Florence stargazing just as she expected. Neither of them spoke for a good long while.

'I'm sorry,' Florence eventually said.

'There's no need to apologise. I would be tearing my hair out in your position. Feel free to scream all you need.'

It raised a brief smile from Florence.

'I'm so afraid for her.'

'You're talking about what happened to you in France. The rape I mean.'

'Yes.'

Clemence swallowed before speaking. 'I do understand. I have never spoken about it, but it happened to me too.'

Florence turned to her.

'My father. When I was fourteen.'

'Oh my God!'

'It stays with you, doesn't it? An offence so humiliating, so frightening.'

They stood in silence for a while just staring at the heavens. Both of them joined together as women who'd known what could happen and had suffered at the hands of a brutal man, although Clemence dared not tell her the whole story. And now here was Florence, terrified for her daughter and in agony at the possibility of history repeating itself.

'Come,' Clemence said. 'Are you ready to go in? Maybe eat a little.'

Florence reached up to touch her cheek and nodded.

At supper Jack joined them again and Florence seemed calmer than before. Perhaps Clemence's confession had given her the feeling of support she had needed. Perhaps it had made her feel less alone to know someone else truly understood her fear. Either way she was at least eating something and that could only help.

Afterwards, Clemence opened the annexe door and when she saw her mother lying flat on the sofa unmoving, she ran to her. *Not now. Not now. Please not now.* She touched Madeleine's cheek exactly as Florence had just touched her own.

'I'm not dead,' the old woman muttered as her eyes flew open. 'But he is.'

'Who, *Maman*?'

Her mother stretched out a hand to reach for her. 'Him! Your father. And it was not you, it was me.'

'What was you?'

'Oh, don't play fast and loose with me, girl,' she snapped, all patience gone. 'You know very well.'

'Do you mean the fire?'

'I wasn't referring to the fire. You think it was you, but it was me.'

'Very well. If you say so.'

Madeleine frowned. 'Are you the new maid? Please fetch my daughter. She's outside playing with the driver's son, but she needs to come in and wash her hands.' She cackled and winked. 'She thinks I don't know.'

Clemence closed her eyes and shook her head.

Later she was sitting outside on her own. The night was beautiful, balmy, the air so full of fragrance it made her feverish with longing. She hugged herself, but burnt for Theo. Thought of him all the time. Why had she so foolishly sent him away? She heard the hall clock striking ten. She was bone-tired but knew she wouldn't sleep, had barely slept since he'd gone. The pain of his loss on top of her dread and fear for Beatrice was almost unbearable and she needed him. So much. What a coward she had been.

She sat there, silent and lonely, and hearing snippets of conversation as Jack walked with his sister-in-law in the part of garden lit by lanterns.

'It's so good to see you,' she heard him say to Hélène, his voice a little slurred.

'You too.'

'Once Bea is found, you and Étienne must come to stay. You never have.'

'Just the way it turned out.'

'Nothing to do with the past?'

Hélène chuckled. 'Not at all. We'd love to come and stay.'

'If it's . . .' He paused. 'If it's bad news, Florence will need you.'

'You think?'

'I . . .'

And then their voices faded as they moved further away.

Love ties us women up in knots, Clemence thought. Love of our man, our child, our life. Even her love for her mother had been multi-layered, full of deep-seated contradictions, testing her at times and occasionally turning her inside out. For Madeleine had been the mother who had not helped when she had most needed her. When she had screamed for her. Begged for her.

CHAPTER 38

Vicky

Marrakech

Vicky had been standing at the window for ages, staring at a peacock strutting in the hotel's gardens. It was late morning and overcast and it suited her mood. She was staying in a room interconnecting with her mother's at the hotel and had never experienced such luxury. Breakfast in bed on a silver tray, bedclothes turned down at night, and a Belgian chocolate wrapped in gold foil left on a little saucer. Although Henri's chateau was grand, their lives had been nothing like this and Élise preferred a degree of austerity, or simplicity, as she referred to it.

Vicky turned away from the window and lay down on the unmade bed. Staring up at the ornate ceiling, her mind flitted back to her tall blonde cousin every few minutes, even when she was trying not to think about her. She would give anything for Bea to be found alive and well, but the unanswered questions constantly speeding through her mind were tormenting her. Why had Jimmy been shot? Where was her cousin? Where was she?

Think about something else, she told herself.

Anything else.

The film. Think about the film.

She recalled hearing how Alfred Hitchcock had filmed part of *The Man Who Knew Too Much* at this hotel, and she has seen it in London with never a thought she might one day lie on a bed in a room here. Now the plot seemed not a hundred miles from her actual life; there had been a murder and an abduction here too . . .

The film had starred James Stewart, whom she adored, and Doris Day, whom she tolerated. A kind of suspense thriller, better in a film than in real life though. In real life the suspense made her feel sick.

An image of her early childhood rose in her mind. A time before Henri, when she and her mother had lived with Hélène in their higgledy-piggledy stone house in the Dordogne. It had limestone walls and shuttered windows – she had helped paint those shutters dusky blue, getting more paint on her clothes than anything else. As soon as she was allowed to roam a little on her own after her seventh birthday, she would race out of their gate and head for a small field edged by wild poppies, where the waddling geese made her giggle. She'd been so happy, but that same year Élise had married Henri, and Hélène went off to live with Étienne in Paris, so their old home was put up for sale. Later, when Great-Aunt Rosalie died quite young, she left her Maltese home to Hélène, Élise and Florence. Hélène went to live there with Étienne and the devastating changes were complete.

She heard a knock on the interconnecting door. 'Come in,' she called out and her mother entered.

'*Maman*,' she said, sitting bolt upright. 'Why have we heard nothing about Bea yet?'

'The moment anything changes, we'll hear, I'm sure.'

'Can't we just go to the kasbah now?' Vicky pleaded. She couldn't understand why they hadn't gone already. Privately, she wondered if Élise was putting off actually meeting Clemence.

'Etta says your grandmother's driver, Ahmed, is it . . . ?'

'Yes.'

'She says he'll be coming to Marrakech to collect us as soon as there's any news. We'll go to the kasbah with him. Look, I understand how you feel. I am determined to see my sister as soon as I can. In the meantime, we have matters to deal with here. You have the sketchbook?'

Vicky barely nodded.

'Come on, *chérie*. Chop-chop!' Élise smiled briefly then pulled her off the bed.

'Oh, very well,' she replied sulkily. Why was it that whenever she was around her mother she reverted to such moody behaviour?

Accompanied by the bodyguard, whom Theo had insisted they took everywhere, they headed for the medina where they began the search for Yves Saint Laurent's house, trailing this way and that through the maze of dusty cobbled alleys lined by square pink riads. The body-guard wasn't much use as he had come up from Casablanca and wasn't familiar with the route either.

'We need to ask the way again,' Élise said.

It had been the hotel receptionist who had given them rudimentary directions, but they were completely out of their depth as everything looked the same to them. When they turned off from a dirt square running only into a dead-end alley and found nobody to ask, they were both beginning to sweat. Turning back and coming across an empty plot of land, they walked behind it along another alley leading to a mosque but nothing else.

'Let's just forget this?' Vicky said, pressing her finger to her temples. 'It's boiling and I'm getting a headache.'

Élise reached for her hand. 'Come on, scaredy-cat.'

Vicky bristled, remembering how bossy her mother could be. When they retraced their steps, they found a knot of men huddled together and, in French, Élise asked the oldest one for directions but he just shook his head as if he hadn't understood. Their bodyguard mean-while was questioning a man nearby. Vicky couldn't help feeling apprehensive when he pointed at the empty plot of land.

'It is the lemon garden. And *Dar el-Hanch*, the Snake House, is just over there,' he said.

Vicky hadn't expected Saint Laurent to open the door when they knocked and yet he did. Deeply tanned, sporting heavy black-framed spectacles, his dark hair longish, he wore a white kaftan and white trousers.

Élise took charge, speaking in French. 'I apologise for

disturbing you like this, but my daughter believes she has found your sketchbook.'

'Oh?' He remained standing in the doorway, blocking the room behind from view.

'Would you mind if we came in? We've been walking around for some time trying to locate your house.'

He drew back, giving them space to enter and glancing at their guard.

'He won't mind waiting outside,' Élise said. 'This won't take long.'

The designer led them to a simply furnished room where on one wall a beautiful snake had been painted in blue, green, ochre and a soft rusty brown, the image glowing with light.

He motioned them to sit on the sofa while he sat opposite on an old wooden armchair.

He glanced around. 'We are very rustic. All the furniture here we picked up in the souks.'

Palms sweating, her mouth dry, Vicky couldn't speak.

Élise cleared her throat. 'I am Élise Baudin Dumas, and this is my daughter Victoria Baudin.' She gestured to Vicky. 'You want to explain?'

Vicky opened the bag she had been carrying and without a word took out the sketchbook and laid it on the table.

Wide-eyed, he picked it up, flicked through, and couldn't seem to work out whether to glare at her or thank her.

'I didn't . . . didn't take it.' Vicky got the words out so quickly she stumbled over them. 'I mean, I didn't steal it.'

'You're telling me you borrowed it?'

'Yes. Well no. Not me.'

Vicky glanced at the snake again which seemed to be pulsing. She took a quick breath to steady herself and slowly exhaled.

'I assume you are aware of who did take it?' he asked sharply, his eyes still on the book as he turned the pages.

'My cousin. We tried to give it, or rather take it back to your studio in the Palmeraie, but things became too dangerous, and now we're under protection. We had to leave Marrakech in a hurry. The man you saw outside is my bodyguard.'

His eyebrows flew up above his spectacles. 'Bodyguard!'

'I can't tell you that part of the story yet, but my cousin is missing, and I am at risk.'

Élise took over. 'I think my daughter is trying to say that as soon as she realised what her cousin had done, she attempted to find a way to return the sketchbook without getting the girl into too much trouble.'

He snorted and headed over to pick up a cup from a small coffee table. 'You expect me to believe such a crazy story?' he said.

'It's the truth,' Vicky said. 'My cousin Beatrice is young and naive. She meant no harm.'

With an impatient look he puffed out his cheeks and sighed.

Aware of his annoyance, she rose to her feet. 'Please. I can't tell you the whole story yet. I'm not allowed to. My mother has come over from France to help me. My grandmother is Clemence Petier.'

'Your grandmother would attest to your honesty?'

Vicky sighed. 'She actually hasn't known me for long.'

Élise took over. 'My daughter is a key witness in a criminal investigation. I promise, she is telling you the truth. I'm sorry we can't tell you more.'

He shook his head, looking utterly perplexed. 'Why did your cousin steal it?'

'She was looking at it but heard someone coming and panicked. She had no idea it was yours. I don't know why she picked it up in the first place.'

There was a long pause. Vicky could not look at him. She had no idea how this was going to go.

'Give me one reason why I should not take this further,' he said.

She heard her grandfather's voice in her head – *courage, little one* – and she took a breath, hardly daring to hope. 'I've just finished my fashion design diploma in London, and I have a place at the *Ecole de la Chambre Syndicale de la Couture Parisienne.*'

He whistled. 'Prestigious.'

'I only came here to Marrakech to meet you. I admire your work so much; you have inspired my studies and the career I hope to have.'

He scratched his head and a cautious half-smile flickered over his face.

'It was stupid of my cousin Bea, and now she is missing, and we fear she has been abducted and may be dead. The police are looking for her. A terrible thing happened the night we tried to return the book.'

'Right.' He paced back and forth frowning, hands in the pockets of his kaftan.

Vicky hardly dared hope. The silence seemed to go on for ages. Not knowing what to say or do, she glanced at her mother who was looking at the floor. She forced herself not to do anything stupid. Or say anything stupid.

In the end the great man narrowed his eyes at her. 'It would seem you have more than enough on your plate without being arrested for theft as well. You were brave to come here. Promise to tell me the whole story as soon as you can?'

Vicky nodded.

'Now get out of here.'

Vicky felt such a flood of relief she almost cried.

Still talking about how well their trip to the Snake House had gone, they walked to the riad, but when Etta opened the door, her face pale and drawn, Vicky immediately knew something was terribly wrong.

'This is Élise, my mother. What's . . . ?' she began, but the woman held up a hand to stop her speaking and led them through to the kitchen where she invited them to sit.

While Vicky could barely wait for Etta to tell them what was wrong, Élise, who hadn't been there before, was gazing around at the paintings on the *tadelakt* walls, at the brightly coloured crystal lamps, the Chinese lanterns, and the carved wooden screen keeping part of the room separate.

'That's beautiful,' she said. 'Looks like lace.'

'They call it a *Zouak* screen,' Vicky said automatically, her eyes still on Etta.

The woman did not return her gaze. Instead, she busied herself boiling a kettle, still not speaking, and making mint tea – especially sweet with far more sugar than usual, Vicky noticed.

'Drink,' the older woman said, passing them tea glasses full of the amber liquid and also sliding across a plate of almond biscuits.

'Thanks,' Vicky said, though she didn't feel like eating.

The sounds from the outside world didn't reach into the depths of the house and all Vicky could hear were the songbirds in the courtyard garden. It felt like a moment you knew was coming, a moment just before the world might stop turning and change your life forever.

'I don't know how to tell you this,' Etta eventually said. 'But the police came round earlier. They came here hoping to speak to you after they didn't find you at the hotel.'

'And?' Vicky said in a shaking voice. She'd asked the question but, deep inside, she already knew the answer. Her eyes felt hot and prickly as she took in Etta's stricken face. *Please no. Not Bea.* She wanted to clap her hands over her ears, just like she had done as a child when Élise was telling her off for some minor misdemeanour.

'I'm afraid they've found the body of a young woman,' Etta continued, in a quiet dull voice. 'A white woman . . . I'm so sorry.'

Vicky stared, the pain gathering in her throat and stopping her voice, leaving her mute. She groaned and crumpled onto the table, her shoulders heaving. She was vaguely aware of Élise rubbing her back. Her mother.

And like a little girl, she needed her. She spun around and as Élise's arms enfolded her, she began to howl.

The sound of her shock and grief filled the kitchen.

In those terrible moments, nobody spoke. This was the worst news possible. The unbearable news nobody wanted to hear.

'The body hasn't yet been identified,' Etta added once Vicky's anguished howls had turned into quieter intermittent sobs. 'But they think it has to be Beatrice.'

There was silence again for a while then Élise murmured something about location. Vicky couldn't quite hear.

Then Élise pulled away and spoke more loudly, though her voice choked as she gulped down air. 'Where? Where did they find her?'

'They wouldn't give me any details. They said they were going to head straight for the kasbah to speak to her parents.'

'I must go to my sister. I must be with Florence,' Élise said.

Etta agreed it was the right thing to do and added, 'I gave the police a message for Clemence. I'm sure Ahmed will be here to collect you both quite soon.'

Élise, white-faced, found a couple of clean tissues in her bag. Vicky took them and attempted to dry her eyes, but her tears would not stop falling, dripping silently down her cheeks and onto the table.

'She can't be dead,' she moaned. 'I'll do anything. Please. She can't be dead!'

* * *

Vicky was going out of her mind while they waited for Ahmed. Her body hurt, her muscles felt raw, her chest heavy. She paced Etta's kitchen biting the skin at the edge of her nails and ignoring all offers of refreshment. *Where was he? Where was he?*

In an agony of suspense she couldn't keep still, but the hours passed achingly slowly.

'I am so sorry,' Ahmed said when he eventually arrived, very late and looking unusually rattled. 'I had a flat tyre. I—'

'Oh Ahmed,' Vicky cried out. 'Thank God you're here.'

Her mother interrupted to ask where the body of the woman had been found but he shook his head.

'Not anywhere near the kasbah, but I don't know more. The police wouldn't say. At least not to Clemence or me.'

'Right,' Vicky said picking up her jacket and bag, her voice choked. 'Shall we go.'

He shook his head again. 'Too dark and much too windy up in the mountains now. We will go at first light.'

Etta offered to put him up for the night, but he declined. 'I have cousins to stay with. Do not worry. I will be here just before dawn.'

Vicky slumped back into a chair, feeling utterly despondent. How could she wait that long?

CHAPTER 39

Clemence

Kasbah du Paradis

It had been late afternoon when Clemence watched Jack walking stiff-backed towards the steep downhill track, a single policeman leading the way. They were heading to Marrakech to identify the body the police had told them was that of a young woman, a white woman. She could have wept. A sadder sight it was hard to imagine and feeling her own breath catching and a lump beginning to form, Clemence had looked away.

Florence had whimpered when she'd heard the news, her innermost fear realised. She had reached her arms out for her lost daughter, as if she could somehow – *somehow* – magically bring her back. Holding nothing but air in her arms, she had staggered to the bathroom and vomited, but she hadn't cried. At least not so far.

Clemence had asked Ahmed to drive to Marrakech to collect Vicky and her mother and bring them here. Hélène and Étienne were still up in the High Atlas peaks searching, staying overnight at a remote lodge, so there had been no way to let them know.

Clemence closed the annexe door behind her. Nadia had agreed to look after Madeleine, who had been kicking out at them both, her rage boiling over. The much needed periods of relative quiet were increasingly being ousted by these bursts of ferocity. *Frustration,* Clemence thought; at her condition, at life itself, at the woman who was her daughter, and not her daughter, changing minute by minute. She felt guilty for leaving her mother with Nadia so much, but Florence must be her priority today.

After a brief search of the gardens, she went indoors again and found the younger woman standing alone in the drawing room, staring out at the mountains and holding a cup of coffee.

'You decided not to go with Jack?' Clemence asked softly.

Hollow-eyed, Florence glanced over her shoulder. 'I couldn't.'

'Can I get you anything? Brandy? I could dash a little into your coffee.'

Florence gave her the slightest of nods

Clemence went over to the drinks cabinet, came back with the bottle, added a strong measure to the coffee and handed it to Florence. 'You'd be more comfortable sitting,' she suggested.

'I want to watch the wind.'

'I'll pull up a couple of chairs so we can both see it. The wind blows across from the south of Morocco, though we don't often see it like this in summer.'

There was a long silence but for the sound of Clemence first moving two chairs and then a tiny beaten copper side table and depositing them all close to the window.

Once they were both seated Florence quickly drained her cup. 'It sometimes feels as if things have just happened to me. All my life. Things I didn't instigate. Do you ever feel you have no control?'

'Now and then.'

'Jack tells me I should try to take life as it comes. But when you're a mother it's hard. You want to fix everything so nothing will hurt your child. You want to protect them. Save them from suffering. Even though logically you know you can't.'

There was a brief silence.

'I have no idea how to feel any more,' Florence eventually added. 'I'm numb. Cold. Waiting for the rage, the pain, but there's nothing.'

Clemence listened, words failing her, and feeling ill-equipped to help the younger woman. What could she possibly say?

'I feel half dead inside. Dead. Why?'

'The shock . . . I think.'

Florence gave her a desperate look and pressed a palm against her heart. 'I want to feel something. I *need* to feel something.'

'Nature's way of protecting you. When we find out for sure maybe—'

Florence laughed but it was a brief, bitter sound and her expression had hardened. 'You really believe there's still hope?'

'I don't know. I don't know what to say to help.'

'No.'

There was another pause.

'I'm teetering on the edge of insanity, you know.' Florence narrowed her eyes and shook her head as if in bewilderment then added, 'Balanced just this side of crazy.'

Clemence gently touched her shoulder, but the younger woman did not respond so she withdrew her hand.

'Life is too impossible. The way we love our children! Die for them even, and yet we can lose them just like that,' and she snapped her fingers.

'Yes,' Clemence whispered, all too familiar with what she meant.

Florence glanced at her and then looked back at the wind blowing the shrubs about. 'Gone in a flash, but we live as if it could never be. As if awful things only happen to other people.'

Clemence didn't speak but knew it was true.

'After everything I endured in France, the war, and after watching Victor's execution, you'd think I'd know better. Awful things can happen to any of us. At any time.'

'What's the alternative?' Clemence said, jolted by the sound of Victor's name. She'd only loved him as a newborn baby, but the feeling of emptiness had lasted a lifetime. 'Not to love at all, just to live in fear?'

'Jack was closed-up when we first got together. He lost a little boy from his first marriage, you know, in the war.'

'Oh, how terrible,' Clemence quietly said, thinking of the man walking down the hill and dreading that he had most probably lost another child too.

Florence shook her head. 'How do we survive this? Can you tell me? I don't even know how to breathe.'

'Of course you don't. But you will.'

Florence stared at her, her soft blue-grey eyes huge and pleading. 'How? How will I?'

'Once we are sure one way or another you will build your way, step by . . .' Knowing anything she could say would be inadequate, her words trailed off. And yet Florence had seemed to need a response, her expression utterly despairing. No parent expected to face the death of their child. And no parent should have to. Yet they did. All the time.

'The waiting has been such a torment and there are brief moments, just split seconds really, when her . . . death . . . when her death feels like a relief.' Florence shook her head. 'What kind of a mother says a thing like that?'

Clemence reached out and took her hand, wanting to offer gentle reassurance while realising there really was none.

'One who loves her daughter very deeply,' she said but it was as if Florence hadn't heard.

'I hated myself, in France,' she was saying. 'Blamed myself for what those awful men did. Felt guilty. You'll understand, I'm sure.'

'Oh yes.'

'And I feel guilty now too.'

'No, my dear. You are not to blame.'

'But I didn't keep her safe. I should have kept her safe,' Florence whispered, and the tears began to fall.

Clemence murmured soothingly but they both jumped as Madeleine burst in.

'Bats! Bats!' the old lady screeched, her dishevelled hair billowing about around her face.

Nadia followed right behind, distressed. 'Madame, I am so sorry for the intrusion.'

Clemence sighed and rose to her feet, indicating Nadia should stay with the grief-stricken woman while she hurried Madeleine from the room.

That night, the sound of the wind howling kept Clemence awake until she couldn't fight exhaustion any longer. It was still dark, but quieter, when she woke from a fitful sleep to hear gentle tapping at her bedroom door. Expecting bad news she lifted her lamp, unlocked it, and was shocked to see Theo there, looking tired, his blue shirt rumpled, pale linen trousers dusty, uncertain of his welcome.

'I'm sorry,' he said. 'I drove out, I had to come when I heard they'd found a woman. Is it—'

'We can't talk in the corridor,' Clemence whispered putting a finger to her lips and pulling him into her room.

They stood almost nose to nose, his eyes searching hers, the worry on his face visible. She found herself wanting to weep from the sheer relief of seeing him, even if only briefly, when she had believed she never would again.

'There's no more news yet.' She didn't know what else to say. Or rather she knew what she wanted to say but hardly dared speak the words. She retreated a little. *Why was he here? Had he come back for her? Or?*

'I—' Everything unsaid hung in the air as her words faded and died.

A short uncomfortable silence followed, but then he cradled her face in his hands, something he had always done, and kissed her hard on the mouth.

'Theo?' she said as they drew apart.

He shook his head. 'No.'

'What?'

'No words. I'm not leaving, Clem. I'm not leaving you again. Say what you will.'

She gazed at him, seeing the light cast by the lantern illuminating only one side of his face, the other side remaining in shadow.

'So?' he asked, and for a moment she wasn't sure what he was asking.

'The woman they found,' he clarified. 'I was about to head back to Tangier when I heard the news on the radio. I couldn't get hold of Officer Alami to find out anything more, so I came straight back out here to see if I could help.'

'We don't know anything yet. Jack was being taken to a police station the other side of Marrakech. I don't think they'd have been able drive back at night in this awful wind.'

'No.'

'But *you* must have.'

'It was wild. I slept in the car halfway here to wait until it died down a little.'

'Theo, I . . .' She paused and managed a smile, the sweet surprise of his presence lifting her spirit once again. 'I'm glad you've come back. I was wrong to ask you to leave. Truly.' She remembered the endless times she'd thought about him lying next to her, skin to skin, flesh to flesh. Theo half-naked and laughing when they were younger, but also as he was now too. Older. Wiser. Still wanting her as she did him, perhaps even more than ever before. And she realised this would be their last and final chance.

He looked at her in mock suspicion. 'Goodness! Clemence Petier admitting to being wrong. Can I have it in writing?'

She reached for him, and they held each other. She felt the warmth of him, his blood moving, his heart throbbing against her own. They would find a way. This time they would. Her lips moved but she didn't speak. Deep inside she felt as if she were smiling. The embers of herself glowing.

When they finally drew apart again, she led him to her bed.

'I'm filthy,' he muttered.

'Sheets can be washed. Just take your clothes off. But I'd better lock the door if I want to avoid my mad mother diving into bed with you.'

He undressed in the lamplight and she watched, deeply aroused by his still-muscular torso and lean limbs as he took off his trousers and his shirt. How she loved this man.

Then they were both under the covers, and although she felt lazy and sensual, they didn't make love. She laid her head against his chest and told him how she felt.

'All these years, I've been living simply to protect myself,' she whispered. 'It's only with you that I can regain my spontaneity.'

'What are you protecting yourself from?' Theo asked.

'The things I couldn't bear to think about or speak of.'

'I'm so sorry.'

'Don't be. It's strange but I want to tell you everything. Not right now. And maybe not yet. But I will.'

'My darling, you could be an axe murderer for all I care.'

'Careful what you say.'

He raised his head to search her face in the low light. 'You *are* an axe murderer?' He smiled at her expression. 'My favourite kind of person.'

Hmmm, she thought. *We'll see.* But she knew she would rather die than not tell him the truth now. The whole truth. Then it would be up to him.

She thought of Florence who had gratefully accepted another sleeping pill but who might be lying awake by now, alone in the room she shared with Jack. She should get up, wash, get dressed and be prepared for whatever the day might bring. She could already hear the birds beginning their dawn chorus and the rustling of animals awakening.

He placed a hand on one of her breasts. She groaned but had to push him away. 'Later,' she said. 'But you sleep. I have to get up.'

'Sleep!' He took her hand and placed it on his groin. 'See what you've done to me.'

She laughed. 'Later.'

And by the time she had washed and dressed he was quietly snoring. She settled her eyes on his dear face and felt herself tremble with wonder. Again, the relief she felt at seeing him surged through her entire body. But it was more. He had let loose what had been lost inside her, unchained her ability to love. And she had relinquished her habitual guard. Like a snake she had shed a skin. This was a new beginning. The return of hope. She had no words to truly describe it, but her body felt so much lighter, so much freer. Nothing could match such quiet joy even at this most awful of times. His arrival had held back the underlying feelings of dread, at least for a while, but now she had to face whatever the day might bring. She took a deep breath, touched his cheek gently and left the room.

CHAPTER 40

Vicky

As they made their way to the parked vehicle in the morning, it was just light enough to see, although the sun hadn't risen yet. Next to Vicky, Élise sat with a scarf wrapped around her head, and her face as impassive as usual. Vicky didn't know much about her mother's Resistance work, though Jacques had told her Élise had faced and endured a great deal. Her grandfather was a reserved man who refused to discuss the dreadful war years that had robbed him of his son, but she understood his silent suffering and that of so many others too. He had been clear that her mother was no stranger to death and terrible grief, and Vicky found her stoicism in the face of tremendous distress a weird kind of comfort now. She thought about her aunt Florence and her uncle Jack and how the loss of Bea was going to affect them both. Did anyone recover from a horror like this?

The wind had died down and as the morning opened out, sunny and blue, Vicky found herself staring out at a crisp Moroccan sky, feeling a little relieved to be getting away from the city. Holding herself tight, she had no tears left to cry, though her eyes still felt raw and puffy. Thoughts of Bea continued to race through her mind, dashing and darting, and she couldn't stop them no matter how hard she tried. Image after image. Flickering long gone scenes, like old movies. Half-forgotten childhood laughter. She recalled again the day they'd gone to the Biba boutique, her cousin's blue eyes glittering with excitement, her straight blonde hair gently flicked up at the ends. Looking so, so lovely. How she'd envied her beauty, but when Beatrice had been sure she'd failed her exams and wept about it, she'd felt sorry for her. Everyone had vulnerabilities. Sometimes hidden so well you couldn't even begin to unravel them. She felt a painful spike of guilt and her chest constricted. She should never have come up with the idea of Morocco.

They spotted Berber villages as they rose higher on the winding scenic route, the sharp bends jolting Élise and Vicky back to life whenever they fell into a doze. The mountains looked blue, the valleys pretty with views of fruit-laden orchards but Vicky felt detached from it all. They passed donkeys, goats and chickens scratching in the dirt, plus a few people going about their morning. Élise, who had never been there before, remarked on some of it. Vicky didn't listen or speak but thought about the quarrels she'd had with her mother while in France. During those times she'd often run to her grandfather

Jacques but all he would say was, 'You rub each other up the wrong way.'

'But it's not my fault,' she'd retort.

To which he'd just mutter a non-committal, 'Hmmm.'

There were plenty of signs of life in Imlil village as Ahmed pulled up and parked and they climbed the track, feeling weary and already overheating. At the top they found Clemence pacing back and forth.

'I was keeping an eye open for Jack,' she said.

Vicky couldn't read her face. 'You haven't heard anything yet?' she asked.

Clemence shook her head. 'We're expecting to find out any moment. I'm so glad the wind has died down and relieved to see you safe and sound.'

'This is my mother,' Vicky said. 'Élise, this is Clemence, my grandmother.'

Élise stepped forward and the two women looked at each other awkwardly and in silence.

Clemence must have so many questions, Vicky thought. *Élise too.*

Clemence recovered first and held out her hand. 'You look so like your daughter, it startled me.'

'People say so. Though others say she resembles her father.'

Her mother wasn't exactly rude but was behaving like an automaton; she hadn't even smiled. Vicky felt mortified for Clemence who was well-mannered and clearly braving the uncomfortable meeting as best she could.

'We'll get you settled in your room soon. I hope you don't mind sharing with Vicky?' Clemence said.

'Not at all,' Élise said, still rather cool and restrained.

'There will be time to talk later on. Meanwhile, Hélène and Étienne are still not back.'

'Will they be safe?' Élise asked, frowning. 'Up there in the wild.'

'There's an old traveller's lodge. As long as they've reached it, they'll be fine. It's basic but at least a shelter from the unprecedented wind we've had. But let me fetch Florence before I show you to your room.'

A few minutes later Florence came running out and instantly the sisters were locked in a fierce embrace, both with tears in their eyes.

Once Élise and Vicky had left their things in their room they all settled under the awning, silent and nervous, as they waited for Jack. After a moment Vicky shrieked and pointed at a shadowy corner of the terrace. Clemence, Florence, and Élise all immediately turned to look.

'Whoa! That's what I call a spider,' Élise said, as if Vicky's shriek had somehow brought her back to life.

A shaft of sunlight penetrated the shadow, illuminating a pale six-inch long spider hiding from the heat and hoping to remain unobtrusive.

'Is it poisonous?' Vicky asked with a horrified expression.

'No. But the bite can hurt,' Clemence replied.

Vicky edged back into her chair. 'What the hell is it?'

'A camel spider. Usually found in the desert.'

As they watched it quickly scuttled away.

'Poor thing,' Clemence added. 'It's probably lost, blown in by last night's wind.'

Theo was in the kitchen organising coffee and Vicky

was fidgeting, unsure if she wanted caffeine or would prefer to sleep for hours. A sound made her jump, and hearing footsteps, Vicky turned to see a policeman appearing at the top of the track, his face giving nothing away. Florence and Élise stood up immediately, pushing their chairs back as they did. Vicky could see the struggle on her aunt's face. Desperate to hear the truth but equally desperate not to. Élise moved to stand behind her sister, hands gripping her shoulders as if she might somehow prevent the awful news from reaching inside her. Florence, twisting, glanced round at her and clutched hold of her wrist.

Then they saw Jack appear at the top of the track too.

Vicky watched Florence raise a fluttery hand as if to ward off bad news and felt her own fear spiralling.

Jack ran to his wife and wrapped his arms around her. 'It wasn't Bea. It wasn't Bea,' he repeated, his voice breaking.

Vicky sank back into the chair, her feelings overwhelming her. What did this mean? Could Bea still be alive? Could she? Élise sat down beside her and held her hand tightly. They stared at each other, and it seemed to Vicky that her mother felt as unsure as she did. Of course, it was bloody brilliant the body they found wasn't Bea, but who was the dead woman? And where was Bea?

The policeman came over and they all looked up at him.

He coughed before speaking in French. 'The young woman we found was American. Frieda Collins, the proprietor of a dress shop.'

Vicky gasped and held a hand over her mouth.

The policeman turned to her. 'You knew her?'

'Not well. I met her once.'

'I knew instantly,' Jack said, holding on to his wife's hands. 'The body couldn't have been Beatrice. What remained of her hair was auburn, not like Bea's blonde hair at all. I desperately wanted to tell you, but I had to wait for the police car to bring me back. Nobody would drive up here last night.'

The policeman beckoned to Jack, had a quiet word with him, but didn't say anything about how Frieda had died, and then he left them to it.

Vicky began to cry. Partly from relief, partly from the dread of what might still be ahead. And partly for poor Frieda. She remembered seeing her as she sauntered into the bar, a glamorous woman with a cloud of bright auburn hair, wearing a scandalously sheer silk dress and gold high heels. She thought of the abandoned shop. *Frieda's Frocks.* The empty dress rails, the reams of untidy paperwork scattered about, and the piles of abandoned boxes on the floor. The bald man's face in the window. What had happened for Frieda to deserve such an awful fate? Was it an accident? It seemed unlikely. In that case had someone hurt her? Killed her?

And would they ever find out the truth?

The one thing Vicky did know was whatever had happened, this nightmare was not over.

CHAPTER 41

Clemence

Kasbah du Paradis

When Theo came back out to the terrace carrying a jug of coffee, Clemence saw the shock and distress spreading over his face at the sight of Florence weeping and Jack already steering her back inside.

Clemence jumped up. 'It's not what you think,' she said, and took the coffee pot from him, placing it on the table then drawing him away by the elbow. 'It's all right. They're tears of relief,' she said.

He looked surprised. 'It wasn't Beatrice they found?'

'No.'

'Thank God,' he said.

'Yes of course. But . . .'

'They still have no news.'

She sighed. 'Apparently Frieda Collins was a young American woman who went missing some days ago. Her body would have been decomposing rapidly in this heat, probably why they mistook her for Beatrice, but the dead woman had the wrong hair colour.'

'So, the police found the remains of a young white woman and jumped to conclusions. How did she die?'

'We don't know. All the police would tell us was that she'd been identified.'

'Gives us a bit of a clue though. If her death was suspicious, rather than an accident, she could well have been mixed up in whatever is going on. Maybe even spying on the security services here for the Americans. There's no love lost.'

'Vicky knew Frieda slightly. Do you think the police will want to talk to her?'

'Probably. Tell her not to say anything unless it's to Officer Alami.'

He was about to continue when Ahmed approached them followed by Clemence's mother and the dogs.

'She has been asking for you, Madame,' Ahmed said. 'I tried to distract her.'

'That's fine, Ahmed. Thank you.'

He inclined his head and left.

Madeleine instantly attached herself to Theo, stroking his arm, smiling and telling him about the bats in her head, as the dogs wagged their tails and snuffled around them before racing over to the breakfast table.

'Madeleine and I will take a turn around the garden,' he said.

Clemence nodded and her mother gave her a look of triumph. Theo grinned and linked arms with her. 'We'll be fine, won't we?' he said.

As the pair wandered off, Clemence saw how easily Theo communicated with her mother who was leaning against him, laughing and giggling like a young girl.

Nadia brought out the breakfast of croissants, toast and yogurt.

'Thank you,' Clemence said. 'I'm so sorry but the coffee is lukewarm now. Could you bring us a fresh pot please? And when you have a moment, a breakfast tray for Jack and Florence in their room.'

Vicky and Élise had gone inside too but they would want something when they came out again. Meanwhile, she was glad of a few moments alone to absorb the fact that Theo was back. He was the kindest man, but her usually peaceful life had been turned upside down and she needed a few minutes to herself. She sat under the awning and listening to the cawing of the birds, wondered how she would go about telling him the truth. It really wasn't a simple ordinary thing that you could just blurt out. Should it be just a little here and there to lessen the impact? She had no way of knowing what he would say but however he reacted, she *was* going to do it. She settled down and flicked the pages of a French *Elle* magazine. It had a photograph of Nicole de Lamargé on the cover, taken by Duffy, and had been a special blue themed edition they'd called 'The Blue Wave'. Clemence had bought it for Madeleine.

A few minutes later, Élise and Vicky joined her. Clemence was waiting for an opportunity to speak with

Élise alone but the woman hadn't seemed very approach-
able and Clemence didn't know what to make of her. And
anyway, what right did she have to grill her about Victor?

'Oh,' her granddaughter said, leaning over. 'I haven't
seen that issue yet.'

'Here. Take it.' Clemence passed it over.

'Are you sure?'

'I wasn't reading it, just passing the time.'

'Thank you. Mind if I take it to our room?'

Clemence frowned. 'Don't you want any breakfast?'

'I'm not really hungry.'

'I'll ask Nadia to bring you some orange juice. By the
way, Theo asked me to warn you not to say anything
about Frieda, except to Officer Alami.'

Vicky agreed not to and left.

Clemence invited Élise to sit with her. Nadia brought
out the fresh coffee and more croissants and poured.

Silence followed. And with neither of them speaking the
air crackled with tension. Theo and her mother wandered
over but as soon as he saw Clemence looking uneasy he
backed off.

'Madeleine and I will take breakfast in the annexe,' he
said and shepherded her away.

After a few minutes, feeling even more ill at ease and
unable to either sit still or politely leave, Clemence let out
a long slow breath. 'I imagine you have questions for me,'
she said, certain Élise must have judged her for allowing
her baby to be taken away. Vicky and her mother looked
very alike and, riveted by this, Clemence couldn't stop
admiring the woman's dark wavy hair. With just a few

strands of white, fewer than her younger sister Florence, it was lustrous and thick, and she had huge expressive eyes, almost the colour of cognac.

'Yes.'

'What you really want to know, I cannot reveal, but could you tell me about Victor, instead? If you don't mind?'

Élise stared at her feet and when she spoke her voice was cold. 'You can't *reveal* why you never came to see your son?'

Clemence swallowed hard. 'It was complicated.'

Élise shook her head and looked away. Clemence thought her very prickly and realised she would have to weigh her own words very carefully.

'What kind of a man was he?' she asked.

Élise turned back, eyes narrowed, openly hostile. 'Don't tell me you care?'

'Please, Élise.'

'I simply don't understand how you could just abandon him?'

Clemence sighed. 'It was beyond my control.'

'And later? Once you were a mature adult and had all of this?' She gestured widely at the kasbah. 'Was it still *beyond your control*?'

The scathing tone of her voice made Clemence wince, but she managed to say, 'In a manner of speaking, yes.'

'Very well, I'll tell you what he was like,' Élise said, as if recognising she would not hear anything more convincing. 'He was brave, reckless, kind. And I loved him. I still do. Even after all these years, it hurts.'

Clemence could not speak.

'The day he was murdered by the Nazis was the worst day of my entire life. I thought I would die. I wanted to die. Rage and sorrow completely consumed me. I couldn't breathe. I couldn't eat. And all I wanted was revenge.'

'Do you feel able to tell me how it happened?'

'Why does it matter to you?'

'Because I have never been able to stop thinking about what happened. About him. Because I was his mother once. And because I need to know.'

Élise narrowed her eyes as if trying to work her out.

'There were reasons, Élise, I promise you. Terrible reasons. And I will tell you as soon as I am able.'

There was a long silence interrupted only by the two dogs barking somewhere in the grounds.

'Instead of frightening us,' Élise said, 'the execution made the Resistance stronger.'

Clemence wrung her hands in her lap as she pictured it. 'Was Jacques there?'

'No. He couldn't bear to watch. Victor's death broke his heart, you see. He never married and had brought him up alone. It was just the two of them. He wasn't always the easiest of men but afterwards he helped the Resistance and Vicky adores him. She brought him back to life.'

'Poor Jacques,' Clemence said, her eyes filling with tears.

'I remember feeling sick,' Élise continued. 'Terribly sick, as the prisoners were lined up and tied loosely to specially erected poles.'

'How many prisoners?'

'Four. There were four of them. I felt the world stop

spinning as we waited.' Élise was speaking so softly Clemence had to lean across to hear.

'The firing squad took aim. It seemed to go on forever, even though it was only seconds. One by one, three of them went limp, bodies sagging as they slid down the poles, heads drooping. Lifeless. I . . .'

'It's all right. Take your time,' Clemence whispered.

'One minute they were breathing human beings with families and people who loved them. Everyone in the crowd was sobbing. Only . . . only Victor was left.'

'Was there ever any chance he might be spared?'

Élise shook her head. 'The firing squad took aim again. I remember wanting to scream but my throat had closed, and I was groaning instead. Then, just before he fell, he started singing loud and clear.'

'He sang?' Clemence asked, imagining her son at that moment, knowing his life was about to end.

'"Le Chant Des Partisans",' Élise said. 'The unofficial anthem of the Resistance. He managed one line, before . . .'

Clemence felt her eyes grow hot and blinked rapidly.

'He died still singing as the shots rang out across the square. We all joined in, humming under our breath until the firing squad turned and pointed their rifles at us. In the space of a heartbeat, his life was gone, and my life was changed forever.'

'I think you only love like that once in a lifetime,' Clemence managed to say as her tears began to fall.

'He was the love of my life.'

'Oh, my dear.'

'I am happy with Henri, of course I am, but it's another

kind of affection. He and I . . . well, we're good friends but we both lost our other halves.' She ran a hand through her hair and blinked rapidly. 'I'm sorry you didn't get to know your son. He was a fine man. You would have been proud.'

Élise took a breath, clearly holding on to herself, though she had tears in her eyes too.

Clemence felt so untethered she was trembling, but Élise reached out and the two women who had loved Victor in their different ways gripped each other's hands.

CHAPTER 42

The next day felt like an anticlimax, empty and devoid of purpose after the highly charged emotion of the previous days. Jack and Florence returned to Marrakech accompanied by the police to appear at a press briefing. Vicky and Élise remained at the kasbah to await Hélène and Étienne's return. Except Clemence, riven by sorrow, still felt unbuckled – the details of Victor's death remaining so vivid in her mind, in her heart, and in her whole being. She had learnt to accommodate the loss of her baby within her, and even the loss during the war of him as an adult. Now she had to find a way to live with knowing more about the loss of the man he had become. She regretted never going to the Dordogne to see him, although there had been a reason why she had not. And that reason remained.

When she slipped out into the garden feeling heavy and dull, she drew to an abrupt halt. The bristly-haired wild boars who freely roamed the land had broken through the fencing and with their long snouts and powerful bodies, had ploughed the sun-baked ground in search of food, rooting and trampling as they fed, leaving large areas of earth uprooted and disturbed.

'Dammit,' she muttered, throwing her hands up in the air. Then she fetched a fork to repair as much of the garden as she could.

The warmth on her skin, the clear bright sunshine and the garlic and mint drifting on the clean air made her feel a little lighter. From time to time, as she worked, she gazed up at the rocky mountainside, as if transfixed, steadying herself on the handle of the fork and taking stock of how much her life here had meant to her. It had been the place into which she had poured the love she'd lost. And over time the loss had transformed into love for the land itself. For her home. For the gentle rhythm of her days. And it had been enough. But now? No.

After a little while, Vicky – spotting her grandmother from a window – came out to help. They did not speak much. From the drawn expression on Vicky's face, Clemence guessed she needed the distraction of physical activity just as much as her grandmother. But however quiet, Vicky's presence still brightened her, felt like a gift, a privilege she didn't really deserve. If only there had been a different way back then, she wouldn't still be plagued by guilt and haunted by the fear of exposure. If only her mother hadn't insisted on such a soul-destroying pact. And yet what other choice had there really been for either of them? *But still,* she thought. *How different my life might have been . . .*

They worked peacefully together for an hour but then were forced to stop. With the sun so high in the sky it was sweltering, so they downed tools and turned back towards the house in relief.

'Did you see that?' Vicky said as they neared the terrace.

'What?'

'Over there. I don't know exactly. I just thought I saw something in the trees.'

'I hope it's not the boars back.' Clemence raised a hand to shade her eyes from the sun. 'I can't see anything. May have just been a shadow. When the sun is high like this everything shimmers. You can imagine anything.'

'I can believe it,' Vicky said, unnerved.

As heat-drowsy insects buzzed lazily around the lunch table, nobody spoke. Vicky seemed jittery, strained, tapping her fingers on the table while constantly glancing around, Élise appeared to be lost in thought and even Theo was quiet. Theo and Élise had spent the morning down in Imlil, questioning the villagers. They had found out nothing new, except for one small thing. Apparently, on the day Beatrice had gone missing, a man on a motor-bike with a sidecar had raced through their village and on down the hill at high-speed, killing three chickens. People had muttered that he was riding like a bat out of hell.

'I hope you'll like this,' Clemence said, as Nadia laid the dish on the table and ginger and cinnamon filled the air.

'Smells gorgeous.' Vicky nudged her mother. 'Doesn't it, *Maman*?'

Élise blinked uncertainly.

'It's a Moroccan chicken dish,' Clemence said. 'Traditionally made with pigeons. Ours is chicken cooked with spices, layered with crispy *warqa* pastry shell and a herby omelette.'

'What's that on top?' Vicky asked as Clemence began to serve the pie.

'It's a mix of crunchy almonds, sugar, orange flower water and butter.'

'I thought I could smell oranges,' Élise said, speaking up at last. Her voice sounded empty. Clemence wondered if their earlier conversation might still be playing on her mind and she wanted to say something comforting, though not in front of the others.

'Hopefully Hélène and Étienne will be back soon,' she said instead.

'When do you think we'll know if the press briefing has had any impact?' Élise asked, looking at Theo.

He scratched the back of his neck. 'Could be days, weeks even.'

'The waiting is awful.' Vicky's voice caught as she spoke and she put down her fork. 'I'm sorry. I'm just not hungry.'

'You haven't eaten anything today. You need to eat.' Élise scrutinised her daughter's face. 'To keep your strength up. I hope you haven't been on one of those crazy diets again.'

'Oh, for God's sake,' Vicky muttered and gave her mother a withering look.

'*Chérie*. I didn't mean—'

'No!' Vicky interrupted, with a wretched look. 'What the hell does it matter if I'm dieting or not, when Bea could be lying dead in a ditch somewhere?'

'Darling.' Élise stretched out a hand to her.

'I can't stand it. Not any more. I can't bear it!' She pushed back her chair as she stood and backed away, her eyes suddenly streaming with tears. She turned and ran towards her room, leaving Élise looking downcast.

'Should I maybe go to her?' Clemence asked gently. 'She's been on a bit of a knife's edge this morning.'

Élise sighed. 'Not unless you want your head bitten off. She's best left to calm down on her own. She only lashes out like this when she's terribly upset. It's all been far too much for her.'

There was a short silence.

'Did you make anything of the man on the motorbike story?' Clemence asked to change the subject.

Élise shrugged. 'I really don't know.'

When Ahmed brought Madeleine to eat her dessert with the rest of them, he tried to encourage her to sit in Vicky's empty chair opposite Theo, but she shook her head and poked Clemence in the back.

'Not a single word. Not a single word about the fire,' the old lady muttered, and then cackled as if it were a huge joke.

Clemence froze. Surely her mother wasn't going to reveal the truth. Not now. Not in front of everyone.

Theo glanced at Clemence with a puzzled look, and she realised he had picked up on Madeleine's remark, although the others had not.

'Up! Up! Up!' her mother insisted.

Clemence managed to smile and changed seats.

Madeleine shot her an acid look then looked self-important as she took her place and reached for Theo's hand. With his eyes still on Clemence he patted the old woman's hand in return.

Pudding was diamond-shaped baklava composed of crisp, flaky layers of pastry, a walnut-cinnamon filling and a sweet honey and lemon glaze. Madeleine ate hers greedily and held out her plate for more.

When they'd all finished and left the table, Nadia settled Madeleine down for a rest, and Clemence took Élise aside. 'If you wish to rest in the sitting room, please do feel free.'

'Thank you. I think I will. I want to give Vicky some time alone.'

'You must be so worried, and for Florence too.'

Élise bit her lip to stop the tremble. After a moment she said, 'I am. My sister went through so much in France. It just isn't fair.'

'She told me about France.' Clemence felt a chill at the memory of Florence's confession and knew the time was fast approaching when she would have to confess too.

'Did she? She never usually speaks of it, not even to us.'

'Sometimes it's easier with a stranger.'

That night Clemence and Theo headed towards her bedroom and the marginally cooler air of the fan. A dark blue haze filled the room with narrow splinters of gold from a patio light outside. As she lay on top of the bed in a gossamer-thin nightdress, luxuriating in the sensation of crisp clean bed linen beneath her, she turned to look at Theo in the half light.

I hate that we lost so much time together, she thought, *so many days, weeks, months, years.* Where might they have been had she dared to lay bare the truth about her past? She shifted her thoughts forward to the present. Could she tell him now? Just the thought of it made her feel defenceless, and she had to force herself to swallow back her fear. But she'd had enough of wrestling with this dilemma. It was time.

She braced herself, ready to speak. Maybe it would be easier like this in semi-darkness. But then he said, 'You, my darling, are a sight to behold.'

Clemence smiled.

He pushed up her nightdress and ran a hand over her bare thigh. She shivered at his touch.

'Did you lock the door?' she asked.

'Ah. I'll do it now.' He leapt out of bed, locked the door, closed the shutters, and switched off the exterior light, plunging the room into complete darkness. Then she heard him pulling off his boxers before rejoining her on the bed. He was so gentle yet muscular and vigorous and as he lay beside her, his hand between her thighs, she felt softer, more relaxed than before. Ready. She smiled up at him and he leant down to kiss her before pulling back.

'I've missed you,' he said. 'All these years.'

Clemence stretched up to hold the back of his neck and draw him close again. He resisted and his fingers moved higher up her thigh. With a sharp intake of breath, she felt terribly exposed but allowed herself to yield rather than turn away. She caught a trace of sandalwood and pepper on his neck mingling with the tang of sweat and her favourite orange blossom oil. It was her last thought as, unable to hold on, she arched her back.

Later, when it was over, she began to laugh.

'What?' he said, raising himself on one elbow.

'I'm happy.'

'I'm glad. It is permitted to love even at the darkest of times.'

'Let's cool down a bit.' She got out of bed, turned on the bedside lamp, and flicked on a second fan.

'God, that's noisy,' he said.

'It's old and a bit rickety.' She looked down at him and smiled. 'Like us.'

He laughed. 'Speak for yourself.'

She switched the fan off again and got back into bed, this time beneath the cover.

'Clem,' he said a few minutes later, leaning over and lifting her head from the pillow just enough to be able to see her face more clearly. 'I sensed there was something going on at lunch. You know, something Madeleine said about a fire.'

She nodded and took a long slow breath. 'It's not easy to talk about.'

He removed his hands from the back of her neck. 'You don't have to tell me anything. Honestly.'

She felt unsure, but knew she had to, sooner or later.

'I need to tell you but it's hard to figure out where to start,' she said, knowing what she was about to reveal could ruin everything. He could walk out of the door and this time it would be for good.

'Take your time,' he said, encouraging her gently.

She stared right into his eyes – his tender, warm eyes – and felt terribly scared. This was a secret she had kept for most of her life; how could she possibly say the words out loud? She wanted to cry, run away, anything to force down her spiralling anxiety. Instead, she took a breath and said, 'I killed my father.'

He sprang back. 'Jesus, Clemmie!'

She closed her eyes. 'I knew you'd see me differently if I told you.'

'But what *are* you telling me? It was an accident, right? A . . . fire?'

Clemence squeezed her eyes shut, not able to look at his expression for one more moment.

The day after her fourteenth birthday, she had looked up the word in her dictionary for the first time.

Patricide.

The killing of one's father.

She had read legends and stories about sons who had killed their fathers but could not find as many daughters. Thinking up ways she might engineer a cruel death for her father became a fantasy. A game she had played. Until eight years after her fourteenth birthday when it became more than a game.

She opened her eyes, shook her head.

'I shot my father point-blank, in cold blood.'

CHAPTER 43

Vicky

Vicky tried to focus on the creaking sounds of the house, but the relentless noise in her head was shrill: an intrusive high-pitched whine worse than the mosquito she could also hear. Or maybe it was just the insect. She tossed and turned in her bed, growing hot and clammy, certain her sheets were becoming damper with every minute.

If she hadn't been sharing with her mother, she would have flicked on the light and opened a book or might even have got up to do some more drawing. A song she'd heard endlessly on the radio in London kept repeating in her mind adding to the sound of the whining insect. 'I'll Follow the Sun', by the Beatles – and that one line about losing a friend – she didn't want those words dominating her mind, but even so she carried on humming the tune in her head.

No matter what she did, the longer she lay awake the more overwhelming her desire to get up became. She was boiling and had to do something. In the end, she couldn't bear it and as Élise murmured in her sleep, Vicky grabbed a torch and crept out, soundlessly closing the door behind her.

Her torch lighting the way ahead of her, she tried every exterior door, one after the other. All locked. It was airless inside the house and sweating profusely, she felt trapped and panicky. The heavy nighttime air weighed her down so much more than the soaring temperatures of the day, which were eased somehow by the bright sunlight and a bit of a breeze. At least up here in the mountains they were. This claustrophobic heat now seemed to expand until it become solid and, desperate for cooler air, she couldn't breathe. She stood still for a moment to listen. Nobody else was awake and in the kitchen she spotted a key had been left in the door lock. She quickly turned it and slid open the top and bottom bolts. It couldn't hurt to go out just for a few seconds.

She breathed in deeply as she stepped outside, feeling some relief. It was still hot, of course, and there was no wind, but at least there was air. The noise in her head had silenced, and taking another long slow breath and moving a couple of steps away from the open kitchen door, she glanced up at the sky. The moon wasn't full but was bright enough to cast a ghostly silvery-blue light across the whole garden. It was a little eerie, though not as spectral as the abandoned French villas in the Palmeraie had seemed that awful night.

Vicky watched the leaves as they rustled a little. There was a sudden crack in the darkness. It came again and she froze. Was somebody out there? Everything went silent apart from the sound of creatures padding and scratching in the bushes – she could see the glitter of their eyes. When a rat scurried over her bare foot, Vicky recoiled, coming to her senses. She shouldn't be out here with nothing on her feet. She shouldn't be out here at all! There could be scorpions. The wild boar could be back.

Vicky turned round to return to the kitchen and as she did, she definitely heard movement behind her. But this time from something much larger than a rat. Before she could shout out, a large hand was pressed over her mouth so hard that it hurt, and the man was gripping her body with his other hand.

'Scream, even once, and I will cut your throat.'

She recognised his voice.

Trapped by him, she still tried to scream – but the terror rising in her throat and a mouth which had gone dry suddenly meant nothing came out. This was it. Patrice had finally come for her. Just as she had feared he would.

He stuffed a handkerchief or something into her mouth and tied what felt like a scarf over it. She could feel the steel of a knife's sharp edge against her skin, imagined him slitting her throat open. Saw her blood spurting in an arc across the wall. Felt herself falling to the ground senseless. She didn't want to die. She really, really didn't want to die.

She thought she heard a noise somewhere in the house. Or maybe outside. She couldn't tell. Her racing pulse was distorting everything. Urgent now, he pushed her ahead of him through the house and stopped in the main corridor.

'We will wait here for a moment,' he hissed.

On the edge of passing out, Vicky whimpered and suddenly nothing was real any more. Snakes were writhing in her head, in her eyes, her brain, her mouth – snakes with forked, red-tipped tongues. Was this what he had done to Bea? Taken her at knifepoint. Driven her mad. Killed her.

Hardly able to breathe, Vicky broke out in a sweat and began to shake. *Please save me, Maman. Please make this stop. I'll do anything. I'll never fight with you again. I'll always think about others before myself. I'll never be jealous or unkind.*

'Not . . . even . . . a whisper,' he ordered, interrupting her thoughts.

When it seemed as if everything was quiet, and nobody else was up, he told her to lead him to Clemence's bedroom. 'Don't even think of misleading me.'

Too terrified to disobey, she did as she was told.

At Clemence's door he instructed her to turn the handle. It was locked.

'Tap on the door. Tell her it's you,' he said and loosened the tie from around her mouth for a moment.

'It's me, Vicky,' she mumbled after she'd knocked. He instantly tightened the cloth again.

When she heard the key turn, she shoved the door open with her bare foot as noisily as she could in the hope of warning her grandmother.

Clemence was standing there pale as snow, wearing her

white nightdress and holding a lantern. Vicky's fear rocketed. Where was Theo? Wasn't he there?

'We need to talk,' Patrice growled as he pushed Vicky in ahead of him.

When they were fully inside the room, Vicky could see Theo really wasn't there. Had he got up for some reason? Or was he sleeping somewhere else?

'Well,' Clemence said, her voice chilly but calm. 'This is unusual.'

'You still think I don't know what happened in Casablanca?' Patrice replied. 'You think I don't know what you did?'

'I don't think anything when I'm woken in the middle of the night.'

'Well perhaps it's time you did.'

'What do you want, Patrice?' Clemence asked, still insanely composed though surely it had to be an act?

'I already told you, I want what is mine.' He paused. 'Now, if you don't mind!'

Clemence regarded him coolly. 'If I am to give you what you want, I expect what I want in return.'

'And?'

'You tell us where Beatrice is.'

'How should I know?'

He was a good actor, Vicky thought, surprised she could even think at all with the edge of a sharp knife still held against her throat. He had sounded genuinely surprised.

She snorted. 'Come on, Patrice.'

'Just get on with it. I need the gold casket and its contents right now.'

'Why? Why do you need it?'

'I'm leaving Morocco. Its sale will set me up nicely.'

'Blotted your copybook again, Patrice?' She turned towards the nightstand and, putting the lantern on top of it, sat down on her bed to open the drawer. 'Very well, you've made your point.'

The room tilted and Vicky whimpered again, feeling sick and faint. Everything was pitching and crashing and falling apart, and she had to force herself not to buckle under the awful terror. If Patrice got what he wanted, would he go? Or did he still plan to kill her and Clemence?

Clemence turned back round. Suddenly, everything seemed to happen at once. Vicky caught sight of a gun at her grandmother's side And within another second, Clemence had lifted her arm. A shot rang out, so shockingly loud, Vicky hardly knew what had happened. Patrice screamed as he crumpled to the floor, inadvertently releasing her. She stared blankly as he writhed in agony and for a moment, she didn't even grasp that she was free of him. But then she saw the knife lying on the floor. Saw it had fallen from his grip and she ran towards the door.

Clemence stood over Patrice, still holding the gun. 'Seeing as you have such an excellent memory of the past, you might also recall I am an excellent shot.'

He lay on the floor moaning in agony, his eyes searching for the knife.

'No, you don't,' Clemence said and kicked it out of his reach. 'Try to move again and I'll shoot you in the other knee too.'

On some strange level, her grandmother seemed to be enjoying herself; with a glimmer of understanding, Vicky knew suddenly that Clemence could easily kill Patrice if she decided to.

The door opened and Theo came running in, eyes wide and almost knocking Vicky over.

'What the hell happened?' He was staring at Patrice groaning on the floor. 'Clem?'

'I didn't shoot to kill,' Clemence said coolly. 'It's just his knee. Could you take the ties from Vicky's mouth, please, then pick up the knife and get some rope from Ahmed to tie this bastard up.'

Once Vicky was free, she fell to her knees, retching. Clemence lifted her up with one hand and pointed her in the right direction. In the bathroom, Vicky vomited only once, then splashed her face and stared at her reflection. Her skin was completely white. Back in the bedroom she watched Theo return with Ahmed and together they tied Patrice's wrists together and his ankles too. The man was very pale and bleeding. *One day, I will tell my grandchildren about this,* Vicky thought. *I will tell them how my own grand- mother stopped a killer from killing me.*

Clemence ripped her pillowcase in two, and as he screamed in agony, she tied a tourniquet above Patrice's knee. From her bathroom, she carried an open first-aid box and attached a large pad to the side of his knee where the bullet had passed through.

'Hospital,' Patrice groaned. 'I need a hospital.'

'Not until you tell us what you've done with Beatrice,' Clemence said.

'Haven't seen her.'

Clemence sighed.

'Have it your own way. I don't know about you, Theo, but I'm sure Vicky and I could do with a coffee. Shall we head over to the kitchen?' She moved towards the door.

'I swear,' Patrice was saying, his face screwing up in pain. 'I swear I haven't seen her.'

'Come on, let's get our coffee, Vicky. You'll feel better for it. Theo, lead the way.'

'On my father's life,' Patrice pleaded.

As she reached the door Clemence spun back to study him, cool as a cucumber. 'He's already dead, Patrice.'

'Can't you see I'm bleeding?'

'It's not an artery.'

'Clemence!'

'Tell us where the girl is. For her parents' sake. Then I'll help you.'

'I don't know. Please, I'm begging you.'

'Like Jimmy was begging you,' Vicky said from where she stood by the door.

After they all left the room and stood in the corridor, Patrice began to shriek for help.

'What do you think?' Clemence asked in a low voice.

Theo shook his head, seeming shaken by how cool Clemence was being. 'Hard to tell. Maybe he really doesn't know where Beatrice is.'

'I think we probably do have to get him to hospital.'

'Yes. Ahmed and I can load him onto a mule and get him down to the jeep. That's all we can do. The police will want to know what happened. They'll question you both.'

342

Clemence sighed, beginning to look rather dazed now. 'Give him some brandy first.'

Vicky and Clemence went to the kitchen for coffee and a few minutes later, as dawn was breaking, they sat on the day bed on the terrace to watch as the two men carried a swearing Patrice to the mule. At the sight of him bound hand and foot and being bundled onto the back of the animal, Vicky felt a muscle in her jaw twitching. As the men began the journey down the track, they heard Patrice still screaming at Clemence.

'I'll get you for this, you bitch! I'll get you.'

'Shut the fuck up, Patrice,' Theo was saying, 'or we'll dump you on the mountainside. Great predatory birds up here. Falcons, eagles, hawks, vultures. Nothing more delicious than a man's eyeball.'

Seeing how ridiculous Patrice looked lying on his stomach, head lolling over the side of the mule, Vicky began to chuckle and then to laugh. And his threats to extract revenge only made it worse.

Dislocated by fear, shock, and the sheer relief of being freed from his grip, a feeling of madness rampaged through her. She took a juddering breath, noticed her grandmother's puzzled face and eyes watering and gasping for air, she felt the laughter erupting again. She doubled over and held her sides to stop the stitch. She sounded manic, felt manic, certain this crazy fit would never end. But when she saw her mother coming upon the scene with a look of horror on her face, Vicky's hysteria ended, instantly changing to great gulping sobs. She ran, stumbling and tripping, eyes streaming, towards her.

'I heard the shot,' Élise said, her voice shaking. 'I didn't know where you were until Ahmed told me what had happened and told me to stay put until it was safe.'

Then she held out her arms.

'I'm sorry,' Vicky cried. 'I'm so, so sorry for bringing all this on everyone.'

CHAPTER 44

Clemence

Clemence and Theo had not talked about her terrible confession. Now he was gone, and she had no idea if he would be coming back. She kept going over his stunned reaction and each time she did, her blood ran cold. She closed her eyes and was right back in the awful moment when she had said. 'I shot my father point-blank, in cold blood.'

He'd covered his mouth, blinking in astonishment and she saw the look of horror in his eyes.

'You *murdered* your father?'

'You're shocked.'

'Good God! I'm not sure what I feel.'

'You're shocked,' she repeated, tears forming in her eyes. 'Of course, you are. Anyone would be.'

He groaned and sat bolt upright, head in hands.

'Say something. Please say something,' but she could see he was struggling to find the words.

He took a long slow breath and said, more to himself than to her, 'I'm stunned. I really don't know what else to say.'

She dashed the tears away.

He didn't look at her for a few minutes more, but then he swung round, and his eyes focused on hers with such a look of anguish it destroyed her. 'I'll sleep on a sofa,' he said.

'Theo.'

He held up a hand. 'I just need a little time alone to digest what you've told me.'

He got out of bed, turned on a light, and in total silence grabbed his clothes and left.

He was a good man. She knew that. But would she ever get the chance to tell him why she had done it? Would he come back?

The two police who arrived at the kasbah later that morning were not known to her. The more heavily built one gave her a flinty look as she offered them coffee and a seat in her study.

'We'll stand if it's all the same to you,' he said, without even the hint of a smile.

'And the coffee?'

Clearly the boss, he shook his head.

The other man had pale transparent eyes that seemed to look right through her. He was the one who asked her to explain exactly what had happened. And as clearly as possible she did so.

'So, it was you who fired the shot?'

'I just said I did.'

'And this granddaughter of yours,' the other man said. 'The one you say this Callier man had captured.'

Clemence bristled. 'I didn't *say* as you put it. I'm telling you what happened.'

The man ignored her comment. 'She is still here?' he asked.

'Of course. She was gagged and Patrice Callier held a knife at her throat. She had a terrible shock.'

'We'd like to speak to her, verify the story.'

'She's asleep. Can you not just take my word for it? And there are others who can attest to it.'

He shook his head. 'The girl, please.'

Annoyed, Clemence turned on her heels and left the room returning a few minutes later with a sleepy-eyed Vicky wearing only a bathrobe over her nightdress.

The man asked her to tell the story from the beginning. When she had finished and had fallen silent again, he said, 'You have nothing more to add?'

She shook her head.

'Why did he come here?'

'He believes I have an inheritance belonging to him,' Clemence said.

'And do you?'

'Of course not. He is deranged and extremely dangerous.'

Clemence was relieved Vicky hadn't mentioned Jimmy's murder.

'Victoria's cousin is Beatrice Jackson,' she said. 'The missing girl. Are you aware of any developments following the recent press briefing?'

347

The man shook his head and seeming impatient to get on with his day, he began to move away. 'Thank you. That will be all.'

'But what has happened to Callier?'

'Under arrest in hospital. We are currently questioning the two men who brought him into Marrakech.'

He strode out with the other man following behind.

Vicky sat down, looking utterly drained. 'Will Ahmed and Theo be all right?'

'I'm sure they will. Why not go back to bed?' Clemence suggested, wondering how Theo and Ahmed really were coping with what might turn out to be an interrogation.

'I will. I feel as if I've been run over by a truck.'

'You need rest. Never underestimate the effect of extreme duress on the body. I'll bring you a cool drink.'

Vicky rose to her feet and took two steps but then turned and threw her arms around Clemence. She could feel her granddaughter's tension.

Vicky had been asleep all day, Theo hadn't returned, and neither Clemence nor Élise wanted lunch. It was just too hot. Clemence offered mint tea to her guest and both women tried to unwind in the sitting room, exhausted from talking about Patrice and speculating on where Hélène and Étienne could be. Even though Nadia had closed the shutters, the air was so hot it seemed to draw the fluid from your body. Clemence fanned herself and thought about taking a cold bath. Her mind kept returning to Theo. She still had no idea if he would be coming back and it was impossible to do anything while they were waiting for news of Bea. Clemence had so much on her mind but at least she knew where she had to start with Élise.

She drew a breath and began to haltingly speak. 'When you told me about the way Victor died it was like . . . like hearing a part of me had died too. I know I have no right to feel like that.'

'There are no rights and wrongs when it comes to the people we love. I would be the same if anything were to happen to Vicky. Since I heard about her witnessing her friend being killed, I have constantly feared for her life,' Élise said.

'I know. Me too. Patrice is a far worse man than I ever knew.'

'You knew him years ago?'

'Yes.'

'You said you might tell me more about what happened,' Élise said. 'Was he a part of that?'

'Not really. You're talking about why I didn't go with Jacques and Victor to France, aren't you?'

'Yes.'

'I do owe you an explanation. Can I just start by saying we were living in a time of French colonial privilege? Things were very different.'

Élise's eyes widened. 'Go on.'

'Well . . .' She paused as the door was opened and Nadia carried in a tray with a silver jug of mint tea, a bowl of sugar, and two decorative tea glasses in filigree silver holders. She rested it carefully on a small side table and smiling at them both, left the room.

'She's a good girl,' Clemence said and poured out the tea. 'Do put your own sugar in.'

Élise stirred in one spoonful.

Clemence watched her and said, 'I don't know what I would have done without Nadia and her brother Ahmed. They're like family to me . . . Right, where was I?'

'French privilege.'

'You might say I'm only living here now because of the privilege.' Clemence shot her a wry smile. 'I was born in 1892 and grew up in a feudal world where my father was, to put it bluntly, a despot. Chattels we were, my mother and I, but I was left money when he died.'

Élise was looking at her, head tilted to one side, listening intently.

Clemence took a moment to remember him. The man who believed he could have and do anything to anyone, his hubris equal to his excessive wealth. The man who had been a trusted advisor to the Sultan of Morocco. The man who had effectively chiselled away at her confidence, for his own amusement. And as she remembered, a harsh wind blew through the wounds that had never healed.

'He and the French settlers along with their supporters in France tried to prevent any move towards Moroccan autonomy and looked down on the Moroccans. I kept my friendship with mixed-race Jacques, the son of my father's driver, a secret.'

Élise didn't speak.

Clemence looked at her. Was it her imagination or was the other woman already judging her again? After a moment she closed her eyes and carried on, speaking almost to herself. 'My mother was destroyed by my father. I'm not surprised she lost her mind eventually. He was cruel, hated women – I have no idea why – and he enjoyed controlling her, hurting her. '

'Surely he didn't hate you too, his daughter?'

Clemence gave a bitter laugh. 'Oh yes.'

'Any brothers or sisters?'

'No. Short of throwing herself down our grand marble staircase, I think my mother did everything she could to rid herself of any possible pregnancies.'

'She didn't want any other children to suffer. Is that what you're saying?'

'Exactly.'

'So what happened? Why didn't you leave home, leave for France with Victor and Jacques? Your baby and his father?'

'Jacques had to get Victor away quickly for his own safety and I was . . . I was . . . I suppose you'd say I was incapacitated right after the birth. And remember it was 1914, right at the beginning of the Great War. I was only twenty-two, unmarried and with no means of support. Had I managed to find a way to follow Jacques, my father would have sent men to drag me back. He wanted me at home.

'In any case, it would have ended up being extremely dangerous for Victor. My decision was made entirely for his sake. I had made a pact with my mother, and I had to keep the terms we agreed.'

'I don't understand.'

'It's difficult. The thing is—'

She was interrupted when the door flew open.

'Hélène?' Élise said, rising to her feet as her sister strode towards her.

'Bea. We found Bea,' Hélène said with a catch in her voice. 'We found her!'

Élise gulped. 'Is she . . . ?'

Hélène's voice broke. 'She's alive, Élise. Alive!'

Élise stared at her sister then burst into huge gulping sobs of relief.

The two women hugged. 'Oh my God. I can't believe it,' Élise kept saying, swiping her tears away. 'I can't believe it. Is she injured?'

'A broken ankle. Which explains why she couldn't climb out from where she had lain. But, of course, there could also be other internal injuries.'

They separated and stood beaming at each other both with tears in their eyes.

'Do Florence and Jack know?' Élise asked urgently.

'That's been taken care of,' Hélène said.

'Where did you find her?'

'We spent the first night in an old lodge battered by the crazy wind and late the next day a shepherd looking for some lost sheep found Bea and then us. He signalled we should follow him and took us to where Beatrice must have fallen. I have no idea what she has endured but luckily it was dark, gloomy and damp. It saved her from the heat and the wind. There was a trickle of water from a stream, and that must have kept her alive.'

'Oh God! Oh God!' Élise said.

'The shepherd fetched men from his village, and they constructed a makeshift stretcher. They lifted her out and carried her back to the lodge where I tore my shirt into strips and bound her ankle.'

'I just can't believe it.'

'It was too dark to move on, so we all stayed there for the night.'

'Is she conscious?'

'Barely. She couldn't eat but she was able to sip water from time to time when she was conscious, and I gave her the painkillers I always carry with me on a climb. In the morning we carried her to the village near here. A guy there who spoke some French raced off on a motorbike to alert the police in Marrakech, request an ambulance, and let Jack and Florence know. And another guy with a truck is taking her to meet the ambulance part way.'

'Oh, thank God.'

'She'll be on her way to hospital soon, with Étienne. He knows what he's doing. I should have gone with her too, but I wanted to be the one to tell you.'

'So, what happened to her?'

Hélène shook her head. 'The man who spoke French muttered something about the remains of an old dungeon.'

'You mean the shepherd found her there?' Clemence asked in surprise, stepping forward.

'Yes, I think so.'

'Sounds like it's part of Telouet Kasbah – once owned by the last Pasha, a kind of warlord. But what was Bea even doing there?'

'We don't know.'

'Shall I go and wake Vicky?' Clemence asked. 'She'll want to be among the first to see her.'

'Thank you,' Élise said, but moved as if to hasten after her. 'Maybe I should go.'

'Stay with your sister. I'll bring Vicky to you.'

CHAPTER 45

Vicky

Vicky was only half awake when she heard her grandmother saying her name but couldn't seem to extract herself from the depths of her dream. Wolves were after her. They had been high up in the icy cold of the mountains and she had been running from them. Unable to move forward as the animals gained ground, she'd been slipping and sliding on the snow and ice lying deep beneath her feet.

'Huh,' she said, feeling startled and letting out a puff of air. 'It's you.'

'Vicky, I need to tell you.' Her grandmother's hand pressed her arm, her clear hazel eyes close to Vicky's. 'Bea has been found. She's alive.'

She sat up, fully awake. 'Oh my God! Where?'

'Hélène found her higher up the mountain. On her

way to hospital now – she was barely conscious but was able to drink some water. I'm afraid it's all we know.'

'Was it Patrice?'

'It's unclear.'

'Where's my mother?'

'In the drawing room with your aunt.'

Vicky scrambled out of bed, the intense relief making her dizzy. She slipped on her robe, glancing in the mirror at her eyes which were huge and feverish in contrast to the pallor of her face.

'*Maman!* Isn't it wonderful?' she said as she found Élise, grasping her mother's hands hard. 'We must go straight to Marrakech to see her.'

Élise was about to speak but Hélène stepped in, adding a note of caution when she said, 'Your cousin is severely dehydrated, and we don't yet understand the full extent of her injuries. Only her immediate family will be allowed in at the moment.'

Vicky frowned. 'But I need to go. You must understand. I more than anyone. What happened to her is my fault. I should never have asked her to come to Morocco. And I . . . I—'

'Let's leave it for it a day or two,' Hélène said, interrupting and ignoring her protests.

Vicky shook her head. 'But I *must* know if she's all right. I was the one who led her into danger. Me!' She knew her voice had risen sharply and did her best to control it.

'None of us can know how she is yet,' her aunt said, and continued in the same annoyingly calm, even way. 'Until the doctors confirm her condition, we need to wait.'

'But you're a nurse,' she burst out in response to this. 'Couldn't you tell?'

'I did what I could, but she could have internal injuries, and hypothermia or dehydration are hard to see.'

Vicky opened her mouth to protest again but Élise stepped in. 'I think it's for the best, *chérie*. We really must think of Florence and Jack, give them a little bit of time.'

'You must be exhausted,' Clemence said, glancing at the elder sister and joining the conversation.

Hélène smiled and glanced down at her mud-streaked trousers and dusty walking boots. 'Filthy too.'

'True, you look like shit,' Élise said, and they both laughed. They seemed giddy with relief. 'So, when you've had a shower—'

'And a sleep!'

'. . . we have a lot of catching up to do,' Élise continued. 'It will be good for us all, won't it, Vicky?'

Vicky wanted to scream at her and felt her jaw tighten in anger. Nobody was listening to her. She took some deep breaths to try to control herself and Clemence smiled at her so warmly the anger simply dissolved. Instead, she felt a lump forming in her throat. She didn't want to cry and suppressed a sob. When she swallowed and the lump had shifted, she said, 'I shouldn't have let her go. We should have stuck together.'

'Darling,' Élise said putting an arm around her. 'You weren't to know.'

'Hindsight is a wonderful thing,' Hélène added dryly. 'You did what you thought was best at the time.'

'Come on,' Clemence added. 'If Ahmed and Theo come back with the jeep soon, we can go tomorrow.'

'And if they don't?'

'The next day then. And now I think we all need coffee and something decent to eat.'

Vicky could see there was no point obsessing about seeing Bea and it was the best anyone could offer. She sighed deeply.

'That sounded intense,' Clemence said and held out her hand.

Vicky took it gratefully, while also remembering how fervently she had tried to convince herself of her own invincibility when she first arrived in Marrakech, and how she had prided herself at never being a crybaby. Now look at her. Edgy and anxious. Close to tears almost all the time. *Come on,* she told herself. *You just have to wait until tomorrow, and surely nothing much can happen before then.*

CHAPTER 46

Clemence

When Theo returned, Clemence – overwhelmed with relief at seeing him – immediately ran to embrace him. When she let him go, he gave her a tentative smile and she felt encouraged. He, Étienne, and Ahmed had seen Jack and reported that Bea had not fully regained consciousness. Although she seemed aware of being in hospital at least part of the time, at other times she was delirious, muttering about a man on a motorbike. On the doctor's orders the police had been unable to interview her yet.

After supper that evening, when the others were together in the drawing room, Clemence drew Theo aside. It took courage on her part but if they didn't talk now, they never would. Vicky had remained unnaturally quiet all day, her red-rimmed eyes full of sorrow, and Clemence could clearly see the intolerable strain the girl had been under. Now, aware her own part in Bea's drama was coming to a close, it was time for Clemence to tell Theo the rest of her story.

'What about Madeleine?' Theo asked as he followed her to the door.

'She won't go to sleep until I go in, but Nadia will take care of her for a while.'

Clemence led the way to her study. 'I have brandy in here. Well, Armagnac, in fact.'

They sat down opposite each other on the two leather-bound easy chairs with a coffee table inlaid with mother-of-pearl and ivory between them. Although trembling inside, Clemence felt as if she would die if she didn't find a way to tell him everything. Even as she feared them, even as she would rather run away from them, the demons of the past had come to claim her.

'Brandy is in the bottom drawer of my desk. Help yourself.'

He opened the drawer and raised his brows when he saw the bottle.

'My best *de Montal* Armagnac,' she said.

He poured and sat down again.

She took a long slow breath and focused on him but couldn't tell what he was thinking. She wanted to say, *I'm still me. I'm still your Clemence*, but maybe in his eyes she wasn't. He seemed wary, unsettled. Not quite himself. She felt sick inside, sick of herself and what she had done.

'I want to tell you . . . I really do.' She paused for a moment, closing her eyes, trying to settle her nerves. It didn't help. 'But I'm not sure where to begin.'

His face was solemn, worried-looking. 'There's no rush.'

There was a long pause. She could hear the wind, saw herself out there, arms spread wide, running towards the mountain, running away again. Free.

She stared at her hands, picked at the skin around a fingernail. She would never be free, but she could take the first step now, by telling Theo the whole truth whatever his reaction.

'Well . . . I suppose the best way to start is by telling you that Jacques was not my son Victor's father.'

Looking puzzled but giving her breathing space, he sipped his brandy.

She stared out of the window into the darkness and rubbed her tight shoulders. This was never going to be easy, but it was turning out to be even harder than she'd imagined and part of her still wanted to run.

'Please don't judge me,' she said.

He gave her a small smile. 'I'll try not to.'

For a few minutes she couldn't speak, her feelings galloping so erratically she felt as if she might pass out.

'Here,' he said, seeing her distress. 'Take a sip.'

She did and handed the glass back to him. Then, before she could stop herself, the memory of the dark world from which she had tried to escape and the egregious harm her father had wrought rose up. The hateful long-suppressed words came pouring out as she said, 'From the letter you read you know what happened on my fourteenth birthday. But you see my father didn't only visit my bedroom that one day.'

He paled, covering his mouth with his hand as understanding dawned.

Stomach clenching, she carried on, 'It went on for seven years, sometimes in my bedroom, sometimes in his office. I couldn't prevent it.' Strained, and stretched tight like a wire, her voice didn't sound like her own. 'He removed the bolts from the inside of my door so I couldn't shut myself in and I found out later, he sedated my mother, although she heard me screaming. It would happen on the servants' night off. Not every week of course, but they would never have intervened anyway. They were all terrified of him.'

Theo pressed his knuckles into closed eyes.

'After a while, I learnt how to live, or rather be, outside of myself when it was happening,' Clemence said. 'Outside of my body. Detached. At least up to a point. But then . . . then I became pregnant.'

Theo opened his eyes, stared at her as the truth dawned. 'Dear God!'

'Yes,' she said quietly. 'Victor was my father's child.'

She rocked back and forward on her chair, dropping her head and holding it in her hands. What could he say? What could anyone say? The air seemed to still in the excruciating silence of the room. She had known speaking of it would make it real. Solid. Undeniable. And she felt the dreadful shame of it burning her cheeks. The disgust. The fear. The powerlessness. She had hated herself for so long. And she had hated her father with every fibre of her being. Afterwards she had been sick, every single time, vomiting again and again until there was nothing left except the self-loathing he had left her with. A flash of intense pain ran through her as it all caught up with her; everything she had tried to hide from rearing up within her and before her eyes. Everything she had been suppressing all these years racing back, and she craved the release of unleashing all the rage and fear she had ever felt.

Theo didn't speak.

Shaken, she squeezed her eyes tightly shut, drew a long breath and then looked up again, managing to say, 'He was a vile man, but despite everything, I loved my child.'

He began to say something as if to counter her words, but she held up her hand for him to stop.

'It wasn't Victor's fault,' she continued with a catch in her voice. 'He was an innocent baby.'

Theo rose and paced the room, his fists clenched and his dear face becoming rigid with anger. He slammed a fist into his palm again and again. 'The bastard! The fucking, fucking bastard!'

She waited until he was calmer then said, 'I never wanted Victor to find out that his grandfather was also his father and that his birth was the result of incest . . . and rape.'

She closed her eyes and was catapulted into the past, just as she'd known she would be. There it was, her old bedroom with the pink flowery curtains – huge peonies and little white roses, green leaves curling round them – her blue satin quilt, and the walls she had insisted on papering in a pattern of yellow and white daisies. The single window – closed of course. And her, alone and swamped by disbelief, the first time it happened. Her father pinning her down, stopping her mouth with his fist, smiling coldly as he told her to quit struggling and be a good girl or it would be all the worse for her mother. *Next time we'll tip her right into the well.* It hadn't been long after she'd been forced to witness her mother being whipped at the well in the yard and his words terrified her. *Next time.* When she began to weep, he'd slapped her face, called her an ungrateful slut. She hadn't been able to bear the pain. Hadn't yet learnt to detach and had completely frozen as he forced himself upon her, heaving and panting until the vile act ended.

'And this is what you couldn't tell me all those years ago,' Theo said, his voice hoarse with anguish as he broke into her awful memory bringing her back to the present.

'Yes,' she said, glad of the interruption, her voice low. 'I have never been able to speak of it. Not to anyone. The words would have . . . well, I just wanted to forget. I couldn't of course.'

He inhaled sharply. 'That's why you killed your father?'

She could see the sorrow in his eyes and felt how close he was to tears.

'I wanted to do it for a long, long time but I was too afraid,' she continued quietly. 'Until my mother—'

But he collapsed into the chair suddenly and bent his head, so she stopped. She saw his shoulders heaving but after a few minutes he had controlled himself enough to look up and reach for her hand. 'I'm so sorry. I'm not helping, am I? I'm finding it . . . hard to grasp. For God's sake, what made him do it?'

'He did it because he could. Power. Just that.'

'And your mother?'

'She hated him as much as I did. But she was scared too, every bit as much as I was.'

She shrugged, knowing Theo probably couldn't take in much more. 'Anyway, I was about to . . . well, to tell Élise, but we were interrupted when Hélène came back with the news that Bea had been found. Now I'm not so sure if I can tell her.'

'What about Vicky?'

She bit her lip. 'I just . . . can't.'

The silence returned, far too full of what had lain buried for so long. Clemence felt trapped by, surrounded by it. Couldn't breathe for it. She gulped for air.

'Maybe if we went outside?' he suggested softly.

'In a minute. I just . . .' She fell silent, held her palm over her mouth, focused on her breathing. In and out. In and out.

'Perhaps if you share what happened with Élise,' he eventually said, 'she could decide whether to tell Vicky or not. It directly affects your granddaughter. The bloodline I mean.'

'I know. And it's a terrible curse. It's why I never went to visit them. The more time passed, the more I felt that if Victor could belong in a world in which he believed Jacques was his father, the better it would be for him. He was better off without me.'

'I don't understand why Jacques agreed to take him and become his father, to move to France with him.'

'He was my best friend.'

'Still.'

'It was complicated. Jacques was poor.'

'So?'

'My mother gave him enough money to get away and start a new life with Victor.'

'He just did it for the money?'

She shook her head vehemently. 'No! He did it to save Victor's life. I told you it was complicated.'

His eyebrows shot up. 'Jesus,' he muttered just as Ahmed opened the door flanked by both dogs.

'My apologies for interrupting,' Ahmed said. 'Your mother is asking for you, Madame. She has eaten but . . .'

Clemence rose from her seat wearily. 'Don't worry. I was about to come anyway.'

As she left the room and went outside to head for the annexe, she glanced across at the mountains. Her stability for all these years. She felt relieved to have finally told Theo the truth, and most of her story, but felt drained and deeply shaken too. She stood absolutely still for a moment as she attempted to settle her breathing and muster enough strength to be able to go on.

CHAPTER 47

Vicky

Marrakech

'My goodness,' Hélène said, as the jeep approached Marrakech the next morning to brilliant sunshine and a seamless cobalt blue sky. 'Do you ever see a cloud?'

Her light brown hair was tied back and, out of her climbing apparel at last, she was wearing a loose summer dress in shades of blue. Nobody could call her aunt a beautiful woman, but she had lovely eyes and an air of authority that impressed people.

Vicky laughed at her question. 'Not often. At least I haven't seen many at this time of year. I haven't been here in the winter.'

Ahmed had driven Vicky, her mother, her aunt Hélène and Étienne down from the kasbah so they could visit

Beatrice in hospital, and Vicky was watching her aunt's reaction while remembering how she herself had felt on her first day here.

'The air!' Hélène said.

'I know. Mint, orange blossom and spice. Isn't it gorgeous? And you can hear water everywhere. Most of the riads have fountains in their courtyard gardens.'

'Water is central to Islamic architecture,' Hélène added. 'I had friend who studied Moroccan history. If I remember correctly, water represents purification and life.'

Seeing the city's ancient buildings lit up by the sun in slabs of gold and pink made Vicky's whole being glow. But how naive she'd been when she first arrived here, refusing to take her grandmother seriously when she had warned her of danger.

Hélène reached out a hand to her. 'You okay?'

Vicky kept on looking round. Even though Patrice was under arrest, she hadn't heard if he was already in a police cell or still being held at the hospital. She couldn't shake the unease. When it came to the trial, she knew she'd have to stand witness, but she didn't want to think about how terrifying it had been when he'd held a knife to her throat and she had feared for her life. She'd much rather get on a plane for Paris and never have to come back again.

At the huge square of Jemaa el-Fnaa Vicky watched as her mother and aunt paused to soak in the atmosphere and Élise turned to answer a question from Étienne.

'This is stupendous,' Hélène was saying. 'These spices! It's so very different here and yet so close to Europe.'

'Parts of Malta are pretty different too,' Vicky said.

'Well, yes. Especially Mdina. It has elements of the Arabic world from centuries ago.'

'It's magical there.'

'Visit again. It's been ages.'

'Love to, but only when—' She raised her shoulders in a shrug.

'I know. But at least we can find out how Beatrice is doing today.'

They were due to call on Etta first to avoid arriving en masse at the hospital and run the risk of intruding on Florence and Jack if Beatrice wasn't doing too well. The sun was hot as Vicky led the group through the dusty alleyways to Etta's, where much of her stuff was still in the small apartment. Their first goal was to ask if she had any further news about Bea and Vicky was already feeling sweaty and a bit worried.

Etta answered the door, her petite frame swathed in her characteristic black, with lime green beads around her neck. She ushered them straight into the courtyard garden, through the hall with its stunning blue-and-white tiled floor, to the kitchen. If Hélène and Étienne were startled by the mishmash of overgrown palms, crystal lamps, embroidered wall hangings, untidy heaps of magazines, and books piled high on every surface, they didn't show it.

Élise introduced her sister and Étienne, and Etta smiled at both of them. 'Do sit.'

They each took a seat around the ancient table.

'You'll be pleased to hear I have good news,' she said as she picked up a large coffee pot. 'Mr Jackson called in to ask me to tell you that Beatrice is conscious and receiving visitors, although only family.'

'I'm family,' Vicky said defensively. 'She's my cousin.'

Etta smiled as she poured the coffee and indicated a plate of *ghoriba* biscuits. 'Please help yourselves. And yes, Vicky, she has asked to see you especially. I was horrified to hear about what happened to you at the kasbah. Ahmed told me.'

'Thank you. Did my uncle Jack say anything else?'

'Just that he and Florence are staying at the same hotel as you were, Élise. La Mamounia. He was at the hospital last night when Beatrice woke up fully conscious.'

'How is she?' Hélène asked.

'Very weak, but I'm sure Jack will tell you more.'

'She's been on a drip?'

'Yes.'

'And what about Tom?' Vicky chipped in.

'Ah, well. He's staying with his father now.'

'In the same hotel as my mother was in?'

'No. A riad I believe. He's renting it until Tom is well enough to travel. Heavily guarded, I understand. The police will tell us where it is.'

Feeling a bit dejected, Vicky nodded, but she wasn't at all sure Tom's father would allow her to call. When she thought about it, she was surprised to realise she'd been so distracted at the kasbah she'd almost forgotten about Tom altogether. Almost but not quite. She felt a frisson run through her when she thought about seeing him again. If she could indeed see him.

Etta offered Hélène and her partner a room and they willingly accepted. 'You're very kind,' Étienne said.

Vicky glanced at him and smiled. She didn't really know him all that well, but he was so good for her aunt Hélène.

'What about you, Vicky?' Etta said. 'The apartment is still yours.'

'Can I think about it? I might stay with *Maman* at La Mamounia.' She glanced at her mother. She didn't want to stay on here without Bea.

'Whichever you prefer,' Élise said. 'We can book two rooms, or we can both stay here.'

'Ah, I almost forgot,' Etta added. 'Jack did say they're only allowing two visitors at a time. And only during visiting hours.'

'Can we go now?' Vicky asked.

Etta glanced at the clock on the wall. 'Not until four.'

Vicky sighed. 'But that's ages.'

'Why not rest up in your apartment with Élise while your aunt and uncle get settled in their room?'

Vicky shook her head. 'I can't just sit around. I need to keep busy.'

Élise touched her arm. 'How about we go shopping in the souks?'

'You'll need hats this time of day,' Etta said and went across to a tall cupboard where she withdrew two large sunhats. 'These should do the job.'

A little later, when they'd finished their coffee, Élise and Vicky headed out. Her dark-haired mother looked right at home in the baking heat of the winding street. Her life in France left her with a year-round tan and Vicky could see how beautiful she still was.

An exquisite-looking woman came out of a riad wearing an ochre brocade kaftan, a shaft of sunlight turning it gold. Vicky nudged her mother.

'That's Talitha Pol,' she whispered as they moved on, trying not to stare.

Élise frowned. 'Be careful whom you admire, *chérie*. The world of fashion is not an easy choice.'

'She's not in the world of fashion.'

'Maybe not. But people will follow where she leads.'

When they reached the bustling souks, her mother looked as bewildered as Vicky had first been, and she was proud to explain they were divided into distinct areas. As they wandered, the colour of the light kept changing as the sun's rays, shining through the swathes of differently coloured fabric hanging above their heads, afforded them shade. The fabric tinted the world: russet one minute, yellow the next, then orange, or gold. And where palm fronds criss-crossed overhead the light turned green.

'A sun-drenched paradise,' Élise said, 'and each area feels and smells so individual.'

'I like the spice market best of all,' Vicky said. 'The blast of all those coloured cones. Like works of art. And the Berber carpets too. They're so beautiful, they literally blow your mind. One day I hope to be able to afford one.'

'And the kaftan stalls?' her mother asked.

Vicky laughed. 'I adore them. The colours are so electric and the embroidery exquisite. They've given me so many ideas.'

'Do I sense a plan?'

Vicky couldn't conceal her pleasure. 'I am thinking of designing a range inspired by them but a bit different from them.'

As they turned into the vegetable market just outside the souks, where the stalls were piled high with bright orange pumpkins, enormous lemons, crimson pomegranates, purple aubergines, yellow melons, and golden grapes, Vicky stiffened. She had spotted Yves Saint Laurent and Pierre Bergé, the man he lived with, standing beside a stall of bright red and yellow peppers. She hadn't meant to catch his eye and froze at the look on his face when he recognised her and Élise.

'He's seen us,' she hissed at her mother.

'He's done more than that.'

Élise was right because Saint Laurent was striding towards them, looking forbidding, dressed all in white like one of God's messengers or maybe an angel of death.

'I thought,' he said as he came close, eyes hidden behind square sunglasses, 'you were going to tell me the whole story when it was over. On the understanding I would not take action over who had stolen the sketchbook. Did you lie to me?'

Vicky couldn't speak for a moment, just shook her head, and Élise was forced to step in. 'It wasn't a lie. But you see, only one part of it is over because, well—'

'My cousin has been found,' Vicky interjected. 'She's in hospital and we're going to visit her today.'

'I'm pleased to hear it. And the rest?'

She pulled a face. 'Still not finished.'

He seemed almost to scowl, and she flinched.

'Ah but you have made me intensely curious,' he replied. He removed his glasses, and she could see his eyes had wrinkled up in a smile. Not a scowl at all. 'Curiosity. A good thing, don't you think for a designer?'

She wasn't sure. Curiosity had got her into a lot of trouble as a child and while it was useful when it came to creativity and coming up with new ideas, in her life it had often led her astray.

'It's quite a long story,' Élise added, stepping forward, her gracious French smoothing over Vicky's frozen awkwardness.

'I'm sure. Well . . . I am grateful for the return of the sketchbook but while it was missing, I had a rethink about the designs. I was never quite sure but with redrafting I am feeling much more satisfied.'

Vicky beamed at him. 'I am so pleased. I'm . . . well . . . I'm thinking of some ideas inspired by the kaftans here, but with a modern twist. A kind of London cool meets Moroccan colour. I've learnt so much from being here. I feel as if the vibrancy has set my mind free.'

'I would be interested in seeing those new designs. Finish your training at the *Ecole de la Chambre Syndicale de la Couture* after which get in touch with my assistant. You will have to tell me the whole story *then*, as we return to Paris tomorrow.'

'How would I contact your assistant?'

Yves glanced at Pierre who pulled out a wallet from his jacket pocket and withdrew a card which he handed to her. She gaped at it in surprise: just a little white card with Yves Saint Laurent's name and a number, but it meant everything to her.

They took their leave and Vicky felt like dancing on the spot, unable to believe she actually had a phone number that would take her right into the great man's main office. Yves Saint Laurent represented a year of her life, the year she had written her dissertation, gained her diploma, and been rejected by the man she thought she'd loved. The prospect of meeting Yves had been the one thing that had kept her going and she had done it. Élise seemed delighted for her, smiling and squeezing her hand, and Vicky felt glad she could share this moment with her mother.

At the hospital they climbed the stairs leading to the wing where the receptionist had told them Bea's room would be found. On entering Vicky was astonished to see she had no need to worry about how to get in touch with Officer Alami to find out more about Patrice. For there he was, standing beside Beatrice, who was sitting almost upright in her bed propped up on pillows and shakily holding a cup of tea.

'Bea!' Vicky exclaimed, unable to hide her distress at seeing how deeply Bea had altered. Feeling her eyes grow hot from tears both of relief and shock, Vicky went to her, touching her cool cheek.

'Oh Bea,' she said softly.

'I know,' Bea said as her eyes welled up too. 'I look a fright. I won't let them come anywhere near me with me a mirror.'

Vicky took the cup of tea from her, put it down, and stroked her hair. 'You look fine. Just a bit tired.'

But the truth was her cousin's hair seemed thinner, her skin flaky and so much drier, she was terribly pale and always skinny, she was now skeletal.

'Well thank you for lying,' Bea said, leaning back against the pillow. 'And if you've got over the shock, how about a hug!'

Vicky hugged her gingerly.

Bea smiled weakly. 'You do realise I'm not made of glass.'

'You look a bit fragile, that's all, and you'll be right as rain soon,' Vicky said, though God only knew what kind of trauma her cousin had been through. Bea was trying to seem normal, but her eyes were dull, and Vicky felt as if she didn't recognise her any more. What had all that time alone, most likely fearing she was going to die, done to her?

'I kept hearing voices,' Bea said as if answering her question. 'You know? All around me.'

Vicky wasn't sure she did know. Bea was distracted, clearly dreadfully unsettled, her eyes seeming to focus far away.

'I hear them here too,' her cousin added.

'I'm so sorry,' Vicky said. 'I shouldn't have let you go alone. It must have been, well, I can't really imagine how awful. You've been so brave.'

'I don't really remember all of it. I'm on fluids and all sorts of drugs.' Bea pointed at the drip. 'They make me feel really spaced out.'

'Maybe not a bad thing.'

Then Alami spoke. 'Miss Baudin, if I might have a word once you've spoken with your cousin. I'll be right outside the door.'

Vicky and Bea exchanged glances.

'Do you know what it's about?' Vicky asked when he had gone.

'No. I've only just finished telling him what happened. He didn't say anything.'

'Can you bear to tell me?' she asked tentatively.

Bea sighed. 'To be honest, I'm shattered. Maybe we can talk later?'

'Was it Patrice? Can you just tell me that?'

'Alami asked me the same thing.'

'We all thought it.'

'Oh God, I'm so wiped out.' Bea closed her eyes and shook her head. 'But no. It wasn't Patrice.'

Vicky was stunned.

'It was some bloke on a motorbike who offered to help us with Tom.'

'Moroccan?'

'No. European.' She gulped back a sob. 'I was so stupid to get into his sidecar.'

'Bea, you couldn't have known.'

'He didn't go back to Tom, he . . . he tore up a mountain track too fast. It was terrifying.' Her voice was growing weaker, and her eyes filled with tears.

Vicky stroked her hair and spoke very softly. 'Oh God, Bea. I'm so sorry. You don't have to tell me now.'

Bea shuddered as if reliving the moment.

'The motorbike stalled. I made a run for it. But . . . I tripped you see, I tripped.'

Bea's voice broke and Vicky realised she had been holding her breath while her cousin told her what had happened. She let it out slowly.

After a few more minutes, when Bea didn't say any more, she asked her mother to stay while she herself spoke to Alami.

After the ebullient mood she'd been in earlier she couldn't work out how to feel. Bea would have such a hard path ahead of her.

'Did she tell you what happened?' Alami asked when she joined him in the corridor.

'Only that she got away and then tripped. Then she fell asleep and didn't say anything else.'

Alami looked very grave. 'I'll fill you in. It seems that she fell down a very steep gradient and into part of a ruined kasbah, broke her ankle, and couldn't get up.

Vicky drew in a sharp breath. 'Oh no. Poor Bea! Did the man come after her?'

'She thinks so, but he didn't find her. When she was sure he'd gone she managed to drag herself to where a stream was still trickling. She shouted but nobody heard her cries for help.'

Vicky rocked on the spot, wild with fury at the man who had done this to her cousin. What Bea must have endured! She didn't know what to say. How to respond. Her breathing became ragged, an urge to hit out overwhelming her, anything to prevent this horrible mix of horror and guilt from consuming her.

Officer Alami reached out a hand but she dashed it away, her voice shrill and too loud. 'You should have found her sooner. What the hell did the man want with her?'

'Miss Baudin, you need to calm down. Remember we're in a hospital.'

He had spoken gently, kindly, and she acquiesced. He was right. She took several long slow breaths to try to damp down the awful pain of it all.

'Who can tell what he wanted?' Alami said. 'Money? Sex? A beautiful rich English girl. He was an opportunist, and she was just unlucky.'

'Unlucky? She must have been terrified trapped there alone,' she said, her voice cracking as she pictured it: the long nights, cold and dark. Bea must have felt she would never be rescued. The ankle would get better, of course, but how was she going to heal emotionally? Once the drugs began to wear off, how would she ever get over it?

She managed to keep calm and said in a firmer voice, 'So, are you going to find him? The man?'

He glanced at his feet then gave her an unfathomable look.

'What?'

'It's unlikely we'd ever be able to identify him. Beatrice has no recollection of what he looked like. He was wearing a helmet and had a scarf tied around his lower face, to protect himself from the sand, at least that's what he told her. And she has no idea what kind of motorbike it was.'

'No. She wouldn't have a clue about that.'

'And I'm afraid to say that right now we have other concerns.'

'What do you mean?'

Alami sighed before answering. He looked as if he were in two minds about even telling her, but eventually said, 'Patrice Callier managed to get out of the hospital while waiting for an X-ray of his leg. He left – well, we don't exactly understand how, while the officers were dealing with paperwork.'

'You mean he just stumbled out?'

Alami nodded.

Aghast, she slumped down onto the only chair feeling completely dazed. *No. It couldn't be true. Please. Hadn't they been through enough?* She listened to the usual sounds of the hospital, the clanging and clattering, the rushing footsteps, the alarm bells, and everything sounded horrendously intrusive. Spiking into her. Hurting her head, her heart. Bright lights stinging her eyes, her throat tightening from holding back the scorching tears and the fear stabbing at her chest.

When she glanced up, Alami went to on to explain there would be a twenty-four-hour watch on Beatrice and she herself would be accompanied by a guard wherever she went.

She swallowed hard and shook her head in disbelief. 'So, you're telling me Patrice is just out there on the loose?'

'We don't think he will linger around these parts for long if that helps at all. And remember, he's injured. He won't be as dangerous.'

For a few minutes she thought about it, and neither of them spoke.

She stood up, furious again, adrenaline pumping through her veins. 'No, it really doesn't help. I just don't believe this.'

But then she remembered Tom and asked if Alami knew where he was staying now.

'I can take you there,' he said. 'If you wish.'

'And Jimmy's body. Have you found Jimmy?'

'I'm afraid the line of enquiry went cold. We have a good idea where his body was held initially but there were signs he had been moved elsewhere.'

She shook her head again. 'So apart from Bea being found, by my aunt I might add and not the bloody police, we are back to square one. Frieda is dead, and nobody seems to know why. And Patrice Callier is going to get away with murder.'

CHAPTER 48

Clemence

Kasbah du Paradis

When Clemence went to see to Madeleine, she opened the shutters and one of the windows and immediately knew something was different. Nadia had left her mother's breakfast in the little sitting room, but the old lady was still in bed. It wasn't unusual, but there was a strange odour in the room. Like acetone, overripe fruit, or urine. Rather sickly, unpleasant. She glanced around and understood the smell was coming both from her mother and from a rotten apple she must have concealed under her cover but had rolled onto the floor.

Madeleine lay there, deathly pale: her hair, her skin, completely white, as if she were fading into her pillow.

'*Maman*,' Clemence said as she lifted her mother's bony

hand to feel for a pulse at her wrist. Still there, though faint and fluttery.

Madeleine's eyelids twitched, and she spoke in a weak voice. 'I want to go home.'

'I'm here, *Maman*, and we're both at home.'

'No. *Home.*'

'Let's get you changed, and we'll see.'

When Clemence checked she found the bed was wet, so she helped her mother to sit on a folded towel on a chair. When she'd changed the bed linen she edged Madeleine into the bathroom, removed her nightdress, sponged her down and doused her in her favourite talcum powder. Back in the bedroom, she slipped a freshly laundered nightdress over her mother's head and threw the apple into the bathroom bin. She'd empty it later.

Once Clemence had her mother safely back in bed again, she asked if she wanted her pillows plumped. Madeleine shook her head

'You could have a nice sip of mint tea if you sit up a bit,' she said encouragingly.

But Madeleine was already drifting off again, so she just pulled up a chair and kept her company. As the minutes passed, she found herself evaluating their life together and their estrangement too when Clemence had been unable to forgive her mother. Her father stepped into her mind. His face. His cold dark eyes. His rage.

This is not real. He is not real, she told herself as she shrank back from the dangerous past.

But her feelings of guilt reared up anyway. She had not cherished her mother as a daughter ought to have done.

That *was* real and she felt the weight of it heavily and especially now. She could not turn back time or undo the past, no matter how much she implored the almighty to let her. It hurt to remember how many years it had taken before she fully grasped that her father had forcibly sedated her mother. Madeleine may well have heard her screaming but had been incapacitated, and unable to help. Perhaps even locked in. Or maybe too terrified to try. Clemence should have known this and had been aware her mother had suffered at the hands of Claude Garnier every bit as much as she herself had done.

Madeleine murmured something unintelligible.

'What?' she asked bending her head close, but there was no reply. Every time the old lady closed her eyes Clemence held her breath until the faint rise of her mother's chest resumed once more.

Her mother's death would not be the greatest loss in Clemence's life, for far greater was the love that had died between them and that she could never fully restore despite doing everything she could.

'Because of him,' she whispered. 'All because of him.'

When she had eventually found Madeleine in the French old people's home in Casablanca, she'd been neglected, left to lie in her own filth. It was one of those moments when Clemence knew nothing could ever be the same again. The shock and mortification she'd felt to see her mother in such a condition had shaken her from her long-held anger and resentment. The bitterness, the ugly feelings, the grievances she'd held on to for so long vanished instantly. She'd tenderly washed her mother herself, weeping as she did it, telling her she was sorry over and over, and that same day she'd removed her from that terrible place and brought her home. Since then, she'd been trying to make up for the shameful neglect of her pitiful broken mother.

A memory came back of the days when she'd been a young child. How whenever she'd seen her mother, her eyes would light up and she'd run to her. 'My own little mother,' she'd say and wrap her chubby arms around her mother's legs, or her waist as she herself grew taller.

My own little mother.

How those words stung her now.

She owed her mother so much, not least her little boy Victor's life. Both Madeleine and Jacques together. They had done what she could not.

There was a knock at the door and Theo came in, a question in his eyes. After she had told him why she had killed her father and what had happened all those years ago, he had clammed up. She'd tried to speak with him again, to tell the rest of the story, but he had shaken his head and she had been certain he wasn't ready. Now he looked like he might be.

'Oh Theo,' she whispered, trying to hold back the tears as he came across and held out his arms.

'Is she gone?' he whispered in her ear as he held her close.

She could feel his heart thumping as hard as her own. *Twin hearts,* she thought but didn't say. 'No,' she said, and added, 'I don't think it will be long though.'

'My darling girl,' he said as he stroked her hair and

then held her away from him so he could study her face. 'Would you like me to sit with Madeleine for a while?'

'Thank you. Just while I shower and dress. But let me know straightaway if . . .'

'Of course.'

Clemence hurried to her room, showered in her beautiful bathroom where the beauty of the *zellige* tiles inexplicably made her want to cry. How fragile life was. How precious. No matter how hard it became. And even in the days that would follow once Madeleine was gone, she couldn't help thinking her mother would somehow still be walking beside her. Still wandering the garden with her. Still eating cake. And she realised she had been wrong. The love *had* remained. Her father had not killed it. Diminished it maybe, but not destroyed. Not ever. And it made her feel sure that whatever Theo decided to do, she would always love him too.

Later, Madeleine had rallied a little, although she remained in bed so Theo, with agreement from Clemence, asked Nadia to sit with her for a couple of hours.

He held out his hand to Clemence, led her back outside and into the shade and quiet of her private courtyard. There, as they stood facing each other, he spoke in a low voice. 'I was deeply shocked when you told me what your father had done to you.'

'Yes.'

'It must have been truly—' He paused and shook his head. 'Well, I have no words.'

She drew in her breath, her head bowed. It was hard having to dredge up the past and make sense of such torturous, destructive pain. She looked up and found Theo was gazing at her, his eyes so full of compassion she could have cried.

'Are you ready to tell me about everything else that happened?' he asked. 'I know there's more.'

CHAPTER 49

Shaded from the sun and standing in front of a wall of blowsy climbing roses, Clemence spoke carefully, slowly. 'A few days before my baby was born my mother got wind of my father's plan to have the child removed.' She paused to gather her strength and carried on. 'To have Victor taken from me. And to have him killed.'

Theo's sharp intake of breath was almost silent, but she heard it all the same. 'He would have killed his own child?'

'To conceal his crime against me. The incest.'

The day her mother came to her with the news of her father's plan, Clemence had been reading about a young Roman noblewoman who in 1599 murdered her father, Count Francesco Cenci, who had raped her repeatedly. There had been a sensational murder trial in Rome where she was condemned and later beheaded for the crime. To even think of it had made Clemence shake with the injustice. Beheading seemed so barbarous and although in some cultures patricide was believed to be the worst of sins, Clemence had felt only terrible sympathy for poor Beatrice Cenci. Sympathy and a fascination that enthralled her.

'Clem,' Theo said gently.

'Yes?'

'So, what happened?'

She took a long slow breath and exhaled quickly. 'My mother offered me a way to save Victor. So I made a terrible pact with her.'

'Which was?'

'She would help Jacques to flee Morocco with my baby, become his father, and settle in France. She gave him the money to never return, just make an entire new life. Sorted out the paperwork. Everything.' She took a long slow breath. 'So long as I agreed to get rid of my father afterwards.'

'Dear God!'

There was a moment's silence.

'Why didn't you just flee?' he said.

'Oh, I thought of it, but I didn't dare leave my mother to face my father's rage once he discovered I was gone. I don't know what he would have done to her.'

'Maybe you and Madeleine could have planned to kill your father before you even had the baby. You'd have been able to keep him.'

'We didn't know exactly when he would be born and kept hoping for a solution. We had no idea my father would . . . that he would order the baby to be killed. I'd been thinking I might be able to keep my child nearby.

By the time we knew what my father intended, I was huge. I don't think I could have shot him while so heavily pregnant.'

Theo bowed his head then glanced up at her. 'And Jacques agreed to leave Morocco and take the baby to France, and raise him alone?'

'Yes, as I said before he was a good man. We were best friends. He knew—' She swallowed the lump in her throat. 'He knew exactly what my father was capable of, and he knew I would never recover if anything happened to my child. So Jacques left, and I did what my mother asked of me. I shot my father dead.'

'With Madeleine's blessing.'

'Absolutely. As I said it was her idea.'

'Why didn't she do it herself?'

'My mother had never learnt how to use a gun. She was scared she'd miss. She planned everything else though, carefully, and just hours after my baby boy's birth, she'd already bundled him up and given Jacques everything he needed for the journey, along with a wet nurse who would go with them as far as Tangier. We had to ensure my baby was safe before I killed my father. If anything had gone wrong with the plan, if I failed, and he had found them . . . well you can imagine. As it was, my father didn't have a clue Victor had been born. My mother had held a hand over my mouth so tightly I could not scream from the pain.'

'The pain of giving birth?'

'Yes, and the pain of my boy . . .' She stalled for a moment but then carried on again. 'The pain of my tiny little baby boy being ripped from me. My breasts were full of milk by the next day, and I wept silently. And alone.'

'Oh, Clem,' he said.

'I had no choice. I had to save his life, even though it hurt so much and made me terribly ill.' Her voice grew cold. 'I have never forgiven my father.'

Clemence closed her eyes and all those years of her life she had tried so hard to erase came hurtling back and settled on that single day.

She had entered his study, the sickly smell of overripe apricots lingering in the air and mingling with the smoke from a cigar burning in the huge onyx ashtray. She had stared at him, fear rippling through her. He seemed not quite himself, a little dazed with glazed eyes and a slack jaw. He had attempted to rise from his chair but had stumbled clumsily and fallen back with a look of uncertainty on his face.

'The child?' he growled, seeing her belly flatter than it had been.

She had swallowed, fighting the pain of letting her baby go. 'Gone, Papa. Gone.'

He was a big man, frightened of nothing. But he looked like a beached whale and despite everything she couldn't suppress a burst of bitter laughter. His eyes had narrowed, and he spluttered, his cheeks purple with anger.

'Get out, you little slut!' His voice was slurred, unsteady.

'You're drunk.'

But it was more than that. And she realised Madeleine must have managed to sedate him after all. She had said she would try, and he had become a sitting target. Weak.

She had been expecting her father to keep her under lock and key until the birth. But he hadn't accounted for Madeleine's cunning and her hatred of him. Had underestimated them both.

Clemence had glanced at the onyx ashtray – a gift from the Pasha – and felt a powerful urge to smash it into his filthy face. Smash and smash until every bit of him had turned to pulp. Shooting was too good for him. Dare she move closer, take a step forward? Shivering, though it wasn't cold, and terrified he might still be strong enough to grasp hold of her wrist, she moved, picturing it happen, his hand reaching out. And her unable to take another step. But all he did was groan. So she picked up the ashtray, blood pounding in her ears, and she flung it as hard as she could at the brick wall where it smashed.

His eyes widened in shock, and he tried to get out of the chair, but failed again.

She took her gun from where it had been tucked into the back of her leather belt. She held it up and wanting to make sure he realised exactly what was about to happen she carefully took aim while he was looking straight at her. The truth had finally dawned upon him, and in the moment of his knowing, she had done it. Exhaling slowly, she had taken her chance. Pulling the trigger, she had shot the tyrant in the chest. Her body had jolted even though the recoil was not great, and she'd been horrified by the noise and the smell of burning and seeing her father's dead body and the blood, so much blood. It had been insanely quick. She had closed her eyes momentarily, the image remaining in her brain, then she turned, running from the room, her heart racing.

Afterwards she had a pounding headache and felt sick. She had never believed she could be the kind of person who could kill, but after that brief moment which had changed everything, she knew with enough provocation anyone could do it. Especially if the provocation had been prolonged. She had felt no remorse, just relief that this cruel despotic man could never hurt Madeleine or herself ever again.

'Clem,' Theo was saying. 'Clem. You've gone very pale.'

Clemence blinked rapidly as if in a daze and saw he was standing over her.

He guided her to a chair: she sat, and he urged her to bend over and put her head between her knees.

She did so, and after a while straightened up, feeling a bit better.

'Can I get you anything?' he asked.

'Water, please.'

She watched him walk away, the vivid memories she had suppressed for so long crowding her mind. After it had happened, Madeleine had gone back with her to her father's study, insisting they did it together. They had sent the servants off to a distant market where they was a fair, so nobody had come running. The study was not connected to the main house but in the small building housing the estate offices nearby, yet once outside again Clemence had felt frantic with fear. They sprinkled kerosene around her father, soaking his clothes with it and they set fire to the whole place. A chill had run through her when she saw how far the flames were leaping but she and Madeleine had clutched hold of each other, waiting for the fire to eventually burn itself out.

Now, fifty-two years later, Clemence leant back against the chair, shuddering at the memory.

Theo came back to the courtyard with a tray onto which Nadia had insisted on adding tea as well as the glass of water.

'By the time the servants returned, there was nothing anyone could do,' she said. 'The next day, soon after the news reached him, Patrice's father arrived. We needed to report the death and we lived far from any officials. I couldn't remember if he took the photographs – it's all a bit of a blur – but I'm almost sure I must have watched him do it. All I can really recall is the room itself, reeking, fetid and rank, and me wanting to run and never stop running.'

What had that smell been? She thought it must have been the burnt meat of her father's body and felt repulsed all over again. Recalling the curling wisps of smoke still rising from the ruin, and catching in her throat, she had desperately wanted to never have to see the scene again, but rooted to the spot she had carried on staring as if transfixed by what she and her mother had done. Afterwards Patrice's father gave her a peculiar look and she hadn't known what to say. But he had held out his hand and smiled compassionately.

'Why did he take photographs?' Theo asked.

'I can remember asking my mother why he was there. She said someone had to report the death, and we needed some kind of record in case there were questions about what had happened.'

'Makes sense.'

'He asked where my baby was. I remember that. He was our family doctor you see. I made an excuse, told him I'd given birth early and the baby had died. I told him we'd buried him in our grounds.'

'He accepted that?'

'Yes. He was kind. Looked at me sadly and said to contact him if my mother or I needed anything.'

Theo looked puzzled. 'He didn't suspect anything? Didn't ask more questions about the baby or the fire?'

'He might have, but my mother dealt with it, and eventually he signed the death certificate. Accidental, was his verdict.'

'Did he show you the photos later?'

She shook her head. 'No. I'd forgotten about them until Patrice sent me a package of them recently. That's what got me thinking. Anyway, I wouldn't have wanted to look at an image of my father's charred body. There was a policeman – an inspector I think – who kept coming back, questioning us repeatedly after my father's body was taken away. He kept digging through the remains of the fire too. He was suspicious, and he knew something didn't add up. When my mother's maid whispered that rumours were beginning to circulate on the estate and in the village beyond, Madeleine told me to run, get away. I begged her to come too, but she refused so I left in a hurry, and I met Etta in Marrakech.'

'That was brave of you and Madeleine.'

Clemence shrugged. 'Madeleine maybe. Me not so much. Etta lent me money then later, when our estate was sold, I paid her back and had enough to buy the kasbah.

I don't know how Madeleine found the strength to cope with everything, but she held firm, and the inspector hadn't enough evidence to press charges, whatever he may have privately suspected. But I was still scared that new evidence would crop up, and I kept expecting a knock at the door. Even years later.'

'Oh Clem. I'm so sorry.'

'My father's body was changed beyond belief, but it was not totally destroyed. Blackened ceiling beams had fallen on to him crushing his chest, thank God. I had not understood broken bones from the shot I fired into his chest might have given me away . . . but the fire!'

'Destroyed most of the evidence?'

'Yes. We'd left empty whisky bottles near him, and mother had removed the glass with the sedative in it. And, somehow, she convinced Patrice's father that no further medical enquiries were necessary. It was different back then. Now we might not have got away with it.'

'It was definitely your shot that killed him?'

'I've always thought so, although recently my mother has been saying it was she who was responsible, not me. She only talks about it now, having kept the secret for so many years. I never knew how much sedative she put in the glass or what it was, possibly chloral hydrate or a bromide; in any case it would have been drugs my mother had been prescribed for her so-called hysteria. Maybe it was enough to kill my father without me firing that shot.'

He handed her the water and she took another sip.

'I've always felt so guilty. Terrified the truth would someday come to light.'

'Your mother took care of things after you left.'

'She did. But I never stopped feeling scared I would be tried, imprisoned, lose everything. I was a murderess and had committed the deadly sin of patricide. When Patrice appeared out of the blue a few weeks ago, just as Vicky arrived, I thought it was the beginning of the end.'

'You have been through so much Clem. All by yourself. I'm sorry not to have sensed any of this before but believe me, I will not be leaving your side ever again.'

'My shadow.'

He pulled up a chair close to hers. 'My darling girl.'

'You are aware I'm seventy-four?' she said wryly.

He laughed. 'Still a girl to me.'

Clemence sighed. 'Anyway, you've heard the whole story. I'm still not sure about telling Élise the truth about Victor's real father, which of course was the reason I could never let Victor know me. It was too awful. I have no idea how much Jacques told him. Probably nothing.'

Theo's face was thoughtful. 'Not the sort of thing you'd want to tell many people. Perhaps you could give Élise an edited version.'

'Maybe, but I'm not keen for Vicky to find out Jacques isn't her real grandfather either.'

He reached for her hands. 'We'll have to think it through. Let's just keep it between you and me for today.'

'Patrice insinuated that he knew.'

'Forget him. He can't hurt us any more.'

And right then she felt the huge burden had been lifted from her. It was time now for her to live a different life, free from guilt and shame.

CHAPTER 50

Vicky

Marrakech

Vicky knocked on the door of a typically pink riad. Alami was with her and had insisted he should come inside too.

'Aren't you too busy and important to be accompanying me?' she asked with a smile.

'I said someone would be watching over you. Right now, it's me. And anyway, they know exactly where I am if I'm needed.'

'If I'm even allowed in,' she said, trying to quell the flutter in her stomach.

'You will be,' he said.

'And you know how exactly?'

He winked at her. 'Fount of all knowledge,' he said just as the door opened.

'Yes?' said a man archly as he flicked his black eyes over Vicky. He was European, had a large nose, an impressive moustache, and he was wearing an immaculately ironed pale blue kaftan.

'Umm,' she said. 'I've come to see Tom. I'm Vicky Baudin.'

'I'll ask,' the man said, still haughty, and began to close the door.

But Vicky heard someone else speaking. A confident English voice enquiring about who was outside. Tom's father, she thought. Just her luck.

But Lionel Goodwin opened the door fully. 'Ah, Miss Baudin. My son has been asking to see you. I'm glad you've come.'

She hadn't expected him to be so hospitable and surprised by it, only managed to mumble in response.

Goodwin glanced across at Alami. 'I see you've brought a friend.'

'Yes. He's—'

'Yes. Yes,' he interjected dryly. 'I am aware of who he is. We've met. I expect you'll want to bring him in with you. Come along, both of you.'

He led the way along a beautifully tiled and arched entrance hall lined with mirrors, to a little sun-filled room where Tom was lying propped up on cushions on a chaise longue and wearing his pyjamas. His jaw was still bandaged but less extensively than before and his dark eyes gleamed as he looked at her.

'Hello,' she said, feeling shy as the others left them to it. She could smell essential oils. Patchouli maybe? At least there were none of the medicinal smells of the hospital in here.

'Come and sit by me.' He indicated a tapestry and leather pouffe.

As she perched there it felt terribly intimate, and she became aware that Tom's eyes hadn't wavered; he was watching her intently.

'How are you?' she asked.

'Up and down, I guess.'

'You look a lot better.'

'I'm not on so many medications. That helps. But tell me what's been going on. I only know Bea has been found.'

'How did you hear?'

'Marrakech grapevine.'

'Well, she's doing okay, although she says she's seeing things.'

'Drugged up?'

She laughed. 'Only in the hospital, I hope.

She updated him about everything, including how Jimmy's body still hadn't been found, how Patrice had held a knife to her throat, *and* how he had escaped from police custody.

His eyes widened. 'Jesus! The man is a snake. I'm so sorry. You must have been terrified.'

'I was until my grandmother shot him.'

'You have one cool grandmother.'

She laughed. 'I do, don't I? The police think he'll be trying to get away from Marrakech as quickly as he possible before they can catch him.'

'They're going after him though?'

'Yes, but . . . well.' She shrugged and they fell silent.

There was so much unsaid between them, and she couldn't figure out where to begin.

'Let's not think about him.'

'Fine by me.'

'I talk to you, in my head, as I lie here,' he said and looked a bit sheepish as if confessing a wrongdoing.

'Oh? What do you say?'

'Well. I tell you that I like you very much.'

She narrowed her eyes, trying to work that out. Did he really?

'Don't say it if you don't mean it,' she said.

'But I do.' He gave her a wistful look and then his eyes crinkled up.

'All right,' she said cautiously. 'Anything else?'

'Well . . . I tell you that I want to kiss you.'

She felt her cheeks heating up. 'And do you? In your mind. Do you?'

'Kiss you?' he asked.

'Yes.'

'I do.'

She leant across his body and kissed his lips. 'Like that?' she said and smiled.

The jewel-like stained-glass window threw geometric patterns of colour across his face and she saw she had been kissing lips the colour of cherries.

He reached out and pulled her down and this time the kiss went on for as long as it could when one of them was bandaged up.

'More like that,' he said, and she laughed with a mixture of embarrassment and delight.

'I didn't want to hurt you.' She looked into his eyes and saw he was enjoying himself as much as she was but having crossed a line so quickly, she wasn't sure how to proceed. He was an invalid, after all.

'I'm going back to Paris any day now,' she added lamely.

'Oh?'

'*Maman* reckons the best thing we can do is to leave the country, get away from the danger of Patrice reappearing. And I have a post-graduate fashion place waiting for me, but I forgot to send back the confirmation paperwork and they need to see me. They want to reassess my commitment to the course.'

'You'd have to return as a witness if Patrice is eventually charged with Jimmy's murder.'

'Yes, though at first they said I couldn't leave at all.'

'Well, I have news you might like to hear too. Or I may have news.'

'What? What news?'

'My dad has a contact at *Paris Match*. He thinks there's a chance he might be able to swing me a job there. A lowly job, but still . . . what do you think? It's either that or back to London.'

She felt herself lighting up. 'I think it would be bloody fantastic.'

'We could get to know each other properly.'

'And in Paris which is the most romantic . . .' She felt herself blushing and came to a halt.

He ignored her discomfort and asked, 'Do you have a place to live?'

'Yep. My stepfather, Henri, has a small crash pad there.

He says I can use it until I start to earn money after my course ends. The course starts in September and lasts for a year.'

'Right . . . well the doctors here say I can't do anything for the next couple of months. But let me have your Paris address and I'll get in touch if I do end up getting a job there.'

'I'd like that.'

'Me too.' He smiled at her. 'We're having lamb for lunch today, slow cooked with paprika, ginger, and saffron . . . if you'd like to stay. It's very nice. The lamb just falls apart.'

'I'll have to see. I think we might be going back to the kasbah to say goodbye to my grandmother before we leave.'

'Can I ask you a question?'

'Sure.'

'Do you like old places? Derelict mansions, overgrown gardens, creepy forgotten cellars.'

'Crumbling cottages on windswept clifftops,' she said entering into the spirit of it.

'Yes. Places where you can't see what's happened, but you can imagine what might have happened. I always find those places more interesting than anything finished or obvious. Do you see?'

'I think I do.'

'You're like that.'

She laughed. 'Dilapidated and creepy? Thanks a lot.'

'No. I mean you're there, but I can't quite see you yet. There's more to come. Some girls are all on the surface. When you try to look beneath, there's nothing to see.'

'Not just girls,' she said.

'No. I was wrong to say that.'

There was a knock on the door and the man in the pale blue kaftan brought in a cake covered in slices of candied oranges, and all the paraphernalia that went with the drinking of mint tea. Silver tray, blue metal teapot, sugar bowl and the prettiest tea glasses she'd ever seen.

'Orange blossom and honey cake,' the man said as he pulled up a coffee table with his foot, put down the tray very carefully, and then poured the tea.

While he was doing it, Vicky glanced around the room for the first time. She'd been so focused on Tom she hadn't noticed how truly gorgeous it was. Tom was leaning against pale cushions embroidered in red and gold, and there were more striped and geometric-patterned cushions in ochre and orange piled up on a divan by the window, partly hidden by a painted screen. She wondered if it was where Tom slept. Dozens of paintings of Marrakech hung on the dusky terracotta walls, and he saw her looking at them.

'Mostly from the 1920s and 1930s,' he said.

'You like art?'

'Very much. I may be a political sort of a guy but I'm not a total philistine.'

She felt embarrassed. 'I'm sorry. I didn't mean . . .' She trailed off.

'I'm teasing,' he said with a grin.

One wall of the room opened onto a patio. She squinted into the light and saw bougainvillea, potted palms, orange trees; listening to the sound of water and the birds too, she thought it the most idyllic place for Tom to recuperate.

A telephone rang in another room, but Tom didn't stop looking at her.

'We don't know much about each other,' she said.

'Not yet. I'm hoping to remedy that.'

A few moments later the door swung open again and, as Alami and Tom's father stepped in, the atmosphere changed from intimate to tense.

Alami spoke first, his face serious. 'I apologise for interrupting, but I have just received news that we have found and identified Jimmy Petersen's body.'

Vicky's hand flew to her mouth as the images of the awful night when Patrice had shot and killed Jimmy flashed before her eyes.

'They're sure?' Tom asked.

'Seems so,' Alami said. 'Red hair and the correct dental records.'

'Where?

'Under rubble on a building site. So now we have a body and a confirmed murder to solve.'

Tom blinked rapidly, clearly distressed by the news. 'Poor Jimmy,' he said. 'Poor, poor Jimmy.'

CHAPTER 51

Clemence

Kasbah du Paradis

Early the next morning Clemence and Theo walked in the garden. The sun was already up but so far the day had continued fresh and pleasant. He rested one palm on the small of her back with the lightest of touch, the casual understanding deeply intimate. She caught the drift of wild-flowers carried on the breeze and sighed, turning slightly, and he smiled.

Soon Vicky and the family would be returning from Marrakech, and with Madeleine fading so fast she would be busy. How much longer did her mother have? Days? Hours? Weeks? Clemence had no idea and pushed the thought away.

She headed back to the annexe with small squares of toast and mint tea for Madeleine, putting the small tray on the bedside table, then pulling up a chair on one side of the bed for herself and another for Nadia on the other side. .

'How are you feeling, *Maman*?' Clemence asked.

'They poison the food,' her mother whispered in a tremulous voice.

'We can't have that,' Nadia said.

Clemence tried to encourage her mother to eat but she just shook her head and clamped her mouth shut. Then turned her face away.

'Madeleine,' Nadia said with a smile. 'Would you like a warm drink instead? Some nice, sweet mint tea?'

Her eyes flew open, and she gave Nadia a beatific smile.

Eventually, after sipping a little of her tea, the old lady fell asleep again.

'You're so good with her,' Clemence said.

Nadia smiled. 'I looked after my own grandmother when she was ill like Madeleine. I did not know how at the beginning and kept getting cross with her, but I learnt to be patient. It is the only way.'

'I remember. You were brilliant then and you are now.'

'It has never been a trouble for me to care for others.'

'I owe you and Ahmed so much.'

She and Theo returned to her private courtyard after lunch, enjoying the refreshing tang of citrus and the sweet perfume of roses. He took hold of her hands and stroked them gently. 'Oh, my old hands,' she said, instantly aware of her ageing skin. But he was smiling, a strange diffident kind of smile. Not a confident Theo smile. And in response to the charge building between them, she felt uncertain. Why was he looking at her so hesitantly? She inhaled the scents of her home to soothe herself, smelt the woodsmoke in the air, the herbs in the garden, the dogs at her feet.

'Marry me, Clem,' he said suddenly, ignoring her comment about ageing hands. 'Not right away, but as soon as everything is settled.'

Surprised, she scrutinised his earnest blue eyes. It was unexpected, maybe even hasty. Wasn't it? And could he really bear to be with someone like her, to love and marry her after all he knew?

'Will you?' he asked again and lifted the stray lock of hair from where it had fallen over her forehead.

'You don't mind about my past?' she asked and felt the warmth from his palm as he held her shoulder.

'Clemence,' he said, drawing out the middle vowel as if exasperated, but his eyes were laced with good humour.

She smiled. 'Incorrigible man.'

'But you love me all the same.'

'Well actually, yes I do.'

'What, you do love me?'

'Yes, and the other thing too.'

'Have I got his right? You, Clemence Petier, will accept me, Theo Whittaker, to be your lawfully wedded husband?'

'Yes. You've got it right,' and she smiled broadly because here she was, waiting for her mother to die and feeling all the sorrow of it, but also making this joyful choice for the life she and Theo still had. And then she laughed out loud.

'What?' he asked.

'I started the day yet again changing urine-soaked sheets and now I'm accepting a marriage proposal.'

'You know what, Clem?'

'What?'

'I *love* you.'

A slow, contented happiness made her smile.

'Come on,' he said as he checked his watch before standing and pulling her to her feet. He gave her a slow meaningful smile. 'Siesta time. We have exactly one hour and twenty minutes. Enough for you?'

She shook her head. 'Incorrigible.'

He winked, reached out a hand, and arm in arm they strolled to her bedroom.

CHAPTER 52

Vicky

As they walked the final part of the track, Vicky looked up to see the kasbah walls tinted a deep rich terracotta by the late afternoon sun. And despite the whirling mix of emotions inside her – the relief, the hope, the anxiety – she could not help but gasp at its beauty. The whole complex looked magical, as if it couldn't really exist in the real world, its walls shimmering so brightly that Vicky beamed in amazement. An eagle skimmed the sky and as it did Vicky saw Clemence moving towards them, hands held out, and wearing a kaftan in such a pale lilac it almost looked white.

Vicky ran to her, and they embraced. But as she stepped back, she noticed that her grandmother seemed different. She was smiling and looked happy but there was something else beneath that too.

Élise stepped forward. 'It's very kind of you to have us here again. We won't impose for long.'

'Not at all. I'm relieved to see you both.' Her voice didn't exactly shake but she sounded subdued.

Élise smiled. 'Thank you. It's a relief to be out of Marrakech to be honest.'

The mingled aromas of the garden hung in the still air: eucalyptus, rosemary, jasmine, and roses. Always roses. Vicky took a deep breath. She had promised herself to stay calm but couldn't help herself and the words just burst out. 'Patrice got away from the hospital. He got away.'

Her grandmother's eyes widened in shock. 'I don't understand. Wasn't he under lock and key?'

Élise took over. 'You would have thought so, but he slipped out of the hospital while the guards were busy with paperwork.'

'Dear God!'

As Clemence began to wring her hands, Vicky felt certain her grandmother was not her usual steady self.

'Hopefully the police will catch up with him quickly.' Élise added. 'And two police officers will be up here guarding the kasbah until he is found.'

But it didn't seem to help. Not really. And Vicky didn't know what to say. She exchanged a glance with Clemence and saw her grandmother's vulnerability.

'How is Beatrice?' Clemence asked.

Élise smiled. 'My niece is doing well. She still has to recover fully of course, but Jack and Florence will be there, helping her find a way through.'

As Theo came out Clemence told him about Patrice, and he wrapped his arms around her shoulders so tenderly, as if caring for a child. Vicky could see he really loved her grandmother.

'Is everything all right?' Élise asked, clearly having picked up on the strange atmosphere too.

Clemence swallowed visibly, not meeting her eyes. 'You're in time for supper, but first I have to see to my mother. She hasn't got long, I'm afraid.'

So there it is, Vicky thought. *Poor Madeleine. Poor Clemence.*

'Oh, I am so sorry,' Élise said.

'Come with me if you'd like to see her.'

'Please,' Vicky said. 'We're leaving for Paris the day after tomorrow. We think the police will let us.'

'So soon?'

'Yes,' Élise replied. 'Vicky will be back for the trial once they catch Patrice again. And maybe you could visit us in the Dordogne. See Jacques perhaps. We have lots of space and my husband Henri would be happy to meet you too.'

Clemence smiled but didn't speak. Instead, she led the way to the annexe and opened the door. Madeleine was still in bed, of course, although looking a little brighter than she had been earlier.

'Who are *they*?' she asked in a sharp voice.

'Vicky, here, is your great-granddaughter. You've seen her before. I am your daughter Clemence. Victor was your grandson, and Vicky is Victor's daughter.'

'If that is true, where is he? I don't remember meeting him.'

'No. It was a long time ago.'

'Come here, girl,' Madeleine said.

Vicky stepped forward and leant over Clemence to hear her say in a loud whisper. 'They poison the food here, you know.'

She turned back to look at her grandmother who simply looked sad.

Later in the evening they were having dinner on the terrace, lamps lit all around them and with the strong smell of anti-mosquito citronella and the oil of lemon eucalyptus in burners. In air alive with buzzing insects and with the owls hooting in the woods, it wasn't at all quiet. A shriek from further up the mountain seemed to shatter the peace, followed by another. They all turned towards the sound.

'Jackals?' Élise asked.

Clemence glanced across at her. 'Probably.'

There was a pause.

'Why don't you tell me about your home, if you don't mind?' Clemence said. *Wanting to keep the conversation light,* Vicky thought.

Élise smiled. 'It's a lovely old chateau with views of the River Dordogne. It's been in Henri's family for decades. He restored it with his first wife before the war; she was a wonderful woman who was murdered during the Liberation. He lost Suzanne to the thugs, and I had lost Victor to the Nazis.'

'So you had a terrible loss in common. Such grief is hard to bear but you must have been a comfort to each other.'

'Over time we grew closer and rather surprisingly ended up getting married.' Élise nodded. 'I've been happy.'

'I'm glad you've had each other after such shockingly awful times.'

When Vicky looked around the table she realised there was one thing they must all be thinking of, yet none of were talking about him.

Patrice.

Theo was the one who broke the silence. 'What do we think about Patrice Callier? Does he still pose a threat to any of us?'

Élise sighed. 'I certainly hope not. *Chérie*, didn't the police say he would be heading far away from the area? And don't forget we're under police protection here.'

But Vicky felt herself go clammy at the thought of that man reappearing. She couldn't even bear to hear them talking about him, declined pudding even though she had such a sweet tooth, excused herself, and left the table.

She went straight to the drawing room and in the silent semi-darkness curled up near the window to gaze out at the gloomy purple mountain. Beneath the darkening sky a shadow shifted out there.

'Trick of the light maybe?' she muttered.

She thought she spotted it again. Movement. Deliberate movement. One of the policemen maybe or perhaps a wild animal. She thought about her dream of wolves with icy blue eyes but ditched that possibility. It was probably nothing at all. Because after all it was the liminal time between day and night when nothing was clear, and your imagination could easily go crazy. Was she seeing things that weren't even there?

Hearing footsteps coming up behind her she twisted round, pleased to see it was only Clemence.

'Oh, you're on your own. I thought I heard you talking to someone,' Clemence said.

Vicky felt embarrassed and pulled a face. 'Just talking to myself.'

'You look a bit nervous.'

'I just thought I saw something moving outside. It's probably just my imagination, but do you want to come and look.'

Clemence joined her at the window. Vicky watched her grandmother narrowing her eyes as they adjusted to the gloom. She focused on the mountain for a few minutes but then closed the shutter and shook her head. 'It's nothing. Nothing at all. Probably just a gust of wind blowing things about.'

Vicky nodded. 'I do love it here, even in the wind. I'd love to see the mountain peaks capped with snow one day.'

'And I'm sure you will.'

'I haven't got long here now, and I've been thinking. Please will you tell me why you didn't go to France with Jacques and your baby?'

'You've been very patient about this. I know you asked me almost from the first day you arrived here.'

'Sorry.'

'Not at all. It's time, I think. Would you ask Élise to come in here to join us? I have something to tell you both.'

CHAPTER 53

Clemence

The relentless tide of the past had swept up to the shore again and again, but now the storm had broken. Clemence had unfolded the layers of her story as rationally as she could, while Vicky and Élise sat listening. There was not the slightest sound – even the air seemed to be appalled – and she did not dare look up.

Élise touched her arm gently. 'Here,' she whispered and slipped a tissue into her hand.

Clemence felt exposed, as if the whole world were sitting in judgement, and had not even realised silent tears were pouring down her cheeks.

After she wiped her eyes and glanced up, she saw how shaken Élise really was, but Vicky, drained of colour, her eyes wide, looked horrified.

'Vicky,' Clemence said gently.

But Vicky just shook her head.

Élise glanced first at Vicky and then Clemence. 'I'm so sorry you suffered so badly at the hands of the person who should have protected you.'

'Thank you.'

'It was fortunate he died. God only knows who else he might have harmed.'

Clemence just inclined her head. She had told them the story but not that she had killed her father.

Élise rose to her feet and spoke to Vicky. 'Come on, *chérie*,' she said. 'You need sleep and time to take this in and Clemence needs peace and quiet.'

Vicky got up very slowly, clearly avoiding looking at Clemence who was now standing too.

Élise held out her arms to Clemence and they embraced warmly.

After a moment Élise stepped back. 'I meant what I said about coming to stay at the chateau. It would mean a lot.'

'Thank you. I can't tell you how much I appreciate that.'

A little later she lay on her bed staring at the ceiling, Theo next to her and the dogs asleep on the floor.

'I wonder if I should not have told Vicky,' she said.

He sighed before speaking. 'Imagine if she'd somehow found out later,' he said gently. 'She'd be hurt to realise you lied.'

'Will she come to terms with it though?' Clemence took a breath and closing her eyes, exhaled slowly. 'I wish I'd lied.'

'A lie always surfaces.'

'You mean like the fact my father did not really die in a fire?'

'No.'

They stopped talking and she listened as his breath seemed to slow. She turned towards him, kissed his cheek.

'I'm not asleep,' he murmured and wrapped an arm around her.

He understood how drained and sad she was feeling and while he could be passionate, he also knew when to make love gently, sensitively. Soothed by the gentle rhythm they made together she gradually loosened up and afterwards allowed herself to fall asleep in his arms.

They were both woken by a horrendous racket of gunfire and shouting going on outside the house, and the dogs barking hysterically beside her bed. Shocked out of a deep sleep, Clemence felt every sound jabbing into her body and her mind.

Leaping out of bed, she rushed to turn on the lamp then stood staring at Theo's horrified face.

'What the hell?' he muttered.

She threw on her robe, slid into her sandals, grabbed her gun and pushed her dogs into the bathroom. No one was going to hurt her beloved boys.

'Shit!' Theo yelped as he searched for his clothes. 'Stubbed my fucking toe.'

He cursed again, stumbling as he finally found them, flung himself into them, grasped hold of his own gun, and joined her where she had opened the door. For a moment the shouting stopped. Was it over? And what on earth was it about? She glanced back at the room where flickering light was coming and going through her semi-closed shutters.

'Torches,' she hissed. 'Be careful. We don't know what's going on.'

They made their way along the corridor. Lights had been switched on there and in one of the bedrooms. Someone screamed. Vicky? Élise? She ran and found them rushing to cower in a corner of the corridor.

'He's out there. I saw him,' Vicky said, gulping for breath, eyes wide with fear.

'Patrice?'

'Yes. When I heard the noise, I opened the shutters and looked out of the bedroom window. I screamed and we ran out here. I don't even know why.'

'Go to my room and lock yourselves in the bathroom. The dogs are in there, but they know you.'

'What about you?'

'I'll be fine. Go!'

After they'd slipped away, she followed Theo to the back door, her heart hammering. Where were the two policemen who were supposedly watching the kasbah? Theo opened the door cautiously and they heard the shouting beginning again but couldn't make out the words.

'It's coming from the woods,' he whispered. 'The police must be there. I can see several torches.'

'Don't go out,' she said, but he had already gone.

She crept back along the corridor, frantically checking all the windows and doors as she went. In the dark drawing room, she looked out to see what was going on outside in the blue moonlit grounds. She paused to listen. Silence. Then a single deafening shot rang through the air. The window glass shattered, the sound echoing in her head, as the bullet ripped towards her. It had smashed through the only window that was too tall for shutters and with glacial certainty she realised the gun had been aimed at her. The smell of smoke rose up as she froze momentarily, her thoughts spiralling. Was there a fire too?

But then another bullet came so fast she didn't have time to move. She felt a searing pain in her right arm and doubled over, dropping the gun.

Gasping with pain, she tried to reach for the gun with her left hand but couldn't see it. Damn! The moon had gone behind a cloud. It was too dark in the room now. She felt around but couldn't waste time, had to leave the gun and get out of there, holding on to her wounded arm with her good hand. At the same moment as she felt the warmth of her blood, she saw his torch first, and then him, running, limping towards her, waving his gun. Grinning. Possessed. Patrice, looking like a madman. He turned and she instantly knew where he was heading. He must have seen Theo go out. He'd only fired into the drawing room to keep her away from the open back door. She raced back along the corridor tripping over her own feet, desperate to bolt the door before he got inside the house.

Too late.

She backed away as he approached. Then chaos. Yelling and thunderous banging as Theo charged in. Someone else screaming at him. Ordering him not to go in. Patrice turned, fired, the roar of the shot erupting in the air and in her head. Theo crumpled. He just crumpled. She couldn't see where he'd been shot. Unable to breathe for the pain compressing her chest, she stared motionless. *Please, not Theo. Please God, not Theo.* Numb with shock, her brain no longer working, the ache spread through her entire body. He couldn't die. He couldn't.

Patrice turned back to her and laughed. It took seconds but felt as if it had lasted for hours. She saw the darkness in him, the well of it reaching deeper than ever before. As if in recoil she gasped for breath, coming back to life as fury raged through her. She could do this. She could face him down. She'd come back from the brink before; she could do it again. Besides, she was taller, more muscular, and easily more agile than he.

'Hello,' he said in a slow drawl, almost conversationally.

She stared at him across what felt like a vast empty space. Then it concertinaed and he was just a few feet away. Her father stepped into her mind, and she forced herself not to scream.

'Drop to the floor,' he ordered.

She did so. 'Why are you doing this? What do you hope to gain?'

He laughed again. 'This is so much fun, isn't it?'

'You're finished, Patrice.'

He shook his head very slowly side to side. 'Thought you'd get the better of me?'

Keep him talking, she told herself.

'I don't know what you mean. I have no idea what you hope to achieve.'

He laughed bitterly. 'Oh, but you do. I need money and I need it now. You have it and you have my legacy, you murderous bitch. Time to pay up or beg for your life.'

'This is absolutely insane.'

'I said beg.'

He came closer holding his gun, dragging his injured leg. 'If I'm going to meet my maker, you, Clemence Petier, *you* are coming with me, and that little granddaughter of yours too.'

'Why her?' she said, her blood running cold. 'She's done nothing to you.'

'No reason why,' he snarled.

She spotted a slight movement behind him and saw Theo rising, as if from the dead, wide-eyed and beginning to edge towards Patrice. A shot of pure joy ran through her. He was alive. Alive! She fought to control the surging overwhelming relief. Didn't dare let it show on her face, but her spirit was soaring. She had to keep Patrice talking. Just keep him talking. If he realised he hadn't killed Theo, he'd spin round and really would finish him off.

'What happened to you, Patrice?' she asked, forcing her voice to remain flat and steady.

'Me? What about you? I know what you did.' He waved the gun at her. 'My father always suspected and the police inspector too, but my father took pity on you and your mother and persuaded them to drop the case.'

'He was a good man.'

'He was weak.'

Clemence kept eye contact with him.

'The way you conceal your mad mother all the way out here. You have secrets. And so does the old hag.'

'She's lost her memory. Recalls nothing. And your father got it wrong.'

'Still lying.' He shrugged and pointed the gun right at her. 'It's time.'

Keep him talking. Keep him talking. But her mind went blank. Time stretched out; the moments all sharp-edged, poised to strike. She couldn't think. Then it came to her. 'Why did you kill Jimmy Petersen?'

'Nothing personal. I fix what I get paid to fix. That young man paid the price for snooping into the government's participation in the ben Barka disappearance.'

'You mean you're an assassin?'

He shrugged. 'Call it what you will. That boy was taken out because he knew too much and was about to share it with the world. Could have caused one hell of a stink.'

'Taken out? Is that what we're calling murder these days?'

From out of the corner of her eye she saw Theo raise his gun and only a split second before he pulled the trigger, he gave her an infinitesimal cue. She pitched sideways onto the floor just in time to avoid the bullet. Patrice groaned, reeling from the impact and – thank God – he collapsed, landing sideways on the floor.

She felt rather than saw Theo running towards her, helping her up, though she was trembling so violently he had to hold her against the wall.

'Is he dead?' she whispered.

'Oh yes,' he said. 'Look at him. Patrice Callier is very dead.'

423

She closed her eyes, inhaled, let her breath out in an anguished puff. 'Oh God! I thought you were dead too. Are you all right?'

'His shot missed. I just wanted him to think he'd got me. Where's your gun?'

'Dropped it.'

Astonished he really was alive, she couldn't stop looking at him. This man. Who he was, what he was to her – it meant everything. And who she was to him too. It meant the world.

'You okay?' he asked. 'You're very pale.'

'A bit dizzy.'

Finally, one of the two armed police who should have been guarding them ran in. Behind him, a thin-faced man with a shaved head was being dragged along in handcuffs by the other guard. 'It wasn't my idea!' he was shouting. 'He forced me! I'll tell you everything. I just drove the car. I'm innocent!'

'Fat lot of use the police were,' Clemence hissed, still holding her hand over her injury.

'Just let them think they were marvellous,' Theo said as he glanced around. 'Where are Vicky and Élise?'

'In my bathroom.'

He shook his head and laughed. 'I'd better let them know they can come out.'

'Yes.'

He moved away but then looked back at her. 'God, Clem, your arm. You're hurt. Look at the blood!'

She looked down at her arm and then slid down the wall and everything went black.

CHAPTER 54

Vicky

The bedroom was in semi darkness as Vicky opened the door and crept forward, the shutters allowing only gossamer threads of light to fall across the room, with just a couple of candles flickering on the dressing table. Her grandmother looked oddly peaceful lying on top of the covers with her hands resting together on her chest and her face completely drained of colour. At the sight of her, Vicky faltered. She had been awed to hear of her grandmother's bravery in standing up to Patrice but desolate to hear she'd been shot.

She edged closer.

Clemence was stoic and had hidden her vulner-abilities well but the abuse she had received at her father's hands had marked her, made her wary of loving people. And it explained so much about her that Vicky had not previously understood, especially when she'd first met her. The distance, the unknowability.

'Nerves of steel,' Theo had said with a catch in his voice when he went into more detail about what had happened.

Vicky wasn't so sure.

Her grandmother's eyelashes fluttered, and her eyes opened.

'You gave me a fright,' Vicky said in relief. 'For a moment I thought . . .'

Vicky and Élise had been kept in the dark for a little while. Theo had carried Clemence to the living room, so that Ahmed could swiftly lead Vicky and her mother to the kitchen. They were unaware that Clemence had even been injured until later that morning when Theo eventually explained everything, insisting Vicky's grandmother had needed to rest before anyone could see her. He had dressed her wound. It was slight, just a scratch, he said reassuringly, but Vicky had been desperate to see for herself.

'Oh, I'm fine. Just a minor wound,' Clemence said now, but her voice wasn't as firm as usual.

Vicky perched on the side of her bed and pressed her hand. 'I'm glad you told me, *Grand-mère*. About the past.'

'You don't feel too bad about it?'

Vicky shook her head. At first it had been such a shock she couldn't even speak, but once she'd taken it in, she realised it didn't change anything about the present. And Jacques would still be her grandfather no matter what.

'It's past,' she said. 'Gone. Whatever your father did, it can't hurt me, or you. Not now. We're fine, aren't we? Or we will be.'

Clemence took her hand and squeezed. 'I'm glad you came to Morocco. I'm beyond happy that I've had a chance to get to know you and so proud of you and everything you're hoping to do. So proud, I could burst.'

'Even though I landed all this horror at your door?' Vicky said in a small voice.

'You brought Theo back to me too. Don't forget that. And Patrice already had me in his sights.'

'I came to tell you *Maman* and I are leaving now for Marrakech. We were hoping to leave Morocco anyway but now we're certain there isn't going to be a trial nobody can stop us. She asked me to thank you and she'll write soon to suggest some dates you might like to visit. Theo says you need peace and quiet and with Madeleine so ill, we thought it best to go. Especially as Bea is recovering, and my aunt and uncle will take care of her.'

'Today. Are you going to Marrakech today?'

'Yes. The police have already taken our statements about what happened last night.'

'Ahmed is going to drive you?'

Vicky tears prickling her eyelids. 'Yes . . . I shall miss you so much. Please will you come to Paris when you're better? You and Theo?'

'Of course. It would be a delight.'

'Thank you for helping me. I don't know what I'd have done without you.'

Clemence looked up at her. 'Be brave, little one. Brave and strong.'

'I'm not really sure how.'

'Oh, you already do know how. More than you realise.

Trust your instincts. They are your greatest asset. It's your time to shine now. Go out and share your light with the world and do not listen to anyone who tries to make you feel less that you are.'

Vicky gazed at her for a moment or two, wanting to prolong the leaving but then she blinked rapidly, took a deep breath and said, 'I promise I'll do my best.'

She kissed her grandmother's cheek, walked to the door, and glanced back. 'Love you.'

And she left the room quickly before her grandmother saw her tears.

Back in Marrakech the evening was sultry. They had planned to have supper together, the whole family, but as Jack was late coming from the hospital and Étienne was speaking to Etta about her apartment – he and Hélène wanted to stay on in Marrakech for a few more weeks – for the first half of the meal, it was only Hélène, Élise, Florence and Vicky at the table. Vicky was longing to say a last goodbye to Tom, but Élise had lain a hand upon her arm.

'Could you stay, just for a bit?' Élise said.

Her mother's look was entreating, and Vicky could tell it was important. Once again, she was reminded how beautiful her mother was with her glowing eyes and glossy dark hair with hardly any grey.

Vicky had a sense that they were all aware this was an important moment in time. And as the muted conversation went on around her she sank into her own thoughts. She had acquired an understanding about herself she hadn't thought possible at the start of this trip when she'd walked into a world about which she she'd known nothing. When she had invited her cousin out here, she had cared so much about Russell's rejection. It seemed like nothing now and it was a good lesson to learn. Even painful things passed in the end. You just had to ride them through, and she felt much better equipped to deal with her own emotional ups and downs now.

'Well,' Hélène said, glancing around at her sisters.

Vicky often wondered how three sisters could look so different. Hélène, the eldest, was taller than the other two, and always said she took after her father. She wasn't plain; she was just a bit less striking.

'Doesn't life throw a spanner in the works sometimes?' Hélène continued. 'Who could ever have imagined the journey we've all been on?'

'Quite,' Élise said. 'And doesn't it feel like a lifetime since the three of us were living together in the Dordogne?'

'The three daughters of Claudette,' Vicky said and grinned. 'Daughters of war. You do recognise it *is* a life-time.'

All three sisters laughed.

'Our lovely old house. And all the bunches of herbs hanging from the beams in the kitchen,' Hélène said.

'Hung there by me, I might say,' Florence added. 'Grown, picked and dried by me too.'

'Indeed, you were our little witch.' Élise smiled before looking over at Hélène. 'Remember the way you used to clean like a lunatic?'

'Only when I was feeling anxious,' Hélène added. 'But

oh my goodness, the mess when you decided we should reupholster the sofa, Florence.'

They all laughed again.

'And do you remember when we found *Maman*'s red dress and didn't have any idea of the story behind it?' Élise said.

'Where did you find it?' Vicky asked.

'In an old trunk in the attic,' Élise and Hélène said together, and Florence smiled at them both.

Vicky looked at her aunt Florence. Her blonde hair had a few threads of silver mixed in it these days. It was disobedient, curly hair, and usually tied up, but tonight she had left it loose, and Vicky thought she seemed so much younger now that the terrible strain of the past weeks was no longer showing on her face.

'That gorgeous silk dress all torn up,' Hélène said, 'but it was the start of uncovering our mother's secret lover, wasn't it?'

There was a moment of silence.

'And what a story it was,' Élise eventually added. 'I wonder why through the generations, we women have sometimes struggled to get on. I never understood my mother, though you, Florence, you did. And I know Vicky and I have misunderstood each other too.'

'Not any more,' Vicky said and winked at her mother. But when Élise took hold of her hand and kissed it, Vicky could have cried.

'Mothers, daughters, and sisters,' Hélène said. 'What could be a stronger more complicated bond?'

'We fought, we cried, we loved, but nobody could break

our spirit, not the war, not the deprivation, not the Nazis,' Florence said in a soft voice.

Her sisters nodded in agreement.

'Let's remember the good things,' Florence continued. 'You know? Swimming in the river. Growing vegetables.'

'Looking after your *jolies petites chèvres!*' Hélène and Élise said in unison, and they all grinned, full of memories, happiness and hope.

'And your job, Hélène,' Florence continued. 'Nursing the sick.'

Hélène nodded. 'And then later the way the way you had to search for Rosalie. Our mother's final request.'

'Long-lost sisters. There you are, another rift,' Élise chipped in.

'We were all so young. And now we're all good, aren't we?' Hélène said. 'Despite the rifts over the years. The secrets.'

Vicky was touched by the love the three of them so obviously still shared. Even though their lives had diverged, all of them living in different countries, the love still held. Like glue. And her heart overflowed with gladness and tearfulness at the same time.

'Oh Vicky,' Florence said. 'Don't cry, darling.'

'These are happy tears,' Vicky said as she got up from the table. 'I won't be long. Tom is staying just around the corner. Order me anything you like. I could eat a horse.'

'Ah, young love,' Florence said, and Vicky felt her cheeks burning.

A little later she was closing the door at the riad, having given Tom her address in Paris and having told him that

Patrice was dead. Out in the alley she leant against the pink wall, her head bent, and inhaling the spices in the air she allowed the tears to flow once again.

It wasn't sadness. It was much more than that. It was everything.

Jimmy killed in cold blood right before her eyes, the corrosive fear over what Patrice might do underpinning every day and night, the dreadful accident in which Tom had been so badly injured, Bea lost and found again. So much had happened in such a short space of time. She was friends with her mother at last, had experienced the joy of getting to know her beautiful grandmother, Theo too, and Ahmed, who had ferried them all up and down the mountain so often. To have been part of the magic of Marrakech itself and the beauty of the kasbah was a privilege. And oh, the thrill she had felt at meeting Yves Saint Laurent. And Tom of course. She couldn't tell how their relationship would work out, but she felt so much warmth inside her when she thought of him, it couldn't be a bad sign. Through her tears, she smiled. It was going to be so much fun getting to know him. And she would be back to see Clemence again, she was sure, boarding the night train to Marrakech once more. And the thought of it reminded her of her first night in Tangier. She hadn't admitted it, even to herself, but she had been absolutely terrified; she was so much stronger now.

CHAPTER 55

Clemence

Kasbah du Paradis, a few days later

She sat on the day bed under the awning on the terrace
and gazed at the mountain before her without really seeing
it. In her mind's eye, she saw Madeleine staring at a slice
of her favourite cake, not seeming to recognise it as food,
crumbling it between her fingers and spreading the crumbs
around the plate. Then images of the distant past and her
life with her mother on their estate near Casablanca rose
up, spinning and spinning in her mind. As they settled, she
could see them both clear as day and as real as if it had
only been yesterday. Why was it that the older you were,
the more vivid the memories from years and years before
became, flowing through your mind like water? Never
stopping. And you only truly recognised how very short

life was when you were on the last part of your voyage. Poor Madeleine. She'd had the most awful marriage. But she'd been happy in her apartment overlooking the sea until her confusion and failing health ruined it. Clemence wished she'd known about her mother's decline sooner.

She recalled the evenings when they'd sat outside together surrounded by the sounds of approaching night before the first stars appeared in the sky. Just the two of them talking and laughing until her father arrived home. Both happy to have that time together and free of him. And now her mother's life was almost over.

There had been times before Vicky came to Morocco and before Theo had turned up again when Clemence had almost felt ready to go herself. The corrosive fear of exposure had plagued her life, and the iron control needed to keep the past buried had exhausted her. Now there seemed so much to live for and she wanted to grasp every moment.

Nadia interrupted her memories and her thoughts as she placed a tray on the table and smiled at her.

Clemence thanked her and made herself eat and drink. She was surprised to rather enjoy the sandwich and coffee and felt much better for it. But it was too hot to stay outside for long, and she had managed to spill coffee on her clothes, so she went to her bedroom, showered hastily, and slipped on a clean pale green kaftan.

Back in Madeleine's room Theo smiled at her as she went across to him and stood behind his chair, resting her hands on his shoulders. He reached up to hold her right hand for a moment.

'No change,' he said.

She slipped into the chair next to him and saw Madeleine's skin looking mottled and a bit grey. Watching her mother die was a desperately sad experience. A wave of anxiety passed through her. Was she even able to do this? She hadn't expected to find herself tearful but soon realised she was.

'Sorry,' she said.

'Don't be silly.'

'I realise that it's her time. In my head I know it is, but in my heart . . . well, I can't seem to help it. I'm not usually like this.' There was a catch in her voice, but she managed to stem her tears and take a deep breath.

'I understand,' Theo said.

'Do you? Not sure if I do.'

'You've had a great deal of worry and drama lately. Your defences are lower than they might have been.'

'I suppose.'

A moment later Madeleine's eyelashes fluttered.

'*Maman*,' Clemence said softly. 'Can you hear me?'

Her mother spoke but her voice was barely audible and Clemence leant forward to hear more clearly, but there were no more words, just Madeleine's rasping breath becoming gradually more intermittent.

'Did *you* hear what she said?' she asked Theo.

He shook his head.

Clemence took hold of her mother's cold hand, the thin skin almost completely transparent. 'I'm sorry for everything, *Maman*.' Her voice caught as she fought her tears and then she continued. 'Truly sorry for blaming you. It wasn't your fault. I'm sorry for not finding you sooner. Please forgive me.'

Madeleine's breathing quietened.

'Maybe if she had some water to drink,' she said and gave Theo a pleading look.

'It's too late. She's mainly unconscious. Surfacing just for a few fleeting moments.'

'I can't bear it.'

'You don't have to.'

'I do. I must.'

'She looks quite blissful.'

She gazed at him. 'You think?'

'I do. She's going home.'

Clemence's face crumpled but through her tears she gave him a smile. 'She is, isn't she? At last, she is going home.'

'We all must go, my love. It's just Madeleine's time now.'

Clemence nodded slowly and kept watching to reassure herself that her mother was still breathing. She still was. But a few minutes later she looked up at Theo.

'She's not breathing now,' she said, her voice low and urgent. 'Theo. She isn't.'

He drew close and Madeleine remained still for a minute, and then she took two long shuddering breaths and her face slackened.

Everything went completely silent.

Clemence waited for another breath. Waited and waited, and when it didn't come her throat tightened and she felt the hot tears dripping down her cheeks. She held one of her mother's lifeless hands and kissed it. 'Fly home, *Maman*. Fly home,' she whispered and crossed Madeleine's hands on top of the covers.

She stroked her mother's hair and then she left the room.

It had finally happened. Her life was over. Just like that, and Clemence could barely breathe herself.

Later, she would lay her mother out with Nadia's help. Women's work. Madeleine had already picked out her favourite nightdress some time ago with strict instructions for everything. Despite her confusion she had seemed to know. People would pay their respects. There would be delicious food and talk of a life well lived, even though much of it had been hell on earth. Ahmed would go to Marrakech and the funeral arrangements would be made.

But now Clemence shut herself in her bedroom and wept for her mother, releasing all the guilt and pain she had carried for so long. She wept until her throat was raw, her eyes were swollen, her head throbbed, and her spirit was completely laid bare.

CHAPTER 56

August 1967, one year later

Clemence, feeling listless, stood gazing at the detritus of her life, and shrugged as Nadia held up a painting.

Clemence sighed. 'What do you think? Not great, is it?'

'Leave it,' the girl said, taking control. 'Ahmed can hang it in one of the guest rooms.'

Packing boxes and a trunk littered the drawing room floor and for the final time Nadia was helping Clemence weed out what should be taken and what left behind.

'What about these old kaftans?' Nadia asked, holding one up.

'Cut them up for dusters. And not those three vases either.'

Nadia pointed at a pile of paperbacks. 'You need more books?'

'Always, but you can have those if you want.'

And so it went on. It was hard work but everything would have to be carried down on mules until they reached her jeep, which would gradually transfer everything to a larger vehicle further down the mountain. So Clemence really had to be brutal. Not that she'd ever been a hoarder but still.

'Let's take a break, Nadia,' she said and left the room to walk around the garden and gaze at the mountain. Her mountain.

She breathed in the scents, tasted the flavours, and immersed herself in memories of the fabric of her life. The herbs. The flowers. The lemons lying on the wooden block sliced and ready to be made into thirst-quenching lemonade. The baking hot stones of the mountainside. The smell of freshly pressed bed linen. The icy cool of the shower as it splashed over her naked body and onto her bathroom tiles. The dogs steaming after a walk in the rain. The logs burning in the fire.

They were due to be married in Tangier in September. Vicky and Tom, now fully recovered, would be coming over from Paris together, Élise from the Dordogne and she would be bringing Henri and Jacques with her. Jacques who she hadn't seen for so long. She placed a hand over her heart, the place he had always occupied along with Victor. Hélène and Étienne were off travelling in South America so they couldn't make the wedding, but Jack and Florence were accompanying Beatrice over from Devon. She wasn't quite back to full strength, even after all this time but was determined to be there. Of course, Ahmed and Nadia would be there too.

Vicky had finished her course in Paris and had designed and sewn a stunning wedding dress for her in palest shimmering silk, one of her current designs for kaftans with a modern twist. And although Clemence was biased of course, she could tell her granddaughter was exceptionally talented and would go far.

As for leaving the mountains, Clemence hadn't sold the kasbah. It really would have been too extreme for her. Instead, she had placed Ahmed in charge of managing it as a hostel for climbers. He was delighted to be his own boss and Nadia would live in and work full-time as house-keeper with help from village girls. Clemence hadn't told Ahmed yet, but she had changed her will and the place would be his and Nadia's one day. It was only fair. They were a part of this place just as much as the soil and the air. It was their birthright.

After the wedding she and Theo would be heading to Paris for a short honeymoon before staying with Élise at Henri's chateau in the Dordogne. She would feel the bitter-sweet moments of being in the part of the world where Victor had once lived. She would visit her son's grave, and the thought filled her with a mix of sadness and regret. But she would also have the joy of being with her grand-daughter and the woman Victor had loved too.

She was looking forward to settling down to married life in Theo's beautiful cliff house halfway up Tangier's Old Mountain with an ocean view and a garden. She was glad about the garden, couldn't bear to be without one after living so long at the kasbah. He'd already told her Tangier could be cold and rainy, but the house was comfortable.

'Whitewashed on the outside and comfortable inside,' he had said when he'd first come to Marrakech after she'd called him in such distress. What would she have done without him? He'd offered to sell his house, suggesting they could buy a new place together, but she'd wanted to live in his home, at least for a while.

Tomorrow she would be saying farewell to her life here. It would be a fresh start for her. The kasbah had been a vital sanctuary in a time of need and she would be leaving it with mixed feelings. Longing to stay, needing to go. They would spend the first night away at Etta's riad, eating and drinking black-market champagne, and the next morning they'd be on their way to Tangier. Today was her final chance to make any adjustments to the packing and to find a way to leave the life she had made here.

Dinner was Nadia's speciality. Minced lamb mixed with garlic, fresh coriander, parsley, cinnamon, and ground coriander, then rolled into balls. Cooked and served in a tomato and onion sauce into which, just before the dish was ready, Nadia cracked eggs into little hollows. After such a busy few days – Clemence seeing to the final packing and Theo preparing the house in Tangier – they both enjoyed it.

They stayed up late after Nadia and Ahmed had gone to bed. Theo was yawning but didn't complain and when the sky was so pitch black they could not see each other, they went out to gaze at the stars. She had fallen in love with this place the moment she realised how close to the stars she felt here. It had given her courage at a time when she'd had none.

The dogs followed them out.

'They've worked out something is up. Don't worry, boys,' she said, bending down to pat their heads. 'You're coming too.'

'They won't have as much freedom in Tangier,' Theo said.

'They're old. Decent meal, comfy bed, fireplace when it's cold. Somewhere to do their business. That's all they need.'

'Sounds rather like me.'

She laughed. 'You and me both.'

'Seriously though. We don't have to go. We could live here.'

She shook her head; had been over it so many times. A part of her wanted to hold tight to everything she had here, and that now included Theo. She glanced back at the dark outline of her home and thought of the comings and goings. The losses; the gains. The beginnings; the endings. The love. Always the love. There could be no life without stops and starts, no life without doubts and fears. And yet the love found a way to shine through every single time. Moments of her life at the kasbah kept coming back to her. Fragments, like the way the light angled through the slatted shutters, and the way the mountain shifted from ochre to purple. And the sky. So big and so endlessly blue. And Ahmed and Nadia; her loyal friends through thick and thin.

She and Theo didn't make love and rose just after dawn. She had been too excited to sleep properly, and poor old Theo had been kept awake by her restlessness.

The air early in the day was fresh and the incandescent light so sharp it almost hurt. They breakfasted outside on eggs, fruit and coffee. A peaceful, timeless pause. She felt as if the clock wasn't even ticking as they wandered the garden listening to the bees and the birds singing in the trees. A little brown lizard ran over her foot, and she smiled.

But only half an hour or so later, five relatives of Ahmed's had marched up with their own mules to help ferry the boxes down the hill. They were shouting and laughing, joking as men did, and the sudden change from the peace and quiet to frantic activity struck her in the pit of her stomach. This really was happening. She really was leaving. She watched it all as if rooted to the spot and then hurried inside. When the last of the boxes had gone from the drawing room, Theo called to her.

'Clem?'

'Coming.' She glanced out at the view for one last time, wiped her eyes and went outside.

'What were you doing?' he asked.

'Praying.'

'But you aren't religious.'

'No.'

'Praying that you're doing the right thing?'

She felt a bit too embarrassed to say that she was.

He held her in his arms for a moment, kissed her on the lips and took hold of her hand.

'Ready?'

She nodded. 'Let's go.'

As if they were young children, he swung their arms energetically, and they ran towards the track. She was doing this. She really was doing this. At aged seventy-four she was joyfully running towards her new life just like a little girl, happy, excited, scared.

Thirty years after they had parted in such sorrow, they were beginning again. *She* was beginning again.

She noticed Theo was whistling a tune.

'What's that?' she asked. 'It's very catchy.'

'The Beatles. "All You Need is Love".'

And with a burst of joy, she realised – it was.

AUTHOR'S NOTE

While I have striven to be historically accurate, this is a work of imagination. For the purposes of the narrative, some historical details and timings around the characters of Yves Saint Laurent, Talitha Pol, and Jean Paul Getty (Jr) have been altered. The famous designer was such an influence on my character Vicky Baudin it was crucial he made an appearance in the story, along with the kind of friends he really did have. To my knowledge, YSL never had a studio in the Palmeraie, and reports vary about when he bought Dar el-Hanch, or the Snake House. Talitha Pol and Jean Paul (Jr) married in December 1966, spent their honeymoon in Morocco, and then returned to Marrakech sometime after the novel takes place.

ACKNOWLEDGEMENTS

Night Train to Marrakech is the final instalment in the Daughters of War Trilogy. I want to thank everyone at HarperCollins who has contributed to this novel and the previous two, but especially my amazing editors, Lynne Drew, Sophie Burks, and Cari Rosen. Your vision and rigorous attention to detail has made this trilogy what it is. It has been such a pleasure and privilege to work with you.

I want to thank Caroline Hardman, my agent, without whom none of this would have happened. I feel proud to have been supported by you through the ups and downs of all these stories right up to this, my tenth book. I can hardly believe how lucky I have been.

I can't finish without also mentioning my debt of gratitude to Venetia Butterfield who, when she was at Penguin / Viking, bought my first novel, *The Separation*, and saw me through seven books in total. Finally it is you, my readers, who bring tears to my eyes with your kind words and wonderful reviews. Thank you so, so much.

And now, read the previous books
in the Daughters of War Trilogy . . .

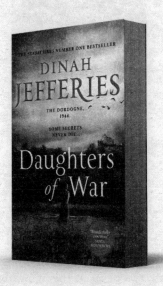

Deep in the river valley of the Dordogne, in an old
stone cottage on the edge of a beautiful village, three
sisters long for the end of the war.

Then, one dark night, the Allies come knocking for
help. Héléne, the eldest, realises that she cannot sit on
the sidelines any longer. But secrets from the sisters'
own mysterious past threaten to unravel everything
they hold most dear . . .

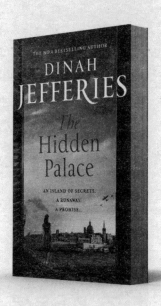

1925. Rosalie Delacroix flees Paris for a dancer's job in the bohemian clubs deep in the winding streets of the tiny island of Malta.

1944. Running from the brutality of war in France, Florence Baudin faces a new life. But her estranged mother makes a desperate request: to find her vanished sister, who went missing years before . . .

A faded last letter from Rosalie is Florence's only clue – and time is running out . . .

Read on for an extract of Book 1,
Daughters of War...

CHAPTER 1

THE PÉRIGORD NOIR, FRANCE

SPRING 1944

Hélène

If only it was late summer, and she could smell the sun-soaked scent of fir and spruce and be able to stand and watch the finches and starlings flitting between the branches. Her optimism might have outweighed the claustrophobic sensation of life leaning in, of ancient lichen-covered stone houses enclosing her as she walked through the village and the light began to fail. And maybe then she would remember they were all just ordinary people trying to make the best of impossible circumstances. Ordinary people longing for the return of a normal life.

Hélène craved daylight, to see more than what lay before her. She needed it to see into the distance, into the future, into her own heart. She needed it like others needed air. But she told herself, when all of this was over, she would still have her whole life before her. Why worry about the worst thing when it might never happen? And surely there would be better news from the Allies soon?

As she left the edge of the village, she glanced up at the indigo sky and heard the early night birds shuffling in the trees. She thought of her sisters, here in France, and her mother in England. Once, when she'd asked her mother if she was pretty like her sister Élise, her mother had said, 'Darling, you have a comfortable face. People like comfortable faces. They don't feel threatened by faces like yours.'

Hélène was only eleven at the time and her mother's comment had hurt her. She had gazed into the mirror for half an hour after that and hadn't known what to make of her face. She had prodded and poked at it, pulled different expressions, pouted, smiled, grimaced, and then told herself it didn't matter. But it had been a lie. It *had* mattered. And now? Her face had matured. She was tall, athletic, with a strong constitution just as her father used to have, but she also had his straight, light brown hair. Ordinary hair. It rankled, but her mother had been right, her features *were* too strong to be pretty, although people admired her kind nut-brown eyes and warm smile. She was the most pragmatic of the three sisters, the eldest, the most responsible. Was it terribly shallow to long for someone to tell her she was beautiful?

The war was a fight between good and evil, people said – although it wasn't always certain which was which. And now her job had become more challenging than she'd ever dreamt. She had enormous respect for her boss, Hugo

Marchand, the town doctor and mayor, and she adored his warm-hearted wife, Marie, a generous soul who always saw the best in people and had been a mother figure to the sisters. But the things Hélène witnessed, the things she heard – the lies, the little deceits, the deeds she could never mention – all of them she'd rather not have known.

After crossing a small field edged by wild poppies, she headed through a walnut grove, picking her way to avoid the waddling geese, until she eventually reached the track and her own gate. She frowned to see the worn wooden gate had been left open.

They never did that.

Their higgledy-piggledy farmhouse seemed to have grown out of the land naturally, its hand-hewn limestone walls soaking up the sunlight so by early evening they glowed, golden and honeyed. She passed the chestnut tree in the garden and glanced up at the foliage-draped façade. The vines remained undisturbed, cascading around the front door just as she'd left them, too early yet for the violet passion flowers she loved. Two medium-sized shuttered windows painted dusky blue flanked the oak door and as the wind got up and the creaky wooden shutters moaned in complaint, she shivered.

She burst through the door, hurrying into the kitchen to drop her bag on the table. From the huge roughhewn beams above her, herbs hung to dry: rosemary, lavender, bay, mint, sage, thyme and more. Hélène raised her head and breathed in their familiar scent, before unlacing her shoes and abandoning them on the flagstone floor hollowed in well-worn patches from centuries of passing feet. Hélène liked to imagine who had been there before her, and on dark nights it wasn't difficult to imagine their shadows still collecting in the gloomier corners of the house along with the cobwebs. But most people were living in the shadows, one way or another, and not just the dead. She shivered again and glanced at the huge fireplace with its carved stone surround; even in spring the house could be chilly in the evening, but the wood burner hadn't been lit.

Back in the hall she thought she heard someone at the top of the house.

'Hello,' she called out. 'Florence. Is that you?'

No reply.

'Élise, are you home?'

CHAPTER 2

Hélène paused for a moment and looked around, feeling uncertain. She was about to go into the sitting room – just in case – when she spotted Élise struggling down the stairs with a bulky bundle, her body tipping back slightly to counterbalance its weight. As usual she was wearing dark, wide-legged trousers, along with a faded blue jumper and brown lace-up boots. With long dark wavy hair and huge expressive eyes, the colour of cognac, she looked just like their mother. Relieved now to see her, Hélène let out her breath.

'You're back early,' Élise said, but then glanced down at her wristwatch. 'Oh, not so early.'

'You left the gate open.'

'I think it might have been Florence.'

'It gave me a scare . . .'

Despite her huge bundle, Élise managed a shrug.

'So, what's that you've got?'

'Just some bits and pieces for a new safe house.' Élise tilted her head to one side and narrowed her eyes at Hélène. 'Do you know you have paint in your hair? Rather a lot, actually.'

'Oh God, really?' Hélène stepped back to glance in the hall mirror and saw the tell-tale white streaks running through her hair and a delicate splatter on her left cheek.

In their hallway, oil paintings and posters peppered the walls, and framed pictures the girls had drawn as children were displayed together. The large mirror, into which Hélène was now frowning, with its ornate carving of grapes and trailing vine leaves, had reflected their faces most of their lives. They were either held up by their mother, Claudette, when they were small, to grin and laugh at their own expressions or, as now, they glanced at it for a quick check of their hair. There was also an older, yellowing photograph pinned there; a shot of their mother with her sister Rosalie not long before she had run away. All three sisters felt the history of the house, the sense of family, and of roots, and nowhere more so than here.

'So how was work?' Élise asked.

'Hugo had me painting the walls of the cottage hospital this afternoon. It hasn't been done for years and, as there are no patients checked in at the moment, it seemed the right time to tackle it.'

'Well, your *extensive* nursing training at the Sarlat Hospital has clearly gone to good use! Umm . . .' She scratched the side of her head in mock contemplation. 'How long was it now?'

Hélène laughed. 'Three long years. And you know it.

6

Anyway, I actually enjoyed the painting today.' She paused then picked up on what her sister had said. 'Why a new safe house?'

'The Germans are getting edgy. And an edgy Nazi is an even more dangerous Nazi. The Resistance is making sure there are enough places to hide out.'

'I wish you would just lie low like the rest of us. Honestly, Élise, you're putting us all in danger of Nazi reprisals.'

Her sister did not reply.

WIN A HOLIDAY TO MOROCCO

To celebrate the publication of *Night Train to Marrakech* by Dinah Jefferies, we're giving you the chance to win your dream holiday with a £1,000 gift card from TUI. To enter simply scan the QR code or search the link the below.

https://gleam.io/competitions/hmEZG-win-a-dream-holiday-to-morocco

Entrants must be 18 years or older. Competition is open to those in the UK only. Competition ends 30th November 2023. Terms and Conditions apply.

HEAR DINAH'S NEWS FIRST
Sign up to the Dinah Jefferies email newsletter for exclusive content, extracts, deals and competitions!
www.dinahjefferies.com